SUSPICIOUS MINDS

SUSPICIOUS MINDS

David Mark

This first world edition published 2020
in Great Britain and the USA by
SEVERN HOUSE PUBLISHERS LTD of
Eardley House, 4 Uxbridge Street, London W8 7SY.
Trade paperback edition first published
in Great Britain and the USA 2021 by
SEVERN HOUSE PUBLISHERS LTD.

British Library Cataloguing in Publication Data
A CIP catalogue record for this title is available from the British Library.

ISBN-13: 978-0-7278-8996-6 (cased)
ISBN-13: 978-1-78029-736-1 (trade paper)
ISBN-13: 978-1-4483-0458-5 (e-book)

All Severn House titles are printed on acid-free paper.

Severn House Publishers support the Forest Stewardship Council™ [FSC™],
the leading international forest certification organisation.
All our titles that are printed on FSC certified paper carry the FSC logo.

Typeset by Palimpsest Book Production Ltd.,
Falkirk, Stirlingshire, Scotland.
Printed and bound in Great Britain by
TJ International, Padstow, Cornwall.

For Nicola.
My beautiful madness; my misunderstood truth:
my endless, immaculate sky.
Please, don't ever get too sane.

Much Madness is divinest Sense –
To a discerning Eye –
Much Sense – the starkest Madness –
'Tis the Majority
In this, as all, prevail –
Assent – and you are sane –
Demur – you're straightway dangerous –
And handled with a Chain –

Emily Dickinson

'Love is a thing full of anxious fears.'

Proverb

PROLOGUE

The little stretch of woodland had seemed pretty, in the beginning. A touch eerie, of course, as all forests should be, but it had still shone with that certain loveliness.

Enchanting.

That was the word. In its embrace, Betsy had felt herself become a fairy tale.

The rustling of the leaves was a soft applause; the gurgle of the river a quiet lullaby. The scent of honeysuckle and splintered wood hung in the air, thick as honey. The long grasses touched her bare ankles. Dragonflies and songbirds whispered and sung their soporific lullabies. Told her to lay down upon the soft, dew-gilded earth. She had flowed into the forest's embrace as if falling into an illustration in a picture book.

Betsy – or *Lizzie* as she had still been then – had felt sure that any passing bears would be kindly souls: great affable lumps painted in a scrumptious chocolate brown. Had no doubt that the red squirrels would chatter in the treetops like dog toys: bright-eyed; coquettishly hugging luxurious tails. She could have conjured up a perfect gingerbread cottage for herself, given time. Could have thought her way inside a red, hooded cape. By the time she left she had been looking for a trail of breadcrumbs.

Later, Betsy had hoped they might perhaps picnic here. She and Jude: pleasure *al fresco*.

It didn't matter that this was where his last real lover had died.

It was their place now.

Theirs.

She saw a tartan blanket, a thermos of tea; triangular sandwiches packed in opaque Tupperware, all plucked from a wicker hamper. She'd visualized *him*, leaning against the old beech tree, both arms around her like lengths of tarred rope, telling her the names of the plants and plucking stray twigs and silvery catkins from her hair. She saw herself barefoot; dirty-kneed in a ragamuffin dress, a tartan shawl pinned with a sprig of holly. Fantasy, of course, but one of her best . . .

'Sweet chestnut,' he'd said, slapping a random tree trunk. 'This one's ash. The brambles have bound their branches. They're holding hands, look. And up there; that bracket of mushrooms – they can cure sore throats. Taste OK, too. Nice in a stir-fry. They tend to explode if you let the fat get too hot, but I like a meal that offers an element of danger . . .'

Come back, Liz. Liz! Oh for God's sake . . . Betsy!

The words come from within her: a chorus of voices, each gasping as if running out of air. She registers pain, suddenly. Pain and loss and fear. There's a fire in her gut: bees swarming inside her skull. She can taste blood; raw liver and old coins. Her gorge rises.

And now she realizes that she is moving . . .

step,

step,

crunch,

crunch,

. . . her stumbling footsteps a chomp of molar upon stone.

And the woodland. The place they had called 'the dingle'. Not in her memory but here, now: *there*, up and down: in front and behind.

She is a captive. She is being shepherded to the place where she will die.

'Slow it down. I don't know why you're in such a rush. There's nothing good up ahead for you.'

Betsy emerges back into her own dreadful reality. Registers the sound of the voice; loud as a breaking bone. Knows herself, suddenly, through the throb of pain and the screeching of fear in her head.

Elizabeth Zahavi.

34.

A size 12, before lunch. A 14 after.

Pretty, once you get past the scowl.

Professional dabbler, mother of none.

'Mad.'

'Bonkers.'

'Off her fucking head . . .'

Lizzie, all her life. Betsy, these past few months. Happy months, mostly. Happier than the years that came before, with Jay, and Anya, and the feeling of being nothing and everything; of being at once dreadful and unappreciated, trapped and unwanted; loving; unloved.

She screws up her eyes. Opens them into a cold, damp darkness. Feels fresh panic claw its way up her aching throat. He'd called this place the dingle – a name that always made her laugh. A funny, happy little word, for a woodland hundreds of years old. It made her think of fairies and bluebells and smelled of crushed honeysuckle and elderflower. Here, in the charcoal depths of winter, the forest has been mercilessly disrobed. The trees stand bare and straight against the night sky; their trunks and branches a jumbled manuscript of stark crotchets and frantic semi-quavers: black on black. The ground is hard as iron in places; soft as bog cotton in others. Betsy's breath, when it comes, hangs about her face like an unwrapped shroud. She shivers like an animal stripped of fur.

She strains her hearing, alert for the sound of footsteps; for help. She fancies she can hear the chuckling of the brook, leading down to the cold, black pool beyond the glade. Cocks her head. Hopes for any distraction from the slow, painful plod of foot following foot. She had thought she heard a solitary robin as they passed the fallen alders, tripping clumsily over the exposed, wormy roots. The sound had become a scream; a vixen's widowed wail, and some part of her had taken temporary leave; retreating into a safe place, far within, where this wasn't happening, and nobody else was going to die.

A memory falls like a dead leaf.

Anya.

Betsy raises heavy eyes, sniffs wetly, foully, and spits blood. She stares ahead. Mist rises from the mulch of the woodland floor; shapeless wisps that coil around the bases of the rain-blackened trees. The moon is a leering eye, half-hooded by a skein of thick cloud. The forest seems older here. Thicker. The trees have fatter trunks and their branches fork off at odd angles, like limbs that have been broken and improperly set. She hears the creak of ancient branches; sees moonlight reflecting back off iron-grey bark. The air feels somehow heavier. When Betsy licks her lips she tastes raw meat. Tastes the blood that runs from her broken nose in gory plaits.

'Anya,' she says, desperately, as she glances to her right and sees the girl. Her hands are tied. Betsy's too.

She glances back.

He's half a dozen steps behind, one hand holding the rope that binds her wrists, the other gripping the stock of the shotgun. It's pointing at the small of her back. If he shot her from this range she'd all but evaporate; disappear in a spray of red meat and white bone.

'That's it, ladies. Not far now.'

They emerge in a small clearing. The trees form a tight mesh, snarled up with blackberries and thorns. She shakes her head, trying to clear her thoughts – hot wasps buzzing inside her skin.

'Please,' she says: an undirected prayer; a comforting invocation, a beseeching for a mercy that will not be found. 'Please, I didn't . . . she didn't . . .'

'Don't bother. I told you. There's no other way.'

The clouds uncouple for a moment and a little yellow light anoints the clearing. There is a hole in the earth; a yawning maw of disturbed ground. A mound of loose stones has been built into a cairn at the far end of the hole. The digger sits there like a metal dinosaur: extended neck, teeth like swords; the rusting paint looking like blood in the moonlight. There's a shove in her back and she starts towards it, her feet moving over damp grass. The light reveals the wildflowers that rise from the flattened ground; purple foxgloves, violet knapweed; a constellation of gold and yellow blooms, winking like the lights of a distant town. She reaches the edge of the hole and leans forward. She gasps, sucking in a lungful of cold air. She smells decay. Spoiled meat and sour milk. She catches a taste of her own scent; all sweat and churned roots.

'Fucking thing . . .'

She glances back. The rope has snagged on a snarl of brambles. The raw skin at her wrists sings with pain. She almost falls, but manages to keep her feet. It's instinct more than anything else. She doesn't want to fall. As long as she's standing, she's still alive. Each step is another heartbeat, each stumble another thump of her pulse.

'Why are you doing this? You don't have to. You can still stop.'

Anya's voice is eerie in its calmness. She's nine years old. There are tears streaking the dirt on her face but there is no tremble as she speaks. Betsy wonders if maybe something came loose when she was hit. Maybe there's a part of the brain that deals with fear, and Anya's has somehow suffered a dislocation.

Betsy feels a sudden urge of something fiery and primal; a raw and perfect need to protect the child from what is to come. Words spill out of her like blood.

'Anya,' she hisses. 'Anya, please, look at me. It's going to be OK. I promise, it's going to be OK. They're trying to scare us, that's all . . .'

She stops talking as she sees what lies ahead. The digger is all right angles and points; damp earth clinging to the teeth of the bucket that has clawed a trench into the earth. She spies a twist of deeper darkness. Even in the swirl of her terror, she identifies it as a yew tree: its circumference vast, its branches splayed out like the fingers of an upturned hand. There are great scars in the trunk; the bark ripped away and the wood exposed. She finds her vision blurring as she gazes into the face of the ancient tree. Sees knotholes become eyes, a porcine snout, a hanging mouth of obsidian black.

'You can't,' she whispers, and the cold wind snatches the words away. 'She's a child. She's done nothing wrong. Let her go and I'll do what you want . . .'

Betsy feels as though somebody has cut a vein at her ankles. Feels her energy, her hope, gurgling into the ground that will soon close over her, and the child she has failed.

'Liz? Liz, what's going to happen . . .?'

She looks into Anya's pale, frightened face: big circular eyes in a mask of blood and dirt. She wants to speak, but nothing comes.

She feels the pressure at her wrists suddenly slacken, and then someone is beside her; the barrel of the shotgun pressed beneath the hinge of her jaw.

'Tacitus.' The whisper wet, in her ear. 'You remember, I'm sure.'

And she does.

They slice the culprit's navel, and secure it to the trunk of a sacred tree. Then they force them backwards, until their guts are unwound about the trunk – decorating it like tinsel at Christmas. As far as the old tribes were concerned, the life of the tree was equal to the life of a man. Maybe they were right.

Betsy needs to see. Whatever it costs her, she needs to look into this killer's eyes and make one last desperate plea. Needs to explain. She understands how it feels to be filled with the whispers of something incessant and demonic; the uncontrollable impulse to sabotage; to cause pain, to do harm.

She turns, her mouth opening, a babble of pathetic entreaty spilling from her bloodied lips.

She experiences a moment of sensory overload; heat and noise and pain and a sensation of being both within herself and without.

Then blackness.

Silence.

Then nothing at all.

ONE

Eight months ago . . .

A nice house in a nice neighbourhood.

A place of Aga. Of Audi. Dyson and Samsonite. Of artisan sourdough bread dipped in cold-pressed virgin olive oil. A place for people with pension plans and life insurance policies and a few little nest eggs tucked away. For people who own their own skis. Where children called Bertie and Imogen refer to ham as '*prosciutto*' and where dads call their children 'the guys'.

There's a big blue Quattro in the driveway at number seventeen: a cycle-rack on the roof, strategically positioned to conceal the two-seater Smart car that huddles in behind.

Inside the big, bay-windowed semi, it's all high ceilings and pale walls. Clean lines. Kitchen glowing like an operating theatre: a palace of Nespresso and Smeg. The NutriBullet blender has been cleaned and tucked away. So too the spiralizer, the uneaten rat-tails of courgette and carrot making the bin look pretty.

Here.

Blue light in a silver-grey room; the furniture all right angles, the curtains thick as fur.

Liz Zahavi. Elizabeth, on paper. *Betsy*, in her heart, though lacking in the self-importance required to make such a drastic change. She'd known a Victoria who rebranded herself every six months. Vicky. Vic. Tori. Toria. It was hard to keep up. Icto was a step too far.

Her brain hurts. She knows that there are no nerve endings in her cerebral cortex, but that doesn't stop her feeling as though there are birds pecking their way out of her wrinkled grey matter like blackbirds escaping from a pie.

She holds herself as if bound with flex, her likeness framed in the TV screen; knees drawn up and head down – her back to the sofa, the window, the world.

Scones, she whispers, inside herself. *You nearly killed him over scones!*

She feels at once embarrassed, apologetic, and absolutely justified.

Air freshener! If those bastards at Febreeze would just work a bit bloody harder . . .

She finds herself furious that the smell of freshly-baked scones cannot be trapped in an aerosol and sold as a room deodorizer. Biscuits too. Would that be so hard? Home cooking, perhaps infused with a subtle trace of furniture polish and that particular, warm-dust fug of vacuuming. The charade wouldn't fool him long, but he might at least look briefly satisfied as he walked through the front door. She can live for months on such minute glimpses of gratification.

Just bake the scones, Lizzie. Tomorrow, just bake the scones. It will make him happy. You'll feel good . . .

She scoffs at herself, offended at the suggestion. Feel good? Here? In this excuse for a life? Trapped with a man whose first worry would be about the curtains if she ran past him in flames?

The little voice takes over, a swirl of memory and projection; a legion of tongues, all oozing scorn.

There's no happiness here, Lizzie. You're stupid for thinking it. Stupid, stupid, stupid. He's right. You'd never get anybody else. Nobody would have you. Nobody would put up with you. Look at you. Getting a bit of a jelly-belly there, aren't you? Why's there all that darkness under your eyes? You look like a panda. You had such lovely skin when you met and now, well, you're all sort of pale. Damp bread. Doughy. Are you using a different shampoo? It looks a bit, well, greasy, I suppose . . .

Lizzie presses her face into the cushion. It's the patterned one – the one she's allowed to cry into. Her tears and snot and wine-soaked spit are too astringent for the velour fabric of the other fabrics. He doesn't object to her crying *per se* – that's what women do, after all – but he doesn't know why she has to spoil some perfectly good scatter cushions with her endless snivelling.

The conversation in Lizzie's head is a constant. It plays like talk radio, dropping in and out of her hearing according to the quality of outside stimulus. Here, now, she can hear damnably well. *His* voice. *Hers.* All the other little Lizzie's that live inside. The toddler: tantrum-prone and lethally inquisitive. The moody adolescent, all huffs and hormones. The student, battling to change the world and railing against inequity, immovable in her righteousness. The twenty-something, suffused with regret; the wish that she'd listened, made better choices, become *more.* And then the reality. The face she wears for the world. Thirty-three. Childless, save her partner's eight-year-old daughter, Anya. A dabbler. Not one to finish anything. Good at a few pointless things but feckless at anything useful. Crap, really. Just crap.

Shut up. Stop. Stop.

She uncurls herself. Feels horribly exposed. She has toddler knees. Fat feet. Dimply hips and buttocks. She doesn't want to look at them. Draws them up again and covers the offending objects with her big, baggy T-shirt. Hugs herself, a wound spring.

She glances at the clock on the mantelpiece, trying to work out how many hours of sleep she can still get if she goes back to bed and tries again. It's 3.06 a.m. So late it's almost early. Her lips tingle. Fingers and toes. Panic, rising. Temper flushing her face and neck.

Not fair. Not fair!

It wasn't as if she hadn't tried. Lain there, still and silent as death, listening to him snoring, his wet lips opening and closing like a lamprey. If he'd held her she would have drifted off, she's sure of it. If he'd just spooned up behind her and laid an arm over her shoulder, or pushed his nose against the nape of her neck, she's sure she could have let go. But he doesn't like to be touched in bed. She's too hot, he says. Too grabby. She makes him clammy. He can't breathe. She always makes too much noise. She doesn't snore, but she makes the bed wobble when she turns over and it makes him feel seasick. He flinches when her feet accidentally brush his hairy shins. Has started to leave out magazines advertising the merits of twin beds.

Don't. Don't be mean about him. He works hard. He drives an hour to work and an hour home again and he puts in proper graft in between.

'Bollocks,' she whispers, in response to her own inner voice, and grinds her face into her knees lest any other disloyal utterances surge free like bats from a cave.

This has been her night-time routine for months now. After they fight, he falls asleep; peacefully, quickly, untroubled by fear of consequence. She, exhausted, cried out, aching to her bones, laying there still as death, until his breathing finds the ursine rumble that tells her it is safe to slither out from beneath the bedclothes and tiptoe downstairs. She knows which steps creak. Which lights are bright enough to wake him. She boils water in a saucepan on the hob, lest the rumble of the kettle should wake him. Makes tea, dropping the used bag in the windowsill composter of which he is inordinately proud. Then she pads through to the living room and sits in the half dark-ness. She has found a way to make the TV screen emit a low blue light, and if she sits close enough she can read, or write, or stare into the surface of her tea and watch the bubbles pop like dreams.

. . . *I mean, what do you want? You've got a nice place to live. A car. You get a job whenever you bother your arse to fill in an application form. I work hard to provide for us. You said you wanted to be, you know, a stay-at-home mum – even though we decided against kids. A housewife, then. A proper partner. I was all for it, remember? And I come home and nothing's done. You said it would all be lovely. You bought all those cookbooks and I got you the blender and the sewing machine and all that stuff you said you needed. And you just lay there, playing with your phone, causing mischief, buying stuff. That card was for emergencies. I'm going to have to take it off you, you can't be trusted. We'll go back to the system as it was. I'll put cash in envelopes – mark them for specific items. If you need anything extra, ask me. I'm not an ogre . . .*

She pulls the cushion to her face again. Bites down until her jaw aches.

By the skirting board, her phone bleeps. It gives her a thrill of pure excitement; a sudden surge of yellow-gold adrenaline. She feels high, suddenly. Life is awesome. Endorphins flood her system. Good memories rise. He'd smiled at her in the way he used to, hadn't he? Back at the beginning, when he fancied her: when she wasn't mad, but kooky, and he liked the way she spoke and got her words wrong and her temper tantrums were endearing rather than a symptom of something dangerously wrong in her head. He'd smiled, hadn't he? Actually grinned. What had she said? What had made the connection? Christ, it was pancakes. She'd been riffing on a theme, warming to her subject, telling him he would never understand her, never really care, that he was too selfish to truly understand what it felt like to be a passenger in their own existence, and she'd thrown words like rocks.

You should be with your mum. Your dad's not going to last forever – when he pops his clogs you can move her in. Cook for you, clean for you, tell you you're her golden child, make you pancakes with syrup on a Sunday morning after you've had a lie-in and a toss . . .

But he'd smiled. It had been OK, hadn't it? It had been a smile that said she was funny. That even after all the ugliness of the past few months, he still thought her way with words endearing.

She shakes her head at herself. Shushes the voices, the memories, the accusations, as she settles back on to the sofa, clutching the phone like a talisman. It's her third this year. He smashed one, wordlessly, methodically, when he found her texting her ex. She lost the other. Left it on the roof of the car while laden down with groceries, trying to fit bags and boxes in the boot of her ridiculous little fridge-on-wheels. Drove off and didn't notice its absence until she tried to call him through the hands-free device on the dashboard. It had felt like bereavement.

The light of the screen illuminates her face. Her eyes, brown like Brazil nuts, sparkle cerise, magenta and blue, as she navigates her way to the icon for Bipped. The website was recommended by the doctors. A forum for people with her condition; a safe, secure online environment, free of judgment: a place to share stories, experiences, to feel less alone. If it were a village, Lizzie would move there. She's addicted to Bipped. It feels like reading her own ghostwritten life story. She hasn't had the confidence to contribute an article yet, but she has given a few crumbs of experiential wisdom to those other users seeking advice and insight. And the advice has been well-received. People have said nice things. One user, Derian_B, said she was an inspiration. That had left her giddy. She'd texted her sister about it. Told her she was thinking of retraining as a psychotherapist – that she wanted to help people, do something that mattered, turn her own journey into a teaching tool. Carly had sent back an eye-rolling emoji, and some dispiriting sisterly advice.

> Just get yourself well. You took three packets of ibuprofen six weeks ago, Liz. You've only just been diagnosed. Remember, you've got officially certifiable levels of impulsivity and paranoia! Just take one step at a time. When can I come visit? Cx

It had well and truly popped her bubble of good feeling. Pissed on her bonfire good and proper. She always was a mood-hoover. She considers her sister. Sneers, nasty and hot. Yeah, OK, so it couldn't have been easy for Carly, who has problems of her own, but they were meant to be family, after all. Sisters, together against the world, like in the books and movies. It was no different when they were kids. Sure, Carly had been the one to find her, to hold her legs up as she dangled in their shared bedroom, turning blue and slack-jawed beneath the light flex, but it wasn't Liz's fault. She hadn't planned it that way. It was Mum who was meant to see. Carly shouldn't have been bunking off school. And she didn't have to act like such a hero after it was all over, did she? She's thirty-one now, two years younger than Liz, and still acting like she's the sensible one.

She stares, hungrily, at the home page. Feels a warmth spread through her as she logs in to the members' area and sees that another fourteen people have marked her response to an ethical conundrum as 'useful'. She feels as though she is standing on a podium, clutching flowers, a medal around her neck and the national anthem carrying her spirits heavenwards; a mermaid surging on a crash of spray.

She re-reads the thread where she has made her mark, a query from a frazzled husband, posted under the tagline: **BPD Partner – I Can't Win!**

> I don't know what to do. Whatever I try to say or do it's always wrong. She won't accept any responsibility for anything. I was her knight in shining armour, the person who made her feel things nobody else could. She was so in love with me it was like being consumed. Now she tells

me I make her sick. That I'm nothing. She says she's been seeing other men and that they'd be better parents to our three gorgeous daughters. What do I do? I can't stand the thought of abandoning her when it's clear she needs me most but she doesn't see she has a problem. The temper tantrums are because I provoke her or say or do stupid things. I try so hard but I'm at the end of my rope. I just need somebody to tell me it will get better.

Liz feels his pain. Understands the frustration. The desperation. The absolute willingness to do whatever it takes to help his beloved wife get well. She'd replied, thumb moving over the keypad in a blur:

You sound like a wonderful husband and father. I'm sure it must hurt horribly when she splits on you like this but I know from my own life that her biggest fear is abandonment and that she says hurtful things because she's frightened of being hurt herself. Try putting boundaries in place, but most of all, don't let her ever think you're losing love for her. I can't promise it will come good, but people with BPD aren't lost causes. We just feel things to such an extent that it makes us a little mad. Stick in there.

She'd re-read the words of advice a dozen times before posting it. A spelling mistake and she'd be lashing herself until she hit bone. Felt pretty damn good about what she'd come up with. She wasn't entirely sure she agreed with herself, but the poor chap needed to hear something positive. He'd earned it, hadn't he? God, how she wishes she could find a post from Jay on one of these forums. Some sign he actually wants things to work.

The thought veers off as she considers the new raft of possibilities. She wonders whether there is a future in this. Whether she could become an online guidance counsellor for those with BPD. She can see herself; cat-eye glasses and a sensible baggy cardigan over a tight vest, dispensing earnest wisdom and insights to a growing global audience. The go-to girl for Borderline Personality Disorder – a regular on daytime TV; perhaps a column in a newspaper or a Sunday magazine. She makes a mental note to check whether such things still exist. Whether agony aunts are now thought of as outdated and sexist. Wonders, briefly, whether she would be deemed a bad feminist for playing up to patriarchal stereotypes about women being the more compassionate, gentler sex.

She sits back, fingers at her mouth, beating out a little rhythm on her lips: three letters, repeated over and over, faster and faster, like a train.

BPD

BPD

BPD . . .

It has been six weeks since the diagnosis. Six weeks since she found a suit that finally fitted. The psychiatrist had given her eight full minutes of his time. Sat with her in the little green room and changed her life: the whole thing taking place two floors up from the same emergency room where she'd had her guts washed out, where charcoal had been pumped into her gut to bind the undigested painkillers – where she woke up miserable beyond enduring at having failed to kill herself properly.

'I've been through your notes. You've been treated for depression. Evidence of self-harm in childhood. The abuse, the instability in your home life, the history of mental illness in the family. Textbook, really. What you told me about these impulsive acts, the huge highs and lows, the inability to rationalize your moods. Have you heard of something called Borderline Personality Disorder?'

She hadn't. Didn't like the sound of it, but wanted, at once, to know more.

He'd given her a leaflet and told her she was going to be put on a waiting list for Dialectical Behavioural Therapy. He'd apologized for how long it would take. Said it could be eight or nine months before she'd get an appointment, waiting lists being what they were. He fancied he could help her himself, but only as a private patient. Sixty quid per session, but absolutely vital for her recovery . . .

She'd said no, naturally. Jay was already cross with her. She'd promised last time that she wouldn't be so silly ever again. He'd had to get cover at work. Had to leave an important meeting. He wasn't one hundred per cent sure how much more of this he could take.

Lizzie squeezes herself tight, elbows drawn in, phone so close to her face she can smell her perfume on the speaker. She is suddenly so afraid that he will leave her that it is all she can do not to rush upstairs and bludgeon him with a bedside lamp. At least then he'd never get the chance to say the words; to make flesh her worst imaginings – the godawful moment when he tells her it's over, she's on her own. He's threatened it plenty.

'You won't be able to sponge off me any longer. And nobody else will put up with your shit. Then you'll really have something to feel suicidal about . . .'

She re-reads the description of her condition. She already knows it off by heart but there is something comforting in the words.

> Borderline personality disorder (BPD) is a disorder of mood and how a person interacts with others.
> The symptoms of BPD can be grouped into 4 main areas:
> * Emotional instability – the psychological term for this is affective dysregulation
> * Disturbed patterns of thinking or perception – cognitive distortions or perceptual distortions
> * Impulsive behaviour
> * Intense but unstable relationships with others
> The symptoms of a personality disorder may range from mild to severe and usually emerge in adolescence, persisting into adulthood.

Liz's eyes start to droop. The words are a lullaby. She's not alone. It's not her fault. There are others out there dealing with the same problems as she is. She sinks into the welcoming hug of people like her. People who understand. People who know she's ill, not horrible; a victim, not an abuser or a bitch.

The phone beeps. She jumps, genuinely startled, as it vibrates in her hand. It's Jay, upstairs, in their bed.

> I presume you're downstairs, talking to all your hangers-on and groupies. Do what you need. I don't want to fight. I've done the sums and I think this counselling is worth it in the long run. So if you want

to find a therapist, I'll pay for it. I want you fixed. This isn't what I signed up for.

Inside her head, an eruption of carnival noise; crackle and static and a sudden surge of feeling; possibility, hope, fear – she feels sick, suddenly, as if an unwanted tongue is being forced into her mouth, and all she wants to do is run up to Jay and smother him with kisses and say thank you, she's so lucky to have a man like him, and she's so sorry about what she said and please don't leave me, please don't lose patience, please don't let me go . . .

She makes a promise to herself, as she falls into a sleep black as treacle, that she will make him pancakes when she wakes.

TWO

From: lizziez_22@hotmail.com
Sent: 10 April 2020 04.46:23
To: Anita_Hood@yahoo.com
Subject: **Re: FW: New Enquiry from Elizabeth Zahavi via Counselling Directory**

Hi.

I think I need your help. A few weeks ago I was diagnosed with Borderline Personality Disorder (BPD) following an act of self-harm/attempted suicide/cry-for-help/etc. I have been through some traumatic experiences in my personal life and feel as though my coping strategies are simply not working any more. I have been really struggling to stabilize my mood and have been feeling erratic, paranoid and anxious all the time. There are some incidents in my past I want to work through. Do you think you could help? My partner has been a true rock for me throughout all this and I want to be able to give him the person he deserves. I've done lots of reading on the condition and so many people seem to think that people with BPD are a lost cause. They say we're manipulative and unmanageable and that people around us should head for the hills, but that isn't what he wants and I don't think I do. I've browsed through a lot of possible therapists but you certainly seem to have a lot of expertise in the field. Weird, I know, but I also like the necklace you're wearing in your picture on the website! I'm sorry for rambling on – please do message me back at your earliest convenience. I'm not working at the moment so am free to see you as soon as practical. I live in Durham but am willing to travel if it speeds up the process. Thank you.

Liz x

From: Anita_Hood@yahoo.com
To: lizziez_22@hotmail.com
Sent: 12 April 2020 09.12:23
Subject: Re: FW: New Enquiry from Elizabeth Zahavi via Counselling Directory

Dear Liz,

Thank you for your email and enquiry, and for the information you have provided.

The issues you describe are certainly something that we could work through together, as well as helping you to stabilize your mood.

It would be helpful for us to meet for an initial consultation first, so that I can get to know a bit more about you, we can think about how we might work together, and this will give you an opportunity to ask any questions you might have.

So that we can do this it would be helpful if you could advise me on your availability to meet? Also what venue? I have a private practice at my home address in Corbridge, not far from the A68, but am in Durham twice a week, though there is a longer waiting list for an appointment. Do let me know which you prefer? I can then get back to you with some options to meet.

Should you have any queries please don't hesitate to contact me.

Kind Regards,

Dr Anita Hood
Chartered Counselling Psychologist

From: lizziez_22@hotmail.com
Sent: 12 April 2020 09.53:11
To: Anita_Hood@yahoo.com
Subject: Re: FW: New Enquiry from Elizabeth Zahavi via Counselling Directory

Hi Anita,

I would be happy to travel to Corbridge. As it stands, any day would be good for me. Apologies for throwing so much

stuff at you in my initial letter – I have a habit of overloading people with information that they don't need or haven't asked for. Am I right in thinking your practice is in central Corbridge? Is there somewhere to park? I've recently been struggling to concentrate when driving and have had a few moments of panic when I cannot navigate my way to my destination. I may ask my partner for a lift, though he works 12-hour days and is unlikely to be able to assist. I'm sure he would if it were possible. I'm very grateful to him for funding our sessions. Sorry, I'm going on again. I hope you know what you've let yourself in for! Lol!
Kind regards
Liz xx

From: Anita_Hood@yahoo.com
To: lizziez_22@hotmail.com
Sent: 12 April 2020 14.08:13
Subject: Re: FW: New Enquiry from Elizabeth Zahavi via Counselling Directory

Hi Liz,
I work from Corbridge Thursday am.
I could meet with you this week at 11.20.
A

From: lizziez_22@hotmail.com
Sent: 12 April 2020 14.23:18
To: Anita_Hood@yahoo.com
Subject: Re: FW: New Enquiry from Elizabeth Zahavi via Counselling Directory

Hi Anita
Yes, that suits me. What is your address and is there a charge for this initial consultation?
Thank you, L

From: Anita_Hood@yahoo.com
To: lizziez_22@hotmail.com
Sent: 12 April 2020 16.11:13
Subject: Re: FW: New Enquiry from Elizabeth Zahavi via Counselling Directory

Hi Liz,
Sessions are £65 and 50 minutes and payable in cash initially. Initial consultations are charged at this rate also.
I do have a 48 hr cancellation policy in place. Sessions cancelled after this time will incur the full fee. I look forward to meeting with you tomorrow.
I'd ask that you arrive near enough to the appointment time and no earlier than 5 mins before this as I don't have reception cover.
Should you have any queries please don't hesitate to contact me.
Kind regards,
Dr Anita Hood

From: lizziez_22@hotmail.com
Sent: 12 April 2020 16.31:55
To: Anita_Hood@yahoo.com
Subject: Re: FW: New Enquiry from Elizabeth Zahavi via Counselling Directory

Hi Anita
Thanks so much. I know you must get all sorts of people turning up and expecting to be fixed and then no doubt forming all of these passionate attachments to you and fixating, but I promise I will be a model patient. I've been chewing my fingernails to stumps waiting for your reply and I must have scared the neighbours half to death when your message pinged through. I don't know if I'm scared or excited. Maybe that's the problem! Ha! Sorry, wittering again. I'm going to make Jay his favourite tonight to say thank you. You don't know what this means to both of us. Thanks again.
L xxx

From: Anita_Hood@yahoo.com
To: lizziez_22@hotmail.com
Sent: 12 April 2020 18.11:13
Subject: Re: FW: New Enquiry from Elizabeth Zahavi via Counselling Directory

Liz,
I also accept payment via bank transfer though this is less desirable. We will talk about your situation in detail when we meet.
Regards,
Dr Anita Hood

From: lizziez_22@hotmail.com
Sent: 12 April 2020 19.06:25
To: Anita_Hood@yahoo.com
Subject: Re: FW: New Enquiry from Elizabeth Zahavi via Counselling Directory

Dr Hood,
So sorry if I sounded like a crazy person in my last message. I've Googled you and seen that you have lots of experience of Inner Child Therapy for Trauma and Abuse Resolution. This may be something we could factor into our sessions, though I don't want to be one of those people who blame their mum for everything. Really sorry to be a pain before we even get to know each other but could you please send me the postcode for your house so I can be super-sure I'm going to the right place? I'm awful at directions and end up going the wrong way, even without the satnav. As I feared, Jay won't be able to take me but he says I'm a grown woman and this is all part of the process. I'm sure he's right – though don't tell him I said that. Lol!
Very best wishes
Lizzie Z xxxxx

THREE

S he'd given herself more than enough time. Set three alarms on her phone and laid out her clothes the night before. Khaki-coloured jeans, a sensible T-shirt and a tight lambs-wool cardigan, its snug dimensions more a result of inadequate laundry skills than her recent carb-heavy diet. She was feeling too sick and nervous to eat, but she'd drunk one coffee at home and tipped the remainder of the cafetière into her travel mug, and she was pretty sure there would be enough sugar and caffeine in her system to keep her motor running until lunch. She gave herself a two-hour window for a journey that could be done in forty-five minutes. Too much time, as it turned out. She was rich with it, able to luxuriate in her wealth of unspent minutes. She had time to spare. Time to take the long way round. To drift on to the scenic route, her radio blasting out Adele and Amy Winehouse, feeling pretty damn good about herself as the little black car zipped along the grey road, blue sky overhead and green fields as far as she could see.

The satnav stopped co-operating ten minutes after she left the A68. She'd been revelling in the view, gazing to her left at a big sky and a patchwork landscape; greys and browns and so many shades of green that she started trying to name them all. Jade. Green. Khaki. Olive. She saw a paddock that reminded her of the duffel coat she had worn to school when she was nine; another, more lurid shade that filled her mind with hallucinogenic flash-backs; the night she drank absinthe with an artist friend and ended up sleeping in the bath, wrapped up in a pedestal mat and a dirty kimono.

She'd followed a sign to a place called Muggleswick. It sounded pretty, and familiar. She'd been to Corbridge this way some time before, she was sure of it. Nothing to worry about, plenty of time . . .

Five miles later she was starting to feel anxious. Jittery. Paranoid. She'd drained her coffee mug and was fairly vibrating with unspent energy. *You've fucked up*, said the voice, almost apologetic. *You're going the wrong way and you know it. Couldn't even get this right. Fucking useless* . . .

She turned the radio down. Started jabbing at the screen of the satnav. The menu wouldn't let her re-enter the postcode and when she tried to prod the first three letters of Corbridge, it kept auto-completing and giving her the route to a village called Cockfield, which would have made her laugh if she wasn't feeling so close to losing it. The little arrow kept spinning, pointing back the way she had come, but each time she performed a three-point turn it went back on its earlier advice and insisted she keep going west. The road looped back on itself, passed over old stone bridges, offered up glimpses of impenetrable forest one moment and then wide expanses of green the next; a great bowl of silvery-blue water identified on the GPS screen as Derwent Reservoir, and overhead a wagon train of gathering clouds.

Now she's sitting in the driving seat like a fist. She's ten miles from Corbridge and getting further away rather than closer. She's telling herself that if she just keeps going, she's bound to get there eventually. *The earth is round*, she thinks, her thoughts a jumble, her vision all steam and tears. *You just have to keep going* . . .

She does. Drifts into Weardale. Looks out through darkening glass at a panorama so timeless that she would not be surprised to see herself transformed: to look down and see herself in Victorian garb, bouncing and swaying in a black-lacquered carriage pulled by clip-clopping horses: a Cathy on her way home to the Heights. She peers at the great swell of stone-walled fields topped with vast, buckskin-coloured moors and the crumbling exclamation marks of abandoned industrial chimneys.

The sunshine folds in upon itself as she pushes into the valley. The blue sky of the main road is snatched away without preamble and in moments the little car is shaking, banging: the thunder of raindrops on metal and glass: the wind screaming as if in pain. She fumbles with the wipers, prods at the air-conditioning as the windscreen steams up and the view becomes nothing but boiling paint; grey and green and brown and the *screech-screech-screech* of wipers flicking away the monsoon like the tail of an excited dog.

Forest now, to her left. Too tall for Christmas trees, but they smell the same. The trunks are pushed up against each other like rockers at a concert; the darkness behind them almost impenetrable. The tyres slip and she jerks right, drifting down into a village that is little more than a row of cottages and one great abandoned Victorian building, its windows smashed and holes punched in the roof. She comes to a halt in the driveway of a big house. A man in a flat cap is holding a wriggling toddler in his arms by the roadside, whispering in her ear and making her laugh. He looks at her, his face an enquiry. Can I help?

She buzzes the window down. 'I'm so lost! I'm really sorry, I think I'm going a bit mad. Or maybe I've always been mad, I don't know. Your son's a cutie. How old? And, erm, where am I?'

Pleasantly, calmly, he tells her where she's gone wrong. Chiefly, she shouldn't have misidentified his darling daughter as a bouncing baby boy. She's in Allendale, apparently. Miles from where she should be. She can go back the way she's come if she carries on another half mile and then does a loop, or she can do a three-point turn and chug her way back up the hill.

'Thank you,' she says, trying to find first gear. 'I'm sorry. She's gorgeous.'

'Yeah, yeah.'

She moves off. Follows his instructions. She's lost again inside thirty seconds. Screams, in despair. Jabs again at the control panel, one hand on the wheel. She's frightened. Furious with herself, disgusted at having failed so spectacularly despite trying so hard. Afraid, too. She has never been a confident driver but in this hygge, rugged landscape the tiny car seems dangerously insubstantial. She imagines great hands taking the corners of the quilted landscape and shaking it out; imagines the gale simply lifting the tyres from the road and pitching it into the air.

'Where the bloody hell . . .?'

The road is getting steeper. She peers at a grubby road sign. Can't make out the name of the three-house hamlet she's passing through. It ended in 'hope', which strikes her as horribly apposite.

The radio suddenly explodes into sound as she passes an abandoned farmhouse. She slaps the controls, changing channels without meaning to. Local news, a pleasant Geordie brogue, giving listeners hourly confirmation that the world is shite.

'. . . protesters react with fury after charges were dropped against a country estate in the Allen Valleys, three years after an incident which left a teenage girl blind in one eye.

'Swinburn Estates, owned by Campion and Candace Lorton-Cave, has been warned by the Health and Safety Executive that they must improve safety measures if they are to proceed with a planned extension. However, a spokesman said the public interest would not be served by bringing charges against any individuals.

'Anti-shoot protesters said the decision was "grotesque" and further proof that those with deep enough pockets are considered above the law.

'The decision brings to an end a three-year saga, which began when a beater working for the shoot was blasted in the face by one of the shooters who pay thousands of pounds a day to shoot grouse. The victim is said to have reached an out-of-court settlement with the estate, which has owned a great swathe of the Allen Valleys since the 17th century . . .'

Betsy slaps at the controls. She can feel her chest growing tight. There's darkness at the edges of her vision, a smell of chemicals and metal in her nostrils; the sound of surf grinding over pebbles surging in her ears. She hears church bells. Glimpses white light. Her feet and lips tingle. She has pills for this. Diazepam. Little white pills to take when the panic threatens to pull her under. They're in her bag, in the boot of the little car. She glances back, her vision a fish-eye lens. If she could just reach them, just stretch her fingers and fumble around for the strap of her bag . . .

The road swings suddenly to the right. She yanks at the wheel, a screech erupting from her lips. A wheel chews at nothing for a moment, and then finds purchase on the greasy black road.

Jab. Jab . . . fingers punching at the controls, music and static and the satnav suddenly speaking in a foreign tongue, some Scandinavian-sounding man instructing her to *lav-en-sving* . . .

Ringing, suddenly. The trill of a call. The satnav has finally located the Bluetooth connection of her phone.

'Liz? You there? I've had a call from your therapist, wanting

to know if you're still coming? What's going on? I had to come
out of a meeting for this . . .'

'Jay?' Her voice is shrill – a squawk lost in the storm. 'Jay,
I've got lost. I'm losing it . . . I don't know where I am and it's
raining and nothing's working and I swear to God I gave myself
enough time, I really do . . .'

'Liz? Elizabeth, I can barely hear you, where are you?'

'Oh shit oh shit, she's still going to charge for the session!
She said there was a cancellation policy. I can't even see!'

'Elizabeth, you have to speak up. Did you say you'd missed
the appointment?'

'I'm sorry, I'm just so sorry – it looked so pretty before and
now it's . . . I don't know . . . like the windscreen's simmering,
boiling, like, I don't know what to do . . .'

'Elizabeth! I have to go back in to my meeting. Call me when
you get into a better signal zone. I can barely hear what you're
saying. I'll see you when I get home. Did you say there might be
maids of honour in the oven? I won't get my hopes up, but . . .'

Liz hears the scream before she registers the pain in her throat.
Looks for the danger before she realizes that it is she who is
screeching, wild and furious, in the cramped, sweaty confines of
the car. She who is gawping out through a shattered spy-glass
at the big yellow headlights of the big silver car. She whose
world is suddenly full of terrible, blaring honk and screech of
horn and brakes. She who is yanking at the wheel, muscles
straining, fists white around the leather.

Somewhere, out in the storm, she registers the sound of metal
on metal; the clang and crunch and the squeal of rubber against
stone; the swell of pain in her shoulders; neck and back as she
is flung forward and back and her head whips forward as if on
springs.

And she is spinning. Whirling. Turning in raucous pirouettes
across the black road beneath a grey sky, her vision full of forest
and stone and sky.

She does not register the little stone wall until the car has
already smashed through it; tyres chewing stone, then air, then
grass and earth and . . . and she is slaloming down the steep
bank towards the frothing, swollen river in the valley floor.

The airbag explodes in a shower of sparks and stars. Her head strikes glass. Fractures it into cobwebs and diamonds, and then it crumples entirely and the cold wet air rushing into the car slaps her like so many fists. Pennies of cold rain strike her face, her eyelids, her lips. For a moment it feels as though claws are reaching out to scrabble madly at her eyes and throat, and then the windscreen is caving in and the branch is spearing the headrest and grinding along her jawline; spears and splinters of ancient wood shooting into the car like a rain of arrows.

And then the awful realization: *I'm going to be in so much trouble . . .*

FOUR

S he can smell sap; an eerie Christmas-tree scent that fills her head with pine needles and sugared almonds. Fuel, too. Pulverized earth. And blood. She can taste it, in the back of her throat.

She lies for a spell. She knows, with atypical certainty, that she is injured. Her face feels wet. She can't be sure whether she is facing the right way up, or if the sensation of moisture at the corner of her mouth is saliva or blood.

After a while, she becomes aware of the sound of her Scandinavian satnav. She wonders if he is telling her she has made a wrong turn, and the thought seems to cut through the thick carpet of numbness that dulls her wits.

She realizes the car has come to a stop halfway down the embankment. Hears the dentist-drill whirr of tyres spinning on nothing. She adjusts her position and pain shoots down her arms, her legs, her neck. She grimaces, and tries again. The airbag lies in her lap, hanging from the steering wheel, all powder and glass.

She fumbles for the door handle and tugs at it with fingers that don't seem to want to do what she tells them. The lock clicks open and she fumbles at the seatbelt clip with her other hand. She pushes the door with her shoulder, glass falling from the frame, drops of blood appearing on the backs of her hands.

She hears voices. Sees the vehicle fill with geometric shapes, cuboids and diamonds of light and shade. Slithers out of the steaming hunk of metal and lands, painfully, on a slope of sodden grass. She lies back. Squints into the leaden sky; raindrops falling in their trillions. She feels strangely peaceful. They gave her a drug in the hospital that had made her feel like this: all floaty and ethereal and no trouble to anybody.

'She's moving! Mick, here, grab my hand, I'm going to go down like Eddie the bloody Eagle in a moment . . .'

She tries to speak. It comes out as a croak. She manages to raise her arms, to wipe her face, and she registers that most of the liquid on her palms is colourless. She pushes her hair back. Pain, there. A lump forming in her parting; a sticky substance at her crown.

'Don't move. Stay there . . . for fuck's sake . . . what were you bloody doing!'

She doesn't know the voice. She pushes herself up into a sitting position and looks at the crumpled shape of the car. A familiar panic rises. *He's going to do his nut, Liz. He's going to go fucking spare!*

'Are you all right? Shit, stupid bloody question. You came out of nowhere – on my side of the road, what were you doing?'

She pulls a face. 'I'm OK,' she croaks. Coughs and spits and tries again. 'I'm all right. I can move. Don't . . .'

Her words are cut short by the sudden, painful impact of a wellington boot thudding into her shoulder. She lets out a grunt and rolls into a ball as a sodden, stocky figure in a waxed jacket scoots past her in a flurry of curses; red face opening in a series of angry vowels.

He shuffles back up the slope. Peers down at her. She looks up into a broad face. Fifty-something, at least. Checked shirt and a coat she associates with the queen.

'Christ, I nearly went myself! Are you hurt? There's blood on your cheek. On your hands.' He moves a light up and down her, peering at her like livestock at market. 'What were you doing? We nearly went right through you! That little thing's no good for here, you fool . . .'

'I'm sorry,' she mumbles. She tries to get into a sitting position. Catches a whiff of beery breath and looks into yellow eyes seamed with red.

She feels a hand slipping behind her head, ungentle fingers in her hair. Experiences a sudden lurching movement, and she finds herself upright, half crouching, pain streaking down her arm. She looks past him. On the far side of the river is an old building. Narrow, two-storeys, holes in the slate roof. There's a light on in the upstairs window, so it seems the house is winking at her. She peers closer. She'd thought it abandoned, like the others that dot the valley. Her vision swims, and clears. She can make out signs of life. Lights. Movement. The flicker of an animal moving swiftly, shadows thrown against the crumbling wall.

'Here,' comes the voice, in her face. 'Look at me. You're all right, yeah? Christ you scared us. Thought you were going to end up in the brook! You're all right. Cuts and bruises and you'll be sore tomorrow but a cup of sweet tea and a lie down and you'll be right as ninepence.'

Liz licks her lips. Shuffles backwards, trying to focus on the face in front of her own. He keeps glancing past her. Painfully, she twists and follows his gaze. There are three figures at the top of the slope, standing by the huge, big rectangle of the vehicle she had clipped. A broken light illuminates the tumbling sky. She squints, head aching. She can make out shapes. A tall figure, oddly tall, holds a large umbrella over two smaller, broad-shouldered specimens. They stand still as cut-outs.

'I didn't see you,' splutters Liz, as the buzzing in her head starts to clear. 'The rain was coming down so hard and I couldn't work the satnav and then you just came out of nowhere . . .'

'Not me, love,' he says, one side of his face twisting, so that the corner of his mouth reaches almost to his eye. Creases appear in his skin. Neatly-spaced teeth peeking out from half-parted lips. 'You were in the middle of the bloody road! I know these roads like the back of my hand. You bounced off the Landy like a ball!'

Temper starts to flare. She's in pain. The car's a mess. She's missed her appointment. Jay is going to be so angry with her and she knows he won't really believe her when she explains that she had tried so hard to get things right. She feels herself filling up with angry words.

'I'm laying here bleeding and you're having a go!'

'You're all right . . .'

'And you're getting your story straight for your insurance claim while I'm still not sure if I can bloody walk . . .'

'You'll be the one who needs a story, you'll be paying for that light on the Landy, I can tell you that much . . .'

'Will I?' She grabs a handful of wet grass and yanks herself upwards. She feels ill-treated. 'You've been drinking, I can smell it. There's barely a pupil in your eyes! Wait until the police get here and then we'll see who's laughing, eh?'

'Don't start with me, lady, I'm the one trying to help!'

'You all right down there, boss? Need a hand getting back up?'

Liz turns at the sound of the voice. One of the smaller shapes is leaning forward. The headlight illuminates a fleshy round face, dark hair brushed forward and snipped neatly in the centre of an unlined forehead.

'Nowt I can't handle,' comes the reply. He pushes his face close to hers. She sees little white flecks of stubble that he missed with his morning shave. Notices a weird strip of coarse white hair growing between his collar and his Adam's apple. Sees flecks of food in the overlap of his front teeth.

'I don't even know if I'm with the AA any more,' stammers Liz. 'I was, but I think that came free with a credit card, and that got cancelled, so . . .'

'You're burbling on, love. Rest your voice.'

'My shoulder feels like I've been hit with a baseball bat . . .'

He gives her a hard look. 'Much experience of that, have you?'

Liz doesn't laugh. Keeps blinking, hoping the fog will clear. Hears him clap his hands and rub them together, decision made.

'You're all right,' he declares. 'No lasting damage. We'll say no more about it. You can get the car back up the bank with a tow rope and a tractor.'

She can hear static. A crackle of voices, as though an old transistor radio is picking up interference. She can't seem to concentrate. Had she heard right? Was he just going to leave?

'A tractor? What? I mean, pardon? I mean . . .'

'You're just waffling now, love. You'll sort it, I'm sure. Pretty lass, people will be falling over themselves . . .'

She can't seem to process the words quickly enough to respond with anything helpful. She rubs her forehead, unsure she has heard right.

'Me? I can barely bloody stand up – you sound like you're going on your merry way!'

'Like I said, I've got places to be, and you're OK. Somebody will be along in a minute. I live at the Manor House in Carrshield, a couple of miles that way. Send me the bill if you're going to be a cow about it. Car like that, though, I've done you a favour writing it off.'

Liz feels as though the world is shifting beneath her feet. She realizes the rain is slowing down – the tectonic plates of grey sky slowly parting to reveal a streak of blue.

'You can't just piss off and leave me. I don't know where I am!'

He gives a nasty smile at that. 'Modern woman, aren't you? Strong, independent, shouldn't need any help from a man.'

'Are you out of your pissing mind?' she shouts, her nose almost touching his. 'I'm calling the police, I swear it . . .'

'Good luck getting a signal,' he says, and pushes past her, reaching down for fistfuls of wet grass to haul himself up the slope.

Liz is too stunned to say a word. In the silence, as the raindrops dry up, she hears the sound of a low, throaty engine; the revving of gears; the whispered shush of big tyres moving over long, wet grass. She turns in the direction of the noise. From lower down the valley, not far from a twisted copse of trees, a quad bike is speeding towards her, bumping expertly over the divots and trenches. The man has stopped climbing the slope and is glaring at the nearing shape. A hard-to-read expression clutches his face. He looks at once hateful and afraid.

'There you go, love,' he spits, hurrying further up the slope towards the road. 'Knight in armour coming to save the day. You've survived one brush with death, another might do you good. Watch yourself with that one. He's got blood on his hands.'

'No, look, you can't just . . .'

He's already too far away to hear. She watches, despairingly, as the tallest of the spectators offers a hand and yanks him back on to the road. Watches as he folds the umbrella and the quartet wordlessly climb back into the great shining shape of the vehicle. Puts her hands in her hair and almost cries with the pain and frustration of it all. Turns as the revving gears drown out the sound of the car pulling away in an elegant crunch of gravel and shattered glass.

On the quad bike, a man and a dog. It's a Border collie; black and white, tongue lolling from a happy, pink mouth. It sits behind a man who is looking at her with a gaze of such piercing intensity that it chills her all the way through. She realizes how cold she is; how her clothes cling to her like just-washed bedsheets.

'Bastard left you, did he?' asks the man, his accent North East. 'Prick. You all right?'

Liz isn't sure what to say. So much has happened. Her head

is too full to process it all. She blinks the rain from her eyes and engrosses herself in him. Short grey-black hair, blue eyes, a few days of stubble on a weather-beaten, angular face. He's older than her. Ten years, maybe more. His gloved hands protrude from the cuffs of a battered, military-style, leather coat, hanging open to reveal a work-hardened body in a plain white tee and quilted shirt.

'You all right?' he asks again. 'I just live yonder. You want to come phone somebody? Get yourself cleaned up?' He gets off the bike and steps towards her, blue eyes close enough to see herself in. 'I'm Jude,' he says, quietly. 'This is Marshall. We live in that tip of a place across the river. I'm asking if you want some help. What's your name?'

Liz doesn't know why she chooses to introduce herself falsely. Will never be able to adequately explain why she chooses to leave Liz on the damp valley floor.

'I'm Betsy,' she says. And it feels true.

FIVE

U p close, he smells of leather and damp dog. Arms around his waist, face pressed against the wet fabric of his coat, bouncing over the muddy ground, she has plenty of opportunity to consider his aroma. Her eyes are shut tight, and the roar of the engine and the rushing of the wind fills her heard with a noise that does not need examination. Unencumbered, she devotes herself to scent. There's wood shavings in there; that sawdust smell of hamster cages. Wood smoke, perhaps. That mustiness of clothes dried in a damp room. And there, on the traces of her olfactory map: the sweet green musk of marijuana. She wonders whether he would notice if she poked out her tongue and tasted the seam of his jacket. Grits her teeth and wonders what the fuck is wrong with her.

A hand, gripping her arm: rough leather on her exposed wrist. She opens her eyes instinctively. Stifles a squawk as he turns the quad sharp left and she feels the soggy furry bundle of Marshall press against her back.

She realizes he is speaking to her. Raises her head from his back and tries to catch the echo on the air.

'Up there,' he says, again, and nods up the slope. 'Sorry if it gets bumpy, I'll try not to shake you to pieces.'

She squints up a lonely stretch of green, a drystone wall snaking along a ridge to her right, shielding the rutted track from the worst of the wind. It drops away a little further ahead, then rises steeply again to where she can make out the half-dark oblong of the house she had seen from across the river. He twists the throttle and the quad surges forward. A straggle of dark hawthorn slashes at her face and hair, the road narrowing; high grass and cow parsley sprouting tall between the tyre tracks. She hears the grass whip by. Sees a stem of some unknown wildflower bleed green across the dark fabric of Jude's sleeve. Swollen grass heads and dandelion clocks burst in tiny explosions of smoke.

Above, the sky is a great anvil. In the distance, a stripe of scarves: billowing, grey; distant rain moving fast.

Liz feels her stomach heave as they surge back up the far side of the rise. She glimpses a steep-sided ravine; white water surging through ancient rocks and fallen trees, and then they are swinging hard left into the muddy forecourt of a building that glares down like an Easter Island face. It's a perfect rectangle: a fairy-tale tower; rough-hewn sandstone and mossy stone slab roof. Three storeys, maybe twenty foot by twenty foot, but it has the forbidding air of a siege fortress and looks as though it could boast a portcullis and moat at the far side. She squints upwards. Some of the windows have been smashed in the upper floor. Deliberately, by the looks of things. Tattered strips of glass hang from a mullioned framework. Jude looks up too.

'Bastards,' he mutters, turning off the engine. She can feel tension in his body; see the strength with which he grips the throttle. 'Bastards.'

The silence that follows is a physical thing; a damp blanket of absolute soundlessness that makes her feel as if even a whisper could be picked up by the breeze and amplified to a roar as it crossed the fields.

He is gone for a moment. Drowsy, dizzy, she watches as he crunches across a tatty courtyard to a big, iron-studded wooden door. She thinks she must be hallucinating. Blinks and tries to clear it. It's still there, a huge, red-brown bird, head lolling, chest mangled; its vast wings nailed either side of the doorframe as if crucified.

The world spins again. She sees him unpin the bird and take it in his arms like a child. Sees the way he screws up his eyes, doing battle with tears, as he crosses the yard and deposits the great, destroyed creature in a plastic sack that hangs from the wooden gate. He shakes his head. Spits.

'There you go,' he says, and she feels his arms around her, gentle. She sees herself as a dying bird, her wings broken, plumage blood-spattered, his big gentle hands delicate against her frail bones.

She feels herself being helped down from the bike. Her feet squelch in thick, chocolatey mud. She shivers, uncontrollably, as the wind charges up the track. She sways where she stands, the house moving forward and back in her vision. She feels woozy. Empty. There's a strange humming feeling in her lips, as though she has been fiercely kissed or softly slapped or eaten something spicy.

'I feel really odd,' she mumbles, but it sounds thick and far away. She looks across the forecourt to where the dog is running in happy circles. Jude is standing still, waiting for her to follow. She can't make him out. There is three of him. Nine. A procession of paper dolls, their hands joined, strobing like silhouettes in a spinning zoetrope.

From nowhere, a rush of paranoia. Of hypochondria. An absolute flood of apocalyptic worst-case scenarios: her mind becoming an open medical journal chock-full of horrible propositions. A fractured skull. A swollen brain, soon to manifest itself with bloodied eyeball and the trickle of vibrant red from her ears. No, a brain tumour. An aneurysm. An approaching fugue state, certain to plunge her world into mute incomprehension and incontinence. No, something new, something as yet unidentified, the explanation for all of it, for the BPD symptoms; the erratic behaviour, the mood swings. Alleluia, an epiphany, a truth, suddenly revealing itself here, now, miles from home, alone with a strange man; a man who isn't Jay, a man that Jay wouldn't like; a man close enough to smell, to leave his scent on her; to mark her like an animal; a wolf, all fur and claws and pheromones.

'Oh, there . . . wow . . . that's torn it . . .'

She falls forward, banging down on to one knee, a silly half-smile on her face; church bells and ice-cream-van chimes singing in her head. She feels bloody stupid. Feels sick. Feels weirdly, oddly high. And then she feels wet and cold and the world tastes of dirt, and her face is sinking into the mud with the same sensuous ease that her consciousness is drifting into darkness.

SIX

She wakes to the sound of shrieking: a shrill crescendo; an inhaled scream. At the same time she registers rough wetness on her skin. Like thrown playing cards, her mind fills with pictures. She sees a huge, rough-tongued beast, crouched over her, scenting her, lapping wetly at her exposed face.

'Fuck off . . . fuck the fuck off . . .'

She flails, her legs tangled up in something, lashing out as if she has kicked a wasp's nest. Pushes herself backwards, eyes fluttering open, expecting to see red-seamed eyes and an open, hungry mouth.

Jude is staring at her, one hand holding a warm, damp cloth, muddied where he has been trying to softly remove the crusted dirt from her cheeks.

'What are you fucking doing?' she asks, her arms tightening at her sides – one knee coming up, coiled to kick out. She hears the rustle of wool on silk. Glances down at herself. She's under a blanket, laid down on something soft. The cushion beneath her face smells of damp dog and wood smoke. It smells of Jude.

'You swear a lot,' says Jude, quietly. 'And you sing in your sleep.'

He's crouching in front of her; a boy staring into the depths of a pond. His gaze is intense, as if checking her bones for fissures and cracks.

'No I don't. I never sing in my sleep.'

'You do. It's nice. A lullaby. *Alive-alive-O.*'

'No way. I've got an awful voice. I sound like a goose.'

'Very gentle voice, you've got. There's a blues singer from Dublin sings like that. She doesn't swear the same as you though.'

'Soz, Dad,' says Liz, and it sounds so ridiculous to herself that she starts laughing. It's a bright, manic sound and Jude gives a twitch of a smile in response. 'Sorry, I don't know what I'm saying. I feel so out of it. Have I been asleep . . .' She stops herself, memories surging back. 'I heard screaming.'

He pauses, considering. 'Curlew,' he says. 'You don't know their call?'

She scowls, irritated at the notion she should know what he is talking about, while furious at herself for her ornithological inadequacies. 'That's a bird, I presume.'

'Yes,' he says, softly. 'I don't hear it as a scream. Yeats wrote a poem about them. Said it reminded him of a lost love.'

'Yeats,' says Liz, raising a hand to her head. She opens her mouth wide, trying to pop her jaw, then stops, embarrassed at herself. 'Yeats,' she says again, hoping something will present itself. 'The Cranberries did a song about his grave.'

He smiles again, showing neat white teeth, evenly spaced. 'Yeah, I think they did.'

Liz starts to sit up. Considers herself. Her legs feel cold and uncomfortable. She's still wearing her wet trousers. Her cardigan's gone though. She's still got her T-shirt. She makes up a narrative, drawing swift lines between the key points. He saw the crash. He came to her aid. He brought her home so she could call for help. She had a funny turn. He brought her inside. Wrapped her in blankets and did his best to clean her up. She checks the story for things to worry about. Can't see any obvious impropriety. Considers it again from a second perspective. Jay's seems most suitable. She got lost. Had a crash. Abandoned the scene of an accident. Went off with a stranger to his isolated farmhouse in the middle of nowhere. Swooned like a storybook princess. Came to half-dressed, being wiped down by a handsome man spouting poetry . . .

'Erm . . .'

'Your cardigan's drying. I did my best to clean you up but you're still a bit, well, streaky. How do you feel?'

'I'm not sure. Odd. Misplaced. Sore. But kind of OK too.'

'It was the adrenaline wearing off. Horrible feeling. I've gone down like that myself. After it's all over, after the rush or the euphoria or whatever, you find yourself shaking like a leaf.'

'I thought it might be one of my panic attacks,' says Liz, carelessly. 'It felt like that, a bit.'

Jude shrugs, not unkindly. 'Either way, it can't have been very nice. No bad dreams? People sometimes get them here, though I reckon people scare themselves half to death thinking about ghosts in the walls and it's hardly surprising they don't get much kip.'

'I thought the cloth was a big tongue,' she says, closing one eye. Her head is still hurting.

'There's nothing I can say to that,' replies Jude, scratching at his forehead. His voice has a pleasing timbre; a lullaby quality that threatens to pull her back into sleep unless she clings to wakefulness. She considers the shape of him as he moves away, taking the damp cloth through to the half-dark area at the far side of the room. He dumps it in a deep sink and busies himself with making tea. There's a black kettle rattling away on a proper old Rayburn cooker. A big, brown teapot sits atop a pile of books and paperwork that seems one loud cough away from avalanche.

She changes position. Slowly, she takes in her surroundings. The crusted dirt on her face pulls at her skin as the growing smile lights up her features. She's in something akin to a farmhouse kitchen-diner, though the only place she has seen a room like this before was on a day trip to the Beamish Victorian Museum, and in the occasional BBC costume drama. She feels as though she has woken in the nineteenth century, and it's clear she hasn't landed anywhere well-to-do. It's low-ceilinged and dingy; the only light coming from the pot-bellied log burner standing in the kind of chimney place that she imagines being a breeze for Santa each Christmas. The floor is all flagstones and loose timbers, mismatched planks stained black by exposure to the outdoors in some former life. There are only two windows, and these pitifully small, set in colossally deep alcoves that have been padded out with dusty cushions. She's lying on a low, three-seater sofa, directly opposite a window that frames a gloomy landscape; miles upon mile of green delineated by grey walls and the occasional copse of trees. The rain is coming down again. She feels safe here, somehow. Feels as though she has found a little safe space and crawled inside it while a tempest rages outside.

'You take sugar, I presume?'

She bristles, unhappy at being read. 'What makes you say that? All girls take sugar, do we?'

'I asked if you wanted sugar,' he says, without turning.

'Oh,' she says, deflating. 'Misheard. It's the sound of the storm. I can barely hear you.'

He brings her a mug of strong, brown tea. Hands it to her without a word. She follows him with her eyes as he sits down in a rocking chair by the window. She sips her tea. It's strong and sweet, just the way she likes it.

'This place is amazing,' she says, through the steam. Her eyes keep alighting on new peculiarities. There is a wooden spinning wheel by the long table in the gloom of the kitchen. A wrought-iron range hangs above; all copper saucepans and patterned metal kettles. By the fire a deep chest, black metal hinges and untreated wood: a woven table runner hanging off one end; scuffed paw-prints turning its creamy pattern a mess of earthy browns. The walls are decorated in mismatched prints, an eclectic mix that reminds her of the John Derian coffee-table book she had failed to persuade Jay to buy for her last birthday. Huge roses in a brocade frame; eye-test charts in a language she doesn't recognize; anatomically precise cross-sections of human organs and limbs, interspersed with sprigs of dried flowers and random pieces of cracked mirror, reflecting random flashes of red-gold light on the higgledy-piggledy walls. There are dried grasses in empty ordnance shells by the fire. Porcelain dolls stuffed haphazardly atop a low table, a dog basket beneath. And everywhere cobwebs, a fog of them, hanging in every angle: parabolas of dirty lace.

What are you doing Liz? You're chatting with this bloke like it's a date or something. You've been in an accident. Nobody knows you're here. What are you doing, you silly girl!

She shakes her head, two bright spots of colour suddenly giving her face a doll-like aspect.

'My car,' she says, pulling herself upright. 'I need my phone. I need to phone home. I had an appointment.' Her vision fills with the sound of metal on metal and the horrible slalom down the hill. She pulls at her hair, the frustration needing to find an outlet. She doesn't cut any more. Doesn't burn herself or starve herself or fill her guts with tissue so as to always feel full. But she's never stopped the hair-pulling.

'It's in hand,' begins Jude.

'He went and left me! I know the crash was my fault but he basically said if I wasn't dying it wasn't his problem. Told me to send him the bill and buggered off!'

Jude turns away from her, his words thrown back carelessly. 'There's an old saying. If it walks like a tosser, and talks like a tosser, it's probably a tosser.'

Liz finds herself smiling. 'That Yeats too?'

'Occam's Razor,' he says, smiling, and although she doesn't get what she presumes is a joke, Liz grins, knowingly.

'Yeah. Ha.'

'I've got a copy of the manuscript showing William of Ockham, actually. Wouldn't know where to put my hands on it.'

'Yeah? I'm like that. Honestly, the amount of phone chargers I lose in a year is insane. Jay would be tearing his hair out, if he had any. Plenty of chest fur and his back looks like a pedestal mat, but it's hardly the same, is it?'

He laughs at that, a genuine, happy sound. 'You've got a gift with words. Are you a writer? Something creative, I'm sure.'

She pulls a face. 'I'm still working it out. Done lots of things but it doesn't always suit. Creative? Maybe. I used to think so. Jay would say I just create chaos. I create headaches.'

'I'm not warming to Jay,' says Jude, smiling. 'Husband?'

Liz shakes her head. 'Long-term boyfriend. He was married before me and it put him off the whole idea. She took a lot of his money when they divorced. You can understand his reservations, I'm sure.'

Jude scratches a hand through his hair. Looks at the fire and then back at her. 'I don't know enough.' He shrugs. 'Walks like a prick, talks like a prick . . .'

'Don't,' she says, and means it. 'I shouldn't say mean things about him. He's my rock really. He put up with a lot. I'm a nightmare. I've got a few loose wires.' She taps her head. 'Bats in the belfry, he says.'

'Yeah? I like bats. And I'm good with wires.'

'Are you a farmer, or something?'

'A farmer-or-something just about covers it, yeah. I'm just like you. Don't know what I am. I was meant to be one thing and now I'm not, but whatever I am, I think I enjoy it. Hope I do.'

He stretches out. Marshall, who has clearly been secreted away waiting for an opportunity, scurries in and leaps on to his master's lap. He gives him a heartfelt stroke, scratching behind his ear.

She smiles. 'You sound as mixed up as me. Would you believe me if I told you I was on my way to see a shrink? I got so lost. Got in such a tizzy and the next minute that big car clipped me and I really thought that was it.' She pouts, a petulant toddler. 'Is it wrecked? Proper wrecked.'

'Friend of mine is on his way to tow it to the garage in Stanhope. They're built to crumple and it did its job.'

Liz looks crestfallen. 'Jay got me that car because he couldn't stand watching me try and park a normal-sized one. I don't even know if I've kept the insurance up to date.' She sits forward, face in hands. Pain shoots down her arm. It awakens other dormant injuries and at once she feels like she is a patchwork person; a quilt of alternating wounds.

'I brought your bag down from the boot. A few other odds and sods – I wasn't sure what you'd need.'

'Odds and sods,' says Liz, quietly. 'My grandad used to say that.'

'Wise people, grandads.'

'Mine was. Loved the outdoors. Loved adventure. He'd have loved this place. Is it like . . . a castle?'

'It's like a castle, yeah,' he says, smiling with his eyes. 'It's called Wolfcleugh Bastle. A fortified farm, really – very popular around here in the old days when you had to defend what was yours.' He thinks about what he's saying and laughs, as if at a private joke. 'Nothing much has changed really. Still all about mating rights and territory and who owns which blade of grass. Never could understand it and I'm a farmer's boy. It drove Maeve to distraction and she was from money. Went from being one of the toffs on horseback to getting mucky in the gutter with the saboteurs. Never afraid of getting stuck in. I sometimes wonder whether it was about animal welfare or having a good excuse for a ruck.'

Liz enjoys his voice. She stretches her back, feeling warm and oddly relaxed, the way she remembers feeling before the operation when she was small. She could fall asleep, given half a chance.

'Did you say you were visiting a shrink?' he asks, as he produces a tin of tobacco and starts sprinkling brown leaf into a cigarette paper. It's a dark brown; almost black – the resultant roll-up the sort of thing she imagines a cowboy smoking. He seals it with his tongue, expertly. He tucks it away, clearly not intending to smoke in company.

'You don't approve of shrinks? Should I just man up? Need a kick up the arse, do I?'

'No, I just thought I knew everybody round here? They must be new to the valley. And as for the other stuff, no, of course not. What sort of twat thinks like that?'

'She's based in Corbridge,' explains Liz, brushing over the question. Her eyes drift up towards the mountain of books. She could sit here and read them, one after the other, in the warmth, with this nice man who seems to listen when she talks. 'I'm excessively crap at directions.'

'Ah,' he says, ruefully. 'You're about ten miles out, but that's only as the crow flies. Your satnav let you down, did it?'

'Went barmy,' she says, cross again. 'Just kept spinning and back-tracking and I started freaking out.' She frowns, a memory surfacing. 'Was there a bird pinned to your door?'

He gives a tight smile. 'Endangered species. Raptor. People know I take it personally when they get caught in the firing line. They were probably trying to get my attention. I've got a mate with the RSPB. I'll take it to her.'

'I heard a story on the radio, just before the crash. Do people really pay that much money to shoot grouse? I don't think I know a grouse? Is it like a fat pheasant?'

He smiles at that. 'Yeah, that just about covers it. Half a million will be shot this summer and no end of other animals will be killed by gamekeepers in case they spoil the sport. They burn the heather too. They'd wreck the whole bloody valley if it meant there were more grouse for their rich mates to shoot each summer. Rare birds getting caught in the crossfire is just collateral damage.' He stops himself, aware he's lit his cigarette without meaning to. He grinds it out into a dirty coffee mug. 'Sorry. You'll already have enough reasons to dislike Campion. Don't need more from me. Tell me about yourself. I'm sorry you had to go through all that. Must have been scary.'

She checks his face for any indication he may be taking the piss. Finds none. 'I've got a sort of, well, condition,' she says, confessing. 'I get worked up. I have a kind of excess of emotions . . .'

'A lot of metal in the ground here,' says Jude, thoughtfully. 'Old mining area, I'm sure you know that. Creates a bit of a blackspot. That, and the fact no bugger wants to invest in an area where you could cram all the residents into one half of a football pitch. Can be a bugger getting deliveries but at least the bailiffs and the Jehovah's Witnesses stay at arm's length.'

'It really is the middle of nowhere,' muses Liz, looking around. 'Very *Wuthering Heights*.'

'Bit of a history,' he says, waving in the general direction of the walls, the ceiling; the little courtyard and the miles and miles of damp green valley beyond. 'It's one of those places that exists between the lines. It's at the edge of things. Northumberland, County Durham, Cumbria. Stone's throw from Hadrian's Wall and the Scottish border. Suffered plenty at the hands of raiders from across the Border. Plenty of blood spilled in these fields and plenty men buried beneath them. Farming and mining, that's what this valley has always been about and those who didn't die beneath the ground coughed their lungs up once they were too broken to work. It's like living in a big, old museum half the time. You sometimes get the feeling you'll open the back door and see soldiers going past on their way to crush the Jacobites.' He stops himself, aware he has been talking more than listening. 'Sorry, I don't get much company. Not company I want to have a chat with, at any rate. I've never been the chatty one. I like to listen. Maybe I just want to tell you everything about me so it's all out there. I must trust you.'

Liz feels her cheeks twitching, as though a grin is hiding under the surface. She wants more. Wants him to share confidences. Wants to hear about whoever he shares this draughty, tumbledown, little palace with. She jumps in, unable to think of a subtle way to introduce the subject. 'Is there a lady in your life or is it just you and Marshall?'

He rubs his tongue over dry lips. Pulls a face that's hard to read. 'She died,' he says, quietly. 'There's just me.'

'Oh I'm sorry,' says Liz, automatically. She curses herself. Knows she's just brought the room's mood down by a good few degrees. She eyes him again, unable to make the action inconspicuous. 'She must have been young.'

He scratches at his stubble with his left hand while stroking Marshall with the right. He looks older, suddenly. 'Too young,' he says, shrugging. 'But she lived well. Packed a lot in.'

'Sounds like you still miss her,' says Liz, and tries not to react when she hears the little voices in her head howl with laughter at the idiocy of the statement.

'Doesn't do to dwell. That's what she used to say, though she tended to say it in a fancy Latin way that drove me up the wall. So much cleverer than me. Cleverest person I ever met.'

'Are those her books?' asks Liz, pointing up.

'Aye. I've read a couple. Classics, mostly.'

'Her instruments?'

'No, they're mine.'

'You play? That's a trombone, right, the long curly one? And I recognize the saxophone there. Love the sound of the sax. Sexiest instrument ever.'

He smiles, clearly pleased. 'Yeah. I'm all right. I used to be good. I don't practice enough now but yeah, I was OK. You play?'

She shakes her head. 'I wanted to learn the piano but Jay said it was too expensive, what with his Snowdonia trip.'

Jude is about to reply when he glances towards the window. A moment later she hears the low thrum of a big car working its way up the track. 'Good ears,' she says, approvingly. 'Company?'

'Your carriage,' he says, with a soft little smile. 'Don't expect to get a word in edgewise on the way, she likes a chance to talk at somebody new. She'll drop you home.'

Liz's face twists in puzzlement. 'Who will? Who's here?'

'Sylvia,' he says, with a wave. 'Lives in Sparty Lea. Nice woman when you get to know her. Unfortunately she rarely allows people the time. But she's an old-fashioned sort and happy to help. I asked and she said yes.'

'But my car . . . getting it back, or written off, or whatever, and I haven't got any money to pay her . . .'

Jude stands. Marshall, after a moment's protest, drops to the floor. Jude gathers up Liz's possessions. Her bag, some letters that might be important, a couple of paperbacks and some leaflets. One is an NHS guide to living with BPD. His gaze lingers on it for a moment. Then he hands it back.

'Oh God, I look such a state . . .' says Liz, her anxiety returning like a flood. Thoughts pop in her mind, bursting like hot kernels of corn. 'Did you phone Jay? Carly? Did you tell him what had happened?'

'Did *I* phone your partner? No, that's not for me to . . .'

It feels like there are hot needles in her head. She's being sent away. Sent packing. Bundled up with a stranger and sent out like a tramp. Why had he bothered being nice to her if he was just killing time until her lift turned up? Why mess with her head like that? She suddenly sees it clearly – this was his thing, the rescuing of damsels in distress, buttering them up, showing them a glimpse of a life they could endure, then pulling the rug from under them. What sort of cruel bastard did that? What sort of nasty fucker treated people that way? She scores crescent scars into the cover of the paperback, clutching it so tightly her arms begin to throb. How had he texted this *Sylvia* without her noticing? When had he done it? Sent his nasty little SOS? What stupid, idiotic thing had she said or not said that had shown her up as the silly little chubby-kneed toddler who needed sending on her merry way?

'Are you OK, Betsy? You look a bit stressed out? Sylvia's literally a nice lady from down the valley and she's doing you a favour because she owes me a favour, and that's how the system kind of works around here. As for the car, my pal will call me and I'll call you, if that's OK. Up to you what you tell your partner, that's none of my business. If you're cool with it, I'll take your number and let you know as soon as there's anything to tell.'

She feels different emotions raging inside her. The paranoia of a moment ago twists into a new shape. Is he trying to get in her pants? Is this an elaborate ruse to sleep with her? And Sylvia? How does she know that the old bat isn't some octogenarian pimp, whisking her away to God knows where to be mercilessly plundered by sex-starved geriatrics?

'Betsy . . .'

That name again. The one she'd given him. The one that had felt right. She snatches up a pen from the mess on the table and scribbles down her number. She writes 'Betsy' above it. Marshall rubs up against her, his head finding the palm of her hand. Jude stands almost close enough to do the same.

'Sounds crazy, but I'm pleased you crashed,' he says, and smiles at the silliness of it.

She nods. Isn't sure she can speak again without something unexpected rushing up her throat.

'Well, Betsy,' he says, extending his hand. 'I'll be in touch.' He takes her palm in his. His palms are rough. Fingertips too. It's like rubbing her hand across tree bark.

He gestures towards the door. She stands still, unable to propel herself forward. 'I have to ask,' she says, lips pursed. 'Occam's Razor. What were you talking about?'

He laughs; the same pleasant sound: a grandad reading a joke from a cracker. 'Entities should not be multiplied without necessity,' he says, softly.

'Sorry?'

'A theory, posited by a monk eight hundred years ago. Sometimes, the simplest answer is the right one.'

Oh,' she says, replaying back the conversation. 'Walks like a prick, talks like a prick – is a prick, yes?'

He nods. 'It sounds better in your accent than mine.'

She grabs her cardigan, warm from the fire. It smells of him. 'Thanks,' she says, again, and heads for the door.

He pulls her back, one hand on her wrist. Looks at her for a moment, as if committing her to memory. She doesn't breathe. Can't. And then, as if he has drunk his fill, he lets her go.

She holds his scent in her mouth and nose until she fears she will die if she doesn't exhale.

She holds the cardigan to her face, where it soaks up her tears, and hides her smile.

SEVEN

Sylvia, is transpires, is seventy-four. She completed her first bungee jump the day before her seventieth birthday. Performed her first charity parachute jump three months after. It was her first flight, too. First time in a plane and she jumped out. Fancy that! She left it late to become a daredevil but now it's all she can think about. She's going up in a gyro-copter next summer. It's being paid for by her grandson, Phillip, with a double L, who's doing very well in public relations and has managed to get three articles in the *Hexham Courant* about her exploits. She's raised over £36,000 for Guide Dogs for the Blind and not far off the same again for a special unit at the school in Allenheads, where her neighbour's two daughters go. Lovely girls, they are. Eight and ten. Always call her by her first name but that's the modern way, isn't it? Their mum's been through it, right enough. Never found the right man, but sampled plenty from the menu, though it pains her to say so. Still, maybe that's best. Get your kicks while you can, and all that. She some-times wishes she'd done things differently. Should maybe have moved away when her husband died, but by then she'd grown used to her own four walls and wasn't sure if it would do her more harm than good to uproot herself. He was a decent husband, truth be told, though he was a long way from dynamic. Solid. Reliable. Like a Volvo, or socks from the Edinburgh Woollen Mill. Been gone nine years now. She's heard about dating websites and those apps you can get on your phone to help you find a nice gentleman, but it all seems a bit tacky and she doubts she'll find anybody willing to give her half the thrill of the bungee jump, or do half the damage to her hips . . .

Sitting in the passenger seat, the window cushioned with the cardigan, Liz is aware she has no obligation to respond to any of this information. She is, largely, a receptacle. It's a lot like having sex with Jay. Nothing required of her, save the occasional grunt. She has used the journey to compose sentences in her head. She feels an urge to log on to the Bipped forum and write an entry. She fancies she could make it funny and tragic and full of excitement all at once. She thinks she knows the voice she would use: self-deprecating; pithy, matter-of-fact. Can picture the entry on the page.

> So anyway, first DBT session went well – got lost, nearly died, totalled the car and had to be rescued from a hillside by a dishy farmer on a quad bike. Going well so far . . .

There's a red-haired girl from Oregon who posts on the forum three or four times a week. She's round-faced with dark eyes and loads of different shades of lipstick and she's got thousands of followers to her Instagram account thanks largely to her posts on Bipped. Liz wonders whether she should send her a personal message, asking for advice, telling her what an inspiration she is; hoping against hope that she'll give her a nod of approval and tell her fans that this new girl is an absolute hoot . . .

'Just let me know whether it's left or right at the river,' says Sylvia, merrily, as they drift around the roundabout on the outskirts of Durham. 'I used to come to Durham a couple of times a month but the parking's crazy, don't you think? I love the cathedral though I do resent having to stick money in the "donations" box. Not a donation if you get told to do it, is it? I never understand the parking neither. Every time I pull in to the multi-storey I think I know where I'm going to emerge and every time I'm wrong. Plenty of students, isn't there? Lots of the Asians, I've noticed – not that I've any objection to that, of course. Always seems like a seal of approval to me, when the Asians start appearing in droves. Very good at seeing a place on the up, in my experience . . .'

They're fighting the tea-time traffic. The sky is a washed-out blue; the same shade it had been when Liz had left this morning in such high spirits. She sees herself as she was at nine a.m.; her make-up perfect, coffee mug in hand, playing with the controls for the stereo. The memory extends a long, wormy tendril and winds it around her mood. Begins to tug. She feels her spirits fall. Feels the familiar accusatory voices inside. Why would anybody want to read a blog post by somebody with nothing useful to say? Why would anybody take any interest in somebody whose only notable feature is a constant ability to get things wrong? She can't even imagine telling Jay about what has happened so what does it say about her that she feels more comfortable turning it into an entertainment for strangers?

She glances over at Sylvia. She's a remarkably comforting sight. She's short and plump. She can't help noticing that her neck is exactly the same width as her head. Crowned with her bright red woolly hat, she looks to Liz like a bruised thumb topped with a raspberry.

'I think it would be better if I got myself cleaned up at my sister's place first, if that's OK,' says Liz, and is surprised to hear the thought so confidently expressed when she had not known she was going to say it until it emerged.

'You might be right,' says Sylvia, nosing the car forward and glancing over from the driving seat. She has piercing blue eyes that make Liz think of wolves and ice caves and various other things she has never actually seen. 'People wouldn't bat an eyelid at the dirt if you walked in to the pub round our way, though you'd turn a few heads for different reasons I'm sure. Nasty phrase but any fresh meat gets plenty of the old dogs sniffing, I can promise you that. And a good-looking girl like you? Bloody hell you'd be swatting them away with a stick, you would. Different story here, I'm guessing. I don't like to stereotype but I'm presuming it's all dinner parties and hanging baskets, is it? People doing bread in little saucers of oil – as if that's some sort of treat! I lived in the big city myself when I was younger. Thought it was amazing, right up to the point I needed a bit of help, and then there was nobody willing to give me the time of day. Still, maybe that's just Hartlepool . . .'

'Maybe,' says Liz, as Sylvia is momentarily distracted by a driver inching a large saloon vehicle into a gap just about big enough for a supermarket trolley. 'We don't really do the dinner party stuff. I'm not good with friends.'

'No? Hard to fathom. You seem lovely, though appearances can be deceiving. Had a neighbour, Olive her name was – brought me a plate of shepherd's pie one winter when she had some going spare and it took me three days to remember to get the plate back to her. Turned up on my doorstep with two of her sons – huge brutes they were – demanding to know why I was robbing from their mam! People are funny buggers, that's the knowledge I've got after seventy-four years. And nobody's the same from one day to the next.'

Liz finds herself smiling. 'I've got a few loose wires,' she says, tapping her head. 'I'm too emotional. I jump in with both feet. I can't regulate my emotions. Sometimes I don't know whether I'm going mad. Jay puts up with a lot from me. I've embarrassed him a few times. Done some daft things . . .'

'Haven't we all?' laughs Sylvia, as the great snow-globe shape of the cathedral appears in the distance, looking down on a city of old bridges and surging waterways; a chaotic centre of narrow alleyways and buildings hewed from old, stout bricks.

'Yes, but . . .'

'Sounds like you let other people do much of your thinking for you as it is,' muses Sylvia. 'Emotional? Excitable? Bit of a temper? Sounds like you've been diagnosed as a woman.'

Liz doesn't respond. She'd been livid with Jay when he made the same joke and it feels unfair to extend a different response to Sylvia, however astute it may be.

'Carly lives over the river, up past the big Tesco. Carry on this way . . .'

'You'll have a story to tell her, I'm sure! You were lucky it was Jude who saw what happened. He's the sort you want to see lumbering towards you when you're trapped under something heavy. Salt of the earth, though I don't know if that's still a good thing to you youngsters. He's been through it, poor sod, but he was the first to come and see what help I needed when the bad snows came and he didn't charge me for fixing the roof or doing a bit of rotivating for the family down the way. He's not shy of admirers neither, though I don't know whether the whole "eligible bachelor" thing still rings a bell for you ladies. "Brooding widower" neither,' she says, taking her hands off the wheel to make inverted commas with her fingers. 'He said it was that stuck-up twit Campion Lorton-Cave who ran you off the road . . .'

'Not really . . .'

'If you need a witness for the insurance claim I'm happy to say I saw the lot, and that he'd been at my place drinking meths before it happened. He's the sort who still wishes people used phrases like "squire". Would give his right arm to be called Lord of the Manor. Would be plenty of lads pleased to see him get a slap around the chops but when you live in a community that makes its money from farming, it doesn't pay to piss off the biggest landowner. He'll be on a high right now. Had three years of worry after that poor lass got shot but it's all done now. Not for her, mind. What sort of teenager wants to wear an eyepatch?'

She suddenly puts the pieces together. 'I heard that on the radio! That was him? The same person who owns all the land?'

'Well, if you go back you'll find that it's his wife who's got the bloodline going back down the centuries. Campion's married well, you could say. He's embraced the lifestyle – loves being somebody to doff your cap to. That poor lass who got shot, they made her life bloody miserable. Had to move away. He had dozens of witnesses to say it was her own silly fault and that if the saboteurs hadn't been stirring up trouble it would never have happened.'

'You sound like you dislike him almost as much as Jude does.'

'Nobody can dislike him that much,' says Sylvia, pointedly. She shrugs. 'Friends in high places and some in the low. He has some right nasty sods come to his grouse shoots. Not exactly comfortable in their country tweeds, if you'll take my meaning. Maeve was never scared of him but even she backed down when he brought in the bad lads to make sure the saboteurs saw the sense in going for softer targets. You ask me, she did it because she knew what Jude would do if things carried on the way they were going. Not a man to trifle with, our Jude. Goes quiet for a good couple of days if he has to so much as pull a dying bird's neck but there are blokes in the valley and further afield who'd have it that he's somebody not to mess with. Doesn't back down, that's what they say. Doesn't matter what's in his way, he'll keep walking forward.'

Liz can barely keep up with the stream of information. She realizes they are approaching the estate. She curses, under her breath. They're nearly at Carly's, just as the conversation is reaching the point that Liz has been hoping is its destination.

'Just up here, right, then left,' says Liz, sitting up and pulling down the sun visor to check her reflection. She's dirty and flushed,

but there is a brightness in her eyes that she hasn't seen in too
long. 'I don't like to ask, but his wife – what happened?'

Sylvia gives her a sly look. 'I'm not one for gossip,' she says,
and grins, her lips parting to reveal big, white dentures that
match the twinkling whites in her eyes. 'Nearly four years ago
now, I'd say. There was a mention in the paper when it happened.
It broke him up, and for Campion to suggest there was anything
fishy about it, well, that just shows you the type of man he is.
Jealous, if you ask me. His wife, Candy – she's got a bit of
class about her and she'd take Jude's side over her husband's
any day of the week. I've heard that Campion sent one of his
boys to talk to him when he was doing some work up at the
Hall, hottest day of the year – insisted that he put a shirt on!
You can picture it, can't you? Candy at the window, licking her
lips, and Campion wobbling about in his Bermuda shorts, gut
like a gone-off pear.'

Liz grins, enjoying the picture. Glances through the darkened
glass and sees where they are.

'Right here, and just down there: the one with the nasty front
door.' She can't help but wrinkle her nose. It's a defence mech-
anism, guarding herself against any suggestion that she should
try and be more like her sister.

'Pinkish one?'

'She says it's salmon. Maybe after it's been digested, definitely
not before.'

'I had a sister once,' muses Sylvia. 'Apparently I ate her while
we were in the womb. I had a boil removed when I was four.
Had baby teeth in it, if you can believe that.'

Liz isn't sure how to respond, so chooses silence. Sylvia slows
to a halt outside the little terraced house, its front door opening
directly on to the street. Carly's partner, Glen, had wanted to
swap the hinges so that it opened outwards; annihilating any
passing pedestrian every time he answered the door.

'Nice,' says Sylvia, chattily. 'Windows could use a clean.'

'I'll be sure to tell her,' says Liz, and begins rummaging in
her bag. Her hand touches her phone and a sudden torrent of
thoughts gush into her mind. She hasn't looked at her phone
since leaving the valley! Why hadn't she thought about it before?
Why not check her messages when it entered a signal area? Why

not message ahead? Reassure Jay? Check to see what repercussions there will be with her therapist. She knows the answer instantly. *Fear.* She doesn't want to see what trouble she's in. Wants to exist here, in this little alternative world, with this gossipy old lady and her stories of intriguing strangers. She begins to fumble in her purse.

'None of that,' says Sylvia, with an audible *tssk.* 'I owe Jude, so no charge. And I fancy you'll get a chance to do me a good turn somewhere down the road.'

Liz looks up from her bag, confused. 'I will? I mean, yeah, I do hope our paths cross again – are you on Facebook?'

Sylvia gives a hard-to-read smile. 'I'll be seeing you again, I've no doubt about it.' She nods at the house. Carly has appeared at the glass: glaring at the vehicle that stands, motor-running, at the kerb outside.

'Oh, that's Carly. And thanks so much,' says Liz, flustered. 'And thank him again for me. Jude, I mean. I don't even know his last name . . .'

'I reckon you'd find it out easy enough, but it's Cullen, love. Jude Cullen. Make sure you spell it right when you type it into the internet. And don't look at me like I'm a mind reader, you've been cuddling that cardigan like it's a cat. I'll be seeing you soon.'

Liz climbs from the car, steps uncertain, jelly-legged and aching all the way to the top of her head. This neighbourhood is called Pity Me. It regularly crops up in the list of strangest place names in the UK. It's also a regular joke of Jay's. He delights in telling her this is where she would be better suited to living.

Liz manages a smile for Carly. Glances around; a weird wooziness creeping in at the periphery of her senses. Takes stock. The evening is still cold and blue and there is no disguising that she has well and truly been in the wars. She watches as Carly clocks the injuries and she vanishes from the window at once. Liz sighs, theatrically, wishing she smoked so she could light up and delay the inevitable. She knows exactly what is going through Carly's mind. *What now? What drama are you caught up in? What mess have you created? What have you done wrong that I'm going to have to put right?*

The door swings opens as Sylvia pulls away.

'What the fuck have you done to yourself?' asks Carly, standing on the front step, arms folded, a vision in too-big T-shirt and too-small leggings, both feet stuffed into colossal unicorn slippers and hair scraped tightly back from a face that has always made Liz think of a particularly well-carved turnip lantern.

'Long story . . . I'll . . . not as bad . . .'

Carly's expression changes as she takes in her big sister's injuries. Softens, at the state of her, then hardens again at the thought of there being a perpetrator behind the wounds.

'Sorry I didn't call first,' say Liz, stuck to the pavement and unsure of herself. On the far side of the road she sees a young mum, pushing a vintage pram with huge, thin wheels. She looks like she has another child on the way. Either that, or there's a frozen turkey stuffed down the front of her hoodie. Liz watches her. Knows her. Pities and envies her. This was her terror, when she was young. Being one of them. Being like the girls she grew up around. Being her mum, or her sister, or any one of the pregnant teens who mistook a shag around the back of the kebab shop as a proclamation of devotion, and who pushed out kid after kid just to improve the odds of somebody, some day, giving a shit about her.

She can't seem to get herself to leave the spot. Just stares at her sister, wondering why the hell she thought this was a good idea. She doesn't normally run to Carly in times of crisis. Carly would disagree, but Liz is steadfast in her belief that her little sister has only been involved at the very periphery of her many catastrophes, and that she has protected her from the worst of her mistakes. She steels herself. Coughs some assertiveness into her voice. Tries her best smile.

'Is it OK if I come in? I'm a bit of a state. Car crash, sort of thing. I need to get cleaned up. I think Jay's going to hit the wall . . .'

Carly shifts on the front step. Pulls a face, awkward now. Shows teeth and squints, like she's staring at the sun.

'Close the door, Carly, it's freezing . . .'

It's not Glen's voice. It's Jay's.

Liz holds on to the smell of Jude. Breathes it in, trying to silence the voices that rise in song. Voices that ring out, discordant, as they offer up their hypotheses.

An affair.

They're screwing.

No, an intervention. They've been planning to put you away. Don't go in, there'll be doctors and social workers . . .

No, they're definitely screwing . . .

'It's not what it looks like,' says Carly, stepping back and opening the door wider. 'Honest. Come in.'

Not what it looks like?

Liz hopes to God that her sister is lying. Hopes she finally has the excuse she needs to ditch her partner, and run for the hills. Or better yet, the valleys. One valley in particular.

She follows her sister inside – cardigan cradled like a child.

EIGHT

They haven't been screwing. That much is obvious from the look on Jay's face. Were he to have been caught with his trousers down he would have his face turned to the wall, or be hiding beneath a pillow, feigning sleep. Sex embarrasses him. He's embarrassed by his need for it; his momentary lack of control. He can't reconcile the opposing parts of his self-image; the man in the tie, the careerist, working hard, doing well, paying his mortgage and composting his teabags; he's happy for the world to see this perfectly honed caricature of a man on the up. He can't make room within that picture for what he refers to as 'all the sticky business'. Doesn't like to talk about their 'bedroom antics'. Liz is usually quick to point out that there isn't much to tell. Their couplings are infrequent and workmanlike. He says 'sorry' before the end. Needs to be left alone afterwards. Goes to the bathroom, which at least gives her time to finish herself off.

He's sitting on the leather sofa, looking very much at home. He's dressed in his work clothes; neat white shirt, one-tone tie, brown hair shaved to a precise four millimetres around a pink monk's tonsure of exposed pate. He's slim. Rangy. He always looks a little sour; as though something he didn't enjoy eating is now repeating on him. She never really thought him handsome, though there had definitely been something oddly attractive about him in the beginning. She'd thought him clever. Perhaps even a little eccentric. He'd certainly seemed bookish, and she had imagined him a regular listener to topical debate shows. Presumed him to have some endearing eccentricity; a passion for antique bicycles or Toby jugs. She wrote a script for him in her head. Wrote a life. She filled her shifts this way – daydreaming, fantasizing, cocooned inside her own head as she banged coffee cups and frothed milk, lost in the steam of the coffee shop. She hadn't realized then how much work she had done on his behalf, re-imagining the awkward, slightly haughty man who came in three times a week and who routinely played with his phone while waiting for his skinny one-shot latte. She was already a little bit in love with him by the time she discovered that he was pathologically normal. No eccentricities. No hidden passions. No ambition, save a desire to put in a conservatory and perhaps one day take his Audi around the Nürburgring in Germany. She hadn't known what that was. He'd explained it on their first date; a tense, stilted occasion at the little wine bar by the river. There wouldn't have been a second date if she hadn't been so dead-set on finding out about his hidden depths. He claimed he was in love with her by date four. The words had been nice to hear and she had returned the sentiment almost out of obligation. She got to know his daughter, Anya. Three years old at the time. Awkward and very sweet. Jay didn't really know what to do with her but was cute in his bumbling awkwardness. She met his ex-wife too; a highly-strung, dark-haired specimen, even slimmer than Jay and with a mouth that always seemed to be sucking a blockage through an invisible straw. Liz only decided that he might be 'the one' when he dabbled with the idea of ending things. He said she was too difficult to read – too unpredictable. He never knew if he was coming or going; whether she'd be happy or sad; contented or disgusted. He didn't have the energy to keep trying to talk her into better moods – not when there was nothing, as far as he could tell, actually the matter with her. The idea of losing him turned Liz inside out. She didn't recognize the person she became in the hours that followed his exasperated threat. She'd begged and screamed, snotted and pleaded: cursed his name and vowed to be whatever, whoever, he needed if he would just give her another chance; keep her, not throw her away. He'd kept her, but whatever equality there had been in the relationship before was wiped away. He knew he had her. Knew that the threat of ending things was enough to keep her obedient, grateful and compliant. She, to her eternal shame, was pitifully grateful for the courtesy. Her last three partners had all knocked her around, and for all his faults he didn't do that. Never needed to.

'Been street fighting, Elizabeth?' asks Jay, sitting up. He angles his head to better see the dirt. His eyes narrow as he spies the crusted blood in her hairline. 'See, Carly, I told you there would

be an explanation. Win, did you? Should I see the state of the
other guy? It's in the blood, isn't it? Some people are just
scrappers.'

Carly gives a dutiful laugh. She's always had a decent enough
relationship with Jay. She reckons him a bit boring, a bit *up-his-
own-arse*, but she frequently tells Liz that a lot of people have
it much worse.

'Nice house, little runabout car, bills paid in full and on-time
– you've got it good. He even tells you he loves you! I think if
Glen said that to me I'd die of shock! He does, like – in his way.
They're not good with emotions, are they? Men . . .'

Liz can't seem to make herself move further into the room.
She doesn't really like Carly's house. It's not as asinine and
joyless as Jay's own fantasy front room, but it's not far off. The
TV forms the focal point, wall-mounted above the artificial fire.
There's no art on the cream-and-cocoa wallpaper, save for a big
canvas bearing the motivational slogan *Live, Laugh, Love*. The
coffee table is clear glass supported on the paws of a reclining
otter. It supports three remote controls and two empty mugs. Jay
has clearly been here for a while.

'He was worrying,' says Carly, brightly. 'I was too, though
I've been telling him – you're doing better, aren't you? Big
day today, wasn't it? No doubt needed a bit of time afterwards
to process it all. I'll stick the kettle back on. You're a bit
grubby, actually, Liz. Shall I take that and put it straight in
the washer . . .'

Carly reaches out for the cardigan and Liz, instinctively,
snatches it back. Carly pulls a face. 'Maybe a shower, eh? Then
you can tell us how it went.'

Liz considers the different ways the next hour of her life could
pan out. She could go upstairs, take a shower, clean herself
up, then come and tell them both that she crashed the car and
spent the afternoon with a man she doesn't know. She could
listen to their exclamations. The criticisms. The sighs and the
rising voices and the endless lectures about making better decisions and not continually putting herself in harm's way. Or she
could lie.

'Was OK,' she mumbles. 'Bit late getting started – got a bit
turned around with the country roads. Made it, though. She was

nice. Early days, but maybe it will do me some good. She says I'm not a lost cause.'

'That's good, isn't it?' asks Carly, directing her words to Jay, who is sitting back on the sofa and looking at his phone.

He glances up. 'I messaged you four times this afternoon after we got cut off. Not a word. Carly neither. I needed you to get Anya. Some problem with the after-school club – the woman's got food poisoning or some such. Thankfully Carly stepped in.'

'You picked up Anya?' asks Liz, turning to her sister. 'She barely knows you.'

'That's hardly fair,' says Carly, temper flashing in her eyes. 'I've known her from before she can remember. And I'm not exactly the Child Catcher, about to carry her off – not with three of my own!'

Liz squeezes her hands together, radiating crossness. She doesn't know why she doesn't like the idea of Carly picking up Anya, she just doesn't. Her mind fills with pictures. Sees Anya laughing and spooning ice cream from the carton while Cool Aunt Carly puts on her favourite movie and makes hot chocolate and does all the things that Liz prides herself on being good at.

'Fixed, are you?' asks Jay, again. 'For sixty-five quid I hope so. More, if you consider the cost of asking Carly to step up and get a taxi over to the school. Nightmare afternoon all round. The halfwits in Shipping have calculated the invoices based on a fifty-three-week year and it's all down to Muggins here to fix. Best if you take Anya home and I'll scoot back to the office. Chicken Kievs would be nice, for later, if you still have the energy after all your, y'know, *feeeeelings*.'

'There was a problem with the car,' says Liz, quietly. 'It wouldn't start. I thought it might be the exhaust, but I got underneath and had a good look and it all seemed fine. Scratched myself coming back up. Tried to push it on my own – I'm aching all over. Lady from the café by the church took pity on me and phoned a friend who was heading this way. Car's been towed to a garage. I feel really sore.'

It's not a great lie, but she sounds convincing as she says it. The short, stilted sentences suggest that she really hasn't the energy for too many questions and the whole episode is very much in keeping with her reputation as being bloody useless. Jay rolls his eyes.

'More expense! Right, you stay here with Anya and I'll pick you up when I'm done. That's all right, Carly, yes?'

'Yeah, she's happy playing.'

'The day I've had,' he grumbles, standing up and arching his back. He briefly looks like a bowstring, ready to snap.

Liz stays still. She can't meet his eyes. All she wants is to be left alone with her phone and a decent Wi-Fi signal. She wants to put her head back in the valley where she briefly became somebody else.

Jay bends down as he makes for the door. Seems to think about kissing her cheek, then wrinkles his nose as he sees how grimy she is. 'Don't let Anya see you like that,' he says. 'She always holds you in high regard.'

Liz stays still after the door has closed and the sound of an Audi, parked a little way up the street, has rumbled away. Then she turns to Carly, who has both eyebrows raised, and her arms open. 'Car broke down? My arse . . .'

'I can't,' says Liz, raising her hands in defence. 'I can't have you being shitty with me. I've no energy.'

'Shitty with you? Liz, I was just worrying. You don't think my head was full of horrible thoughts? Jesus, you've been suicidal for bloody ever and today you go missing after seeing your shrink!'

'I didn't even get there. I crashed. I thought I was going to die. I don't even know if I was scared of it or wanted it. And a man was horrid, and then another man was nice, and . . . and . . . and . . .'

'It's an old T-shirt,' Carly says, her whole face softening, so that for a moment she looks like their grandmother rather than their mam. 'Come here.'

As Carly folds her arms around her, Liz lets it out. Cries, her face against Carly's chest, all snot and tears and salty dirt, until she's sure there's nothing left.

NINE

They've been drinking for a couple of hours now. Carly's on the white wine: a decorative raspberry floating in the top of her glass, pilfered from a bar in town in protest at the cost of the Chardonnay. Glen has a can of cider in his meaty fist. He's changed out of his work overalls and into a T-shirt and shorts and with each sip his bare legs drift apart a little further, spreading out with the sluggish inevitability of tectonic plates. Their eldest, Suki, has been sixteen for a few weeks now but drinks her peach schnapps and lemonade like somebody pretty experienced in the art. Liz, on the floor, back to the wall, is sipping the last of the whisky liqueur that she had bought for Carly last Christmas. Stag's Breath, it's called. Warm and gold and honeyed, it never fails to bring out the colour in her cheeks, or to nudge her softly towards a languid, dreamy state of mind. She isn't hurting any more. Carly made fishcakes, mashed potato and beans for tea: sprinkling half a block of Double Gloucester over Liz's portion, with a wink that said 'I remember how you like it'. Liz had wolfed it down. Necked two paracetamol as a palate cleanser before tucking in to Viennetta and blackcurrant jelly. She feels pleasantly satisfied. It's nearly dark outside and the streetlamp is casting a soft-yellow glow through the front window. Anybody walking past can see in from the street but Liz is taking no care to offer an affected picture of herself. She's feeling uncommonly comfortable in her borrowed clothes: vest, tracksuit top and a plain corduroy skirt; all a little too big. Were it not for the fact that she will be the first to identify the problem when Glen's legs reach maximum separation, she could almost consider herself relaxed.

'Mum, can we watch . . .?'

'Yeah, you know the password.'

'Is Anya allowed . . .?'

'Yeah, but nothing more than a fifteen. Don't put any horrors on, she's not ready.'

'Thanks, Mum. Crisps?'

'If you can't find them you've eaten them.'

Liz is always slightly in awe of the way her sister has taken to parenthood. She's a true Mamma Bear; fiercely protective of her own precious cubs. She works part-time in the convenience store on the corner of the road but somehow manages to find a way to make sure her kids are always washed, clothed, fed and watered, and Liz has never been able to identify an area in which any of the three children could consider themselves lacking. Glen makes just about enough money delivering furniture for an international sofa company, and Carly could get a First from Oxford if they offered degrees on how to make the most of the Benefits system. She gets literally everything they're entitled to, from supplements to rebates. She's offered to do the same for Liz. Thrown words at her that mean next to nothing: PIP; Universal Credit; Working Tax Credit. Liz has all but turned her face to the wall. It's all too complicated and it muddies her thoughts. At least with the envelopes that Jay leaves on the mantelpiece, she can feel the cash in her hand. It's real. Authentic. If she were suddenly self-sufficient she fears she would have all but run out of excuses to leave.

'You look all dreamy, love,' says Glen, smiling at Liz. He's a big chap, all curves and concentric circles, with a hairless head that he shaves and polishes to a bowling-ball gleam every morning and night, lest somebody suggest he is losing his hair. He's been with Carly for years now and is the dad of her youngest, Kai. Suki's dad hasn't been seen since he knocked Carly up at fifteen. The middle kid, Elemental-Chi, is half Caribbean and head-turningly attractive. She's ten, and Carly remains convinced that her middle child is the product of some passing energy force that chimed in harmony with her energized womb, rather than a bang on the beach with a limbo dancer whose name is lost in a cloud of rum and cokes. Glen loves them all the same, and Liz fancies that he would extend the same love to Anya at a moment's notice if circumstances necessitated it. He enjoyed teasing her at teatime; gently making fun of her nice manners, asking whether her designer spectacles were available with windscreen wipers, or whether the posh school she attends had chosen a green blazer to hide the snot on the sleeves.

'Dreamy?'

'Aye. Sitting with a smile on your face. It's nice to see. This farmer chap, is it? Bit of a handsome devil, I'm guessing. I mean, you're a woman with needs, aren't you? And I suppose now you've got used to the idea that I'm a one-woman man, it's only fair to have a new fantasy . . .'

Liz shakes her head, smiling; a smudge of blush creeping into her cheeks. Glen likes teasing.

'One-woman man?' scoffs Carly. 'Which woman's that? Anyway, leave our Liz alone, she's had a hell of a day, I told you at dinner.'

'Still can't see how you end up almost at Allenheads when you set off for Corbridge. That's a skill and a half.'

Liz pulls a face. 'I got turned around.'

'We don't need to hear the gory details,' grins Glen. 'However you and your farmer made friends, I'm just pleased it's put some colour in your cheeks. It's a nice part of the world out that way. Weird, like. Old. Not much changed in centuries, really. I've delivered out that way a few times and it does feel like driving into the past. Plenty money out that way though. There's an Arab prince owns a great big mansion. Got some of the best grouse shooting in the country, so I've heard.'

'I don't like grouse shooting,' declares Liz, with feeling. 'They get fed to bursting then scared into the air so rich men with guns can blast them to smithereens. Loads of other animals die. Rare birds. It's cruel.'

Glen puts his hands up in surrender. 'I think I may have run over a grouse or two but until they find a way to coat a dead one in breadcrumbs, I'm not to blame. Didn't know you felt so strongly about it. I heard about that lass who got shot. On the news this morning. Lost an eye and had to move away but somehow it's her fault for, well, I dunno . . . not having a bullet-proof face, I suppose. Somebody's slipped some cash into a pocket or two, don't you think?'

Liz's face fills with Campion Lorton-Cave. She thinks of what Sylvia shared on the journey. Remembers the red kite, nailed to the doorframe and the look of pure cold rage in Jude's eyes. God how she wants him to call.

'Don't listen to him,' advises Carly. 'He's just pleased to see a happy face in his living room.'

'He likes his girls to smile,' grumbles Suki, sitting in the armchair in her hooded dressing gown, playing a game on her phone. 'Apparently I've got a face like a slapped arse. Or a cow with indigestion. What's the other family favourite? Oh yea, like I'm hiding a turd under my tongue. That's a real treat, that one. Said it when Nev was here.'

Glen grins, delighted with the memory. 'He's the same age as her and he's called Neville. I mean, who does that to a baby?'

'Here he goes . . .' warns Carly, smiling at him indulgently. 'Off on a roll.'

'I'm in no position to talk, not when I've got to order birthday cakes with Happy Birthday Elemental-Chi once a bloody year. Suki, of course, is a proper treat for the social media generation. She may have eight thousand followers but most of them think her name rhymes with ducky.'

Liz sips her liqueur. Glances to where her phone is charging, plugged into the wall by the magazine rack: home to an Argos catalogue, the *TV Times* and the phone book. If Liz didn't know better she would think Carly was trying to make her living room a near-replica of the foster home where she had felt happiest. A quiet, spacious house; an older couple, churchgoers – eager to do their bit by this angry, vengeful little girl who'd been moved around so many care homes and foster placements that she rarely knew where she was waking up from one day to the next. They did well by her. Got her into a nice local school and got her grades up. Helped her make some decent friends and supported her in her extra-curricular passions. They even came to watch her judo matches, wincing theatrically each time she hurled a bigger, broader opponent to the ground. They only let her down when she fell pregnant, urging her to give herself the best chance at a future by taking the difficult, un-Christian path. Carly had told them to shove it. Had her daughter, called her Suki, and forged her own path. Liz has never been able to decide whether she would have been better served in life if the couple had taken her too. Sometimes she wakes up and she's still at that window, watching her little sister leave with the purple-haired social worker who had promised, faithfully, that she would never stop looking for a placement that would allow the sisters to stay together. This was temporary, she said. And even without Carly, she was better off at The Abbeyhouse. She was safe, and clothed, and her grades were exceptional; she was making friends and her artwork was amazing, and, well, surely this has to be better than the way things were . . .

'You look a bit smitten, actually,' says Glen, returning to his favourite topic. 'That's how Carly looks when we're watching *X-men* and Wolverine takes off his top. It suits you. So do Carly's clothes, actually. I'd best put a cushion on me lap or you'll be getting an eyeful . . .'

'You are a pig,' snorts Carly, punching him on the arm with enough force to leave a bruise. He doesn't flinch. This is how they talk. How they play. How they love.

'It's the whisky and the paracetamol, I'm sure,' smiles Liz. She looks again at the phone. There's a blue light flashing on the top. She almost throws herself on to her belly. Manages to stop herself from wriggling towards it, Commando-style. 'That'll be Jay . . .' she mumbles.

'Aye, he's a proper Mr Charisma your fella,' laughs Glen, draining his cider. 'Last time he was here he started talking about that bike of his. Not a motorbike – no, there I would have something to say. A bicycle. A bloody bicycle, at his age! What's next? Skateboard? Space-hopper? A bike is for the under-nines to go and get milk from the shops for their mam.'

'Millions of people love bikes,' says Liz, instinctively rising to Jay's defence. 'Look at all those Olympians. He's really into his fitness.'

'Yeah, but I can think of better ways to spend two and a half grand. I don't care if it is light enough to lift up on a finger, he's been had.'

Liz furrows her brow, a pulse twitching at the corner of her mouth so it seems as though she is smiling and itching her cheek at the same time. 'It wasn't that much, no way . . .'

'He said it was. All that Lycra too. I mean, no man looks good in Lycra, do they? Least of all somebody who looks like a half-sucked breadstick. Me, on the other hand, I'd be a right bobby-dazzler.'

'You'd look like a bag of mixed veg,' says Carly, absently,

as she glances at Liz. 'Don't listen to him, it's none of our business . . .'

Liz slithers to her knees. She's looking forward to her bed. She fancies Anya must be feeling pretty tired too. She ate enough to give a hippopotamus heartburn at tea-time and the rustle of packets coming from the kitchen-diner suggests she and her semi-cousins are snacking heavily while watching Netflix on the laptop. She pulls herself up and straightens her skirt, crossing to retrieve her phone. She's never been this good at pleasure-delay before. Normally her impulses outweigh her sense and she will embark upon long text conversations or notes-to-self with only three per cent left on her battery life. She's let the phone climb to full capacity, delaying the exhilarating bliss of checking her messages until she has the energy. She looks at the screen. Half a dozen emails from companies offering discounts and vouchers or enquiring about whether she wants to renew memberships. An alert to inform her that an Instagrammer she likes has uploaded a new video. Facebook notifications, reminding her that she hasn't uploaded anything to the page she started months ago when she was briefly thinking of becoming a party planner. And a text. A text from an unknown number.

'Back in a jiff,' says Liz, brightly. 'He won't come in. Jay, I mean. Apologies in advance but he'll just honk and we'll have to come out . . .'

'Go on, you'll ruin your pelvic floor,' says Carly, waving a hand. 'I'll get her stuff together.'

Grateful, Liz almost bounds up the stairs, closing the door behind her and wiggling the little bolt into place. Her heart is racing, head spinning. She feels sick and giddy, as though she has sprinted uphill after drinking too much pop. The backs of her knees are clammy, her palms so sweaty she can barely grip the phone.

She suffers a paralyzing flash of clarity. Sees the words on the BPD forum; the instruction to people like her to make good decisions; to learn from the mistakes of the past and not jump in with both feet. She knows herself well enough to identify her own triggers. She does *this*. Falls fast and hard. Gets hysterical with excitement then tumbles into depression and ennui. She fixates. Idealizes people to the point of obsession, then dismisses them as nothings and nobodies as soon as they show her some attention. She doesn't want to admire anybody who would be friends with somebody like her – even while considering herself far too good to waste time on the myriad people who would like nothing more than to be a bigger part of her life. The fact that she has a name for the condition doesn't change a damn thing. Having BPD is an explanation, not an excuse. She still has to try and modify her behaviour. She owes it to Jay to try and get better – to see things his way; the right way. Owes it to him to stop being so bloody unmanageable. She should just call the therapist, reschedule, knuckle down to getting better, and start thinking about the future. Maybe start another college course. A night class. Something.

She opens the message from Jude.

> Hi. This is Jude. Hope you're feeling as well as can be expected given the incident. Just checking Sylvia got you home OK. Don't know why but the place seems noticeably empty since you went. Sorry, rambling on. I'm in the pub. Had to get a decent mobile signal and stopped for a wee one. I'll be here a while longer yet, I reckon, so if you're able, or fancy it, do message me back. Sorry if I've woken you, or anything. Marshall sends a woof. X

Liz has to suppress a squeal. He'd gone out just to be able to message her. He was concerned for her. Worrying, even. And the place was empty without her! She feels suddenly exhilarated: high on him. She rubs at her hair, pushing it back from her face, ignoring the pain that darts along her hairline and crown. She checks the time the message came through. Twenty-four minutes ago. He'll still be there. Waiting. Maybe sipping from a whisky, reading a paperback, glancing at his phone every few seconds to check for a reply. She can see him so clearly it's almost eerie. Can see a barmaid, motherly and big-haired, gently probing about his thoughts being a million miles away tonight. And she can hear him confessing, quietly, that he's met somebody he can't stop thinking about.

She thinks about how best to compose a reply. Who she wants to be. What she wants to happen. Her head doesn't co-operate. As soon as she starts to type the words come out like projectile vomit: feelings and confessions and wishes and regrets. By the time she's done, Jay has been honking the horn for over five minutes, and Carly has resorted to throwing items of footwear at the bathroom door from the foot of the stairs.

Oh wow, I really didn't think I'd hear from you again! Sylvia is just so lovely and she gave me a full rundown on valley life, so rest assured I know all about your dirty secrets now! Sorry, that's weird. Do you have dirty secrets? I sort of hope that you do. Sorry again, I've been drinking. There's a licquer/liquor/lickewer I like called Stag's Breath, which doesn't look very feminine now I see it written down. Blame the pain-killer combo for any weirdness that comes out. I need to thank you properly for all that you did to help me this afternoon. I normally have to know somebody a bit longer before I let them see me face down in a puddle, ha-ha. And you're in the pub, are you? Bit jealous. I'm at my sister's. We have one of those weird relationships. I love her one minute then want to cut off all ties the next, but I guess that's all part of my condition. Did I tell you about that? Probably should. It's called BPD, and means I'm basically halfway between neurotic and psychotic, but at least I'm not dull. Anyway, I'll let you look into it, if you're interested, so you know what you're letting yourself in for if we do start talking. Incidentally, how's the car? And how's Marshall? He's so lovely and totally in love with you. It must be the eyes! Thanks again, and soz for being weird. ☺ x

Then she presses Send.

In the car, on the way home, she gets a reply. It sends a vibra-tion right the way through her. Jay scowls at her from the driving seat as she looks, eagerly, at the screen. Has to bite her cheek to keep from smiling.

You are fascinating. Feel free to message me your
deepest and darkest. Really pleased we have met,
Betsy. You're a poem. Xx

In her stomach, the glow of liquid gold.

TEN

It's a little after midnight and Liz is sitting at the kitchen table with a full pot of tea and a packet of biscuits. She's changed into her nice pyjamas; the soft pink, cotton ones with the dark-blue piping, which always makes her feel a little bit glamorous. She's wearing slipper-socks: largely so the sight of her feet doesn't make her feel suddenly hideous and trigger an episode of nuclear self-loathing. She's brought a lamp in from the dining room so she can sit in an appropriately soft-yellow light, rather than the harsh white glare of the strip-light overhead. She feels naughty. Indulgent. The only thing spoiling the atmosphere is the smell of Deep Heat muscle spray, which she doused herself in when she caught sight of the purpling bruise across her shoulder and down to her chest. It looks nasty enough to be checked out by a doctor, but Liz is pretty good at self-diagnosing. Most times, pain is nothing more or less than itself. It's not an indicator of something else. A bruise is just a bruise, a break is break. It all heals. Skin is more resilient than the soul. If nothing else, Mum taught her that.

She pours the tea. Adds a splash of milk. Dunks a biscuit. She looks like a piano player preparing to attempt a complex piece by Debussy.

Then she types his name, carefully, into Google. She finds what she's looking for on the second page: an article in the *Northern Echo*, four years ago, under a headline that makes her catch her breath.

Death of Weardale Activist 'Could Have Been Avoided',
Says Coroner
By Alison Willison

A well-respected environmental campaigner found dead by ramblers at a Weardale beauty spot 'should never have been left alone', according to a coroner.

The body of Maeve Ducken, 41, was discovered in August at Swinburn Falls – a waterfall hidden in secluded woodland between Wearhead and Sparty Lea, a mile from where she lived with her husband.

Ms Ducken was well known in the community. She stood for the Green Party in recent elections and had led a campaign to block a proposed housing development in the isolated valley, as well as being an activist for animal rights. She was a noted anti-hunt saboteur and gave evidence at several prosecutions for contraventions of the Animal Welfare Act.

Ms Ducken, who had suffered from epileptic seizures since undergoing an operation on a head injury, was taking strong painkillers at the time of her death. She had been warned about being left alone, operating machinery or taking on too much work.

However, on the day of her death, she left the family home following a 'petty row' with her partner. She is thought to have suffered a seizure, which caused her to fall and hit her head. She was found by ramblers staying in a holiday cottage nearby.

Erin Potts, of Kirmington in Lincolnshire, told the court: 'She wasn't responsive. She was white and wasn't moving and as soon as I saw her I knew there wouldn't be a happy ending. There was blood on the moss that coated the rocks. We'd almost gone over on the moss ourselves a few times that day, it was very, very slippy. It took some time to summon help because of the remoteness of the location and we had no phone reception. My husband stayed with her while I went to get help, which is when I saw the man who identified himself as her partner. He was in a terrible state having been out looking for her. I didn't know how to tell him but it would have been wrong to keep him in the dark. When I told him we'd found a body he just went to pieces in front of me.'

Partner Jude Cullen, 43, who shared Wolfcleugh Bastle with Ms Ducken, said: 'She was always so stubborn. That's what I loved. It was who she was. When she set her mind to something there was no stopping her. It didn't matter how many times I urged her to slow down, she only ever did what she thought best. I think she thought she was too busy for anything bad to ever actually happen. I all but pleaded with her just to have a quiet day: not to walk the dogs or muck out or go and try to save the world. I thought she'd taken my advice but when I came back from taking a shower she had already left the house. She'd do that sometimes – she had her favourite places to go. I was worried because she'd been getting such awful headaches. Then I went looking. I met the lady on the track coming from the wood. The way she looked at me it was clear she'd seen something awful. Nothing's been the same in my life since.'

Coroner Suzanne Bramall said: 'I've seen the medical report and am satisfied this death was a tragic accident, but it's an accident that could have been avoided. The doctors were quite clear about the importance of keeping on top of her medication and taking as much rest as she could. Had she been adequately looked after or taken to hospital when her headaches began to get worse, I'm sure she could have still been here today.'

After the hearing, Mr Cullen was involved in a confrontation with members of the victim's family. Speaking to the *Echo* afterwards, Ms Ducken's mother, Evelyn, said that her daughter's death had devastated her.

She said: 'Our relationship wasn't always an easy one but she deserved better than to die alone in that miserable place. She was always headstrong but when you love somebody you sometimes have to do what's best for them rather than what they want and her partner simply didn't do what was required to keep her alive. Look after her – that's all we ever said to him when they got together. A light has gone out in the world.'

Mr Cullen, approached for comment at the rundown farmhouse that Ms Ducken converted from a ruin, told the *Echo* he had no comment to make, and asked to be left alone.

Liz feels as though her mouth is full of tissue paper. She takes a swig of tea and rinses her mouth. She can feel her heart, banging off her ribs like the foot pedal of a bass drum. A flurry of emotions spin inside her; a blizzard of conflicting feelings. She feels defensive for Jude. Sad, for Maeve. Angry at her family for turning a tragedy into something ugly. She's at once energized and slightly fearful. The reporter has all but accused him of being somehow complicit in the death. She feels other questions begin to slither in to her consciousness. Different surnames. And his quotes. He'd hardly dripped with love, had he? Sounded almost sick of her stubbornness; her pig-headedness.

She picks up her phone. Taps out the message slowly, savouring every letter.

Hey. Still up? Confession time. I Googled you. Can't find the words to do it justice but I'm so sorry for what you've been through. She sounded like a good person. No offence, but your in-laws sound horrible.

She finishes her tea. Pours another. Feels a frisson of excitement as she witnesses the little tick symbol turn grey. He's seen it. Read it. Now three little dots, an ellipsis signifying pleasures to come.

Hey yourself. You aren't running screaming for the hills, then? It's not like the way it was made out. Her mum couldn't stand me. Still can't, though I'm not missing out. Sorry you've had to wade through that to decide if you want us to be friends. Modern life, isn't it? I'm not a fan of most of it. Anyway, how's your neck?

Liz makes herself comfortable. She can hear his words being whispered against her skin. Reads his messages in his accent.

Sounds like a bitch. No offence. I can't even blame the alcohol now. Horribly sober. In the kitchen, drinking tea, thinking hard. I do that. World-class over-thinker. Ruin everything for myself. Can't leave stuff alone.

Nothing wrong with having a big brain. A muscle unused is a muscle wasted. And anyway, you've got an excuse (sorry, an explanation!) – this BPD malarkey sounds like a barrel of laughs.

Oh, you did see the leaflet then? Yeah, I'm clinically impossible. Always feels good to be diagnosed as unmanageable, paranoid and emotionally unstable. Totally what I'd put on my dating profile if I could be bothered.

That's one way to read it. Another is that you're always going to be the most fascinating person in the room. All sounds a lot like monochrome people telling you off for being multi-coloured. All the people I admire are a little bit out there. It's more exciting trying to cling on to a racehorse than to plod along on a donkey, don't you think?

Ha! At least I'm not a donkey – despite my great ass. OMG that was so cringe. Forget that.

Did you read anything else about me? There's not much there any more. I think you'd have to go as far back as MySpace to see that I existed.

What's that?

Man that makes me feel old. Was a place for people who were into music. They uploaded songs and stuff and some people did well. I was a session saxophone player. The jazz quartet I was in did quite well. Not well enough, but y'know. I'll dig out a link and you can listen, if you want.

Liz doesn't wait for the link. Her thumb dances over the screen. In moments she is looking at an impossibly outdated attempt at a website: purple and green letters on a black screen. She scrolls down. Grins, wildly, at Jude as a younger man. White shirt, unfastened bow tie, braces, waistcoat, trilby. Cool, in a dated kind of way.

The surge of self-consciousness, the prickly heat of jealousy . . .

She wonders how many groupies he worked his way through. Remembers him telling her how her singing reminded him of a singer in Dublin. She feels a heave of hatred for her. Has no doubt that whoever she was, he'd been there, done that. She feels too hot again. Doesn't know where she wants to steer things now. It's too much. All that's happened, all she feels. Too much. She needs to shut down before the wires in her head start going out. Wonders if stress can bring on a seizure. Sees herself, dead on the rocks beside a pretty little waterfall, her blood dripping slowly into the murky depths, flowering like waterlilies, drip after drip after drip.

Suddenly exhausted. Going to hit the hay. Why do people say that? Anyway, aching suddenly. Speak soon, maybe. See ya, bye. x

She sends the message and then pushes the phone away from herself. It skitters away like a hockey puck. She drops her face to her hands, convinced that she has done the right thing and the wrong thing; been kooky and cool and a weird cold bitch all at once, and that he's probably sitting there wondering what just happened. She should message him again. Make another pot of tea. Maybe send a picture of herself looking suitably abashed. Yeah, that would work. Get a laugh, start again . . .

She looks up. Jay is standing over her, holding out the phone as if it's a dead rodent; a look of absolute superiority twisting his features.

'Say hello from me,' he says, and turns away. His white T-shirt, neatly ironed, hangs off his frame like a flag of surrender.

'Jay, I was just talking to some people in the forum . . .'

He's gone.

She looks at her phone.

So has Jude.

She makes a pillow of her arms and lays her head on the table. She is asleep in moments. Her last thought is that she has forgotten to take her anti-depressants.

You don't need them, Betsy. You feel alive. Good. On fire. Tomorrow, let's change the world.

ELEVEN

She dreams of smashed glass and the dark, slimy earth beneath old trees. She dreams of red blood on green moss. She dreams of Mum.

Betsy? Fucking Betsy?! Ha! You're too big for your boots, my girl! Think you're something special, don't you – nose up in the air like your top lip smells of shit. I'd be something if it wasn't for being lumbered with you. The mess you made of me. Never even wanted to be born, did you? Hung on to me with your fucking claws and tore me up. Imagine what I'd be if I was free, eh? Betsy! You're disgusting. Come here: come here and let me show you what you are . . .

The name a sneer, a grunting pig-faced snort; Mum's face up against her own.

Who do you think you are? You're no better than any of us. Do you know what I'd have been if not for you? You're my curse, girl. A curse. And you still haven't learned your lesson. I'll have to show you again . . .

When she wakes, her skin feels aflame. The crack of muscle on muscle, bone on bone, is still echoing in her ears.

She can still feel the foot on her throat, slowly closing off her trachea.

She can still hear Carly, too young to understand, hugging herself, sobbing and telling Mum to stop, please stop, you're killing her . . .

She sees herself, perverse in her refusal to surrender; snarling up at the woman who beats her, snarling back, telling her to bring it on, to hit harder: steel-eyed in her determination to take whatever she can give and not let the hurt show. She wonders, dazedly, if it was that beating which the neighbours heard. That beating which led to the final call to the social services. That call which led to them finally, blessedly, being taken away. She doesn't think that it was. Something came after, she's sure. Something worse. Something she doesn't think about and which turns her to stone whenever her thoughts threaten to rattle at the locked door in her skull.

'Did you do my packed lunch?'

Jay behind her, crisp and clean, a small piece of paper stuck to a scab on his freshly-shaved cheek.

'Shit, sorry, overslept, I'll . . .'

He shakes his head. 'Make sure she's not late for school.'

'What? No, the car . . . Jay, I swear I was just on the forum . . .'

'I don't doubt it. That's what sickens me. Your little sycophants, all falling over each other to tell you you're ill, you're a victim, that the world doesn't understand that you're trying your best . . . I'm sure it does you the world of good. Just remember, when every single other person is telling you you're the problem, what are the chances they're wrong?'

He walks out without another word.

Anya, muzzy-headed, pads in from the living room, already dressed in her posh school uniform. She smiles in greeting; still too much her father's daughter to offer a hug. 'You were crying in your sleep. Are you OK?'

Yes, decides Liz. *Yes I bloody am.*

She looks at her phone and sees the message that's waiting for her.

You were in my dreams last night.

She replies at once, more than content to lie.

OMG – You were in mine . . .

TWELVE

Liz has been growing steadily more agitated for the last half hour. Anya is due at school on the far side of Durham by 8.50 a.m. *'at the absolute latest'*.

It's now 8.05.

Liz has never been a punctual person. School, for her, started around nine-ish and the best she can offer when making plans is a firm commitment to 'be there on Tuesday'. Yesterday's failed attempt to reach the psychiatrist on time has shown that whatever she is, she is destined to arrive at every appointment in a state of panic: red-faced, sweaty, gasping for water and hoping that whoever she has been meeting will extend her the courtesy of not buggering off after a mere ten minutes. It feels worse when she has responsibility for somebody else. Anya isn't used to being late. Her mother, Marie, is a very organized person. Organized to the same degree that Liz is scatterbrained. She's a far better fit for Jay: a true zealot in her devotion to straight lines, neatness and bleach. At first, Liz had thought Jay had fallen for her because she was in every way the reverse of the woman he married while too young to know what he had let himself in for. It was only later that she realized he actually held her up as the ideal partner, and expected Liz to use her as a role model. She has battled, daily, ever since; trying to outdo her in terms of domestic magnificence, before outright rebelling at the notion of wifely servitude and challenging herself to see how slovenly and chaotic she can be.

Liz feels herself growing hot and twitchy with each syllable that Anya's mum breathes down the phone. If she weren't trying to pull on socks, eat a piece of toast and tie up Anya's hair, she would be able to focus all her energy on hating the snooty cow. She realizes she has a crumb on her nose. Tries to lick it off.

'And you told him?' says Marie, her irritation morphing into outright peevishness. 'He knew you had no means of transport? I find that rather hard to swallow, Liz, if you don't mind me saying so.'

Liz can't seem to swallow the toast. Her tongue feels fat, her mouth dry. She has the phone tucked painfully between ear and chin, a triangle of bread and Nutella clamped between her teeth, one sock dangling from her toes like a used condom, a hair bobble splayed around her fingers. Anya, standing by the mirror in the hall, is watching it all in the reflection. She and Anya get on well. Liz doesn't try to be a mother and Anya enjoys having somebody ditzy and endlessly inappropriate in her life. If it weren't for Liz, life would be nothing but homework and healthy meals, swimming club and chores. Thanks to her almost-stepmum, she knows an impressive amount of swear words and is able to treat the bullies at her school the way a confident comedian treats hecklers.

'What can I tell you, Marie? I'm sort of going a bit doolally here. Is that a word you know? Sorry, I never know whether something's an actual word, or just something I've made up. Like, I thought if it was cold, everybody said "brrrskarooni", but apparently not . . . sorry, I'm rambling . . . I don't have a car – I was in an accident. I'm aching all over. I'm sure he just forgot, or I dunno, maybe it was a test . . .'

'Please, Liz, don't say "dunno" around Anya. A lot of time and money has gone into her elocution.'

'Soz,' growls Liz, petulantly, and is rewarded with a proper grin from Anya. 'My bad.'

'The reason she's there, Elizabeth – as I carefully explained to him yesterday – is that I am not presently available. I am in London. At this exact moment I am walking to thc lift that will take me to breakfast and by nine a.m. I will be in an Uber heading to a meeting in Hoxton, so quite how you expect me to solve this problem is beyond me. Why can't you just call a taxi and accompany her on the journey?'

Liz has read up on Dialectical Behaviour Therapy. She knows there are ways to train oneself to stop temper flaring. She hopes one day to master the art. But here, now, she is still a novice.

'Because I don't have any money to pay for it!'

'What do you mean you don't have any money?' asks Marie, as if the very idea is preposterous.

Liz screws up her eyes. 'I'm not working, am I? And I don't get any benefits because Jay says it's not necessary and that I don't deserve them because I've paid so little in to the system. He leaves me envelopes for what we need and sorts out the bills himself online. He won't put my name on the account and won't let me have one of my own and if I want something I have to persuade him of the merits . . .'

Marie's tone softens as she tries to calm her down, but Liz is on a roll now, her voice speeding up.

'I don't want to point the finger but he's like this because you went off with his money! And it's messed me up so fucking much that I can't hold down a job long enough to be self-sufficient, which means I'm trapped in this excuse for a life!'

There is silence at the other end of the phone. Liz glances at herself. She's pale and clammy, her skin like a wild mushroom at dawn. She jerks herself away from the mirror as if her reflection were about to reach out and throttle her.

'I'm sorry, I didn't realize it was like that,' says Marie, quietly. 'Is Anya there with you? Now?'

Liz is gulping, sucking in air. The room is spinning. She knows she's gone too far. There will be hell to pay for this. 'I'm sorry, I shouldn't have—'

'Call the school and say she's ill,' says Marie, without preamble. 'An unspecified infection works best. Don't say she has a stomach bug or they will insist on her staying off for a full forty-eight hours. She has a pretty good attendance record, so let's not make a habit of it.' She pauses, catches her breath. 'Is that how he treats you? He holds the purse strings?'

'I shouldn't have—'

'That bastard. I'm sorry. I can't believe he's had you thinking I took the money when we split, Liz. Do you know how hard I had to fight just to get the most basic child support? He took the house. Both cars. Fought tooth and claw to make sure I didn't get his pension or any spousal support – all because I dared to tell him I didn't love him the way people should be loved. He was the one who couldn't deal with money. I paid off more credit card debts for him than I can count. Things are a bit more cordial now but he still pays the absolute minimum – not that I need his help. Seriously, Liz, Anya thinks the world of you but you have to do what's best for you. We've never really chatted, have we? Perhaps when I'm back we could talk?'

Liz holds the phone away from her face, tears pricking her eyes. Why now? Why finally start talking to her like a functioning human being? She doesn't know how to react when people are nice to her. And could she possibly be right about Jay? He's always been so steadfast in his assertion that she took everything he had. That it was him who gave her the start-up cash for her blossoming PR business. He who did everything to look after Anya before she decided she could do better and walked out on him with barely a backward glance. It feels like there is a battle raging inside her skull. How can she know who to believe when her very nature dictates that she cannot trust her own impulses?

'If you're sure,' mumbles Liz. 'I'm sorry I swore like that. I'm probably exaggerating. He does his best. I'm not an easy person . . . I'm sorry we've never talked properly . . .'

'Am I staying off?' whispers Anya, in the mirror. She looks excited, grinning out from under her mop of curls. Liz nods, and a stab of pain shoots down to her fingers.

'I'll call later on, chat with Anya,' says Marie, her usual clipped tones returning. 'And if there's money in an envelope for goodness' sake spend it on something fun.'

Liz hangs up. Risks a glance in the mirror. There is colour in her cheeks again. A strange jingle-jangle sound in her head, as if somebody is dangling a gaoler's keys just behind her eyes. She knows the feeling. The medication she takes is hard to come off. The BPD forums are full of first-hand accounts of feeling nauseous, strung out, dizzy. She just has to push through it. Keep drinking water and wait for her chemical levels to stabilize. She's sure she was right to miss her dose yesterday. She doesn't like the way they make her feel numb one moment and weirdly high the next: a combination which she founds rather ironic, given that they were prescribed to battle those very complaints.

'Duvet day?' asks Liz, watching Anya in the mirror. She grins up at her and Liz feels the overwhelming urge to put a hand on her head and ruffle her hair as if she were a Labrador. Mum used to do that to her and Carly, on her good days. She'd scratch her behind the ear and she'd play-act that she was a happy dog, her leg jerking up and down in satisfaction, letting out contented woofs. Mum always said she was a proper little actress. The words came to mean something else when she grew a little older

and a little less cute. By ten, '*actress*' became a synonym for
'*whore*'. Then it disappeared from her mum's vocabulary alto-
gether, replaced by straightforwardly poisonous invective: the
syncopated *thud-thud-thud* of '*slut-bitch-whore*', and the slash
of leather on her skin.

'Duvet day,' confirms Anya, delighted, and reaches up to wipe
away a smudge of Nutella from Liz's cheek.

Liz freezes at the touch. Jerks back. Tries to make up for it
with a hug that feels more like a stiff headlock. Feels so guilty
about the whole bungled affair that by mid-morning she is baking
scones by way of apology; the house filling with a scent that
would make Jay tumescent with satisfaction.

She doesn't hear from Jude until nearly lunchtime. He'd told
her in his early-morning texts that he would be in a bad signal
area for a good chunk of the day. She'd said she would try and
struggle on without him, and then sent half a dozen sad-faced
emojis followed by a '*ha-ha-ha*'.

When the knock at the door penetrates her consciousness she's
halfway through her first attempt at a blog post for Bipped. She
suddenly feels as though she has a lot to say. She needs advice,
sure, but she wants to share, too. She wants to hear that the things
she is imagining doing, are not an act of self-sabotage. She wants
to know that she can trust her feelings. Wants to be told that she
should go for it, or believe in herself, or at the very least, have
a nasty argument with some dissenting voice who tells her she's
being selfish and cruel and should be grateful for what she has.

'I think that was the door,' says Anya, munching her second
scone and licking jam off her lips. 'I can get it, if you . . .'

Liz fills up with a flood of desperate optimism. Might it be
him? Could he have tracked her down? Could he be standing on
the doorstep, rain on his shoulders, a shy smile on his face,
wondering whether she might be free to go for a walk: an old-
fashioned suitor turning his hat in nervous hands. Oh God, what
about Anya? How can she buy her silence? What excuse can she
make up to be allowed to do what she wants most?

She runs from the sofa as if fleeing an attacker. Smooths herself
down in the mirror by the hall, noticing the pink circles on her
cheeks. She looks OK. Jeans, a baggy jumper, hair artfully
mussed. She yanks at the door handle. Turns it the wrong way,

then makes a meal of doing it right. She's laughing at herself as she pulls open the door and lets in the crisp blue light of the day.

'Well, hello . . .'

The man on the doorstep isn't Jude. He's taller. There's a harshness to him; a slab of meaty face scored through with deep lines that drag down the corners of his mouth. His nose, a crooked beak, makes her think of a budgerigar. He's wearing a dark jacket, a logo on the lapel, with black jeans and boots.

'You'll be Elizabeth,' he says, and his accent doesn't match his appearance. 'Zahavi? Am I saying that right?'

Liz grew up in a series of environments where a knock on the door was an augur of bad times ahead. Bailiffs. Coppers. Debt collectors. Social workers. The bad lads from the flats, asking for a little favour or trying to track down Mum. These past years, Liz has managed to persuade herself that not all unexpected guests are after something bad. She routinely answers the door with her best smile, prepared to give generously to charity collectors or door-to-door salesmen (if such a glorious anachronism should find its way to leafy Durham) and each Halloween she makes more of an effort with her costume than most of the kids who come and knock on the glass. But there is something about this man who strips away her more recent experiences and puts her back in that stinking corridor, hiding behind a plywood door, bolted and triple-locked; listening to boot after boot thudding against the wood, her hand over Carly's mouth, tears stabbing at her eyes as she waits for the return of silence and safety.

'Zahavi, yes,' says Liz, and keeps the door open just far enough to see out. He's standing on the neatly tiled porch, casting a lazy eye over the brickwork, the double-glazed bay window. He's sizing them up. Pricing them up. Weighing the value of the house and its contents. Behind him, a blue van idles at the kerb. She can't see its occupants without extending her neck.

'Thought I had the right place. That's good. Any chance I can come in?'

Liz pulls a face: confused, an embarrassed Englishwoman frightfully sorry to not be entirely *au fait* with the particulars of the enquiry. 'Sorry, what's it regarding?'

'Rather not do it on the street, love. Neighbours around here are the sort who get a hard-on over the clarity of their security cameras. Probably some prick buzzing us with a spy-drone as we speak.'

'Sorry, I'm in the middle of something. My partner should be back in a second . . .'

'Will he?' says the man, and something like a smile pulls at his mouth. 'Fair enough, I'm just trying to do as I was asked. Your blushes, not mine.'

Liz stiffens as he reaches into the waistband of his jeans. Scenes from a dozen different movies play out in her mind.

'Here you go,' says the man, and hands her a square envelope. It's tied with a length of soft leather, elegantly double-knotted. 'Go on then, I've got places to be.'

Curiosity gets the better of her. She reaches out and takes the package. The envelope has a creamy texture, as if it's been handled by somebody wearing lotion. 'What are you giving me? Is it for Jay?'

'I just do the drop-offs and the pick-ups,' he says, shrugging. 'More pick-ups, if I'm honest, and few areas quite so nice. I'll not keep you any longer – not if you're expecting the hubby home.' He gives a nod, an oddly courteous gesture, then walks briskly back down the drive. Liz watches him climb into the passenger side of the van. A moment later it pulls away. Liz retreats inside.

She sits on the bottom step for some time, unusually cautious about opening the package. She keeps glancing at her phone. She realizes she's missed a call from Jay. Suddenly remembers that she never got round to actually phoning Anya's school to report her absent. There's a voicemail from an unknown number. Nothing helpful.

'Sod it,' she mutters.

The leather is soft as calfskin. The envelope smells of bergamot and lavender. She unties it, deftly, and opens the flap with one eye closed, braced in case she has somehow been chosen as a target for a group of polite and unambitious letter-bombers.

Inside the envelope, a stack of notes. Four fifties, and the rest in twenties, neatly stacked and wedged together with a silver clip embossed with a flower. Her heart quickens as she slides the money out on to the step. Behind it is a plain white piece of card, the edges embossed with a gold fleur-de-lis.

An apology. Not an acceptance of guilt, you understand, but a way to put a nasty business behind us. If I was at all discourteous following our meeting yesterday then I will ask you to forgive an ageing man with frayed nerves. Yours, **CLC**.

Liz reads it through twice. Counts the money. An even four thousand pounds. Tries to think of any way it could be from Jude. It's not. She knows, at once, it's from Campion Lorton-Cave. It's a silencer. A bribe. A bung. He's sobered up, realized what he has to lose, and decided to dip into his deep pockets and fling her a sweetener.

The money feels magnificent in her hands. She rubs it between finger and thumb. Machine fresh. He must have drawn it out specially. But how had he known where to find her? Her full name? She answers the questions as soon as she poses them. She's very much at home in the digital age. Every bit of personal information can be found online if you just know where to look. He'll have taken a picture of her licence plate while they were still imperilled on the slick hillside. A close-up of the rear window would have shown the pile of unopened post she routinely flings into the car when leaving the house in a hurry. Name, address, even a postcode if you could get the resolution high enough on the screenshot. It makes sense, she thinks.

'Are you coming back in, Liz?'

'Just a moment,' she yells, startled, in reply to Anya's question.

'Dad's forgotten his laptop, by the way. It's pinging away under the sofa. Do you think he'll be mad? He guards it like it's made of gold.'

It takes a moment for Liz to get a hold of herself. She knows she should call the police at once. Tell them that a strange man has just delivered her some cash, clearly intended to bribe her into staying silent about the alcohol on the breath of the country gent who ran her off the road. But would they believe her? She's a proven hysteric. She gets paranoid, can't control her moods;

can't always decipher the truth from the fantasy and is only six weeks removed from a suicide attempt. She has nothing to lose by taking the money. Nothing to lose, and four grand to gain. Four thousand pounds. Not a fortune, but enough for a little car and plenty change left over to keep her head above water for a little while. Would he come looking for her, she wonders? Would Jay actually bother himself to try and track her down?

She tucks the money back in the envelope, re-wraps it with the thong and slips the package into the waist of her jeans, the way she had seen the courier do. It feels rather pleasant, like the palm of a lover pressed softly against her tailbone.

Her phone bleeps as she makes her way to the living room.

I can't concentrate. Need to see you. Can we meet?

A delightful shiver runs through her, as if her skeleton were suddenly conducting electricity. She knows what the answer will be but she can't rush her reply. Something else, something even more important, is clanging a big metal bell at the centre of her head, a demented town crier desperate to be acknowledged.

His laptop! He's forgotten his laptop! And if it's bleeping, it might be unlocked . . .

She's so excited, she wonders if she'll even be able to type.

Fancies that she will muddle through.

THIRTEEN

A little after four p.m., Carly arrives to take Anya back to her place. Jay's house is no longer a good environment for a child. Liz had been able to communicate that much, at least, during the last of their stuttering phone calls: crying and wailing and blowing bubbles of snot and tears into the handset. She'd used words that Carly hadn't heard since they were children. Carly had told her not to do anything rash. Said she'd be there as quickly as she could. Insisted that Anya be put on the line and managed to persuade Liz to promise on an orphan's eyes that she had no plans to start necking painkillers and vodka. Liz had agreed to the terms of the pact: a curious hangover from a childhood where a promise counted for nought unless somebody's eyes were at risk.

Liz has done most of this evening's self-destruction away from prying eyes. Anya has been in the living room most of the day, working her way through box sets and occasionally venturing into the kitchen to make healthy snacks without leaving so much as a crumb or a dirty knife to offend her father's sense of order.

Liz has been upstairs, tucked away in their bedroom, working her way through Jay's internet history, his emails, his bank statements and private correspondence. Her phone has rung endlessly. Jay has called more times in the past few hours than during the rest of the year combined. She takes a perverse enjoyment in picturing his face: blushing crimson, a little boy caught out.

Bing

Beep

Brrrr-brrrr: the landline joining in.

She knows that he knows. He's realized that he's left his laptop at home. Knows that she will have been unable to help herself from poking around inside: as inviting as an open diary. Knows, too, that she will have peeled away the carapace of what he shows to the world, and feasted her senses on the rotting malignancy beneath. And he knows that there will be a price to pay.

All this time! All this time believing he would come apart if she left him; believing that underneath his meanness and greyness there lurked something like true love; that for all his faults he was a good and reliable man who put up with more than most and who did at least appreciate that, on her good days, she was somebody worth keeping around.

'Christ, you look like somebody's taken a hammer to a badger,' says Carly, cautiously poking her head around the bedroom door. She's still wearing her work uniform; muddy-blonde hair escaping her ponytail like fronds of seagrass. 'Come with me. Spend a night or two on the sofa. Let me look after you . . .'

'I don't need looking after,' hisses Liz, teeth locked. The pain in her neck and shoulders is intense, a dull agony; mean fingers kneading at her skull as if probing for weakness.

'I know you don't,' says Carly, entering the room in increments. She looks around, weighing up the décor. 'Is this the Passion Palace? It's a bit, well, Travelodge. Not very you, is it?'

'He likes it plain.'

'And you like it loud and chaotic.'

'I don't know what I like. But I let him have everything he wanted. I've never been a nag to him, never tried to guilt-trip him in to being different and by Christ you know I'm good at playing that game – I learned from the best.'

Carly fully enters the room. She can't seem to work out what facial expression to pull so she just stands there, distractedly picking at a mole on her forearm. 'People stray. You've strayed.'

'Not once,' says Liz, shaking her head. 'Not properly.'

'Come on, those text messages you were sharing with the writer bloke you met at the gallery? You may not have done anything physically but you went all the way in your head.'

'I just needed . . . something. Something has to be better than nothing, doesn't it?'

'And you got proper funny over that girl. Izzy, was it? Moroccan-looking lass? When she started going out with your ex, that soppy prick Ryan? You lost it over that. It's no wonder Jay smashed up your phone, Liz.'

'Well, this is so fucking helpful!' spits Liz, turning away and throwing herself on to the bed, holding the pillow to her face. She doesn't need to be reminded of her own foolishness. She's already mortified about the whole shameful debacle with Izzy. She'd set up fake social media profiles, uploaded screen-grabbed images, stalked every aspect of a stranger's life, just because she had learned that a partner she no longer cared about was 'blissfully happy' with his new romantic interest. Liz had posed as a tattooist from Vancouver. Her name was Roy. Into Harley Davidsons and Foo Fighters and brimming over with compliments about Izzy's tattoos, her eye make-up, the way her eyes glittered like fireflies whenever she sent him pictures last thing at night: her boyfriend's shoulder in the back of the shot, dozing serenely while his blissful happiness was quietly torn apart. It had all come out in the end. Liz had owned up. By then Izzy was as obsessed with 'Roy' as Liz had pretended to be with Izzy. Guilty, Liz had eventually sent all their messages to Ryan: thousands of raunchy texts and photographs. She still feels bad, sometimes. Misses Izzy. Misses being Roy.

'I'm not judging you, Liz. You're ill. This is how you are. But this stuff you've found, surely it has to be a good thing. You've been looking for a way out – you've always had one foot out the door.'

'He's got six different accounts full of money, Carly! And he makes me live on handouts and then be grateful!'

'You've made mistakes before, Liz. And it's his money, isn't it? I mean, he looks after you.'

Liz sits bolt upright, genuinely intent on doing harm. Carly is already braced for the blow. Liz stops herself at the last moment. Sees her phone, buzzing merrily away, at the foot of the bed.

Carly, grateful for the distraction, glances at the screen. 'Jude,' she reads. 'Who's Jude? Is that your farmer?'

Liz lays back down, her body language stating in no uncertain terms that the conversation is over. Carly waits a moment then lifts herself off, all sighs and long-suffering martyrdom.

'If you want to talk to me I'm just a phone call away. Whatever you decide, you're not on your own. You're my big sister and I love you but for God's sake try and work out what it is you actually want. It's not all roses and rainbows, Liz. Real life gets in the way. And you've got what so many people would want. You've got a roof, and nice things, and all you have to do is keep things tidy. I know it's not thrilling but every time you try something exciting it's too much for you and you end up breaking down. You're trying to get well and I admire that but sometimes do you not think that you'd be better just getting on with it all?' She pauses, as if trying to decide on a good exit line. 'Maybe a baby is what you need?'

Liz screams. Scrunches up, foetal. Can't bring herself to speak. Doesn't move again until she hears the front door close.

She sips water from the beaker at the side of the bed. The strange jangling sound in her head is getting worse: a weird kind of arcade game beeping sound every time she turns her neck. The phone is ringing again. Jay, this time.

She slides her hand under the pillow and touches the stack of notes.

The latop, the source of so much rage, is on the bottom stair so that it will be the first thing Jay sees when he walks in. When he touches a key or moves his finger over the mouse he'll be greeted with the sight that will, she hopes, bring him to his knees. She could have chosen any one of the websites that he has been routinely visiting. Could have called up the details of any one of the camgirls to whom he has been paying handsome sums: dropping digital currency in the slots of blonde Americans with names like Gaby, Kandiss and Allura. Barbie girls: fake tits and big lips, waxed to a level of pink hairlessness that Liz has tried herself, in an effort to tempt him, and which led to nothing more than awkward silences and a painful rash.

She's found his chain of messages. It's clear her hard-working partner spends most of his day with his hand in his pants: having explicit chats with men – and women – from all over the world. He's shared with them what he likes. What he wants to do to girls like Gaby and Kandiss and Allura. What he does to himself while enjoying their attentions. There are pictures, before, during and after. They're quite artful, in their way.

As much as she would like to make him blush about his sexual hobbies, they are not the source of her rage. Her disgust is entirely down to what he has to say for himself when masquerading as *Bluejay_225* – a regular contributor to a social media group set up to support the long-suffering spouses of people diagnosed with BPD.

She can see his words swimming, muzzily, on the air in front of her. Can repeat it almost from memory. One post, among the thousands he has bashed out in a spirit of frothing self-pity and outright fucking lies!

> Me again, back to strike a blow for common sense. Does anybody else think that this whole 'I've got a syndrome' thing is just victim culture taken to the extreme? I'm sick of people behaving like absolute evil bitches and then taking no accountability. I swear she wakes up in the morning and the first thing she asks herself is how she can drive me to the verge of insanity and then play the victim. She's so clingy and needy it makes my stomach heave, then if I do summon up the courage – and watch enough porn to get myself ready! – then she'll find something to argue about, or she will have been slobbing around eating crisps and biscuits and turning her jelly-belly into Santa's Sack. I gave up even trying to please her ages ago. Now I just have to work out how the hell to get her to piss off when my daughter has such a thing for her, as if she's kooky and bohemian rather than just some common little scrubber off the estates. Apologies if this seems a bit ranty but she has driven me to the point where all I can fantasize about is coming home and finding her gone, but even then I swear she's so vengeful she'd find a way to say I'd knocked her about or abused my daughter or convince herself I was secretly a rapist and a serial killer! Stick in there gang, I swear, whoever you're stuck with can't be as bad as mine!

The words evaporate. She thinks of the Cheshire Cat. Feels sleepy and exhilarated and wonders whether Jude is real or just somebody she made up to explain to herself how she got home from the valley. Wonders whether, perhaps, she lies there still, wet and lonely and dying a little more with each fading tick of her pulse.

Liz jerks upwards and grabs the phone. The world tilts and whirls and for a moment it seems that she can see out of her own ear. She wonders if she has suffered a contusion. Whether she is bleeding inside her skull. Wonders what Jay will do when he walks in and finds her dead on the bed, blood pouring from eyes, ears, nose. For a moment she imagines writing a letter to the police, informing them that this thing was done to her by her partner. Pictures him in prison, silently crying, afraid to venture into the showers, growing a rind of dirt that would make him gag. She shakes the thought away. Wonders if she is any more than her illness.

'Betsy? Betsy, are you there . . .?'

She looks at the phone in her hand. Unthinkingly she's answered it. Jude's voice, tinny and faraway.

'Betsy? I don't want to be some weird stalker but you went from sharing every thought in your head to just disappearing, and well, I asked a friend to go on Facebook and they saw you'd posted something about being, what was it – absolutely crushed – and I've been ringing, and, well . . .'

She raises the phone to her ear as if it were a shell and his voice the sea. Her own voice, when she speaks, is dreamy and far away. She wonders, briefly, whether she might have taken too many painkillers, and why the water on the table tasted of vodka.

'Jude . . . hey, ha – that's a song, but backwards . . .'

'Betsy, are you OK – you sound really out of it.'

'Your friend Campion sent a man to give me money. I feel sort of rich.'

A pause. 'He did what, Betsy? Say that again . . .'

'I think it's over with Jay. I don't think it ever really started. I've wasted so much of my life. I'm damaged . . . it's weird you're paying me this much attention, really . . . what is it you're after, deep down?'

'Betsy, I don't know you well enough to know if this is normal but you sound in a bad place. Is somebody with you? I'm not far away – I can come and be with you . . .'

'Be where? Be here? I don't think that would be a good idea, Judy-Judy-Judy . . .'

'Betsy . . .'

The corners of her vision are moving slowly in. She feels bone-tired. She doesn't want to talk any more but words keep pouring out, half-formed, dreamy . . .

'He just thinks I'm a malingerer. A sponger. A cancer. He keeps me here because it's easy for him. Gives me pennies when he's got all these accounts. He's been talking to all these camgirls and he won't even go near me . . .'

'You sound all slurred,' spits Jude, from somewhere nearby.

'I used to think I was OK-looking, and he used to fancy me, I know he did, but I think I just disgust him now.'

'Is somebody there, Betsy? Tell me again about the money. You said Campion sent it?'

'Yeah . . . think I'll book somewhere nice and drink until it runs out. You could come and visit. No funny business, mind.' She attempts a comedy voice but it cracks halfway through. 'I'm not that sort of girl . . .'

She hears the key in the lock. Somewhere on the edge of consciousness she remembers sending Jay's stream of filthy messages and pictures to his mum; his ex-wife; his work. She can't be sure why she thought it would be a good idea.

She hears him bellow her name. Hears a crash and then the heavy stamp of work shoes thudding on his perfect carpet.

She closes her eyes and drifts away. Floats off somewhere that is all blurry outlines and soft, pastel-coloured clouds.

Time passes. She's sick, but manages to cough it up without choking. Rolls, by pure fortune, into some approximation of the recovery position. Wonders where all the noise is coming from. Why the clouds are turning to knives; the softness suddenly abrasive and needle-sharp.

She is only dimly aware of the door bursting open. Barely registers the sudden vicious hands in her hair, yanking her off the bed and on to the floor. She can't be sure if she's remembering or experiencing. Mum used to wake her like this when she'd had a bad day, or a bad night, or just wanted somebody to smack around until the edge had been taken off her temper.

He's in her face, now. Crazy eyes and a vein throbbing at his temple. He's screaming in her face. Were she able to fully form her thoughts she would remark upon how unusual it is to see him so animated. She has always longed to see what lies beneath the surface. Has poked and prodded and gone to great lengths to see what he looks like when he's not trying so hard to be his own vision of respectability.

She realizes that she can't breathe. There are hands at her throat. She can't swallow. Her tongue is all swollen and there's dampness on her jeans, and all she can see is the pure hatred in his eyes. Jay's eyes. Eyes that threaten to pop right out of his skull.

She has been in this position so many times that muscle memory takes over. She spent great chunks of her childhood trapped beneath the great fleshy bulk of her mother, ham-hock forearm under her jawbone, spit flecking her features. She knows how to go limp. How to play dead. How to scare her attacker into realizing the enormity of what they are in the process of doing.

She becomes a dead weight. Feels her pulse slow to almost nothing. Lolls, deathly, on her side. Sees him shuffle back, hands in his hair, tears streaking his face.

He'll stop now, she thinks. *Now he sees . . .*

Time passes. Seconds turn to minutes as he sits there, his eyes wide as coins.

When he places his hands around her throat again it is a deliberate, calculated act. He takes the time to stare at her. To look into her half-closed eyes with intensity that she has only seen at the very climax of their love-making.

Feels him close his hands like the wings of a bird.

She starts to thrash. Kick. Reaches up and claws at his hands, his face.

Doesn't register the bang-bang-bang on the glass. Hears voices both near and far away, ice-cream vans and church bells.

Then the door is flying open and Jude is hauling Jay off her: slamming him up against the wall. Hitting him, hard. Harder. Smacking his head off the wall and kicking him below the jaw as she slithers to the carpet.

Then Jude's arms are under her neck and her knees and he is lifting her so carefully it is as though she is made of cobwebs and snow.

She locks eyes with Jay as Jude carries her outside and into the soft black caress of the evening. He's crying. Bleeding. Snivelling into himself like a boy who's been beaten up in the playground in front of the girl he likes.

She feels sorry for him.

Guilty.

Disgusted with herself for making all this happen.

Then she is giving herself to the darkness, and to Jude.

FOURTEEN

Six months ago . . .

Betsy is beginning to enjoy waking up early. The world smells rather wonderful just before the sunrise: the air golden with ozone and honeysuckle, elderflowers and dew. She tries not to let the lingering whiff of horse shit and damp hay sour the experience. She wonders why she never noticed such olfactory wonders when she simply stayed up through the night. She fancies it may be something to do with the off-and-on-again quality of sleep; the cranial reboot, the shutting down of yesterday and the beginning afresh of today. She keeps running through half-remembered idioms about the importance of going to bed at a decent hour. Amends them for her own amusement. *Early to bed, early to rise: summons a farmer between your thighs . . .*

She has taken to falling asleep early too. She tends to drop off not long after nine and sleeps in a state of dreamless, cashmere blackness, only stirring when Jude chances to step on a creaky board during one of his night-time sojourns around the old farmhouse. He sleeps little. Reads or listens to music. Writes, should fancy take him, though his pages are routinely reduced to cinders by the morning. She sometimes feels as if he has set himself up as a sentry at her door: that he is up to guard her, and the house, from intruders. She doesn't like such thoughts. The bastle's most glorious feature is its remoteness. There are perhaps half a dozen little farmhouses strung out along this ridge of the Allen Valley so visitors to their door are rare. She's barely spoken to anybody since Jude brought her home: an injured bird needing its wings reset and a safe place to rest. Sylvia popped by, leaving a hamper of home-baked goods and a sponsorship form for an abseiling challenge. A handsome man in a pink shirt and splendid quiff came and knocked repeatedly on the door while she cowered upstairs and waited for him to leave. And there had been the guy with the braid in his hair: a shaved head but two rat-tails dangling down from his hairline. Cargo pants, a big baggy jumper and a balaclava rolled down around his neck like a scarf. He'd had plenty to get off his chest. Jude had cut him off before he made it to the courtyard but Betsy had still heard snatches of their conversation and none of it had sounded friendly. His name was Moon. He'd been a friend of Maeve's. An environmental activist. He wanted to know if Jude was pleased with himself: whether he felt good that he had robbed 'them' of their best chance for justice. Jude never lost his temper. Just kept telling him that it was none of his business and that maybe one day he'd understand. Moon had half lost his mind over that. Demanded to know whether he'd done a deal with the devil. Whether he'd turned his back on everything they'd ever stood for. He demanded Jude hand 'it' over, whatever the hell 'it' might be. And Jude had told him 'no'. Then he'd walked back into the bastle and left him standing there, throwing insults at the great walls like rocks. Later, when Jude came up to the attic room to check on her, he didn't mention it. And she didn't ask.

Today, as with so many yesterdays, Betsy has woken at dawn. The birds that flutter and swoop around the bastle can be relied upon to sing her into wakefulness, though it is not the Disney melody that she would have expected. The sound is an orchestra tuning up: a raucous assault of squeaks and squawks and strangled yells. Betsy is starting to be able to identify the individual species from their songs. She can pick out the song thrush, the blackbird and the wren, but she has invented her own names for some of the less melodious performers. This morning she definitely heard the song of the *Screeching Little Bastard* and the *One Man Band Falling Down the Stairs*.

Jude is teaching her the so-called proper names, although she has no way of verifying the factual accuracy of his claims. Some of the birds he mentions sound distinctly made-up, but even when she questions the veracity of his claims she does so with glee: delighted at the very idea there could be such a thing as a chiff-chaff, a long-tailed tit or a willow warbler.

She and Jude are not yet a couple. She wants him; wants him so badly that there are times it feels as though there is a heat from her neck to her ankles, but she is so certain that it will happen she is able to enjoy the agony of waiting. She knows it's important to him that she does not give herself to him out of some sense of obligation or gratitude; that she must concentrate only on getting well, or the closest thing to it, before embarking on something as potentially damaging as a new relationship. The agreement doesn't stop the growing tenderness between them. They often eat together, facing one another at the little kitchen table, talking about nothing and everything. Sometimes, on the sofa, she stretches out her legs and puts her feet in his lap, and he'll stroke them like a puppy while reading his book, and she will smile, half-embarrassed, behind the pages of her own. She has been his 'house guest' now for seven weeks. She feels as though she has put on a stone and grown three inches, though any old acquaintance who saw her today would remark upon nothing more than the glow in her cheeks and the absence of coal-black darkness beneath her eyes. She feels as though a few years have been shaved off her age. For seven weeks her life has been entirely free of obligation, command or responsibility and so far, she hasn't taken any steps towards spoiling it for herself by insisting she be allowed to do more. Truth be told, this is the first time in her life she has been cared for by somebody who has not made her feel guilty about it. She likes it. She won't always like it, but for now it feels rather nice.

Her bedroom is next to Jude's. The wall that separates them is pretty thick but she has worked out that her bed – a grand, wrought-iron affair – is pushed up against the same stretch of brickwork as Jude's, so viewed from above, it could be seen as one giant bed separated down the middle by a brick divider. It's a thought that comforts her. Most nights she drops off to sleep with her hand against the rough wall. As her flesh warms the brick, and she slowly drifts into a dreamlike state, the wall becomes flesh. By the time she gives herself to sleep, she knows she is touching him. Can feel him. Can breathe him in. Can picture him, on the far side of the wall, touching her in return. In such moments she wishes he was a less decent man.

Too-wheet-too-wheet . . .

Betsy identifies the familiar song of the *Lesser Spotted Whistling Little Shite*. She fancies that it's around six a.m. She sits up. Stretches: a big Hollywood yawn. A satisfying series of clicks and pops emerge from her rested joints and muscles. She looks around her bedroom. Now the smile comes. She still hasn't got used to this seismic shift in circumstances. She lives in a fortified farmhouse: a centuries old slab of crumbling brick and timber. She's becoming an outdoorsy type. She feels good about the dirt beneath her fingernails and the twigs and hay in her hair. She hasn't shaved her legs or armpits since she moved in. Still cleans her teeth twice a day, in case today is the day he kisses her, but a lot of things she considered crucial to a life well lived now seem entirely redundant.

She looks around, even happier today with the room's layout as she was when Jude first showed her what could be hers, if she wanted it. He'd seemed oddly nervous when he'd made the proposition, gripping his hat as if it were a steering wheel, looking into her so earnestly that she'd turned away in case he was somehow able to read her secrets through her eyes. He wasn't offering himself: that was what he wanted to make clear. Not that he wouldn't be honoured, of course, but she was too vulnerable, too emotionally drained, to be thinking of anybody but herself until she got back on her feet. It was important to him she understood that he had no ulterior motives. He wasn't taking advantage of somebody in a susceptible position. There was to be no payment in kind. He was offering her a place to stay until she decided how she wanted to live and there was nothing expected of her save a promise that she would start taking her pills again, and that if she started to feel the black clouds gathering in her mind, she would tell him before she chose to do anything about it. He didn't want to find her dead, he said. He wasn't sure he could take that. Not again.

Betsy – as she is starting to think of herself – cannot recall saying yes, or recollect very much about what the doctor advised, a little agitatedly, as she was signing herself out of the hospital, but she knows she must have said yes as she has been here ever since. She feels good. Better. Something has happened to her bad thoughts. She can't seem to grab hold of them. Every time she considers the negative aspects of these past few weeks and months, the thought flits away from her: a greased eel. Jude is good at telling her not to worry, that they'll deal with this, and that, and anything else that troubles her, once she's done the most important thing and got herself well. Part of her finds it all a bit much – his attentiveness a little overbearing, his manner disconcertingly intense. But she cannot help thinking that if this were all a dream, she would have no desire to wake.

Still, Betsy has no doubt that her dark thoughts will soon find a way through. That will be a payment of one kind or another for the gentleness of these past few weeks. She cannot imagine Jay leaving things as they stand. He'd come to the hospital the day after she was admitted. Told the doctor he was her husband and received chapter and verse on her injuries. Told the shrink that the bruises at her throat were from the cord of her dressing gown and that it was he who had cut her down. It had all gone into her medical files. They'd almost had her committed to a mental health facility before Carly convinced the doctor that she would be coming home with her and would be watched round-the-clock. She'd asked Liz time and again: *Are you sure he attacked you? I mean, he's not like that, is he? A prick, yeah, but not violent! I won't be cross, just tell me. Just tell me, please . . .*

Liz spent her four-night hospital stay trying to piece together the chain of events. Jude had been there, she knows that for certain. He'd saved her. Knocked lumps out of Jay. Driven her to hospital. But why was he not there when she woke? Where was the money she'd stuffed in her back pocket? Carly had been able to offer no answers. She'd managed to convey to the nursing staff that she didn't want Jay anywhere near her but she'd managed to come out of the exchange looking like a hysteric, with Jay the long-suffering party. He'd refused to explain the great purple bruise on his face, though he managed to inject a quality into his silence: a suggestion that this had been done to him by a certain party who may or may not have been struggling with some inner demons.

By the time Jude turned up at the hospital, Liz had almost convinced herself that he was a figment of her imagination. She had no independent proof that he truly existed. She'd begun to wonder if perhaps he was some symptom of her madness: a projection; one of the voices in her head made flesh and blood. And then he was beside her; that earthy smell, leather and soil and engine oil. And he was looking at her like she might be just a little bit magic. He'd made his offer. Told her he had space for a house guest. Helped her dress herself, then held her hand as they took the lift to the exit and made their way to the battered 4 x 4 in the car park; Marshall waiting patiently in the passenger seat.

Seven weeks on, this little square room feels like home. The exposed floorboards are stained almost black but the rest of the cosy space is made up of warm colours. Rag rugs overlap either side of the soft, springy bed, the eiderdown a heavy affair in splendid reds and golds. An oil lamp sits on a pedestal table within arm's reach, and little toppled columns of hardback books form stepping stones from the bed to the big, old, wooden door. Gold hooks on the back of the door are eclipsed by the old fur coats she found in a downstairs wardrobe and which she uses as ostentatious dressing gowns when taking a late-night trip to the toilet. Sometimes she vacates the bed to go and lounge on the blue chesterfield against the far wall, its scarred leather surface mostly covered up by the colossal crocheted blanket with its gypsy-rose motif. She always feels rather decadent when reclining, as though she should have a cigarette in a plastic holder and be wearing her hair in a sleek suffragette bob, rather than the short, choppy pixie cut she has given herself with a pair of dress scissors.

'Morning. Are you decent?'

She smiles, ear to ear. He always asks her the same question before softly opening the door. His knock is a quiet, respectful thing, as if frightened that he may be about to wake a small child or disturb a sleeping bear cub.

She arranges herself neatly, sitting up, back to the headboard, quilt puddled around her middle, big sloppy T-shirt hanging decorously off one shoulder. She rubs her hand over her face as he enters; a cafetière and bottle of fresh orange juice on a tray, along with toast in a rack, a butter dish and a selection of jams. When Betsy is up early enough to return the favour, she intends to pick wildflowers and put them in a glass half full of water, just to give the tray that little extra touch of class, but she considers herself amply satisfied with his efforts.

'Oh Jude, you don't have to keep spoiling me like this, you've done so much . . .'

He places the tray at the foot of the bed and looks at her in that way of his: not quite smiling but his eyes radiating delight in her. There's something timeless about him. She entertains fanciful notions that he is a spirit trapped in a haunted house; a manifestation from another time. She has so many questions for him but doesn't know where to start asking. She cannot fathom the transformation between the musician she saw online, and the quiet, rough-handed man who always seems to be resisting the urge to reach out and stroke her hair.

'No bother.'

'But you must have so much to do – I'm such a nuisance.'

'I like making you smile in a morning. I'm sure you'll return the favour.'

'Haven't you got to be shaving the piglets or feeding the sycamores or something?'

'That's the joy of living on *farmer time* – you get to decide what pace you want to go.'

They go through this same conversation most mornings.

'Do you mind if I . . .?'

She nods, motioning at the foot of the bed. He pours himself a coffee, adds a splash of milk. Eschews the option of sitting on the bed in favour of crossing to the window, opening the curtains, and looking out through the small square frame; a tapestry of blue skies hemmed with a thick tasselled foot of rippling greenery. Betsy ignores the view. Looks at him instead. He's wearing his summer workwear: an old T-shirt, tatty moleskin trousers and work boots. His Akubra cattleman hat gives him a cowboy aspect. It's dark with old sweat and will be darker still by the day's end.

'Sleep well?' he asks, as she pours herself coffee and spreads a homemade gooseberry jam on buttered toast.

'Until the birds started auditioning for X Factor, yeah,' says Betsy, tucking in.

'Aye, the nuthatch is an acquired taste,' smiles Jude.

'That's a bird yes? The one that sounds like Space Invaders? It's called a nuthatch? That is *so* what I would call the gusset in a pair of boxer shorts.'

'I know you're joking,' he smiles. 'I take comfort in the knowledge that you're joking.'

'I told you, I wouldn't know the difference between a robin

and a penguin!' says Betsy, licking jam from her finger. 'I only know a turkey because it's bald and has an onion up its arse. That's rather hard to get wrong.'

He takes a gulp of his coffee. Considers her. 'You've got a shine about you today. You always do, but you've got that glow. They'd have burned you as a witch in the olden days.'

Betsy focuses on her toast, playing things cool. Manages to breathe in a crumb. She holds in the resulting cough, which chooses her nostrils for an emergency exit and a moment later she is coughing, spluttering, sneezing and utterly malfunctioning in front of a man who thinks she glows.

He pours orange juice. Helps her sip it. Wipes the tears from her face with a rough thumb.

'So smooth,' wheezes Betsy, her chest sore and features burning. 'I'm the coolest person I know.'

He sits back down, shaking his head. 'You fancy helping out today? It's one of the nicer jobs.'

Betsy narrows her eyes, unsure how to wear her face. Helping out? Was he serious? So far she thinks of herself entirely more hindrance than help. When she'd first arrived he'd made some vague suggestion that she help out a little, just to see whether country living was for her. Thus far, that has consisted of doing a little invoicing on Jude's behalf, ordering feed from a supplier – a task she got spectacularly wrong – and trying to tidy the living room in a way that did not actually give off the impression of her trespassing on his inner sanctum. This has involved lifting up books and dusting beneath them, then replacing the books so he doesn't notice. She has taken a lot of Brasso to his musical instruments, only to learn that this could cause vintage instruments to turn from a gorgeous brassy gold to a kind of mottled pewter hue in the space of twenty minutes. She was midway through cleaning one of the visually impenetrable downstairs windows with an abrasive cloth when Jude had informed her that it was frosted glass.

'I'm game for anything, but I'm a liability, you know that,' says Betsy. A sudden thought spurts up, geyser-like, from a part of her mind that has been dormant for weeks. She scratches at her head, prickly heat at her pulse points, her scalp tightening. 'Sorry, sorry, I just got this look at myself, this moment of clarity

– what am I doing, Jude? Look at me, sitting here like Lady
Muck, letting a stranger look after me, hiding away in the middle
of nowhere like a teenage runaway!'

'Are you OK, you've gone kind of grey?'

She ignores him, words tumbling out in a rush. 'God, I wonder
what all your neighbours think of me! I mean, I'm not bothered
what people think, or maybe I am – Jay always said I was
obsessed with approval but that can't be true, can it? I mean, I
went out of my way to be the opposite to what people are
supposed to be. I dunno, I mean, well, how do you make yourself
criticism proof? That's the hard bit with all this social media
stuff. Kids are having to find ways to be so unremarkable that
there isn't a single thing for people to pick them up on, but then
they run the risk of being accused of being Average Joes, or
whatever. This jam is amazing, by the way. It's sort of tart, but
not. It wakes your mouth up. Actually, that reminds me, I think
I used your toothpaste. It's the pink one, isn't it? Tastes absolutely
vile, what on earth do you use that for? Maybe I should get my
own. We should probably talk about money, and stuff. I eat like
a horse so I need to contribute, don't I? The shop's in Allenheads,
you said? Or there's the Tesco in Hexham. I can't put it off, I
need to show my face, but I sort of feel embarrassed, like I've
duped you into giving me a place, and I haven't, have I? I mean,
I know it's weird, how quickly it's all happened, or hasn't
happened, but that's just circumstances rather than choices,
and . . .'

She realizes Jude is smiling at her. Realizes she may need to
stop talking in order to take an actual breath. She sags, suddenly
very tired. She wants to slink back down into the cushions. Wants
him to climb in beside her and stroke her hair until she falls back
to sleep.

'I don't think I'm interesting enough for the neighbours to
give me or my companions a second thought,' says Jude,
thoughtfully.

'Oh, I'm one of many, am I?' asks Betsy, in a way that she
hopes is playful.

He shakes his head. 'Sylvia's the gossip, and she's on your
side. Thinks you're brilliant. Hasn't stopped popping up under
false pretences, desperate to see how you're settling in.'

Betsy finishes her coffee. 'I feel bad for Carly. She really would have looked after me.'

'She would,' nods Jude. 'She still can, if you tire of this. If you're wanting to go to the shops you'll pass into a signal area and you can call her then. Tell her you're doing OK. Send her some flowers or something. I've got your money downstairs.'

She crinkles her brow. 'My money?'

'The package from Campion.'

'Oh!' she says, unsure how to respond. 'I wasn't sure if I'd lost that. Or imagined it.'

'It fell out of your trousers on the way to hospital.' He cocks his head. 'You didn't think I'd taken it, did you? I wouldn't touch money from that bastard and I sure as hell wouldn't steal from an unconscious woman.' He turns away, hard to read. 'Jesus, people really have messed you up, haven't they? I hate the idea of people damaging you.'

Betsy studies the pattern in the bedspread. 'I wind people up,' she mumbles.

'Everybody who's hurt you, mistreated you, looked at you like you're anything less than spectacular – I want to show them just how wrong they were.'

There's something about the way he says it which causes the hairs on Betsy's arms to rise. Shivers, involuntarily, and Jude immediately changes his demeanour, waving away the darkness in the air that has briefly gathered about him. 'We can talk about that now, or the past can be left where it belongs.'

'Does he know I've gone? Did he call in the police? Does he think I'm missing? I'm getting a bit twitchy, if I'm honest. My head's a bit jangly. I mean, he did go for me, didn't he? Tried to squeeze my throat shut? And you came. I know you came for me, and there was a hospital, and now I'm here and I think I'm happy, but I don't even really know what you do, or anything about you, and . . .'

Jude returns to the bed. Sits down. She gets a whiff of him. It's a warm smell that makes her think of a badger's burrow: cosy and dry and the sort of place where a lost soul could make a safe, secure little home.

'You didn't answer my question,' says Jude, softly. 'Do you want to help out? I've got to do some felling at the dingle.'

'The dingle?' grins Liz. 'Is that a real thing?'

'Yeah. A little woodland, just up the valley. The beck we get our water from runs through it. Beautiful at this time of year, and occasionally profitable.'

'What do you do?' she asks, unsure where this is heading. 'Shave bears and sell their fleece or something?'

'Bears?' he asks, frowning. 'You realize they don't live in Britain, don't you?'

She tuts at him, as if he's been a little insulting. 'Of course!' she says, then adds, under her breath, 'I do now.'

'That's a relief. Anyways, the golf club likes to serve hedgerow specialties when they're available,' he continues. 'Delicacies; gorse lemonade, hawthorn bread, stuff that sounds good in a fancy cookbook. They've asked me to rustle up some elderflower champagne. There's a great clump of the stuff at the dingle. You can pick while I fell, and then we can make it together. It smells wonderful.'

Betsy pours the last of her coffee into the mug. 'A lot of that was just noise, Jude. I heard "rustle" and "clump" and "smells wonderful" and that must mean there's a sentence to be had, but I'm not going to bother looking for it. Anyway, if you're willing to take the risk, I'm game.' She smiles, feeling better. 'Dingle all the way.'

She sees her left hand rise and move swiftly forward, fastening over the hard, grimy knuckles of his clenched right fist. She can't stop herself from pushing for more. 'Is it healthy, do you think? Just shutting out the world and acting like none of it is happening?'

Jude lays his head on one side, giving the matter some thought. 'Who knows what's right? Like you say, everybody wants to be criticism proof. You tried one way and it nearly killed you. Maybe try this for a while, eh?'

She drops her gaze to the bedspread. 'She had nice taste, your Maeve. Her things are lovely.'

He looks puzzled. 'You've never said her name before. And I know I haven't.'

'I Googled her. I told you. The day it all . . .'

'So you'll know what people said.'

She looks away, wishing she hadn't spoken. 'I'm sorry, I didn't mean to . . .'

She feels his rough thumb stroking the soft skin of her palm. 'It's all OK, Betsy. Ask me what you like.'

'I will,' decides Betsy. Her grin becomes impish, her whole manner teenage and full of mischief. 'And you're going to take me up the dingle, yes?'

He grins, a flash of white teeth and a crinkling of the eyes. 'You are the strangest person I've ever met. Don't ever change.'

'You won't always say that,' mutters Betsy, trying to keep things light, and failing.

'Yes,' he says, eyes fixed on hers. He says it like a prophesy. 'Yes, I will.'

FIFTEEN

The dingle is every bit as charming as its name suggests. Jude did give Betsy the option of taking the quad bike, but he had also offered the chance to enjoy what he had referred to as 'a little walk up the hill' – a sentence that had sent Marshall into great paroxysms of excited barking. Betsy had felt unable to disappoint him, and besides, a walk had sounded nice. They left the bastle just after seven a.m., Betsy in a colourful patchwork dress that Jude had laid out across the lid of the colossal wooden hamper at the top of the stairs. She hasn't rummaged around in its depths yet, but she plans to. It's an antique piece, easily big enough to hide a family in, and the first place she'll head in the event of a rising flood. She has a sneaking suspicion that it is full of Maeve's old things, but she has enough of a grip on herself not to go looking for landmines to sow in their Eden. Not yet, anyway.

They've made their way down the hard dirt track and the wooden footbridge across the river – Marshall bounding ahead – then begun their ascent up the green slope, patterned with white and yellow flowers and cut into occasional squares by patches of dry bracken. Jude has pointed out old lead mine workings as they walked – showed her the remains of a house unoccupied since the First World War. *Our place was like that*, he'd said, casually. *Just a ruin.*

Twenty minutes later – exhausted, limp and oozing moisture like a malaria sufferer – Betsy is beginning to regret her decision to walk. Jude has dictated the pace, which hasn't been much above a leisurely amble, but Betsy has never been good in the heat and today the sky has been travel-brochure blue; the sun a big blurry golden medal on a sailor's suit. By the time they spot the line of trees that point the way to Swinburnhope Wood, Betsy is starting to hate nature with a passion she had previously reserved for Nazis and traffic wardens. It comes as a true relief to finally duck under the leafy parasol of the trees and to hear the low applause of the river chuckling its way over rocks. The temperature drops almost at once. Betsy takes her first deep breath since leaving the bastle. Reminds herself that it is unlady-like to spit.

She looks up, foggy-eyed. The dingle is almost unreal in its loveliness, as if it has been designed as a Hollywood filmset. Butterflies and dragonflies flit like faeries between flowers of yellow, blue and white, while the trees tower so high above that their tops are out of sight. The grass and moss beneath her feet looks inviting as a feather-bed and she can hear the pleasant gurgle of water splashing over rocks somewhere nearby. There's a path, of sorts; a slim track that heads in the direction of the running water, the branches of the sweet-scented evergreens forming an arbour overhead. Betsy feels an urge to string it with fairy lights.

'This is amazing,' she says, catching her breath. 'It's beautiful, really. Is it . . . yours?'

He flashes her a grin, Marshall springing around his legs. 'Ownership is a hard thing to explain when it comes to a wood-land. Nobody should own something like this – it belongs to everybody. But if you're asking me whether, on paper, it's part of the area I look after, then yes, it is.'

'That was a complicated answer,' smiles Betsy. 'I've noticed you're good at that. You tell me things in a way that makes me feel like you've answered, when really you've just given me more questions.'

'Do I?' He looks troubled by the accusation. 'Maeve used to say I didn't know how to communicate.'

'You fought a lot?' asks Betsy, eagerly.

'I didn't fight,' he says, quietly. 'She did.'

They traipse on in silence, enjoying the relative cool of the forest. She hears birds she cannot remember noticing before. Somewhere, bees drone fatly in the undergrowth. She looks up at Jude, shading her eyes with her hand, and realizes he is smiling. He seems happy here. Peaceful. It is as if this is where he belongs.

'Down yonder,' he says, gesturing through the trees. He seems unconcerned by the multitude of different insects that are landing upon the faint sheen of sweat at his neck and bare forearms. 'I've a bit to do but I'll talk you through it.'

She follows him, her feet sinking into the soft grass. She wants to take her shoes off, feel the caress of the dew-dampened moss upon her bare soles. She realizes he is speaking to her – that she has been lost in her own thoughts.

'. . . of course, the family could have helped out but they're the sort who make you pay a higher price emotionally than they ever do financially and I think it would have killed her to have gone cap in hand . . .'

Betsy plays catch-up in her head. He's telling her about his ownership of the wood. The realization collides with another thought which ricochets off, and a moment later the importance of this particular woodland is sending off great neon flares in her mind.

This is where Maeve was found, she realizes. *This is where she died.*

'There's a stand of holly bushes down that little snicket,' says Jude, pointing with his head and turning to make sure she's doing OK. He looks at home here, a spring in his step like Marshall's. 'It's called a hagg.'

'What is?'

'A stand of holly trees. These are big brutes. Tall as firs. It's something farmers don't really bother with any more but the branches make a great winter feed. There's a grant you can apply for if you're willing to show other farmers how best to do it, but it hasn't made its way up my to-do list yet. A hard job. Scratched to buggery I was last year. Worth it, though.'

Betsy isn't sure what's required of her, so just keeps following him, pushing through the sharp, sticky trees like a jungle explorer. Flies keep landing on her sweaty neck and her feet are starting to ache inside her unsuitable trainers. She tries not to think about how cheery he seems as he treads through the place where his wife died.

'This is where we had the drama with the pigs,' says Jude, pointing out a tangle of bracken and fallen trees. 'Friend from up the valley – she asked if she could wild-graze. The pigs I mean, not her personally. They're good for a wood, turning the ground, chewing up the nasty bits. They're also escape artists and love getting up to mischief. There was a couple of saplings just there and they went through them like a lawnmower. Turns out it was to cause a distraction. We found the biggest of the brood sunning herself on the river bank, looking like a Brit on holiday.'

He stops long enough for her to catch up. Without speaking he takes her hand. He's bone dry and Betsy feels embarrassed at how clammy her palms are.

'I can hear water,' she says, and her voice is swallowed up by the trees. She has the feeling of being in a greenhouse on a hot day, as if there isn't enough air and the leaves are sucking something vital straight out of her lungs.

'That's the burn,' he explains. 'Drops down into a lovely little pool. There's trout. Big fat lazy ones that might well have wallowed for centuries. It's a bit scary taking a dip for the first time – you can never be sure there isn't a monster down there waiting to take a good slurp of your ankles.'

Jude leads them to a sparse stretch of wood and pushes back a spray of spindly branches as if opening a door in a posh restaurant. She ducks under his arm and finds herself at the water's edge, watching the clear water tumble down over green-furred rocks to splash joyfully into a deep, dark pool. It looks to Betsy like real ale, not yet settled in the glass. She follows the river with her eyes, watching as it tapers and then veers to the right, following the treeline. Dragonflies hover among the myriad insects that form a speckled haze above the surface of the water.

She looks to Jude, and finds him closer to her face than she had anticipated. Embarrassed, she giggles and starts to babble about it being pretty, and how it would be nice to picnic here, and then he is reaching past her, eyes never leaving hers. She spins on the spot, half slipping, and sees him reach inside a hollow a little way up the trunk of a silver-black tree. He withdraws his hand from the hole in the trunk, holding a lethal-looking implement. Betsy stiffens, instinctively, and Jude gives her a soft smile, his eyes crinkling.

'This one's a billhook,' he says, handing it to her. 'These are secateurs. I'm not talking down to you, I just don't know what you know. You know loads of stuff I don't. Anyway, just down there a little way there's a tall, spindly tree with thousands of white flowers on it. They look a bit like lace. Do you know cow parsley? Hogweed?'

'What do you think?' asks Betsy, laughing.

'OK, I was going to say it's a bit like that. But anyway, there's none of that here so there's no risk of you not getting the right one. They smell amazing. I just need you to lop the flower heads off. The higher up the tree you can reach the better. Honestly, don't look scared, it's a nice job and you will smell like summer by the time you're done.'

'Where will you be?' asks Betsy, noticing a tone in his voice that indicates imminent departure.

'I've got some of the less pleasant jobs to worry about,' he says, his manner indicating he would rather be here, with her. 'Got to try and get the mini-digger up the track while the weather's good enough not to clog up the tracks. I'll need it come winter but I won't be able to get it up here. Forward planning – I'm trying to get better at it.'

'A lot of what you say goes over my head, Jude, I think you should know that,' says Betsy, feeling foolish. There's an excitement fizzing inside her suddenly, a desire to do well, to impress. She glances at the blade in her hand: a great curve of shining steel ending in a point that could cut flesh like paper.

'I won't be long,' says Jude. 'If you get done before I'm back just enjoy yourself. I'll leave you Marshall, just in case you get a bit jumpy. No reason you should, it's a lovely wood. I've put a lot of myself into this place over the years.'

She suddenly doesn't want him to go. She has so many questions and yet, in truth, no desire for answers.

'Marshall. Stay.'

Betsy looks down and Marshall settles down in the long grass at her feet, pink tongue lolling happily. She looks up and Jude is already disappearing back into the wood; shadows dappling his back. He doesn't so much leave her sight as become completely absorbed by the forest: his outline disassembling into leaf and shadow and bark.

'Well Toto,' says Betsy, looking at the dog. 'Looks like we're not in Durham.'

SIXTEEN

Betsy follows the smell of summer and honey until she finds the white flowers. They're familiar. The scent, too. She's drunk elderflower gin, she remembers. A bright, fizzy sort of flavour.

'Come on then,' she mutters to herself. 'Just lop some heads off. How hard can it be?'

She giggles at that, imagining Jude coming back to find her embarrassingly thumbless and the woodland churned to potpourri.

With her back to the river, her feet planted on a patch of damp grass that leads down to the water, she selects a spray at random, and with a note of apology, neatly decapitates it with the secateurs. She doesn't feel confident in using the billhook. She drops the floral head on the grass at her feet and selects another. Soon she finds a steady rhythm: picking, cutting, dropping, losing herself in the pleasant monotony of it, working up a pleasing sweat, setting herself the target of reaching higher, pushing further through the greenery. She drifts into a state of near-meditation, listening to the crystal splashing of water upon water; the high drone of the bees; the mosquitoes, pausing only to slap at her damp skin when something tickles at her exposed places.

An hour passes. More, perhaps. Betsy realizes it has been a long time since her mind has been so quiet. There is a timelessness to this place, a near mystic sense of permanence, as though this little wood could be the fulcrum around which the whole world turns. If she were to lie down among the ferns she fancies she could see dragonflies big as eagles fighting in the skies with archaeopteryx and pterodactyls, and surprises herself that her mind is able to offer up such rarely used relics of her vocabulary.

She stops to catch her breath. Wonders whether it is safe to drink the water from the pool. Feels a brief pop of irritation that Jude didn't think to bring a drink, then immediately chides herself, wondering who the hell she thinks she is to be so ungrateful.

Her thoughts take on a familiar pattern and she does nothing to stop them, carefully picking her way further down the riverbank towards the pool. The surface is a mirror. It makes her think of playing cards: the Queen of Hearts reflecting back upside down. Beside her, Marshall noses her hand, demanding a stroke. She rubs at his ears. *This is OK*, she thinks. *This is nice. I like this.*

Marshall stops, suddenly. Hunkers down. Betsy, on impulse, stops perfectly still, half shielded by the overhanging branches of some silver-green tree. Across the pool, a group of brown trees stand sentinel over a steep, bracken and pine-needle strewn floor. The forest beyond the water is sepia in tone; the greenery seeming to have bled itself dry. It makes her think of rust and bloodstains.

Somewhere a little way up the slope, she spots movement. The bees stop their frenzied humming; the songbirds briefly halt their calls. Betsy stares, unsure what to expect. She wonders if perhaps a deer may be making its way gingerly towards the water. She wonders if she will be able to suppress her squeal of delight if so. Or a bear. Could a bear be snuffling its way through the branches? She isn't entirely sure she believes Jude about the absence of grizzlies.

Marshall emits a low growl, taking his role as guard dog seriously. Betsy lowers herself to a crouch, listening intently as the shadows take on more obvious outlines. She hears low voices. A man and a woman. She's doing most of the talking. And then there are shadows dappling the surface of the water and she is watching as two figures push through the trees.

Soundlessly, Betsy shuffles back, one hand pressed to Marshall's back. She knows at once that something is wrong. From her position among the long grasses, half obscured by reeds and the great, sweet-smelling mound of elderflower heads, she takes in the curious apparitions across the river. The woman, leading the way, is athletically built and her thigh muscles, bulging against taut black combat trousers, are tree-trunk thick. She wears a short white shirt, the sleeves rolled up, and has tied the tails just above her midriff to expose a stomach so tanned and toned it makes Liz think of fresh clay scored with a pizza wheel. She has a blonde Mohawk; the back and sides of her head speckled with a day's growth of dark hair. She's glowering at the water as if it has just insulted her mum. Just behind her is a short, stocky man, his face a sweaty beetroot disappearing necklessly into a black T-shirt. He's grunting. Even from here, she can tell that he's half done in from his exertions. And Betsy can see why. Across his shoulders, where a Waitrose mum would wear a pashmina on cold days, he is struggling with the weight of a huge, dead ram.

Betsy sucks in a breath as the message reaches her brain. He's carrying a sheep. A big muttony mass of muscle and wool. A ram: fleece so thick with black blood and flies that it looks to Betsy as though it has been bludgeoned with a pot of jam.

'You could have took a fucking turn.'

'I did the hard work. Stop moaning. We're here.'

'I've been bitten through to the bone.'

'Count your blessings. Might do you some good. Maybe it's a radioactive one and you'll wake up with sheep powers.'

'Ha bloody ha. What's the point of all that muscle if you've got me doing the lifting?'

'I'm largely decorative. And you're doing fine. I'll pick you up – you keep hold of the sheep . . .'

'If I didn't love you!'

'Aye, but you do.'

'Here, grab hold.'

Betsy watches, her hand pressed into the sweat of her bare arm. She knows she's done the right thing in making herself scarce. She would not profess to be an expert on rural matters but she fancies that something about what she is witnessing is very, very wrong.

'Just drop it in – that's what he said.'

'Seems wrong, Donna. Nice spot like this.'

'You reckon? You're easily fooled, babe. More violence in a wood like this than you'll find on the worst streets in Glasgow. Lift up a rock and you'll see something eating the guts out of something else. Peek into a nest and you'll see baby chicks pulling caterpillars apart with their beaks. I watch *Bambi* and all I see is a horror movie waiting to happen.'

'You're fucking great company today, girl.'

'It's the heat. And something bit me somewhere unmentionable.'

'My heart bleeds. I'm wearing a necklace of bites . . .'

'Heave it then. Go on. Give it the full John Cena.'

With a grunt of exertion, the man shrugs the dead ram into the perfect stillness of the pool. Betsy feels a shower of rank pond-water spray across where she lays. She raises her head, watching the dead animal. It disappears, momentarily, then bobs back up; a drowned cloud: a woolly island spoiling the picture perfect serenity.

'And this'll do the trick?'

'Dunno, Mick. But it's what we've been asked to do. So it's done. Shame Punch wasn't around. Would have been nice to get a look at him.'

'Better us than the others. You've seen how Rufus is itching for an excuse. Hard to keep him on a leash.'

'I know family's family but he sickens me, Mick. Not a good bone in him. Evil all the way through. It's going to end in blood.'

Mick doesn't reply. Just stands there, staring at the sheep, slowly sinking into the depths. He looks dejected, as if he's disappointed in himself.

'Seems a low move, if you're asking me,' he says, as the woman joins him. 'I mean, this is where she died, innit? You leave flowers. You leave a teddy. You don't leave a dead sheep.'

'Not our place to worry, babe. Money's good. And this is better than unleashing Rufus, isn't it? A bit of dead livestock and a few broken windows is always going to get my vote over burning the house down while he's nailed to the roof . . .'

Beside her, Betsy feels the low throaty rumble of a dog tensing to strike. She pushes him down. Whispers, softly, in his warm pink ear. 'Easy, Marshall, easy, easy . . .'

Marshall swivels his head and gives her what she takes as an enquiring look. It demands to know why she is lying here, scared and furtive, while these two take liberties on Jude's land. She feels the hot coils of guilt fastening themselves around her belly. Surprising herself, she glances down at her left hand. She's holding the billhook. Holding a length of steel sharp as a Siberian gale.

There is a sudden shout from across the river. She glances up and sees that Mick has his hand to his eyebrow, his face a great twist of pain.

'Jesus, that felt like a bullet!' hisses Mick, taking his hand away long enough to show off a crimson smear of blood and a rapidly swelling eye. 'Shite – another inch and that would have been my eye . . .'

'Where did it come from?' demands Donna, glaring around. She squints across the pool. 'Howay then! Got something to say have you? Have you?'

She turns the other way, glaring directly at where Betsy lies, prone, trying to blend in with the earth. Eyes move across her hiding place like searchlights.

The sound of something slashing at the air: the thwack of stone upon flesh.

'Fuck! Fuck, they've done the other one!'

Through the grass Betsy sees Donna turn back to her companion, who is now holding the other eye. She hears stone strike stone, then ricochet into the water with a splash. Donna jumps back, raising a hand to her Mohawk, where a distinct hole has appeared.

'You cheeky bastard!'

'Stones, Donna!' screams Mick, gesturing at his face with his index fingers. 'Stones!'

'I know he's chucking stones you silly bollocks, I just can't see where he is!'

'He wants you gone, you prick!' yells Donna, addressing the dingle in general. 'No more warnings, no more little hints. Gone. Next thing that goes in this pool will be twice as pretty and no less dead, I swear to . . . aagh!'

She jerks back, clutching her kneecap. The sound of stone hitting hard flesh makes Betsy think of a horse being whipped.

'Come on,' hisses Mick. 'We've done what we had to . . .'

'He's there,' growls Donna, her face red with pain. 'Somewhere just over there.'

'Donna, come on,' says Mick, again. Twin lumps are growing on his eyebrows and smears of blood are marking his cheeks. 'Another time.'

Betsy watches them plunge back into the woods, breaking branches and crunching through dead bracken. She stays still until the last of the shouts and echoes have died away. Then, slowly, she raises her head.

Jude is perhaps twenty feet further down the river, slowly

climbing to his feet. He has a length of black elastic dangling from his left wrist. From his right hand, small stones fall like pennies.

Beside her, Marshall wriggles upright and bounds, energetically, to his master. Betsy has only a moment to study his face before he sees her and alters it to one suitable for company. He looks terrifying. The set of his mouth, the white fire burning in his gaze; he glares at the dead animal in the pool with such ferocity that Betsy momentarily thinks of his eyes as the barrels of a sawn-off shotgun: everything within his gaze should prepare for violence.

He flicks on a smile as he sees her. 'You've worked up a sweat,' he says, softly, as she approaches. 'Good job on the elderflowers there. Built enough to hide in.'

'Jude, that was really intense – who were they . . . they did it on purpose, I don't . . .'

Jude gives a little shake of his head. 'Public right of way. You get all sorts of dickheads ambling through. Trying to be funny, I reckon, though they might not laugh so loud next time.'

'No, they were talking as if it was personal, as if it was a message . . . they mentioned a person called Punch. Who's Punch? This is where you get your water, isn't it? And where Maeve . . .'

Jude puts a cool, rough palm upon her face. Looks into her. 'It's OK, Betsy. I swear.'

'Jude, don't treat me like I'm made of sugar, if you're in trouble I want to help you!'

He smiles, grateful. 'We'll talk later, I promise. We've a mucky job now. You can help, or Marshall can walk you home.'

Betsy doesn't have time to answer before Jay wades, fully clothed, into the cool embrace of the pool. In moments he is up to his waist, then chest, and with powerful strokes he reaches the dead ram. Ducks under. He surfaces, dripping, and places his hands in the animal's fur. Pulls it, as reverently as he can, towards the bank.

Betsy and Marshall glance at one another and suddenly the madness of the past few moments seems far away and inconsequential. All she wants is to be in the cool deep embrace of the pool. She wades in from the bank, Marshall splashing excitedly beside her. The cold takes her breath away. Her skin tingles. Something slithers through the fabric of her dress, nudging wetly at her hip. She gasps, and begins to giggle; teeth chattering, fizzing with cold in her every cell. Jude grins as he sees her. Laughs, wetly, as he hears her shrieking – the pondweed flirting with her ankles.

'Oh God, it's so cold! Oh my God . . . and deep, and the rocks are . . .'

She reaches out, grasping for something to hold onto, and then her hand closes on fur, then matted, sticky wool, and she disappears for a moment into the cold brown water, and then Jude is pulling her to the surface. And then her mouth finds his, and his hands find the shape of her beneath her wet clothes, and in moments all is mud and grass and tongue against tongue, and she feels as though a sort of magic is working within her, around her, deep inside her.

For a time, there is only pleasure. A bliss of connection; the sure and certain understanding that this, this fleeting *now*, is true contentment.

Here.

In the place where his wife died.

Where he seems so very much alive.

SEVENTEEN

She kisses him on tiptoe. He is no taller than she is, but she parts from his embrace the higher of the two. His lips exaggerate her limbs. She finds herself elevated; feet arched, a ballerina *en pointe*. It seems as though she is a mere vessel for something bigger than her own dimensions – that she must stretch and twist and wriggle to make room for the sensations that unfold inside her, as her mouth opens into his.

'You're a sunflower,' he says, and his lower lip touches hers. 'You're heliotropic. A sunflower, searching out the sun . . .'

There is a fleeting contact; a dragonfly upon still water, as his embouchure forms the soft 'f' of flower. If she were able to live within a single moment it would be thus – half a heartbeat; a breath made flesh.

He is holding her the way she needs. She cannot fall. She is anchored here, pressed to him. She thinks for a moment of fossils and wings; brachiopods and footprints in ancient stone.

Within their kiss her senses feel heightened, as if every part of her is made of the skin that grows back after a scald. She feels intensified; she can isolate every individual sensation, from the wet grass that touches her ankles and calves, to the tickle of a loose hair – brushed free during their first caress – alighting half upon her collarbone and half upon her white blouse. She fancies that if she concentrated she would be able to pick out the sound of each separate raindrop as they tumble through the tall trees with their storm-blackened trunks and spill on to the mossy roof of the squat, tumbledown hut in which they take shelter. It was a farmhouse, once. Eight generations of men and women – only ever two surnames on the deeds – but empty since 1946, when the last of the Durrell men cut their losses and walked away. It's a crumbling grey rectangle; the roof more holes than slate. Spindly trees poke their branches out through the glassless windows. The inside is sheep shit and weeds; an artwork drawn in broken bottles and indecipherable graffiti.

'Where are you?' he asks, and his eyes are so close to hers that she feels dizzy looking into them. She blinks, and he withdraws a little, as if chastened. He rests against the damp stone wall. She feels his arms leave her waist.

'Your mind,' he asks, again. 'Where did you go?'

'I was thinking of stones,' she says, grinning. 'Fossils. I'd like it if we turned to stone together. Have you seen the shapes barnacles leave on rocks? Or the patterns of leaf skeletons in soft rock? I'd like us to be like that. Do you think if we lie down long enough we could just sink into the ground and it wouldn't matter any more? We'd just be together. Just one entity . . .'

She stops talking, annoyed at her own inability to precisely articulate her thoughts. Since meeting him she has become increasingly aware of the gulf between emotion and language. She occasionally feels that her declarations of love will sound asinine to his ears. It is as if the language of her passion necessitates a more physical, demonstrative depiction. Sometimes she longs to crush a peach within her hand and hold it to his lips for him to lick. She wants to shake apples from a tree by swinging on the branches. She wants to stick her head under the surface of a still lake and take a bite of the moon's reflection. Wants to say . . . I love you *this* much.

'Like towels,' he says, twitching a smile. 'Neat, hotel towels, stacked on top of one another. We'd be like that. It's a nice picture.'

'I haven't stayed in many hotels,' she says, and there is an apology in her voice, as if she has let them both down with such an omission. She pictures him as he was when he toured the world as a musician. Her mind floods with ugly erotica: Jude pleasuring and being pleasured; a flickerboard of images; fifty shades of flesh.

'You will,' he says. 'You'll stay in the finest hotels all over the world. You'll dry yourself with pure luxury. I'll take you places where they've trained pandas to hug the guests dry.'

'You're going to have to work hard to pay for that,' she says, and stares out through the empty window at a landscape that drifts on, endlessly, until bleeding into the sky. 'I don't really understand how you make money. I know you cut down trees . . .'

'I try not to cut down trees,' he says, and he nuzzles his head against hers, the way she has seen horses do. 'I'm a qualified tree surgeon, not a lumberjack. Major difference.'

'Soz,' she smiles, and slaps her wrist. 'Bad girl. I just sort of told Carly you're a farmer. But you're not, are you?'

'I'm not even a tree surgeon really,' he says, chewing on his lip, thoughtfully. 'I don't know what I am. Everything I thought I was – I look back and realized I wasn't.'

'You've done a lot with your life,' says Betsy, and she feels him adjust his position so he can press himself against her; his cheek against hers, arm around her waist. 'You're a great sax player.'

'Thanks,' he says, quietly. 'I was OK. I'm not now. I'd love to be as good as I was when I was twenty-one.'

'Are your family musicians?' she asks. He hasn't spoken about his family much. Doesn't speak about anything personal unless she pushes.

'My dad likes the harmonica,' he says, and she senses him smile at some memory. 'Mum could bang the pans together like she was Keith Moon midway through a drum solo. Not an easy woman. I'm sure there'd be a proper name for it nowadays – Dad just said she was highly strung.'

She considers this. 'That sounds quite cynical,' she says, a little frostily. 'Jay never really understood mental health problems. I know that the things he got right were just the law of averages. All he really wanted was for me to behave. To be grateful. To be normal.'

'That's the last thing I want,' says Jude, stroking her stomach. 'I like your craziness. I'd rather deal with the fallout from your fires than live a life without a spark. Whatever your brain does to you – however it tries to ruin things, I'll always see past it. I'll always see the real you, underneath.'

She shakes her head. 'You don't know how I get. What I'm capable of. It's only a few weeks since I was necking tablets like they were Tic Tacs . . .'

'But you're happy now?' he asks. 'You feel good, inside?'

She nods, meaning it. 'But when I split – I think up such terrible things. I get so paranoid. I used to believe that Jay had a whole other family – a whole other life. I had software put on his phone to track his locations. I would ring his work and do fake accents and try to get one of his colleagues to drop him in it by admitting he was out with Suzie from accounts . . .'

'I'll never give you reason to doubt me,' says Jude, in her ear. 'I know what trust means to you. I won't spoil it.'

She readjusts herself, taking her weight on her left leg so she can lean against the damp wooden timbers of the doorframe. The wet earth has squished over the lip of her sandals and there is brown mud on her cold toes. He likes her toes. He told her so as he peeled off her damp socks on the riverbank. Likes all toes, as far as she can tell, but hers in particular. She has reconciled herself to such accommodations. He likes necks, but hers is best. Likes the scent of female shoulder blades and wrists.

She glances up as a sudden flash of colour catches her eye; a flash of earthy brown streaking through the heather that rises above the dry-stone wall. 'Look,' she says, squeezing his forearm. 'A deer.'

'A doe,' he says, nodding. 'There's a family of them in the wood that joins up with the dingle. The stag's a real bruiser. Intelligent eyes.'

'I suppose you and I have different views on hunting,' she says, hoping that she's wrong. 'Seems horrible to me. Cruel. I know you don't like grouse shooting but aren't you countryside types into your blood sports?'

He looks at her, hurt. 'Why do you say that?'

'Just what I've read, I suppose. Sorry, I wasn't trying to insult you, or anything . . .'

'You know Maeve was an activist for animal rights, yes?'

Betsy curses herself. Why had she said that?

'Sorry, I do know that. I don't know why I said that. I say daft things sometimes. I'm sure you will too though.' She wonders if she can distract him from thinking bad thoughts about her by making him think he has done something to upset her in return. 'I've let stuff slide with you, haven't I? You don't need to make me feel like a shit about it.'

She turns away from him, whipping her neck so fast that it makes a noise like somebody stepping on a twig. She listens to the sound of his breathing. Wonders whether he's going to say sorry and hopes to God he doesn't.

'I hate all the tally-ho stuff,' he says, as if the unpleasantness hadn't happened. 'Hate anybody looking down at me from horseback and acting like I'm a peasant and they're Lord of the Manor. But there's far worse than foxhunting. Snares – they're what eat away at me. People who think they're safeguarding animals and then go set these barbaric traps. They say they're catching foxes but I've seen badgers with the snare dug in their leg all the way to the bone. Housecats too. Maeve used to spend half her life dismantling them, walking the countryside pulling up traps and handing in snares. Never did a bit of good but it's better than doing nothing at all.'

'Is that how the bad blood started with Campion?'

Behind her, she feels Jude tense at the very mention of his name. 'Yes, in a way. He runs one of the biggest grouse shoots in the area. Not as big as he wants it to be, but he hasn't given up hope yet. Feeds the birds up until they can barely fly, then his rich mates blast away at them until they're not much more than mince and feathers. Seventy-five pounds per bird, at least. You can see why it's a rich sod's game. I've always hated it. Did some work as a beater for the shoot at Slaley when I first moved back north and couldn't stand being a part of it. Maybe that's when I started rubbing people up the wrong way.'

'Sylvia said you've got a few enemies.'

He shrugs. 'I know there's always somebody trying to impress their mates by spilling my pint or treading on my toes at the bar. People have selective memories here. There are grown men, fifty and sixty years old, who still give a damn about whether or not they're thought of as the hardest man in their valley. You think toxic masculinity's a new thing – believe me, men have been fighting over mating rights and territory since time began.'

'Campion fled like a scolded cat when you came to help me that day,' remembers Betsy, smiling. 'Those men with him. They didn't hang around either.'

She hears Jude let out a dry little laugh. 'Likes to surround himself with macho types. His gamekeeper's not a bad sort but the number two, Brendon – he's more of an odd-job man. Been inside for taking a baseball bat to an animal rights activist. He knows people worse than himself and pays them well to do what they do best. He's the one who hires in all these hard cases to scare his tenants into paying their increased ground rents, or insisting they open up parts of their land for Campion.'

'Opening their land? How do you mean?'

He sighs, as if he's been keeping the words inside him for a long time. 'He's got his plans,' he says. 'Wants to put an access road all the way up the fell to where his new grouse butts are – right through half a dozen farms, including the bastle. He's been putting cattle grids in on the bridleway, just so riders stop going up a path they've had access to for centuries. Been some bad accidents. One poor yearling snapped both legs and there was a three-hour wait to put it out of its misery. Brendon and his mob just stood there. They've got everybody on board now – all willing to turn a blind eye to what he's doing because they're too scared to do anything else.'

'And you?'

He laughs, drily. 'Be a cold day in hell before I give that man anything that makes him happy. I've told him to do his worst.'

'And you're not scared?' asks Betsy.

He shrugs. 'I don't see how that would help.'

She snuggles into him, feeling safe and warm and good.

'What's that tree called?' she asks, nodding at the specimen with the purple leaves.

'Andrew,' he says, and reaches out from his side of the doorframe to take her hand in his. Impulsively, she raises his fingers to her face and kisses them. Neat, soft fingertips, clipped pink nails. He smells of soap and wood polish. Smells like the garden after a storm.

Over his shoulder, she watches the deer fade into the landscape, looking for her stag: the gentle brute with the big intelligent eyes.

Back off, she thinks, and turns to kiss him. *He's spoken for.*

EIGHTEEN

During the years that she invested in trying to make things work with Jay, Elizabeth Zahavi developed a rich and multi-layered fantasy life. In her mind, she experienced idyllic outings, luxurious dinner dates and erotic assignations with all manner of made-up people – her projections of perfection utterly eclipsing the minor enjoyments of her reality. It led to accusations that she viewed the world as some sort of Hollywood movie; that she would be happier living her life in a different time, when being spun and dipped and kissed roughly while wearing petticoats were all that a person needed to feel fulfilled.

Life's not life that, would be Jay's stock reply, whenever she suggested a barefoot stroll on a moonlit beach: a half-bottle of champagne and a tartan rug laid out in preparation at some secluded cove. *You'd say it was too cold. Flies would bite your ankles and you'd bitch about being itchy for the rest of the week. You don't even like champagne – it gives you indigestion. And where would I park? Have you tried getting sand out of the upholstery? You look at the world through rose-tinted spectacles. You can't handle reality. You can't handle a grown-up relationship . . .*

Betsy allows herself a wry smile as she pictures him now, pontificating about the real world and her ingratitude for not being satisfied with what she's got. Here, now, she feels vindicated in her belief that there is another way to live and to love. She never actually pictured this precise scene, but she knows that if it had flashed through her imagination as a proposal for a perfect evening, she would definitely have plucked it from the slideshow and given it a once-over.

It's early evening; the sun still working hard enough to give the soft blue sky a shimmering, hazy quality. The view from the little courtyard garden at the rear of Wolfcleugh Bastle seems somehow fabric in texture, as though the big sky and the endless, empty moors are made up of different coloured wools: mohair, alpaca, merino. Everything seems soft, as if the world has lost its rough edges.

Betsy is sitting in a white plastic garden chair beneath a pergola that is coming away from the ancient brickwork. The few roses that cling to the trellis are being throttled by a mass of some tangled creeper, but there is a prettiness to the way the two intertwine and overlap, as if it were all part of a courtship ritual that will lead to a splendid new species. She's barefoot, wearing one of Jude's work shirts, the sleeves rolled up to her elbows. She keeps smiling. Keeps giving deep, contented sighs.

She sips her drink; some purplish hedgerow concoction enlivened with a healthy measure of bathtub gin. Her lips, tender and slightly swollen, sting pleasantly each time they come into contact with the glass. She feels good. Soft and dreamy. She's barely taking much in, just lolling, head back, half-watching the curve of the dirt track that ducks and weaves and rises towards the front of the farmhouse, and then on up the lane to where a couple of holiday cottages stand empty. Beyond that is another of the seemingly inexhaustible supply of abandoned houses, then nothing much at all until the dingle and the burn. The home of Campion and Candace Lorton-Cave lies beyond the valley. Were she a sniper, she could lie on the bastle roof and make all of Jude's problems go away.

She listens to the nothingness. It's never truly quiet here but she can make out no noises of modernity; no car engines or too-loud television sets or the chirruping of mobile phones. She hears birds, and the drone of bees, and the occasional scratching of paws against wood. If she strains her ears she can just make out the soft lullaby of Jude singing while he works in the kitchen. The smell of the elderflower champagne adds a golden lustre to the air; a sticky, sugar-sweet aroma that sweetens her lips.

'You look comfortable. You look lots of things too. Irresistible, mostly.'

She turns towards the voice. Jude stands by the kitchen door, watching her, a pleasing light in his eyes. His forearms are patterned with elderflower petals and he gives off the smell he brought back with them from the burn: leather, sweat, the ripe green tang of moss and riverbed.

'Kiss,' says Betsy, dreamily.

'Not until I shower. I'll repel you.'

Betsy pouts. 'I thought it was "repulse".'

'Neither sounds great,' he says, and reaches into his shirt pocket. He pulls out a joint, expertly rolled. Lights it without another word and sucks the smoke deep into his lungs. Breathes out a thin plume of grey. He holds it out to her, eyes asking if she wants to try.

Panic shoots through her, shredding her serenity as if with a blade.

Why's he smoking that? How often does he do that? He didn't even ask if I was OK with it! Is that what he needs to get through the day? How can she believe him when he's off his head on that stuff? Is she not enough? Why isn't he as happy as her, sitting here, high on him . . .?

She reaches out and takes it from him. Takes a puff. She hasn't smoked since she was a teenager and even then all it had done was make her feel sick and then put her to sleep. This stuff doesn't taste like that. It's smooth and slips into her lungs like honey. She breathes out without coughing. Feels a warmth spread through her and in moments she is telling herself not to worry about the detail that everything's good, that she's safe and desired and maybe something more. That everything's, well, groovy . . .

'Groovy,' she says aloud, and starts to giggle.

Jude grins, enjoying her. 'Music?' he asks.

'I've got Spotify on my phone if the signal's working,' says Betsy, though her words sound distant and thick inside her head. She slithers back into the chair, staring past the empty stables. 'You should play for me. Did I tell you I kept listening to your music? Kept looking at your picture on the website too. You were very handsome. Still are. More so. I bet you got so many groupies, didn't you? I'm kind of paranoid about that, if I think about it. That you've had lots of women and I'm . . . well . . . I mean I'm not going to get married in white, but . . .'

'Sorry, were you saying something?' asks Jude, emerging from the kitchen and unspooling a long extension cable. He plugs in a battered old CD player – the sort she imagines painters and decorators used to use before the iPod came along and made the world less untidy. There's a crackle of static and then the sound of piano, sinewy and deep; a poem of sound written entirely on the black keys. 'Bartok,' says Jude, and takes a seat on a wooden crate: old and well-made. It might once have carried beer bottles or ammunition.

'I like it,' says Betsy, listening. 'Sad, but beautifully so.'

He grins at that, as if she's said something insightful and wise. 'I've always preferred the minor key. My dad used to tell me to play something cheerful when I was practicing but it just feels a bit . . . well . . . flimsy to me. I like music that reaches in and touches you where you're vulnerable.' He takes another drag on his joint. 'Sorry, just occurred to me – are you cool with this? I don't smoke much, I'm just kind of in a good place right now.' He twinkles as he says it. 'You've already made me high – this is just a chaser.'

Betsy doesn't reply. She feels like she's floating above every-thing, looking down at two people falling in love without knowing the first thing about one another. She makes one of her endless pacts with herself. *Don't overthink it. Don't analyse it to death. Don't deconstruct it because it might not fit back together again.*

Jude notices her look in the direction of the stables. 'Something sad about an empty stable, don't you think? Like a ghost ship. You know something's happened and that it can't have been good. She'd hate to see them like this.'

Betsy feels herself descending. Floats back down and into herself. She wants to be properly present if he's going to talk about his dead wife. She's awake enough to see the wisdom in continuing to look half-asleep and fully stoned.

'I don't know much about horses. They scare me a little.'

'Scare me too. Never been a rider. I can muck out and I know how to lead one by the nose but I'm with my dad on this one – you can get the same experience bouncing up and down on the sofa and throwing money out the window.'

A breeze rushes up the valley, rustling leaves, sending birds squawking into the air. Betsy shivers as it cools the sweat on her brow. She feels the air pressure drop, as if rain is on the way; this afternoon's brief downpour a mere prelude to a Biblical tempest.

'You don't have to talk about her if it's difficult,' says Betsy, hoping to God he doesn't take her up on the offer of remaining mute.

'It's not difficult,' he says, looking past her to where the moor starts to climb. 'It was for a while. I think I went a bit mad after it happened.'

'All the best people are mad,' says Betsy, quietly. 'I used to have a T-shirt that said that. Jay didn't let me wear it.'

Jude cocks his head. 'How did he stop you?'

Betsy thinks about it. 'He didn't get in my face about things like that – just made it impossible for me to enjoy them. If I wore something he didn't like he'd make me hate it too – poke me in the stomach and say it showed off my tummy, or sneer at me for trying to be cool, or hang with the kids, or whatever.'

Jude sucks in another lungful of smoke and starts picking the flower petals and seeds off his arms. 'So that night – that was the first time he went for you physically?'

Betsy answers in Liz's voice, a reaction so swift as to seem like a hypnotic suggestion. 'I pushed him too far. The stuff I sent his work, his contacts, his mam – it humiliated him and for him that's the worst possible thing. He has to measure up to this vision – the status symbols, the house, the flat-screen TV. His mum made him like that. He's a good dad really – he was my rock for a long time . . .' Her voice fades as she talks, the words losing their meaning as she regurgitates lines she has said countless times before. 'I think he would have stopped,' she says, flatly. 'I have to think that.'

Jude doesn't say anything. Just turns his gaze back up the valley to where his wife died, and where today, he and Betsy became something so much more than lovers and friends.

'I'm sorry – I interrupted,' says Betsy. 'You can tell me about her. You know I've read the article about what happened. Sylvia said to make sure I did. I think she could see I was falling for you and wanted to make sure I knew what I was letting myself in for.'

Jude shakes his head, a half smile at his lips. 'You wouldn't get many facts from the way it was reported. Lies, mostly, and guesswork the rest. Truth is, she was here and then she wasn't. She was alive, and giving me her usual routine of telling me what I'd done wrong, and then she was stomping off in a huff, and then the next thing they're showing me her body and she's turning from alive to dead before my eyes; the colour draining out of her the way ice lollies go when you just suck the juice.' He shakes his head as he considers the memory. 'People need somebody to blame. Some people blamed me.'

'And you?' asks Betsy. 'Who do you blame?'

He doesn't reply. Edges his crate forward so he can reach her bare foot. Strokes his rough knuckles against the soft sole and stops when she shivers.

'It must be killing you,' he says, looking into her eyes in that intense, earnest way of his. 'Not asking. Not letting yourself be the person you are. I appreciate the gesture, Betsy, but Sylvia's right – you deserve to know what you're letting yourself in for. I know you will have trouble trusting me on that and I don't expect it to serve as some miracle cure for any problems you've faced in the past, but I want us to be together. That's suddenly more important than anything else.'

Betsy wishes she could look back into his eyes with the same intensity but she suddenly feels uncomfortable and twitchy, as if there are little electric charges going off inside her. She can't work out how best to reply, even while a choir of voices within are screaming at her to reply that she feels the same about him. Instead, she sets her face into something resembling seriousness, and tries to put her thoughts into some kind of order.

'I feel safe with you. Then I don't. And I don't know if that's because I've got BPD and mess things up for myself, or if my paranoia is like a superpower and it's warning me to get away from you.'

Jude reaches out and wraps his hands around hers. She's still holding her empty glass and he takes it from her and puts it down at his side.

'Long story short?' he asks, softly.

'Long as it needs to be,' replies Betsy, and her fingers fasten around his, holding on as if he might pull away.

'This is her place,' says Jude, turning a slow circle with his head to take in the bastle and its land. 'She'd been here for years when she and I got together. Did most of the work herself. It was a ruin. A proper ruin, like the ones all over the valley. The landowners around here get it in the neck for making it so difficult for people to buy up these abandoned houses and turn them into modern homes but there are ways around it if you're determined enough. This place belonged to an old couple who live over Ireshopeburn. They used the land a little but nobody had lived in the bastle since the end of the First World War. Maeve fell in love with the place when she was up from London visiting her mum . . .'

'They're local?'

He shakes his head. 'Warwickshire, ancestrally speaking, but they're not short of money. Her mum owned a couple of holiday properties up here. Rented them out or came to stay herself when fancy took her. And Maeve had always been a countryside girl and wanted somewhere she could keep horses and ride and teach and be as far away from what some people call the real world as possible. She managed to get the money together to make an offer on this place, even while everybody else said she was mad to do so. The council's planning department were never going to approve any plans to do it up – there was no precedent for it. But she did it anyway. Moved in to a place that wasn't much more than a hole in the ground and four tall walls. Pitched a tent in the grounds and set to work. There are photos of all that she did. Half-killed herself grafting away clearing the site. She had to prove there was a "functional and financial need" to live here, because it was listed as an ancient monument and they preferred it to be a ruin than risk somebody ruining it, which is her phrase, not mine.'

Dutifully, Betsy smiles. She feels cold, suddenly. The clouds, high and gold, are racing up the valley; turning grey and purple: a bruise on drowned flesh.

'She got a lot of people on her side,' he says, and Betsy notices that his hands, clasped within hers, have gone still. He is somewhere else now, remembering. 'Got the planning officer at Hexham council eating out of the palm of her hand and the local businesses and most of the farmers supported the application. She wanted to run a trekking centre – that was the plan, and managed to get agreements with a lot of official bodies that she would do it all in a way that encouraged wildlife and would have managed the land in an eco-friendly way. She couldn't have done more.'

'But?'

'Campion,' he says, eyes flashing like flint against stone. 'He made a formal objection to the planning committee.'

'Why?'

Jude laughs, drily. 'Because he gets great joy from being a complete and utter bastard, Betsy. That's what he lives for. He's got a lot of clout in this valley. Used his wife's name to open a few doors and turned himself into Toad of Toad Hall. The local copper has been in his pocket for years. Half the planning committee too, if the rumours were to be believed.'

Betsy rubs her thumb against his dry, crackled knuckle. 'She got her application rejected. She wasn't going to be allowed to live here, or do it up, and she'd spent every penny she had on buying a ruin.' He looks away, eyes downcast. 'They came to an arrangement,' he says, and the word seems to disgust him.

'You don't have to tell me . . .'

'She went to him cap in hand and asked what she could do to get the committee to support the application. And he was enough of a bastard to tell it to her straight. He wanted a share of the profits, and he wanted a share of her.'

'Jesus,' whispers Betsy, her face twisting.

'It went through like a dream at the next planning meeting,' sneers Jude. 'She got what she wanted. Started work. Turned this into what you see. By the time we met she was doing good, taking parties out on treks, teaching kids to ride, applying for land management grants and renting out land to farmers. She was doing what she set out to do. All for the price of letting that sweaty bastard enjoy her for a few seconds of her time.'

Betsy shakes her head. She remembers the sensation of being used; of her body being a cash machine. It twists her guts. She needs to stop him talking before she throws up on her own bare feet.

'How did you meet?'

Jude shrugs. 'It had all gone wrong. For me. I hadn't been good enough. Band did OK, I did OK, but I was creeping towards cruise ship territory career-wise and I was living wrong. Drinking. Too much powder up the nose. I couldn't rely on my fingers to play the way they had before. I came home for a while. My dad still farms at Heddon-on-the-Wall. I grew up in this life. Born to be a farmer but left to study music at university and didn't come back until I was pushing forty. We met in a bar over Edmundbyers way. I was living here within six weeks.'

'You do like your passionate beginnings,' says Betsy, with a meanness she instantly wishes she could take back.

Jude looks away. Grinds out the dead joint on the heel of his boot. 'I think we were happy. More happy than sad, anyway. She was always cleverer than me, and I'm not saying I'm a dunce, but she always had a million ideas running at any one time and had this fire in her, like she wanted to change the world. I couldn't keep up sometimes. She'd studied Classics at Durham and did another degree in Forestry Management just because she thought it would look good when applying for land grants. She was exhausting. And she could be nasty when things didn't go her way. One moment I was her everything and the next I was some sponger, some loafer, trying to get her money. I didn't even know she had any money! And when she left me this place . . .? I swear, I never knew. Sometimes I felt more like a punching bag than a partner and I was only just working out how to co-exist with her properly when the accident happened.'

'I'm sorry, Jude,' says Betsy, because she feels that she should.

He nods thanks he doesn't seem to mean. 'Afterwards, Campion came to see me. Nice as pie at first. Sat in my kitchen and I didn't know he wasn't like any number of other locals coming to pass on their respects. I knew of him, course I did, but it wasn't until that moment that I found out what he really was. He took delight in telling me, of course. Sat there with his feet up, one of his blokes standing by my back door, drinking my tea, enjoying my hospitality, and then he tells me about the arrangement. All he'd done for her in the beginning. And he wanted to make sure I knew that now, her debt was mine. Maeve had signed it over to me, you see – the house, the land. In her will, it all came to me. Which would have been a nice surprise if it hadn't come with a side order of Campion. As far as he was concerned, the profit sharing arrangement was going to continue, even though I couldn't possibly run a trekking centre without Maeve because I knew next to nothing about horses. I was too overwhelmed to speak – especially when he started telling me how hard she'd worked to get him onside in the first place. Told me in great detail.'

Betsy experiences a rush of pure hate. She squeezes Jude's clenched hands. 'You can stop, Jude. I'm sorry I pushed . . .'

'I was numb for months, Betsy,' he says, despite her protests. 'I didn't know what I wanted. I sold the horses and it wasn't long before the tax man and the bailiffs were knocking on the door saying they'd been tipped off I hadn't paid my full death duties and was skimming on my taxes. I got audited and had to pay a huge chunk to make it all go away. Equipment started going missing; stock I bought for the fields got savaged; got ill. And Campion just kept sending down little reminders that he was owed, and was running out of patience.'

'And the grouse shooting?'

'Maeve fought that until her last breath – I was damn well going to honour her wishes. He wasn't having it. I tried to be as reasonable as I could. I said I'd do jobs for him in part-payment until things worked themselves out. Ended up at his big house managing his woods and taking orders from these halfwit city lads he'd brought out to get the local tenants to do what he wanted.'

Betsy puts the pieces together before he speaks. 'His wife? Is it Candy? Sylvia mentioned . . .'

Something a little like a smile rushes across Jude's features. He looks momentarily bashful. 'She needed somebody to talk to. Maybe I did too.'

'You slept with her?' asks Betsy.

He shakes his head. 'No. I liked her, I suppose. Liked her enough to want to be her friend and nothing more, and if I'm honest, she wasn't really my type. But the fact that Candy maybe wanted to – well, that didn't do much for Campion and from then on it was out and out hatred. He wants me out of here. Wants me to suffer. He's got people for whom it's a full-time job. Debt collectors trying to recover goods, enforcement officers trying to seal off the house and evict me.' He stops talking and shakes his head as some realization pains him. 'I shouldn't have brought you here. You should have gone to your sister. I'm a selfish prick for putting you in the middle of all this.'

Betsy leans back in her chair, digesting it all. 'The money he gave me,' she says, at last. 'He sent a man with it. A big man. And those two at the river . . . he has more of them too? Jude, you can't be everywhere at once. What are you going to do?'

He extricates his hands and rubs his palms across the stubble at his jaw. 'Sell up, maybe. Not to him if I can help it, but nobody else will buy with him hovering over the sale like a cloud. I've been keeping on keeping on just for bloody-mindedness but now, maybe . . . I don't know. I woke up this morning and thought of you. I've thought of nothing but you since we met. But then I picture us here together, you and me, and I get this feeling in me that you get when you're a kid and you realize Christmas isn't far away.'

The air temperature drops again and Betsy feels the first droplets of rain spatter on the bare flesh of her legs. She doesn't make any attempt to move. Nor does Jude. She realizes that he's asking her a question, even without the words ever finding a shape. It's there in his eyes, in the lingering scent of elderflower and pondweed; in the song of the birds in the hedgerows and the dark emptiness of the stables; in the spaces between the notes that bleed from the CD player. He wants to know if she will be here, with him. If he can be hers.

'I'm hard work,' she says. 'Whatever I say to you now, I don't know I'll still be cool with things next time something triggers me. I'm jealous of her already. Jealous of her, and the rich cow in the big house. You've got no pictures of her but I feel like she's watching us. Like she's in every corner. I don't know if I can feel like I'm at home here, but I think I can feel that way as long as you're always near.'

'There are pictures,' he says, softly. 'I took them down off the walls when I brought you home. Chucked them in the dresser in the hall. I want you to know that the past is just that.'

Silence, then. And the rain. The proposition, still unspoken, between them.

She doesn't think for long. Whatever doubts she harbours, she will put them aside for another day. He is what she wants. *This* is what she wants.

'Why did he give me money?' she asks, at last.

Jude pulls a face, slightly embarrassed. 'Candy. I didn't know

she'd go for it. I just told her what had happened and asked her
to have a word with her husband.'

Betsy's face hardens. 'And anything in return?'

He shakes his head. 'You never have to doubt me, Betsy. You
can trust me all the way through to the bone. I'll never give you
cause to fear me straying, I swear it.'

They're good words, and Betsy enjoys them. Doesn't believe
a solitary syllable, but enjoys them nonetheless.

The rain begins to fall in earnest now, pitter-pattering down
from a grey-blue sky, sending up tiny clouds of vapour as each
droplet smacks into sun-baked earth. Betsy raises her face. Enjoys
the kiss of the rain against her skin.

'Betsy . . .'

She shifts position. Takes his hands. Pulls him forward and
raises her damp hands to his wet cheeks and holds his face to
hers. Just before she kisses him, she gives a nod of assent.

Yes, it says. *This is what I want.*

At a little after two a.m., Betsy slips naked from her bed. Jude
has joined her in the spare room and sleeps soundly, soundlessly,
as if attuned to finding himself in new company. Nothing was
said, but they wordlessly agreed it better that he move down the
hall to her room, rather than her joining him in the bed where
he used to sleep with perfect, pretty, firebrand Maeve, with her
fight and her determination and her two degrees and her big brain
and her *I've-got-loads-of-money-why-don't-you-come-be-my-
houseboy* smile.

She tiptoes downstairs, bare feet at the edges of the boards so
as not to give out a creak. The kitchen reeks of the elderflower
champagne, brewing away in two big plastic containers on the
table top; stems and dead flowers surround the base like floral
tributes at an accident site.

She gives Marshall a stroke. Listens, carefully, for any hint
that Jude may have noticed her absence. Smiles to herself as she
imagines how she will wake him when she returns to bed. Sends
up a silent little wish that she will find him sleeping on his back.

Quickly, noiselessly, she moves through to the Welsh dresser.
Opens the cupboards. Rummages through for the photo albums;
the moonlight bleeding through the dirty hall window turning

the plastic and cellophane pages into so many multi-coloured mirrors. She finds what she's looking for in moments. It's there on the third page of the first album, as if it has recently been placed at the top of the stack. It's a picture of Maeve, impossibly beautiful, sunlight turning her mop of curly hair into a halo of gold ringlets that complements the perfect white smile, the tanned skin and the immaculate swell of her chest. She's stunning. Sexy, but in a wholesome way – as if she is not averse to being pleasured from behind while rolling out pastry in a farmhouse kitchen.

Betsy doesn't even register surprise when she sees that Maeve has been photographed wearing the same dress that Jude tore from her today; ripping the fabric away from her as if it were aflame.

She replaces the picture. Goes back to bed. Presses herself against him and hopes he won't wake. Lies still until morning, hoping that his warmth will bleed through to the place inside her where, suddenly, she feels very, very cold.

NINETEEN

Days slide by. Nights too. They eat when they remember to. Get dressed only to walk Marshall or to take slow, meandering strolls upon the moor. Jude points out abandoned buildings, interesting trees, old mine shafts and crumbling bridges; his hand never unlaced from hers. They become an island, for a time. Betsy does not miss contact with the world beyond their boundary wall. She feels drunk. Mesmerized. High on pleasure and contentment and the sensation that every cell in her body is exploding and re-forming each time he looks at her in that way of his: as if she is a rare bird that has fluttered into the woodland – multi-coloured feathers dazzlingly conspicuous against the green-brown foliage. She feels safe. Feels good. She waits until he is asleep to tell him that she loves him but she does so with absolute conviction; whispering in the dark, staring into him as if trying to see the bottom of a well. She longs for *always*. For the first time in her life, she wants only this. Only now, in perpetuity.

One morning she wakes to coffee and poetry. He has written her a verse; black ink on a scrap of card, torn from a cereal box. The words leave grooves in the card, the nib pressed in so hard that his fingers must have been white as he wrote.

Days that Laze.
Days that drift, reeds upon water: lilies falling upon gathered rain.
Such evenings are damp eyes and violet stones.
Lilac poppies, spinning as Dutch sails.
Fields of canary yellow, crying beneath the weight of sky.
Such evenings my chest softly splinters.
Aged oak, paint as old parchment, piled with skull upon skull of ancient rock.
Ribs a creaking cage: screeching hinge atop whispering tomb.

I *feel*.
I who searches for dock leaves before the nettle kisses flesh. I.
Wrapped tight in muslin.
I breathe. Breathe as if emerging from ice.
Gasping kiss, drunk deep.
Cleansed. Risen. Effervescent.
A sky of tender lightning.
You. Did this. Built this.
Breathed upon Dead embers. Folded brown paper into a
bruised rose.
You.
Rain and flame upon dry earth.
A kiss of shattered glass.
You.
My immaculate sky.

She holds the card against her chest and pushes herself against
it, as if trying to push it inside her skin; to brand it upon herself.
Nobody has written her a poem before. Nobody has told her that
she is rain and flame. She is unaccustomed to being deemed
responsible for another's effervescence.

She tucks it inside her pillow, like a rosary. Hopes it will keep
her safe from bad dreams.

Asks herself, just once, whether it has been written for her,
or whether he first used it to woo Maeve.

Weeps for the ugliness inside her, even as she lingers upon
the beauty of the words.

TWENTY

The serpent slithers into her Eden in the first week of July. The day has been bright and blue and the darkness that blankets the land at one a.m. is as impermeable as a closed eye.

Betsy, sitting up in bed, is making her night-time vows to the curve of Jude's back and shoulder. He doesn't snore, but she has already come to know the patterns of his breathing. She knows he is sleeping deeply, and she is glad. Here, now, he is untroubled by the dreams that sometimes cause him upset when he is in a shallower sleep. On such nights he wakes afraid, his skin goose-flesh, as if he has dreamt of pale hands reaching out for him through dark glass. He never cries out. Never speaks of what has frightened him. But he reaches out to Betsy and hugs her to him; an infant clutching a favourite toy. He sucks the warmth from her; fills himself up with it, then sleeps undisturbed until a little before sunrise. He is never there when she wakes, though there has not been a morning when he has not left her some tiny offering; a pretty feather; a plucked wildflower; a speckled eggshell or an acorn cup. A poem, like the one she traces with her finger each morning.

'It's never been like this,' she whispers, in the voice a nun might use for prayer. 'Please don't let me spoil it, Jude. I know myself. I know that I'll try and ruin it all with horrible thoughts. It's all too good right now, isn't it? We don't fight. Nobody comes near us. I don't think about anything real. But can it stay like this? What happens if I wake up and something's triggered me? I know there will be a time when I think I hate you. It's so ugly to imagine it now but something in my head delights in flipping switches on me. I don't know how you'll react. I told you about the BPD but maybe you were just all caught up in the good feeling. We were so intense, weren't we? Nothing, then every-thing. I have things I want to tell you and things I want to say to me but I just know that one wrong word and all my barriers will come up. It all works when you're near me but what happens when you need to go away for work or something? I don't want to be some needy, nagging wife. I looked after myself for a long time – people don't ever give me credit for that. Yeah, there were foster homes and care homes but you're on your own, really. It's duty, not love. I made myself strong enough that nothing could harm me. Not betrayal, not abandonment, not rejection. But I hardened myself against all the other stuff too. People said I was a cold fish; that I couldn't love properly, hug properly, live properly. And then just when I think I've found what a normal life looks like I crash down inside myself and they're telling me I've got this syndrome and that syndrome and that I've got too many emotions. How can I have too many emotions? I hope you understand. I really think you do but how can I trust you? I don't know what this is to you. Why you chose me. What you really feel . . .'

She realizes that her voice is getting louder. She doesn't want to wake him. She stops talking and winces as she hears Marshall release a low growl from the kitchen. At first she thinks she may have roused him, but when he repeats the sound she realizes that it is not a gruff bark of irritation, but a low snarl of warning. He's heard something.

Betsy sits perfectly still. Should she wake Jude? Tell him that the dog has scented an intruder? She considers it and registers a sudden, fierce desire to be seen as capable, independent. She slithers out of bed, the floorboards pleasantly cool against the soles of her bed-warmed feet. Naked, she crosses to the window, tip-toeing around the edges of the floorboards. There is only one small window in the bedroom, set back in a thick recess and half-obscured by curiosities and little objet d'art. She has added pretty stones and a small bird skull to the old bottles and Victorian knick-knacks scavenged by Jude and his wife. In such ways she is taking possession of the house in tiny increments; shuffling, inch by inch, into its embrace. She took delight the first time she swept away the dust from the corners of each room, as if she were scooping up the microscopic skin cells and hair fibres of her predecessor and casting them, joyously, on to the breeze.

She leans forward, her skin scraping against the rough brick.

Peers out into the earthy darkness; the silver scythe of moon and the dusting of stars serving more as a painting than a source of illumination.

Downstairs, Marshall growls again. She squints, screwing up her eyes so tightly that her cheeks almost touch her eyebrows.

Slowly, achingly, the night gives up its secrets. The courtyard and stables come into focus: the planters; the beer crates; the abandoned machinery, all delineating into eerie blocks and right-angles sketched in perfect black.

There are two shadows near the stables. A tall, willowy figure leads the way; great orangutan arms and a stooped gait, as if his bulbous head were too great a burden for his frame. The other is stocky. Muscular. He moves with purpose, unafraid to be seen.

Betsy knows she should feel afraid. These are the bad men. These are the people who want to make Jude pay. If she wakes him, he will go out there. He will challenge them. There will be violence. Blood.

Something catches her eye; a shape that she cannot make sense of. She feels as though she is staring into a fire and among the faces and dancing faeries has glimpsed something wholly unfamiliar. There are trees just before the stone wall that marks the courtyard. Plum, greengage, cherry. She already knows the shape of their branches; their distinctive silhouette. Tonight, in the raven blackness, something has been strung within the branches.

She slithers back from the window. Jude is standing directly behind her. He is wide awake. Naked. In his hand, the silver gleam of the shotgun. Where had he hidden that? she asks herself, panic rising. Was it under her bed? What sort of man sleeps with a gun?

'Go back to bed,' he says, softly. 'I'll go see.'

'They're gone,' says Betsy, forcing some joviality into her voice. 'Slipped over the wall. Tall man and a stocky chap. Campion's, do you think? They had nothing with them so there's nothing stolen. Maybe they were just lost. Trespassers, eh? I'd leave it, Jude. Come back to bed, pull the covers over, forget they were there . . .'

He reaches out and strokes her forearm. She shivers. His hands are cold as the grave.

'I won't be a moment,' he says. 'Marshall's downstairs.'

'Great guard dog,' laughs Betsy, nervously. 'Shouldn't he have been barking the place down?'

'They're hunters, Betsy. They're good at this. No noise. No scent. They get up close. They can be standing over you before you even know they're there.' He stops himself, aware of the effect his words may have. He gives a smile that doesn't reach his eyes. Hands her the gun. She takes it as casually as if he had asked her to hold his shopping. It's as cold as his touch.

'I don't want this! Jude, I don't like it, let's just imagine I didn't see . . .'

He turns away from her. Gathers up a shirt and shorts from the chaos on the bedroom floor, and makes his way through the dark arch and down the stairs. Betsy stands still, unsure what is expected of her. Eventually she follows him. Pads silently down the wooden stairs and steps through the open door; the chill of the dark air feeling delicious against her bare skin.

She sees Jude standing in front of the trees. He turns back, as if to tell her to move back, but seems to change his mind. He just gives a sad little shake of his head.

'What is it?' whispers Betsy, standing beside him. He puts an arm around her. Takes off his shirt and wraps it around her like a blanket. Rubs her arms like a dad trying to warm up a child on a snowy day.

The dead thing hangs between the boughs of the two sturdiest trees. Lengths of twine have been used to tether the branches to the gory celebration of bone and ragged flesh. Thick wet ropes of gut hang down like gruesome bunting from a splayed ribcage. The pelt has been stretched out like sails; holed in places but stretched taut across the branches, as if in flight. Amid the carnage of pulverized meat, Betsy sees the gleaming white of tooth, of eyeball, of jawbone. She stares. Sees lightning flashes of white amid the branches. Antlers. Huge, like so many axe heads – a great spray of curving spikes.

Suddenly she knows what she is looking at.

She feels bile rise up her throat as the scent hits her; a rotten, carnal scent.

'Oh, Jude . . . Jesus . . .'

She narrows her eyes. Something is dangling from the sagging hammock of entrails. She moves towards it and feels Jude pull her back.

'Is that . . .?'

'A stag,' he says, quietly. 'Somebody trying to be funny.'

She looks at him. His eyes are sunken; the irises black, like a shark's. 'No,' she says. 'That's a puppet. A puppet attached to its guts . . .'

This time she shrugs him off. Marches toward the monstrosity and peers into its depths. Raises her hand to her nose and inspects the gruesome, hook-nosed manikin which had been tied, hands splayed, to the looping intestine of the dead stag.

'That's Punch. From Punch and Judy.' She looks back at him, horrified. 'Jude, why would somebody do this?'

'A silly joke, like I said.'

'No. No, people don't do this!' Her voice is rising, her skin itching with icy sweat. 'Jude, this is something else. This isn't a dead sheep in the river, this is . . .' She searches for the right word. Finds it and wishes it were different. 'This is something evil.'

Jude turns away as Marshall pads, loyally, to his side. Settles down at his feet as if this were the most normal thing in the word. Jude tuts as he looks at the tree. 'Peeled the bark, too,' he grumbles. 'Tacitus was bloody right.'

'Who the hell is Tacitus?' asks Betsy, wanting to stamp her foot.

'Roman senator. Historian. We've got a copy of his Annals somewhere . . .'

'Jude!' yells Betsy. 'Why are you talking about Roman anal?'

He gives her a smile, like she's joking. Pulls a face when he realizes she's not. 'Sorry,' he says, quickly. 'Just something he wrote about the Germanic tribes. Any man found to have stripped the bark of a living tree would have his navel sliced and the skin nailed to the bark. Then he'd be marched backwards around the tree until he unwound himself. Don't know why I thought saying that out loud would help the situation. Forgive me – I have my idiot moments.'

Betsy rubs her arms, feeling frightened and angry and endless shades in-between. Jude sees the change in her and comes back to where she stands, lifting her face so he can meet her gaze.

'You have to trust me,' he says, quietly. 'For this to work, you have to.'

'But this . . .!' she protests. 'Why would somebody do this?'

'There are bad people in the world. I'm not one of them.'

'How can I know? I don't know you, don't know what makes you tick, what you're willing to do . . .'

'Enough,' he says, the two syllables mushed together into one barked command. 'Enough,' he repeats, and she has the feeling that he wants to stroke her hair like a dog that has been reprimanded.

Swiftly, wordlessly, he crosses to the woodpile. Pulls the hatchet from the stump. He slashes at the twine that binds the stag to the trees. Takes her hand and pulls her, firmly, away from the trees. The dismembered animal crashes to the ground; twigs and blood and rotten flesh.

'A joke,' he says, again. 'Come back to bed.'

He walks past her; back to the open door with its warm, soft light. After a moment, the smell of dead flesh lingering on her skin and hair, she follows him back inside.

Soon, in the darkness, there is only the gnaw and crunch of Marshall's teeth, dutifully grinding through bone.

TWENTY-ONE

B ehind the wall, their scents obscured with dung and fish-meal, the bad men watch. Brendon, tall. Rufus, stocky. Both capable of great harm.

Brendon did not wish to stay to see the results of their handi-work. He would have been happy to deposit their little gift and be gone before the smell woke the occupants. But the other man, the one named Rufus, had stayed to watch.

Shapely, he'd thought. *Pleasant curves and a mucky look about her, as if walking about without your drawers on wasn't asking for trouble. Looked like a sweet fit. Looked like she'd come out to show herself off; to flaunt it, like they all do, when they're youngish and prettyish and when they've worked out how pitifully biddable a man can be when his dick's hard . . .*

Brendon hadn't said a word as his colleague fumbled about in his trousers and silently enjoyed himself. He could hear him smiling in the darkness. Heard the hiss of ecstasy as he completed his handwork. He never reprimands him for his moments of self-indulgence. They have done terrible things together and neither is in a position to chide the other for taking their pleasures where they find them.

Tacitus, he thinks, making a mental note to look him up. *Knew his fucking stuff . . .*

They stay, hunkered down in the long grass, until long after the dog retreats inside. Then they make their way back down the valley to where their car is waiting; the rear seats stinking of spilled blood and sawn bone. Not all of it is animal.

They drive for an hour. Stop, and make a call. Dump the phone in the water as they cross the bridge on a forested curve of road. They park up, tired. They don't speak. There is nothing to say.

When sleep comes, it is untroubled. They have done their job well tonight.

For the tall man, the rewards will be financial.

For his companion, his hands still smelling of meat and blood, the money is largely unimportant. He needs enough to clothe himself, to feed himself, to pay for occasional accommodation, but the amount of notes in his wallet is not how he judges himself. He lives for his work. Lives for the opportunity to cause fear. Cause pain. He delights in the dismantling of beautiful things. Nothing matters save the opportunity to take out his frustrations on flesh. It had been Jude Cullen's flesh he was looking forward to spoiling, but the woman now has his interest. There's a fire in him; an urge he can't satisfy alone. She looks like she's been hurt before. The way she carries herself; the set of her shoulders, the angle of her hips – she had been braced for pain or danger as if both were old friends.

He feels momentarily blessed, as if some benign deity is arranging things in accordance with some impassioned prayer.

Jude. Oh how he wants to wipe the look off that saintly cunt's face.

And her. The woman who shares his bed. The woman lit by moonlight. Each thrust, a knife through her man's heart . . .

He promises himself he will wait.

Some things are all the better for letting the anticipation build.

TWENTY-TWO

Four months ago

There's a rickety old excuse for a barn about five hundred yards over the low boundary wall at the rear of the bastle. To Betsy, it looks like it sprouted from the earth, and is slowly sinking back into it. It's not as old as the foundations of Jude's place but it still gives the impression of having long stood sentinel over this slope of dirt and grass. It's witnessed much during its long vigil. Jude has told Betsy all about the lead mines that honeycomb the land beneath them. Less of a filthy job than coal mining, but filthy nevertheless. That was how Jude had described it. It's known suffering, this valley. Seen much life and no little death. The mine at Allenheads was one of the biggest in Europe. The locals paid the price for such success. Boys grew up fatherless; life expectancy was short. Only the few prospered. Grew rich. Became important. And when the decline came, they bought up the properties and land of the men who could no longer afford to keep them. Gave it all over to farming. Then to hunting, and grouse. The rich got richer. The poor stayed poor. And so the wheel kept turning.

These days, the barn sees little. It's just another abandoned building: a weight pinning down the flapping corner of this great brown pelt of land. Jude rents the field out to hill farmers looking to keep their flock somewhere with guaranteed feed during the colder months. Betsy enjoys watching the animals snuggle up together in the lee of the drystone wall, or to waddle fatly into the comfort of the barn, staring out through the open windows like characters in a picture book.

Betsy's always a little cautious about opening the gate to the field. She still hasn't got used to the idea that this is home. She feels a constant need to ask permission in case she accidentally transgresses some countryside code, though Jude would be the first to tell her to come and go as she pleases. He wants her to know she has no duties. No chores. No responsibilities. She's free.

'Yeah,' she mumbles, watching a grouse waddle through the heather beyond the field. 'Free as a bird.'

It had all sounded lovely when he said it the first time. No duties. No presumptions. Now she feels overwhelmed by it all. It is as if she's been ordering her meals from the same three-item menu all her life and has suddenly been handed a list of options thick as a phone book. She doesn't actually know what she wants. She'd help Jude more if she could, but if she's honest with herself, she doesn't really know what he does. Some days he leaves on the quad; others he takes the battered old Land Rover, the back full of chainsaws and harnesses and spiked boots that weigh more than Marshall. He gets by, she knows that, but she has no way of gauging whether he has money to spare, or whether every day's a challenge. He doesn't talk about any of it. And her paranoia loves a vacuum. She can't make up her mind whether she suspects him to be a secret millionaire, a drug dealer, a hitman, a gigolo, or somebody so utterly destitute that he's picked up a vulnerable woman with the aim of pimping her out to the hill farmers. All seem equally possible, and similarly outlandish.

'Betsy!'

There's thunder rolling in over the fell. The sky is chewing itself up; the wildflowers closing their petals as if it were night-time.

'You might want to hurry before it . . .'

Jude's voice, bellowing out from the downstairs window of the barn, is drowned out by a sound like splitting oak. Where moments before there was a grey-blue sky, suddenly the air has taken on a purplish hue, the air sparkling with microscopic crystals. Her hair crackles with static. Her fillings suddenly sting. She glances right as a fork of lightning, bright and nuclear, rips the sky into fragments; a greasy grapevine of blood vessels gleaming in her vision as she puts her head down and runs towards the barn.

The rain falls like pennies, scything down from a sky that seems somehow Biblical in hue and intent. She has never seen clouds move so fast. They turn in on themselves like so many sacks of eels, and the air pressure drops so suddenly that for an instant Betsy can't hear properly, as if she's on a plane that's hit turbulence and briefly dropped from the sky.

'There's a rut there, babe – watch your step!'

She narrowly avoids stepping in the trench. The ground is hard and the tracks from the quad and the sheep have churned the ground into a meringue of peaks and dips. She bursts through the open door, laughing, her hair plastered to her face. He's waiting for her, grinning widely. He's got a joint in his left hand; a ceramic bottle in his right. Marshall is lying flat on a damp bale of straw, ears pressed against his head, still enough to pass for a rug.

'You OK?'

'Yeah, yeah. Damp. Bit breathless. I saw you from the window and . . .'

He looks past her, winking. 'Simon, Vik, here's her Ladyship, Duchess of Wolfcleugh, and light of my life.'

Betsy twirls back towards the doorway. Sitting there in white plastic garden chairs are two men she doesn't know, and whom she certainly hadn't been expecting when she climbed over the stile and drifted off towards Jude like a moth sensing fire. She feels flustered, suddenly. Runs back the last moments to check for anything that might have shown Jude up, or embarrassed herself.

'She's everything you said and more,' says a tall, good-looking, twenty-something with an impressive quiff and intelligent eyes. In his pink-and-white checked shirt and with his good cord trousers tucked into Wellington's, he's the kind of young country gent she'd ordinarily expect Jude to steer clear of. He looks like somebody featured in a *Daily Telegraph* picture special. And yet Jude is grinning at him like they're cousins. She spots the joint in her partner's hand and understands why. He reaches out and cups her around the waist, his skin unexpectedly rough against her hip.

'She could do better,' growls the other man, appraisingly. He's older. Fatter. Mixed race, perhaps. He's got a perfectly shaved head, glistening like a peeled apple. He's a bit of a mess: Bermuda shirts and hairy legs stuffed into old walking boots. He's wearing a bodywarmer over a couple of unravelling jumpers. He gives a nod at Betsy, for politeness, but doesn't move.

'I didn't know you had company,' says Betsy, looking to Jude. 'I was going to say I'd made you something to eat. Just some leek and potato soup, but it's up there when you want it. If you want it, I mean . . .'

Jude grins at her. Looks at her as if he'd like to eat her with a spoon. He takes a swig from the bottle and she can't decide whether the act makes him seem somehow sexy and roguish, or just a middle-aged man getting stoned and drunk in the barn when he said he was out working.

What if the bad men come, she's thinking. *What if today's the day* . . .

'You, my darling, are extraordinary,' he declares. 'A peach. A pumpkin. A penguin. That would be amazing. Will it keep a while longer, do you think? We were just setting the world to rights, that's all.'

Betsy grins, indulgently, swallowing down her distaste at seeing him so unlike himself. 'Of course. I'll head back up . . .'

'Don't be silly,' says Simon, starting to stand. 'It's coming down in sheets. One lightning strike and you'll end up like a charcoal outline and that would be a hell of a waste.'

'Simon here is the chivalrous sort,' says Jude, and to Betsy's surprise he waves his friend back into his seat. He takes Betsy's hand and pulls her over to where he stands. From her new vantage point she can see the rain surging past the doorway, billowing like sails. The earth is turning to swamp as she stares. She glances back to Jude, then past him, at the huge assemblage of old furniture stacked up against the far wall. Jude follows her gaze.

'Stuff she planned to do up and sell on,' he explains, looking away. 'Mostly knackered now, though the oak's still good. Oak's hard as iron after a couple of centuries. The older it gets the harder it gets . . .'

'Exact opposite to my problem,' says Simon, sucking on his joint, and giving a bark of laughter.

Vik spits. Puts a finger to his nostril and pushes out something vile, for emphasis.

'*She*, you say? Who's fucking "*she*", eh? Cat's mother? By *she*, you mean your partner, yeah? Actual lady of the manor. You think she'd be OK with this, do you? Your fucking pride, Jude . . .'

Jude pats at the air, not letting it bother him. The air splits again; lightning turning the sky a scorching white. Marshall shivers. The sheep, huddling in the far corner, begin to bleat, nervously.

'Don't listen to Vik,' says Jude, in Betsy's ear. 'He's got things he needs to get off his chest. He'll feel better for it.'

'I should go,' begins Betsy.

'We're here for a quiet word, that's all,' says Simon, pointedly, to the man beside him. 'Jude's been very gracious, hasn't he? Opened the good stuff, all very civilized. Happy to listen to our proposal . . .'

'Simon here is a land agent,' explains Jude, taking another swig from the container. It's old. Pot. Two-tone. There's a stamp on one side: a face with writhing snakes for hair. 'Remind me to tell you all the synonyms for "land agent" once we're alone.'

Simon gives something like a bow. Looks at her, patronisingly, as if to tell her she's a lot cleverer than he would have expected.

'What I explained, Betsy, is that Jude has made his point. He's stood his ground. Nobody could accuse him of turning tail or giving up without a fight. But the development of the valley requires everybody to be of an accord. Certain landowners in this valley have plans that could make a lot of people financially comfortable for the rest of their lives but if one person holds out, the whole project stalls. He's willing to pay not just the market value, but over and above. Not bad for a house you didn't even know was coming to you until the will was read out . . .'

'What do you think he's doing in the meantime, eh Jude?' growls Vik, kicking out at nothing. 'Rent rises. Job cuts. Bringing in cheap labour from God-knows-where. And Brendon's got that madman on a frayed leash, I swear to you. The squire can't hold him back. He's a psycho to begin with, but he's got it in for you in a big way. Don't act like this place is your fucking dream. You're being a twat about it because he fucked your wife!'

Betsy shoots a look at Jude. He's swaying, as if there's nothing on his mind except happy thoughts and butterflies. She looks in his eyes, expecting to see his pupils expanded to the size of Kalamata olives. They're normal. Fine. His breath tastes of tobacco and of the gum that he chews to disguise it. No alcohol. No marijuana. Heart rising, she glances at his visitors.

Both men look as though they are struggling to hold their sentences together, although Vik is clearly not the type to become more mellow the more he smokes.

He's putting this on, she realizes, suddenly. He's just pretending!

'That was completely unnecessary,' says Simon, apologetically. He swings the chair on to its back legs. Starts rocking; a schoolboy at the back of the class. 'Nobody likes to pry into another man's business, Jude. People talk, you know they do, and you lost friends when you were going through your – shall we say – downhearted spell. You did things you may now regret. But there are plenty still grateful to you for standing up for them, and few have anything but a good word to say about poor sainted Maeve, God rest her. But it's clear you have a new life now. A new partner, and what a partner she is. So why not make the most of this opportunity? Start again, with money in your pocket. Campion will take care of this place, I guarantee it. I know he's made all sorts of outlandish threats but there are checks and balances in place. We just need you to rescind the agreement he had with Maeve, that's all. Then sell up and head on to pastures new. The impact on the environment will be minimal.'

'Don't be expecting his missus to come to your rescue again, lad,' growls Vik, stubbing out the end of his joint. 'That ship has sailed. Don't neglect the few people you've got on your side, that would be my advice. If you thought you had some leverage on him you've shown you're not willing to use it, so I'd do the right thing while there's still a pleasant option open to you . . .'

Jude's eyes flick towards Simon at the exact moment that he plonks the front leg of the chair back on to the hard earth of the barn. There is a bang. It's nothing compared to the sound of the storm, but the resulting explosion throws Simon back off his chair and into the stinking hay behind him; his trousers ripped to shreds; blood speckling his legs. To his side, Vik throws up his arms in defence as the last of the blast scorches his cheek and ear, sending him tumbling the other way.

Jude moves fast. Brings the ceramic bottle down on the side of Vik's head. Vik gives a grunt and topples to his stomach.

Simon has one hand to his face and the other grasping his leg, shuffling back against the wall.

'No,' says Jude, and kicks him in the side of the head. 'No, it's not for sale. No, I'm not leaving. No, I don't give a shit what you say. And no, I'm not fucking scared of anything you send after me because there is nothing in this world you could do to me that I wouldn't repay a hundred times over. I know you can't hear – that'll be the perforated eardrum – but I sense you get the gist of my message.'

Bleeding from the nose, a boot print on his cheek, Simon tries to pull himself upright. Jude seems about to let him go, then something seems to grip him – some sudden mania that refuses to let things be. He drags Simon by the hair, and throws him on to the ground where his seat had been moments before. Without a word, he stamps on his back. Betsy barely hears the explosion this time, the sudden tremble beneath the ground, but she sees the result. Simon squirms back, holding his stomach, jagged shards of plastic and shell sticking into the perforated pinkness of his stomach and chest.

'I'd get that seen to,' growls Jude, in his ear. 'And I'd think about sending Betsy here some flowers. That was a shitty thing to say.'

He turns. Whistles. Marshall leaps down from the hay bale and runs to his master's side. Betsy stands perfectly still, unwilling to be as similarly well trained. He comes back. Looks into her eyes, raising her face so that his lips brush hers.

'It won't always be this way. But he's not having it. He's not getting this as well.'

'What . . . what were the explosions . . .?'

'Poacher traps,' shrugs Jude. 'Pressure-triggered. More rock-salt and dust than anything else. Nothing deadly. These pricks will be sore and deaf for a couple of days but they're not incap-acitated, and if they say a word to anybody in blue, they might want to explain why they were here smoking weed laced with Spice on a Wednesday afternoon. Shows up in your piss for weeks, lads, and I promise you, the hallucinations are going to make you wish you'd climbed back inside your mothers. I under-stand that feeling. Everybody who's been inside your mothers had nothing but good things to say. So, be good lads, keep the wailing down, and then report back to that red-faced bastard that the seller is not particularly keen.'

'I thought you were stoned . . .' asks Betsy.

'So did they,' smiles Jude.

He takes her hand and leads her back through the rain. The lightning writes scripture on the violet, roiling skies.

By the time they are back within the courtyard, the darkness of the past moments has been washed away like dirt. They are back within their bubble. Back in their fairy-tale castle.

Only afterwards, as he watches the broken men limp away over the field, tracking their move with field binoculars, shoulders squared like a boxer's, does she ask herself the question that screams inside her every cell.

What exactly are you capable of, Jude?

Just how far would you go?

TWENTY-THREE

A filthy, late-August day.

Leaden skies pressing down upon the land: a vast grey ceiling held up by the shadowy, pencil-stroke pillars of distant rain. The valley seems otherworldly on days like this; the lip of the moor teasing infinite possibilities beyond the horizon. Betsy can imagine a dragon suddenly screeching overhead, streaking fire; or a lumpen megalosaurus waddling down from the brim of the far fell.

They're driving into Hexham – the closest thing to a town that the area has to offer. It's a half-hour's drive but Betsy, comfortable in the passenger seat of the battered, old-school Land Rover, is happy for it to go on indefinitely, or at the very least, until she gets hungry. Jude, driving, is having one of his chatty days. She loves it when he's like this. He's never exactly taciturn, but there are certainly times when he seems far more comfortable in silence. She'll catch him sometimes, staring at a point somewhere in the distance or in the flickering heart of the fire, lost in his own thoughts and only returning to their shared reality when she says his name or rises to kiss his cheek. She often wonders if she bored him. He always listens to her, but sometimes it seems as if he's using a part of his brain to take notes while the rest of him is somewhere else entirely. He always seems startled to see her in his home, as if he has momentarily forgotten she is here. He seems delighted, though. Seems uncommonly thrilled to find this beguiling, bewildering soul pottering around in his kitchen, returning his smiles and occasionally looking at him as if he might be a little bit magical.

Today he has given himself a half day off to take Betsy into Hexham. He has errands to run – a phrase that sent Betsy into great cataclysms of pleasure – and, in his words, believes the rest of the world should be allowed to enjoy her too. She'd rolled her eyes at that, but she'd been pleased too, even as she made a mental note that his view of the '*rest of the world*' might not extend far beyond Hexham.

'. . . amazing view from there, once you get past the treeline,' he's saying, one elbow out the window, cigarette smoke drifting out and spotty rain swirling in. 'Saw a stag perfectly silhouetted against the moon one night – one of those moments that's so impeccable you want to grab the nearest human and say "look", as if the world has meaning and everything's going to be OK. If you carry on over the lip there's a place called Old Man's Bottom . . .'

'Fuck off, no there's not,' laughs Betsy, grinning so widely she can see her own cheeks in her peripheral vision.

'I swear, there is,' he says, glancing to his left and smiling at her. 'Man, you look exceptionally good. Very Mary Quant.'

Betsy frowns. 'I don't know her. Is she from the valley?'

He eyes her, suspiciously. 'You're taking the mick, aren't you? Making fun of the old man and his outdated references. Fine, you look like Velma from Scooby Doo.'

'Is that the farm over the valley?'

'You *are* joking . . .'

She slaps him, enjoying herself. 'Of course I am, you idiot. Do you like the fringe? I think I got it right. It's not quite symmetrical but it was the best I could do with a bowl and some meat scissors.'

'You're exceptional,' he smiles. 'And yes, there is a place called Old Man's Bottom. If you want to be really po-faced about it, it's Oldman Bottom, but that isn't anywhere near as much fun. Had a pint one night with an old boy who remembered delivering milk from his dad's dairy herd down that way when he was a nipper. It was him and another bloke – chap who'd lost an arm in a shotgun accident. Could milk the herd with his toes. That's not a transferrable skill.'

'Every story to do with farming seems to involve a hideous injury,' muses Betsy, straightening her skirt. It's a grey, houndstooth affair with a neat pleat, matched with a tight black roll-neck and a short waistcoat. She's started to enjoy rummaging through the big old chest on the landing. There always seems to be a different outfit available: a new persona to slip into. She feels rather chic today. Sleek, too. Would like a neat raincoat, a pair of jet-black sunglasses and a cigarette in a holder, but the box of delights offered nothing suitable so she's had to make do with Jude's old parka. She likes stuffing her hands in the pockets and riffling through the detritus of his life, pulling out receipts from agricultural stores, scraps of paper with scribbled phone numbers; tobacco papers and the wrappers from extra strong mints.

'Any job worth doing comes with a few risks,' says Jude, as the wilderness of the valley starts to disappear into the rear-view mirror and they begin moving quicker over better roads.

'Accountant?' asks Betsy, teasingly. 'Advertising? Public relations? Marketing?'

'Exactly,' he smiles. He looks at her, staring through her in that way of his, as if reading her DNA. 'What about you, Betsy? What are you going to be?'

'When I grow up, you mean?' She closes her eyes, wishing she had learned a neat answer. 'Thought about that so many times and I'm still clueless. You've seen it – I'm a dabbler. I get into something and it has my total focus and passion and then suddenly it's like somebody has pulled the plug and I just don't care anymore. I've always been the same. Afraid to see things through, I suppose.'

Jude doesn't reply. Turns his eyes back to the road. She looks at him, waiting for him to speak. She can see there is a sudden tension in his jaw.

'Is that what I'll be?' he asks, his voice a little distant. 'An enthusiasm? A sudden impulse?'

Her instinct is to give him a reply that will reassure him, but some tiny voice in her head stops her from offering a mindless platitude. She would rather see how he responds to the ugly truth.

'I can't imagine these feelings ever drifting away,' she says, talking to the side of his face. 'It's all-encompassing. Scary, sometimes. If I'm honest I always kind of thought that this fiery, all-powerful love was a bit of an invention, something to sell movies and poetry books. But what I feel now, for you – it's so intense as to be out of control. But for all that, I know there will be times when I doubt myself. Times I doubt whether you're right for me, or whether we're right for each other. When I have my days of self-loathing, I wonder whether you're only attracted to me because we're two bad people and we each see something reflected in the other.'

Jude runs his tongue across his teeth. Flicks his cigarette butt out of the window. 'Two bad people? How are we bad people?'

She shakes her head, wishing she hadn't spoken. 'I just mean I get all sorts of thoughts, you know. And often they seem crazy and paranoid and other times they seem like a total and unmistakable truth. And we've hardly had an easy beginning, have we? Dead animals in the stream, dead stags in the tree, people trying to hurt you, to buy you . . .'

'It won't always be like that,' says Jude, and she can see how much he hopes it to be true. 'I don't know how else to be, Betsy. They want something. They're trying to take it. I give up or I fight. And I don't know how to give up. I feel like I'm from a different age, or something. I don't understand how people look at themselves in the mirror. They roll over. They let people tell them how things are going to be. I can't live that way. I don't think I'm bad, Betsy. Stubborn, maybe.' He glances at her. 'You're not letting the whispers get into your head, are you? About Maeve?'

Betsy stares through the glass. They pass a squat grey farm; a woman in her eighties bringing in washing while geese squawk around her ankles and a goat tries to put its long face into the pocket of her apron.

'There was a man one day,' says Betsy, quietly. 'I saw from the window. Shaved head and little rat tail plaits.'

Jude makes a face. 'Moon,' he mutters. 'He thinks he's an animal rights activist. He's not. He's a thug who's found what he thinks of as a noble cause. He worshipped Maeve. Wants somebody to blame.'

'He said you'd sold your soul to the devil,' prompts Betsy, wincing inside as she wonders if this will be the day that he loses his temper.

'He's convinced I could have helped them get a conviction against Campion. The girl who got shot, during the grouse shoot – during the protest. I was there. So was Maeve. Moon says he filmed it all and gave the footage to Maeve. Now that's a piece of evidence that even Campion couldn't make disappear. Moon reckons I've got it and chose to withhold it. You know me, Betsy. Do you think I'd do Campion a favour?'

She stares at the side of his face, longing to reach out and stroke his jaw with the knuckles of her hand. She stops herself. She doesn't know what she believes.

'Anyway, I'm curious – how are you bad, Betsy?'

She waves her hand, annoyed at the turn in the tone. 'I don't need a therapy session, Jude. Some things just are what they are.'

'I hate that phrase,' he mutters. 'Maeve used to say that. "It is what it is" – that was another. Nothing has to be what it is. If things aren't right, you change them. If something's bugging you, you remove that thing from your life. If something scares you, you turn the tables. Make it scared of you.'

Betsy shakes her head, angry with him. 'What, so people with mental health problems should just toughen up? Jay used to say that, if you're wanting to play that game.'

'I didn't say that. That's the last thing I mean. Listen, I . . .'

'Don't tell me to listen. I hate being told to listen. It's like you're saying "heel" or "sit" . . .'

'How is it like that? That's mad, Betsy.'

'Yeah, well, newsflash – I fucking am!'

Jude sighs. Clamps his teeth together. His body language suggests he has nothing else to say.

They sit in silence for a time, passing through a straggle of villages before drifting down into Hexham. Compared to where they've been, it feels like driving into Vegas. All of the vehicles are driving with their headlamps on; there's a crackle to the air, a fizz, that speaks of a gathering storm. Betsy, glaring out through the dirty glass, watches as a mum does battle with a collapsible pushchair on the pavement by the park; a toddler on her hip dressed for summer and with near-blue lips to show for it. Instinctively, she strokes her stomach, holding herself. Mourning.

Betsy had been looking forward to Hexham. There's a crypt beneath the abbey; a museum in the old gaol. Jude had mentioned maybe going for a drink in a bar he knows or taking a walk by the river. She'd even got excited about popping to an actual supermarket – purchasing junk food and freezer meals and maybe buying extra data for her mobile phone. She winces as she remembers that she's left the money back at the bastle. She curses herself, silently. Feels her own temperature rise as clearly as she sees the air pressure drop. A huge fat raindrop hits the windscreen:

a jellyfish momentarily splattered across the glass. And then the deluge comes.

'Jesus,' mumbles Jude, turning the wipers to full. He looks in her direction, his demeanour altered by the sheer power of the weather. The rain is so heavy it's somehow funny. 'Still fancy a stroll?'

She leans over and rests her head on his chest, the Land Rover inching forward in a line of virtually static cars; the air the colour of dirty water; the rain an avalanche of pearls. He strokes her hair and she nuzzles into him.

'I'm sorry if what I said spoiled the mood,' she says, softly. 'I told you about the BPD. I don't know how it will deal with me being happy, Jude. There'll be times when I'm anything but. It would be lovely if you could somehow heal me by loving me but it's not like that. You couldn't fix diabetes or a broken leg just by cuddling me twice as hard, could you?'

She feels him nodding. 'I get carried away,' he says, his lips brushing her hair. 'I'm a romantic, I guess. It's a curse. Dad never knew what to make of me. I could beat any farmhand in an arm wrestling match by the time I was thirteen but I played the saxophone and wrote poems and liked drawing pictures of feathers and eggs. Didn't make sense to him. Couldn't work out if I was a man or a pansy.'

'I hate all that stuff,' says Betsy, squeezing him. 'Toxic bullshit – the idea that if you have feelings it's somehow emasculating – that you're more of a man if you treat your partner like property and hold your tears in until your heart gives out.'

'I've never worried about what people think of me,' he says, sucking his teeth as the car in front nabs the parking space he had set his sights on. 'Never really fitted in anywhere. At university I was the farmer's lad; on tour I was the bumpkin who hadn't seen the world; back here I was the lad who'd turned his back; the soft lad who fell short and came home to something they thought of as second rate. I don't rise to it. It's impossible to make yourself criticism-proof. People will say horrible stuff regardless. Long before social media, the world was full of wankers.'

'What do you think people say about me?' asks Betsy, settling back into her seat.

He smiles, shaking his head at her. 'Probably that you don't know what you're letting yourself in for. Or that I've abducted you or bullied you or bought you. No doubt they'll have it on good authority you were in a relationship when we met. There'll be some who think I've brought you home just to piss off Campion.'

Betsy furrows her brow. 'Why would that piss him off?'

'He wants me out, doesn't he? And here I am setting up a new life in the bastle. With you – the love of my life, who I only met because he can't drive.'

Betsy grins. She'd like to squeal. *Love of my life*, she repeats, endlessly; the words a train running upon tracks.

'People won't think it's too soon?' she asks, ever eager to bring a wasp to the picnic.

'Too soon? What, since Maeve? I doubt it, but nor do I care.'

'Would she have wanted this, do you think?' asks Betsy. 'Would she have wanted you to be happy?'

He laughs at that, drumming his fingers on the steering wheel. He doesn't look at her. 'I don't know how often Maeve thought about my happiness when she was alive so I doubt she's giving it much thought now she's dead.'

Betsy takes a moment. He'd looked hard as he'd spoken. Looked as though there was something there, beneath the surface; his face wearing the same expression she glimpsed in him when she caught him gazing into the fire or staring off towards the woods.

'The argument you had,' she says, and genuinely can't seem to help herself. 'In the newspaper article, the day she died . . .'

He shakes his head. 'We didn't argue. Not really. She told me how things were and I had the choice to like it or lump it. She wanted to go see her horse up at the trekking centre. Her head was thumping so she took her meds. Maybe she took too many. Either way, she wasn't listening to me when I suggested staying in. Said I would run her a bath, take care of her, put the flannel in the freezer and hold it to her eyes, the way she liked. But she wouldn't be told. Wouldn't let me take her either. Walked off while I was having a shower and I didn't know she was gone until I came out wet and saw her boots missing and her coat gone. Her laptop was sat there on the table, like she'd just stood up and walked out. I didn't see her alive again.'

'I'm sorry,' says Betsy, automatically, though her tone is hard.

She doesn't like the images in her head. She winds the window down, letting the rain and the wind surge into the car, cooling the heat in her cheeks and plastering her newly-trimmed fringe to her forehead. When she looks at Jude again her face is pale as bone. 'What had she been doing online?' she asks, and it seems important that she know.

Jude glances at her, confused. Shrugs, as if it doesn't matter. 'Probably on Skype with her mum, or something, I can't remember. She spent plenty of time on the damn thing once the next farm over got their satellite Wi-Fi put in and gave us the password. Always campaigning for something, liking stuff on social media, tapping away at the keys like she was practicing the piano. I swear, she once asked me to stop playing my saxophone as she couldn't concentrate on what she was doing. She was only on Facebook, for God's sake.' He shakes his head. 'I do remember, actually. I think she'd been burning a CD. I remember the disk drive was halfway out.'

'The disk drive?'

'It's a very old laptop,' he says, ruefully. 'She liked doing mixtapes, or the not-quite-modern equivalent. She had a gazillion songs on her laptop and she'd do a playlist for people and burn it off.'

'Burn it off?'

'Sorry, I forget you're the same age as my socks. You save it to disk, then you can put the disk in one of these delightful old things called a CD player.' He taps the dashboard, home to his own stereo system. 'Bit of Curtis Mayfield by way of Madness and Echo and the Bunnymen in there, I think.'

Betsy doesn't reply. Something in her mind is uncoiling itself. She winds the window up and notices that they have passed through the town centre and have reached the big, brightly lit rectangle of the hospital. 'Having me surgically removed, are you?' asks Betsy.

He takes a ticket from the machine and swings into the car park, nudging the boxy old 4 x 4 into a space. 'Repeat prescriptions,' he says.

'Prescriptions,' smiles Betsy. 'Prescriptions, prescriptions . . . can I stop now?'

He grins at her. Can't seem to resist her. Leans in and kisses

her, hungrily, damply. 'You coming in?' he asks, as they part.
'It can take an age.'

Betsy nods. They climb down from the car and step into the
gale. He takes her hand, automatically, fingers intertwining, and
they run across the forecourt, rain bouncing up almost to their
knees. They reach the big glass awning and shake the raindrops
from their clothes and hair. Betsy makes him laugh, shaking
herself like a damp dog.

She follows him in to the pharmacy in the entranceway: bright
and white and clearly designed to resemble the inside of a fridge.
There's a queue of damp, mouldering pensioners inside the pharmacy, waiting in line at the till. More sit in the soggy school
chairs at the centre of the square space, wiping raindrops from
spectacles with the hems of pleated skirts or doing battle with
mobile phones, sending dramatic messages to loved ones declaring
themselves safe despite the tempest.

'Ah shite,' mutters Jude, miserably. 'Why don't they ever have
enough staff? There's a coffee shop down towards A & E. Do
you want to go get something? This is going to be painful.'

'What is it you're getting?' asks Betsy, taking the fiver that
he has extricated from the pocket of his tatty jacket.

'My prescription,' he says. 'Oh sorry, what is it for? Venlafaxine.
225 mg. My *happy pills*.'

'Happy pills?'

'Don't worry, they're not to suppress my inner psycho. I just
get dark episodes sometimes. These keep me from sinking into
the swamp, y'know?'

Betsy gives him a tight smile and hurries off down the huge,
empty corridor. He's on depression medication, she tells herself.
He's got mental health issues of his own. He's still grieving his
wife – his perfect, mixtape-making wife. He doesn't need you
on top of all this . . .

She sees him just before he sees her. Mick. The lump who'd
thrown a dead ram into the beck. Fading bruises on his forehead,
as if he's had horns snapped off. He's got his arm folded across
his front, a sling holding it in place like a wing, and he's the
unhealthy grey colour of somebody enduring a good deal of pain.
He grimaces, and Betsy sees that he has cotton balls wedged,
bloodily, in a gap in the top row of teeth.

He doesn't know you, she tells herself. Just keep walking.
She puts her head down. Carries on, her heart racing.
'Ere, boyo, hold on, daft lad.'
Another man emerges from the mouth of A & E. He's slimmer
than Mick at the waist but bigger at the shoulders and neck.
He's got big arms beneath a muscle shirt and black jacket; a
bulldog face with deep-set eyes. He licks his lips, foully, as he
struts past her; a noise like a lizard lapping up water. He barely
glances at her; his eyes focused on Mick.
'Forgot your 'scrip, you prick.'
Betsy glances back. Realizes she has walked right past the
coffee shop.
'I'll get you a drink and Mars bar, put a smile on your face.'
'How do I eat that, eh?' Mick's voice thin, pained.
'I'll chew it and spit it down you. Come on, don't be a girl.
We'll get your medicine, take you home, get you snuggled up
with Donna. She might even slip you a length . . .'
'Don't.' His protests are weak. 'Don't talk about her like
that . . .'
'Fuck, you are softer than kitten shit, aren't you?'
Betsy watches them disappear into the coffee shop. Mick hadn't
given her a second look, but there had been something about his
companion; something in the air around him, some whispered
familiarity. She fancies she can smell something corrupt; the
faintest trace of spoiled meat.
She feels her heart racing.
Senses trouble coming as surely as the storm.

TWENTY-FOUR

B etsy hurries back down the corridor, moving in the odd, stiff-legged style of somebody keen to move quickly without attracting attention: a brisk walk interspersed with shuffles of speed.

Back at the pharmacy, Jude is third in line, clearly bored to the point of self-harm. There are two pensioners in front of him and a mum with a four-year-old behind him, and Betsy knows that at any moment he will gallantly step aside and let the mum go before him, just because he's that type of chap. It makes her proud, and irritated, and annoyed with herself all at the same time.

'Oh, that was good timing!'

Betsy turns at the sound of the loud, bright voice. Sees Sylvia making her way towards the pharmacy. She's in the company of a sturdy woman in her fifties: short, bottle-black hair and a sensible raincoat over a woolly jumper. Betsy has to force herself to look pleased by this sudden, extra interruption. Is this a bloody drop-in centre, she wonders, agitated. No company for ages then I see too many familiar faces all at once!

'Sylvia, hi,' she says, and automatically approaches to give her a kiss on the cheek. 'Awful day, isn't it? Thought we were going to be washed away . . .'

'Oh I wouldn't,' says Sylvia, putting her hands up to warn her off. 'Virus. Not nice. Keep your distance and smear yourself in anti-bac, that'd be my advice. Not unless you've got a penchant for explosive bowel movements and want to spend a week living on nowt but hot water and Oxo cubes. You'd think I'd have lost weight, wouldn't you? Honestly, I've evacuated parts of myself that haven't seen daylight since 1950!'

'Oh you poor thing,' mutters Betsy, dutifully, glancing back down the corridor and then to Jude.

'Jude here, is he?' she glances through the glass. 'Oh poor sod. They do like to make you wait in this place.'

'I'm Val, by the way,' says the woman beside her, pointedly introducing herself. 'Best not touch me either.'

'Hi. I'm Li . . . I'm Elizabeth. Betsy.'

Val narrows her eyes, putting a face to a name she has heard before. 'Oh, you're Jude's new friend, are you? How are you finding the valley? Godawful bleak at times, isn't it and the winters either kill you or make you stronger. I stuck it out for a bit but I've moved to Allenheads now, just for the convenience. Of course, the husband will insist on taking the car out with him each day so when I need to get myself in to do a big shop I have to rouse poor old Sylvia here, although it does give us a chance for a natter . . .'

Betsy can feel sweat prickling at her back. She doesn't want to talk. She wants to get to Jude, quickly. She nods, showing she's paying attention, and tries to manoeuvre them towards the pharmacy.

'I heard about the bother at the pit-head,' says Sylvia, looking sympathetic. 'Why can't they just leave be, eh? I mean, she's gone, he's just trying to make a life for himself, but Campion just can't let things go.'

Through the fog in her head, the words catch her attention. 'What bother?' she asks.

Sylvia and Val exchange glances; two gossips caught out. 'Oh well, if he didn't mention it . . .'

'Go on,' says Betsy, her face serious. 'If you know, I should know.'

Sylvia breathes out through her nostrils, irritated with herself. 'More of the same, love. He was doing a bit of stone-dyking at the Dalton farm and Campion's debt collectors were up there, collecting – brandishing some bit of paper like they were police. Coming in to recover goods, that was what they said. There was some argy-bargy.'

'Argy-bargy?'

Sylvia shrugs, meaningfully. She'd love to know more. 'Way I heard it, they left without what they came for.'

'Oh the gossips in this valley . . .' says Betsy, with a forced brightness that comes across as thoroughly manic.

You silly, silly girl, Lizzie. Better than your old life, is it? Better than the comfort you had before?

The voice, silent for days, whispers in the dead centre of her head. Grows louder. Finds its favoured form. Screams at her in a way that makes her want to wrap her arms around her head and plug her ears.

What have you got into, Liz? What do you know about this man? How can you be in love with somebody who lives like it's the Middle Ages – fighting people off his land, taking on enemies? What does that make you, eh? A damsel in distress? Look at yourself, in your borrowed clothes. And he's not been telling you the truth, has he? Hiding things from you. Keeping you in the dark. Treating you like a fool . . .

'Would you give me a moment?' she asks, breathlessly.

'Of course, you go on – queue like that there's no bloody rush . . .'

She hurries to his side, bringing him out of his trance by slipping her hand into his. He turns to look at her. Sees no hot drinks. 'Shut, is it?' He looks past her. 'Oh look that's Sylvia. If I'd known I could have brought her in, she hasn't been so well . . .'

'The man who threw the sheep in the river,' she whispers, urgently. 'Mick. Coming out of A & E. They've got a prescription, so . . .'

Jude doesn't alter his expression. Just looks at her, the same smile of welcome on his face. Then he gives a little shrug. 'I've no problem with anybody, Betsy. Don't worry.'

'He's got somebody with him. Called him "boyo".'

Jude's features harden. It's only a moment, less than a heartbeat, but she sees something in his face that frightens her. It's not just hate. It's a look she recognizes from childhood; a sudden retrogression; a backwards evolution into something primal. She sees the ape in him; the *Homo sapien*. Sees in his eyes the desire to do harm.

He shakes his head as if trying to dislodge water from his ear. She grips his hand.

'Let's come back, eh?' she urges, desperately. 'The rain's easing off, we could still do the walk by the canal . . .'

'Mr Cullen?'

They look up. Both pensioners are being dealt with by a harassed-looking teenager with glasses and red hair, leaving Jude to the attentions of the fierce-looking manageress. Betsy dislikes her at once. She looks as though somebody has drawn drag queen eye make-up on a Soviet shot-putter. She has the look of somebody who enjoys her authority; the type to wear a lanyard like a sheriff's badge.

'It's OK, it won't take a moment,' says Jude. Turns to the pharmacist: 'Jude Cullen. Repeat 'scrips, please.'

The manageress looks at him in the way that only the truly officious are able to: conspiring to make the most innocent of heart feel as if they are turning up for their daily dose of methadone. Haughtily, she taps at the keyboard and then busies herself sorting through a shelf of white paper parcels, looking for the medication. Betsy realizes that Jude's whole manner has changed. He's breathing as if his nose is blocked, his irritation at the service becoming more apparent. She tries to catch his eye so she can smile up into him but he's just glaring at the woman behind the counter as she fiddles through baskets of pills and paperwork.

'Cullen,' he says, again. 'Same as last month. And the month before.'

'Terrible, isn't it?' says the pensioner to their left. She's small, with candy-floss hair. 'Every bloody month. Back and forth to the surgery, back and forth, they don't talk to each other and then they blame the computer.'

'You did order it, yes?' asks the pharmacist, looking at Jude as if he is trying to pull a trick.

'This again?' he asks, rolling his eyes. 'You order them for me. It's a repeat. I repeatedly need them. I repeatedly take them. I ran out yesterday, so I'm here to pick the new ones up. I don't want to be a twat about this but I can't understand why this is always so hard.'

'There really is no need for foul language, Mr Cullen.'

Jude looks baffled. 'What foul language?' Realization dawns. 'Oh "twat"? Come on, that's almost a surname. It's just – this doesn't always have to be so difficult . . .'

'We have systems in place for a reason, Mr Cullen.'

'This isn't a system. This is the opposite of a system.'

'*Well, fucking well.*'

Every head turns towards the door. The man who has spoken is the same meaty lump who had called Mick 'boyo' in the corridor. He's standing with his hands on his hips, like a cardboard cut-out of a superhero, beaming at the back of Jude's head as if all of his Christmases have come at once. Behind him, Mick looks pained. Worse, he looks embarrassed. He's cringing under the spotlight glare of so many sweet old ladies.

Jude lets out a sigh. It seems to come from a deep, dark place.

Suddenly, Betsy feels as though the pharmacy has been transformed into an Old West saloon. The way Jude turns from the counter is with the resignation of a gunslinger tired of people using him to try and earn themselves a name.

'Now then,' says Jude, managing some approximation of a smile. 'Been a while.'

'Few years, I reckon,' says the man at the door.

'My heart's been bleeding for you. Does me good, seeing you look so bright-eyed.'

'That's me, Punch. Wide awake and very able. I should be wearing one of those facemasks, like the Chinese do. Keep the germs out of my nostrils. Stinks like God's waiting room in here.'

He glances at the mum and her child, both holding boxes from the two-for-one offers on hair colours. He addresses her in a loud voice. 'I wouldn't bother if I were you, love. You can disguise the grey but even if you do, there'll still be a nasty surprise for whoever gets your knickers off. Not unless you wax yourself down to the wood, and that's not a look I'm into. Always a bit suspicious, I am. Why would anybody want their missus to look like she's got a kid's minnie? That's our word for it. Some people say "cunt".'

Mouths open in unison; lips parting and a chorus of appalled vowels spilling out. Betsy watches as Mick steps forward and puts a hand on his companion's arm. The other man shakes him off and stares back into the room, overwhelmingly pleased with himself.

'You're looking old, Punch,' he declares, eyeing up Jude. 'They do say grief can age a man, but then, so can liver damage. Heard about the missus. Brought a tear to my eye.'

Jude doesn't rise to it. 'I'd heard you were back. Heard I was supposed to be shaking like a leaf.'

'*Out*,' he replies, his tone gently reproving. 'Not back. Out.'

'I was trying to spare your blushes in front of the nice people, though I can see that isn't something you worry yourself about.'

'I am what I am,' he shrugs. 'Descartes said that.'

'No, Gloria Gaynor said that. Descartes said "cogito ergo sum". I think therefore I am. And you don't think, lad. So therefore, you're probably not.'

There are some titters from the assembled spectators, all of whom are watching the exchange like a tennis match. Behind the counter, the manageress looks to Betsy as if this unpleasantness is her fault, indicating with her drawn-on eyebrows that she should better control her man.

'Shall we come back for these, Jude?' she asks, quietly, holding his arm. There's no tension in him. He seems perfectly relaxed.

'Nearly done,' he says, not taking his eyes off the man in the doorway. Behind him, Mick is staring down at his own feet, clearly trying to wish himself somewhere else. Jude flicks his eyes towards him. 'You OK there, Mick? Been in the wars, have you?'

'You talk to me, Punch,' says the man who shields Mick with his bulk. 'Everything that's coming, it won't be little brother any more. It'll be me.'

'Taken the king's shilling, have you?' He makes a show of slapping his own forehead and dumbing down the sentence for the hard of thinking. 'It means "joining up". Yeah, thought I recognized your handiwork. Subtle as a brick to the face. Aye, I guess Campion owes you. But I warn you, there are easier ways to make money.'

'None so enjoyable, though.'

'Would you like your prescription, Mr Cullen?'

Jude turns to the pharmacist. He takes his wallet from his pocket and touches his bank card to the machine. Gives Betsy a squeeze. 'This chap is an old friend,' he says, loud enough to inform everybody in the room. 'Never the sharpest tool in the box but he can carry out simple tasks. Dig a hole. Fill it in. Dig a hole. Hit somebody with a shovel. Gets his shoes on the right feet if you give him time to concentrate. He's never quite forgiven me for not being impressed by him.'

'Come outside, Punch,' the man says, his voice thick as honey. 'I'll impress you, I promise.'

Betsy can feel her heart thumping. Can taste the violence in the air. 'Punch?' she asks, then remembers the doll in the dead stag's innards. 'You didn't tell me you had a nickname . . .'

'Oh you're in trouble now, Punch,' laughs the man. 'Got you in bother, have I? Soz about that. To be fair, she'll probably forgive you. Got her eating out the palm of your hand, I can see that. Hope you can keep up with her. Brendon said that when he gave her that envelope she half threw herself at him. Affection-starved, that's what I think, though she must be desperate to shack up with somebody who killed his wife.'

More gasps from the spectators, and one or two reproving stares. Betsy senses movement. Sylvia is thumping her way towards the door, Val hurrying along behind.

'You're one of those, are you?' asks the man, warming to his theme and giving Betsy his attention. 'I can see it. Definitely one of those.'

'One of what?' she asks, and her mouth feels dry. She can taste iron. The air feels as though it's full of static.

'Better looking with your clothes on. I mean, you looked peachy with your arse out but you are banging today. That's a lovely outfit.'

She feels the change come over Jude, the tension bleeding into his arms. She shakes her head, urgently. 'Don't. He's just a silly man, don't . . .'

'Still got the picture in my mind,' he adds, licking his lips. 'Oh it's beautiful. Candle-white against the moonlight – the smell of rotting venison. I can conjure it all up at a moment's notice. I'm good at that. All those years inside, I had a whole scrapbook of memories to enjoy. Your bitch-wife, for example, Jude. I read that it was a stroke that done her in, result of a bad head injury. Subdural haematoma – that's it, isn't it? Can't have been easy to make it happen but I admire the craftsmanship. I'll have to tell you exactly what I see when I picture her dead – see if I've got it as accurate as it should be . . .'

'Well, you're a bit of prick, aren't you?' says Sylvia, poking Mick aside and addressing her comments to his companion. 'Stop showing off. There's a queue. I've already told the security guard there's a pillock in here causing trouble. I'd have it away on your toes if I were you.'

He turns to her, unhappy at being interrupted. 'What's it to you?'

'I know you,' continues Sylvia, unperturbed. 'You were one of the thugs Campion brought in to stop the saboteurs. Loved the rough stuff, didn't you? And from what I remember reading in the papers, that's not the worst of your habits.'

'You stop talking,' he spits, getting in Sylvia's face. 'You shuffle on and buy your incontinence pants somewhere else.'

'You don't talk to her like that,' says Betsy, genuinely angry. 'Say what you like about me but—'

'And you close your mouth unless you want something sticking in it,' sneers the man, flashing eyes and teeth. He drops the act. Snarls, from the heart. 'You do know what he is, yeah? Know he killed his fucking wife.'

The eyes spin back towards Jude, his knuckles white where he grips the counter. 'You are one evil little man,' says Sylvia, shaking her head at him. 'Go on, security guard's coming . . .'

'Come on,' hisses Mick, tugging at his sleeve. 'Not now. Not here.'

'A friendly woman, his dear departed,' says the thug in the doorway, enjoying himself again. 'Very accommodating. Came to quite the understanding with Campion, didn't she? The things we do for love, eh? But she isn't here to pay that debt any more, is she? And Punch, you aren't my type.' He leers at Betsy. 'So, love. Guess it's up to you.'

Betsy knows that the words will unleash something in Jude but she doesn't move quick enough to stop him. One moment he is motionless at the counter. The next he has crossed the floor and wrapped his left hand around the man's throat, pushing him back into Mick, who cannons back into Sylvia and Val.

They go down like dominos, Jude on top, pushing the man's face into the floor. He hits him, once, twice, slamming him in the kidneys and ribs with his free hand. He's saying something as he hurts him. 'Never again,' he hisses. 'Never again . . .'

Betsy runs towards the melee, the whirl of arms and legs and curses, and tries to put her hands on Jude's shoulders. He glances back to see who is touching him and the man beneath him squirms an arm free, reaches up and rams his thumb into Jude's eyeball, pushing as if trying to shove a cork into the neck of a bottle.

Jude gives a hiss of pain, and then the man is pushing him over, his hair in his hands, bringing his knees up and Jude's head down, knocking him to the floor; stamping at his chest, screaming in his face, taking his head in his hands and slamming it into the floor with thud after sickening thud . . .

'How you going to keep her safe when you're in hospital, eh Punch? Who'll be her big strong man when you're shitting in a colostomy bag?'

Betsy doesn't even think. She lunges at him, raking her nails down his face. She takes a handful of his cheek in her right hand and twists. Lashes out at him with her other hand, kicking, biting, doing whatever she can to hurt him. He roars in pain and shoves her away, his strength uncanny, and then there are shouts and men in blue, and Jude is pulling himself to his feet, blood leaking from his forehead, and Mick and his mate are rushing towards the exit.

She stands still, panting, blood thudding in her ears, heart a great fist slamming into her ribcage. The room spins. She has to stop herself from throwing up on the dirt-streaked floor.

She looks across at Jude. He's staring at her: one eye a burning coal, the other hidden bloodily behind his hand. A security guard tries to put an arm out to help him and he shrugs him off. Looks to where Sylvia is lying, holding her hip, groaning with pain.

Jude shakes himself. The look of pure rage disappears as if beneath the surface of a pool. He crosses quickly to where Betsy stands. Wraps his arm around her waist. Presses his forehead to hers, blood smearing on her pale brow. 'Thanks,' he mutters, breathless. 'He was lying. You know he was lying.'

'It doesn't matter,' whispers Betsy. 'It doesn't matter.'

And the voice, loud as rushing water: *Yes it does, Liz. He's a killer. You saw. He can't protect you and he's a bloody killer . . .*

TWENTY-FIVE

They take the long way home. Betsy drives. She's never handled a car like this before and the vibrations from the chassis seem to run right up her arms from the steering wheel and rattle her whole skeleton. She feels nervous on this road. Last time she drove here she clipped Campion's big beast of a 4 x 4 and ended up spread-eagled on the fell. But Jude is in no position to drive. He can't see out of his right eye. It's filling with blood; pink tears occasionally seeping out to run down his face. He scowls through the passenger window, saying nothing. His bearing is a clenched fist. He's barely spoken since they left the hospital. It was Betsy who persuaded the pharmacist and security guards not to call the police. She'd promised to take Jude straight down the corridor to A & E. She'd rather basked in the compliments of the witnesses who said that she'd handled the whole thing brilliantly and had gone for the nasty little thug 'like a wildcat'. Jude heard some of it. Heard the grannies saying that men were just animals and that it was a good job she was there to stop him from getting badly hurt. She can see how hard he's trying not to let his ego take control of his personality. He's trying to be the poet. The musician. The man who brings her coffee and wildflowers and lets her stroke his hair as he lies on her lap and talks about the future. He doesn't want to be the kind of man who would point out that he'd have won if she hadn't got involved. Doesn't want to get into that macho bullshit, even as every cell in his body is telling him to do so.

'We could stop for a bit,' says Betsy, and her jolliness sounds strained. 'No rush for home, is there? We were going to have a walk.'

Jude swivels his eyes in her direction. The bloody red iris looks horrible. He's necked some painkillers and wiped the blood from his head with his shirtsleeve. He's pale. She wonders if she would be better off taking him straight home. She knows she was wrong to listen when he said he didn't need to go to

A & E. He has a head injury, that's clear. He must have con-
cussion. A damaged cornea. He must have at least one broken
rib. He'd only said it once, but he'd said it in a way that
left no room for argument. 'I've had worse. I just want to go
home.'

He gives a tired smile, grateful that she's trying. 'There's a
layby a mile or so up the road. Little walk down to the river.
Fresh air might be nice.'

'Great. Tell me when. Are you really sore?'

'You've done worse than this to me,' he says, trying to make
a joke of it. 'First night together, you left me looking bloodier
than this.'

'Shut up, I did not.'

'Ferocious, you were. You always are.'

'You'll make me blush.'

'Take me somewhere quiet and I'll make you do more than
that.'

She finds herself smiling. The dark skies have lifted a little
and with sunset still hours away, the day is rallying; the air
cold and blue.

'That's a red kite,' says Jude, looking past her and nodding at
the big brown bird that turns in lazy circles above them.

'It's massive!' says Betsy, slowing down to peer through the
glass. 'I can't tell how far away it is because I've never seen a
wingspan like that!'

'They nearly went extinct,' says Jude. 'Took a lot of work to
get the numbers back on the rise and there are still nasty sods
who think it's a great day if they manage to shoot one. RSPB
does its best but some people's instinct is to see something
beautiful and smash it. I've never understood that.'

There's something familiar about the bird. She concentrates.
Thinks about that first day: the huge feathery mass pinned across
the doorway. She swallows drily. Something ignites inside her.
She can't pretend. No more fairy tales, no more hiding away in
their castle. She wants to know what he is. What he's truly
capable of.

They drive in silence. Then Jude gives a vague wave. 'Up that
little track, on the right.'

As instructed, Betsy turns the car down a pitted dirt track; a small stretch of grey and brown among the endless green. The car rattles them around like bricks in a washing machine. She sees the pain in Jude's face and takes a perverse pleasure in it. She jerks them to a stop on the brow of a hill, staring out across a vast expanse of heather-clad hillside. To their right, the green fields are speckled with wildflowers; a confetti of multi-coloured petals. Ahead, a dry culvert: a man-made stream covered over with slabs of stone. Rabbits peak out from the places where the stone has caved in. She wishes Marshall were here. She'd like to see him chase rabbits. Catch them, one after another. Right now she would like to see every fluffy little fairy-tale creature ripped to bits.

Painfully, Jude manoeuvres himself out of the car. Betsy joins him. It's colder than she'd imagined. They're high up and the wind cuts like a lash. He takes her hand. Pulls her towards him. 'You're bloody hard work sometimes,' he says, with a smile. 'You don't give an inch, do you?'

'That's me,' she says. 'You'll never find anybody like me.'

'I know,' he says. 'So I'd best do all I can to keep you.'

His face swims in her vision. He's so close his features are blurry and indistinct; the pool of blood in his eye expanding and dilating. She tries to keep things light. But the fire inside her is rising, growing, threatening to overwhelm her. What she feels is something like hatred. Like fear and rage and an absolute willingness to do whatever she must to keep herself safe. At the same time she cannot understand herself – why take herself somewhere secluded with a man she is beginning to truly fear? Why not drive them somewhere loud and boisterous and full of witnesses? She wants to scream into the sky, to roar at the heavens that she has had enough. She wants to understand herself. Make good decisions, stop being so damnably insane.

She mutters, 'What he said . . .'

'About Maeve? Look, that nasty bastard has been trying to goad me for years. Some people have it in their mind I'm a tough guy and people like him want to test it. He knew her, a bit. Back before my time. She was with a group of hunt saboteurs. Brendon had rounded up some thugs to stop them. It all got a bit out of hand and Maeve got a blow to the head. I wasn't there. I didn't see it. But it led to the seizures and the seizures led to her death.'

'So how come people are saying you were somehow to blame?'

He sighs. Rolls a cigarette, expertly, despite the biting wind. Lights up and exhales his woes, heading off down the track towards the brow of the fell. She falls into step beside him, still holding his hand. 'Betsy, you've got every right to ask questions. You've been through all sorts of hell with Jay and now you're with a guy who's got more enemies than friends, but it's important to me that above all else, we have trust. Can't you just trust me?'

'I love it when you tell me my rights, Jude,' she says, with a nasty little smile.

'There you go again,' he says, tiredly. 'I've done nothing wrong. I don't know what I've done to make you doubt me.'

She stops, throws up her arms. 'You don't know? How about the sheep in the river, the dead deer in your tree, putting me in your dead wife's clothes, not telling me that you'd thrown Campion's men out on their ear up at the farm you were working at . . .'

He sucks angrily on his roll-up, grinding his jaw. 'I didn't do that. Those things are happening, but I'm not culpable for that. I don't deserve to get it in the neck for that.'

'What?' asks Betsy, screwing up her face and shaking her hand free. 'What does that even mean? I'm supposed to weigh all that up before I speak, am I? I'm supposed to decide what I feel, not just feel it?'

'Of course you are,' snaps Jude. 'Thoughts and feelings are worlds apart. I have mad impulses; crazy moments of paranoia, but I think about them before I let them out. They're just suggestions from some part of your brain, they don't have to be commands.'

'That's insane,' barks Betsy, her temper rising. 'Is this how you were with Maeve? If she told you off or questioned you it was invalid unless she could back it up?'

He gives a laugh, thoroughly bewildered. 'Doesn't that sound a bit mad to you, Betsy? Of course it's invalid unless it can be backed up. If you tell me off for being . . . I don't know . . . too fat, or something, and I look down and see I'm a size thirty-two-inch waist, then it means you're going on about nothing, and it's not on me to defend myself. It's just a mad accusation.'

She looks at him, horrified. 'Who thinks like that?'

'I think like this,' he growls. 'Jesus, the amount of shit that's been poured in my ears over the years by people who want me to agree with them about the nonsense they're spouting . . .'

'Nonsense? I'm spouting nonsense now?'

'I wish I could record your voice and play you back so you could hear yourself.'

'Jay used to say that!'

He turns on her, face close to hers, his eye leaking blood, the stub of his cigarette flaring gold.

'Jay needs putting in the ground for all he's done to you, Betsy. Your mother too. They're fucking things up for us because they've left you unable to trust people.'

'I know!' she screams, and stamps on ahead up the track. 'I can't believe I got you so wrong. You think you understand me, but you just know how to say the right things. I had a house. I had enough to pay the bills. It wasn't exciting but at least I knew I was somewhere safe. Now I'm with somebody who acts like we're living in a fairy-tale castle and he's a knight who can protect me from the dragons. Weren't much of a knight today, were you? Not when he was smashing your head in the ground . . .'

She looks back at him as she hurls this final rock. He's standing on the track, chewing his lip, breathing heavily. She knows she's right. He deserves this. Deserves to be told. He's lied to her. Messed her up. Taken her away under false pretences. Jay was boring but he was safe. And Anya. She misses Anya. She shouldn't have pushed Jay so far. She's a nightmare. Always has been . . .

She hears him running up the track towards her. Spins to face him, braced for an attack. He's trying to take hold of her; to cuddle her as if she's a child having a strop. He wants this to stop. She can't let it. She needs this anger. It shows her the truth.

'So quiet about your first wife, aren't you. Shame, is it? Why haven't you taken me to see your family? Are you ashamed of me, or are you just hiding me away? Or maybe you don't want people seeing how you're dressing me up in your dead wife's clothes, trying to recreate her so you can kill her again.'

'Betsy, please, look at me—'

'It's Liz! I've been called Liz all my life. I don't know why I told you I'm called Betsy but I'm not. I'm just Liz. Lizzie, if you like.'

He looks confused. 'Fine, OK, Liz . . .'

'And you, Mr Punch? That doll makes sense now, eh? You're treating me like a fucking mushroom – keeping me in the dark and feeding me on shit—'

'Please, just listen—'

'Sylvia's in hospital because of you. What if she catches MRSA and dies? And the way Val looked at you, as if she knew what you'd been up to. Who can't even go to the pharmacy without getting into a fight? You know I was suicidal before we met, you do know that, don't you . . .?'

'Please,' he whispers, desperately. 'Just look at me, this isn't you talking . . .'

'Yes it fucking is!' she spits. 'This is me. This is what you've fallen for. This is what you've got forever. Not such a picnic now it's not all about wildflowers and blowjobs, is it? This is reality . . .'

She can tell he wants to grab her. To hold her arms and make her listen. He's fighting with himself. All she has to do is push a little harder and she'll see the real him, she knows it. This is the part of herself that keeps her safe; stops people getting close, stops her getting hurt.

'What is it you want from me?' he asks, almost beaten.

'Did you kill your wife?'

'How can you ask that?'

She screams. Throws her head back and roars like an animal summoning the pack. Turns to stamp on up the track. He reaches for her arm, pulls her back.

'I love all of you,' he says, his voice steel. 'I don't like this bit of you, but I love the whole of you so whatever's inside, that gets loved too.'

'Don't,' she snaps. 'Don't mess with my head. My mother used to do that.'

'And she was an evil bitch. The people who've hurt you, none have seen the real you. I do. And I love it all.'

'No. Don't be nice. You're lying!'

'I want you – all of you. Betsy, please, trust me . . .'

'You've got enough problems,' she says, and she feels her strength going. 'I shouldn't be here. I shouldn't be anywhere . . .'

'Betsy, you should be with me. Marry me.'

She looks at him like he's mad. 'What? How can you be asking that after all I just said?'

'Because we're meant. We're right. You make me feel alive.'

'I'm a bad person, Jude. I'm rotten all the way through.'

'No. You're sweet and loving and clever and there's a fire in you that . . . I dunno, it makes me think of an oil lamp . . . sometimes it's turned up high and other times it's down low but you're always the most spectacular, fascinating person in the room.'

She feels sick. Breathless. Doesn't know if she wants to kiss him or jump off the edge of the fell.

'Please, Betsy.' He turns away from her, gazing out across the valley. Turns back to her, decision made. 'We can stay here, or we can go. I've fought to keep the bastle, to keep the land, but if you want us to start again somewhere else, we can do that. Whatever you want. Wherever you want. We can start a family . . .'

She looks up, eyes wet. She shakes her head. 'I can't,' she snaps, her hand clutching her stomach. 'The things that were done to me – I'm all ruined in there. Messed up. I can't even . . .'

He places his hands on her cheeks. Forces her to meet his eyes. 'I'm so sorry, Betsy. For all that's been done to you.' He pauses. Makes his offer. 'Say the word and I'll stop every one of them from drawing breath again.'

She shakes her head. 'Things like that – they scare me when you say them. You look like you would.'

He nods. 'I would.'

'Then how can I trust that you're a good person?'

He grins, relief seeping out of him. 'It might not seem like a code that fits in to the world out there, but it's the only code that makes sense to me. It's really simple. There are consequences for your actions. If I do terrible things, people have a right to try and kill me. And I have a right to fight back. That's how it's always been. But that doesn't mean I'm going to go looking for people to harm. I want everybody to get along. I believe in goodness and kindness and compassion, but I also understand the need to protect that which belongs to you.'

She looks down. Here, now, his words make some kind of sense. Later, she knows she will replay them in her mind and hear the song of a psychopath. 'Those things I said . . .' she mumbles.

He pulls her close. Presses his face to her neck. 'You can be a nasty sod, but it doesn't mean you're bad. It means I'm glad you're on my side.' He angles her head so he can look at her. 'The clothes aren't Maeve's. I think you may have worn her dress once but most of that stuff in the chest is stuff she got in a house clearance. I don't think she ever wore any of it. I've dumped some of her stuff in there, just so I don't have to see it every day, but Maeve wouldn't have worn that. And if she did, she wouldn't have looked so extraordinarily gorgeous.'

Betsy isn't sure how to respond. She feels oddly hurt for Maeve.

'Was that a real proposal?' she asks, managing a smile. 'Only I'd imagined candles? A ring? Maybe a saxophone solo . . .'

'That can be arranged,' he smiles.

She feels bone tired, suddenly. Wants to lie down on the cold ground and pull the heather over herself. Wants all the thoughts to stop, just for a moment.

'I don't want to leave the bastle,' she says. 'You fit there. You're meant to be there. And I love it too because it's so much a part of you. That's why Maeve left it to you, I'm sure. How bad will things get? With Campion, I mean?'

He considers it. 'He'll tire eventually. There are easier ways to make money than sending his bullies to my door. I keep sending them back. And if it comes to it, he knows I have leverage.'

'You have leverage? And you're not using it?' She stops, thinking hard. 'That man. Moon. Was he right? Do you have a video showing what happened to the girl?'

He shakes his head. 'I wish I did. I've got something else. Something that makes me feel ill but if it ever comes to it, if I have to make that choice, I'll do what needs to be done.'

'Be honest with me, Jude. Tell me.'

He looks away. When he speaks again, his voice is quiet. 'He wants to know what I'm capable of. He doesn't believe I'll use what I've got.'

'And what have you got?'

He stares away into the distance, watching the red kite circle in the darkening sky. 'Would you believe me if I said it was best you didn't know?'

Betsy makes a face, anguished. 'There you go again.'

'Please,' he says. 'You have to trust somebody. Let it be the man who loves you to your bones.'

She shakes her head. He's done it again, she thinks. Mollified you. Turned you inside out. And you're going to let him, aren't you? Going to kiss him like it's all forgotten . . .

'Can I still call you Betsy?' he asks, smiling. 'I like it.'

She nods. Pulls him closer.

'Me too.'

TWENTY-SIX

Three months ago

Betsy dreamed of locked doors last night. She woke at two a.m. from a nightmare in which she was trapped inside a labyrinth of sliding panels and portcullises: doors slamming closed and banging open, creating a whirlwind inside her skull. She woke up panting, little half-moon scars scored into the skin of her left arm. She'd reached out for Jude but he wasn't there. She listened out for him, trying to catch the sound of him moving around the house. Perhaps he was writing her a poem. He's stopped doing that. She hasn't really responded to his last few attempts and she can tell that he's losing enthusiasm. It doesn't matter how pretty his words are – she just doesn't believe them. She'd fallen back to sleep long before he returned to bed. Chose to stay unresponsive when he kissed her cheek and left her coffee on the bedside table.

He's been gone an hour, now. He's due at Allendale today, lopping branches at the big house where the shooting parties stay when they're in town. He hates going there for work but they pay well, and on time, and Campion isn't sufficiently well-connected to instruct the owners not to use him. They're richer than he is. More influential. Couldn't give a damn.

Betsy's sitting up in bed, staring through the deep-set window at a day that carries the first faint traces of autumn. The fell has taken on a gingerbread hue; the birdsong is strangely muted. She sees the occasional wisp of smoke puff past, snatched from chimneys where elderly occupants are starting to feel the chill.

She knows, even without looking directly at the thought, that today will be the day. He's not going to be coming back any time soon, and she's put it off for so long that she feels entitled to indulge herself. He can't really expect any differently, she tells herself. He knows you. What you're like. You warned him in advance. Of course you're going to snoop.

And inside, the voice she knows so well: *That's my girl. Do what you do best. Fuck it up for yourself. Make him cross. Make him see what happens . . .*

Twenty minutes later she is dressed in yesterday's jeans and a slouchy sweatshirt, her hair held back with an elastic band. Her fringe, growing back too quickly, sticks straight up. She catches a glimpse of herself in the bathroom mirror as she brushes her teeth and has to stop herself from bursting out laughing. She looks a little unhinged.

She toys with the idea of subterfuge. She could tell herself, and him, that she has been giving the house a good clean. Clearing cupboards, sorting through the old items of furniture, flicking through the document folders in the Welsh dresser, all in the name of domesticity. She screws up her face at the idea. It's her house too, isn't it? She can damn well rummage if she wants to.

By eleven a.m., Betsy has begun to tire. She doesn't know what she wants to find. She isn't even entirely sure what she suspects, but the feeling of being lied to is overwhelming and she fancies that if she can just tell herself that she's exhausted every possibility, perhaps her mind will settle down. He's done everything right these past couple of weeks. There have been no repercussions from the incident at the pharmacy. His eye is almost completely healed and if his ribs are bothering him he's not complaining about it. He might be drinking a little more, but Betsy is too. Their evenings are becoming quite decadent. They drink sticky spirits, often wrapped around one another in the deep copper bath, or naked in front of the fire. She massages the aches from his shoulders; he kneads the tension from her toes. They make love constantly. He says she makes him feel peaceful. She doesn't know how to describe what he makes her feel, but it's something she knows she cannot ever give up. That is why she needs some form of proof: something she can use as a catalyst. Something that will burn what they have to ash.

Annoyed with herself, feeling a bit disloyal, she takes a cup of tea to the courtyard and sits on her favourite seat, watching as the trees shimmy their branches in the cold breeze. Jude planted a garden on the roof of the stables last weekend, bringing up earth from the low field with the digger and depositing it expertly on the flat wooden roof. She'd walked barefoot in the earth and planted seedlings. By spring it will be an explosion of colour. She feels quite giddy at the thought. Spoils it, as she asks herself whether she will still be here.

From time to time she considers picking up her mobile phone. The signal is still terribly sketchy but she can access the Wi-Fi at least. She keeps meaning to call Anya. She misses her, inasmuch as she misses any part of what used to be. She can't honestly say she feels the absence of Carly.

She leans back against the wall. She's been through every book in the house, flicking through the pages looking for letters, photographs, some scrap of paper that will feed into her generalized feeling of being left out. There's no shortage of marginalia in Maeve's old books but nothing that she can incorporate into a conspiracy. Even the inscription in the old copy of some dull classic had done nothing to pique her curiosity. A passage had been underlined, some dry witterings about the old Germanic tribes and their relationship with trees. She'd stopped reading when she got to the bit about people having their navels pinned to tree trunks and their guts unwound. She'd taken a picture of the inscription on her phone. She looks at it again.

'*Flectere si nequeo superos, Acheronta movebo.*'

Carefully, she types it into her phone and looks it up. 'If I cannot bend the will of Heaven I shall move Hell.' It's a phrase worth knowing, but it means nothing to her.

'What are you doing, Betsy?' she asks, aloud, and realizes that the name feels more familiar now. She doesn't need to act like Liz. Doesn't need to snoop around, looking for reasons to prick the bubble of her happiness. She could do something useful. Write an article for Bipped, maybe. Contact Carly and ask if she can maybe get some of her old things from Jay's place. Or she could have a rummage about in Jay's life. See how he's getting on without her. She wishes she had a laptop. She feels disconnected, and for the first time in weeks it's not a pleasant sensation. She needs to check that the world's still turning.

Laptop, she thinks, sucking on the word like gum. A memory rises. Maeve, tapping away at her laptop, the day she died. The half-open disk drive. He wouldn't have thrown it out, would he? A laptop has so many memories. He said he had leverage, didn't he? Leverage Campion didn't believe he would use.

She feels her pulse quicken. She walks briskly back into the kitchen, suddenly aware that she has been making a hell of a mess while rummaging through the chaos.

'Laptop,' she mumbles, as if able to summon it up with a spell. 'Where would you be?'

She almost loses herself in the voluminous depths of the bridal chest on the landing, still full of the clothes she has been helping herself to these past weeks. She delves to the bottom like a pearl diver, prodding around for anything that might be a secret drawer or concealed entrance, feeling brilliantly clever and faintly stupid at the same time. She feels her way around the roof joists, down the back of furniture, fondling under the bed. In the bathroom, she gets down on her knees and squeezes half of herself into the gap beneath the big copper bath. She finds a silver earring; shaped like a horse's head, and puts it into her pocket like treasure.

Dirty, tired, sticky with sweat, she flumps down on to the sofa an hour later, deciding that, on balance, today has not been her most productive day. She gives a sigh of exasperation, glaring down at the haphazard wooden floor. He's done it himself, he said. Old reclaimed timbers that he'd dipped and sanded and laid over a floor of mud and earth.

She angles her head. Follows the grooves between the boards with her eyes. Slithers on to her knees and runs the palm of her hands over the furrows. She can feel a breeze; the flimsiest of drafts, as if a body beneath the floorboards is whispering.

There's a knife sharpener in the kitchen: a lethal-looking length of steel hanging on a hook beside the sink. She retrieves it and tells herself that this is the last time she'll be bad. Her pulse quickens. Grunting, she shoves one end in between two boards. Wood splinters. Frays, as if chewed. She puts her weight behind it and gives a yelp of satisfaction as it disappears into the earth. She hauls at the improvised crowbar. The wood creaks afresh. The nails pop. And then she is flat on her back and a board is sticking up into the air and the house is filling with the smell of disturbed earth and dead flowers.

She looks into the hole. She expects to see a skull. She doesn't know whose skull it will be, but she is so certain that she will be greeted by the sightless eyes of a skeleton, that it comes almost as a shock to see the clear polythene bag, half-covered in dirt.

She's shaking now. Scared and excited and pleased with herself all at once.

She reaches into the hole and pulls at the bag. It's not particularly heavy. She peers at it by the flickering light of the fire. Inside, a blue laptop; a charger; a little silver camera. She squints at it more closely. There's another bag inside this one. Again, it's clear. It contains two rings, both white gold. Betsy closes her eyes.

She knows that she still has hours to play with. And that there is not a chance that the bag is going back in the ground unopened.

TWENTY-SEVEN

The camera offers up nothing of interest. The battery is dead and she can't find a replacement AA or a charger to plug it into the wall. The laptop is more cooperative. Twenty minutes after plugging in, halfway down her second cup of tea, the machine gives a musical 'ta-dah' and the log-in screen comes up. The username is NewWaeveMaeve. The password icon is blinking. Betsy chews her lip. Tries the obvious ones first, typing in the username as a password, then the word 'password' just in case she was a halfwit. Tries JudeCullen and a dozen variations. His date of birth. Thinks of what she knows about the dead woman and plucks words from her limited range of equestrian terms. After twenty minutes she realizes she's getting nowhere. She slumps back in the chair, staring up at the books that line the ceiling eaves. Pulls out her phone and calls up the image of the inscription on the flyleaf.

Cautiously, she types it in, one letter at a time.

Wrong password.

Cursing, she pushes the machine away. Stares at the blinking cursor like it's an enemy. Then she types it in again, and sticks a number one on the end. The screen changes colour. She's in.

The home screen shows a picture of a black-and-white fell pony, silhouetted against a setting sun. It's a pretty picture but Betsy gives it no attention. She ignores the endless Word documents scattered around the screen and instead clicks on the bottom left corner, plunging straight in to the 'recent items' section.

The computer hasn't been used since the day Maeve died. The last task performed by the computer was at 10.17 a.m. She'd been online for an hour that day. Her browser history seems a lot more grown-up than Betsy's own. She visited the *Guardian*. *Huffington Post*. Read three articles in the *New Yorker*. Downloaded a recipe for poppy-seed shortbread from a foodie page. Then she'd clicked on a page called *POWAtothepeople*. Betsy clicks the link. *Protect Our Wild Animals*. It's a news page, detailing recent press coverage of anti-hunt activities. It lists, in reverse chronological order, a seemingly endless catalogue of cases showing the widespread disregard for the hunting ban, going all the way back to 2005. Betsy scans the first few entries.

Hunt Horse Throws Rider in Kent
Police Acting as Private Militia for Hunt
Saboteurs Attacked by Pro-Hunt Thugs
HSE Considering Charges After Beater Blinded

Betsy rubs her face, unsure what she's looking for. Scrolls down. Tries searching for a specific word. Her first try is Maeve's own name. It brings up a profile, a piece that appeared in *Countryside World* magazine in 2014. She chews her lip. Tells herself there is a lot of work to do before Jude comes home, and decides to spare herself the anguish. Instead, she looks at the last task performed by the computer, perhaps an hour before she fell and banged her head and bled into the river where Betsy feels so very much at home.

She 'burned' a disk. Transferred a file from the folder on the C-drive and pressed it to CD. Eight minutes long. And then she moved the footage to the Trash.

Betsy opens the Trash. Restores the file and hits 'play'.

A minute later she shuts it down. She doesn't want to see this. Feels disgusted with herself. Catches her breath. Opens the laptop again.

Maeve is on her back, by the water's edge. It's a hot day. Sticky. Flies are buzzing and she can hear the curlew. And Campion is on top of her, trousers around his ankles, face sweaty with exertion. Maeve has her face turned towards the camera. There are tears on her cheeks but she isn't fighting. There's a look of pain and resignation on her face. There's something curious about the angle of her neck. Betsy feels her stomach clench as she makes sense of it. Campion has a riding crop to her throat – he's pushing down on her larynx, forcing her to look away from him. She's pulling out clumps of grass as her fingers clench and contract, clench and contract: dying spiders.

Betsy closes down the laptop. Slips it back in the bag. Unplugs the charger and puts everything back where she found it. Drops the bag into the hole and sets about filling it back in. The nails are a little bent but she manages to jump up and down on them until everything looks as it should. She realizes she is crying. There's a pain in her windpipe.

Bastard, she thinks.

Says it aloud, in case it helps. 'Bastard.'

Her heart aches for Jude. In this moment, it aches far worse for Maeve.

She spends the afternoon putting the books back, tidying away and generally making things nice. She feels guilty and sad. By the time Jude comes home she's drunk the rest of the Stag's Breath. She greets him with sloppy kisses, over-compensating: trying to make up for her disloyalty by being too much of what he likes.

She feels so bad, she doesn't even mention the missing buttons on his shirt front, nor the blood beneath his nails.

TWENTY-EIGHT

I n the third week of October, Jay turns up at Wolfcleugh.
Betsy has barely used her mobile phone these past weeks,
save for the occasional text to Carly telling her that things
are going well, and enquiring whether she might have a moment
to retrieve her meagre possessions from her old house. She hasn't
thought much about Jay. Her old life has begun to feel unreal.
She feels as if that life happened to somebody else. Being Betsy
is liberating, she has decided. All the bad stuff happened to Liz.

She's emerging from the cool of the dingle when she spots
the car, moving up the track with such excruciating care and
attention that it appears almost static. She's waist-high in brambles: scratched and blood-jewelled in the gap between her green
welly boots and the hem of her shorts. She's stopped paying
heed to such trivialities. Barely scratches at her insect bites or
makes a fuss when she has to ask Jude to tweeze something
sharp and invasive from her skin. She hasn't been here long but
it truly feels as if she has planted herself in this earth. She has
a fanciful notion that if she fell asleep on the damp grass of the
valley, she could be somehow sucked into the earth and absorbed;
perhaps a tree would grow to show where she had lain.

Things are better with Jude. His '*I love yous*' are vocal now,
and the poems are there when she wakes. He writes of nothing
but her and how she makes him feel. How she has changed him.
Saved him. She does not recognize the person he writes about,
but manages to take pleasure in his words, even while wondering
how silly he will feel when he realizes that he's fallen for somebody who doesn't exist.

As soon as she sees the car she feels the old familiar knot of
panic in her gut. He's come to take her back. No, worse, he's
come to tell her that he's pressing charges for attacking him that
last night they were together. She runs through a multitude of
possibilities and none are good. She assesses her appearance and
knows at once that he will greet her with scorn. She's every inch

the country wench. She's always been good at dressing correctly for the role that she is playing and she has thrown herself into character these past weeks. She's got a wicker basket over her arm and a floppy hat pushed down on undyed hair; a tangle of blacks and browns shot through with the occasional fleck of grey. Her hands are grimy, nails unpainted. She wonders if he'll even recognize her.

Jude, she thinks, suddenly. *What will Jude do?*

She lets out a breath, hot and sticky, and quickens her pace. Cranes her neck as she moves down the valley and spots the space where Jude's quad bike is supposed to be. She must have been at the dingle longer than she thought. It has a habit of swallowing her up. It reminds her of entering a church; a cool, sacred space. She has lost countless hours just sitting by the water, dangling her feet in the river, acquainting herself with the flowers, the birds; the creatures that buzz and flutter and crawl. She picks flowers that she likes the look of; plucks berries and fruits and gathers up fungus and brings them home to Jude, who delights in telling her the names of her specimens, and their uses. She is picking up knowledge as a tree draws in water. She has begun to wash her face in elderflower dew; a preservative of youthful looks. Had she anyone to tell, she would delight in informing them that expensive face creams contain the exact same element that can be found on the humble hedgerow flower.

She arrives back at the bastle just as Jay is pulling up. Despite his best efforts, there is dirt on the side panels and grit stuck in the big treads of his whitewall tyres. He glances in her direction as she scurries across the little footbridge and towards the court-yard, looking at the bastle with a newcomer's eye. She feels suddenly embarrassed of her new home. For all the work that has gone into it the place is still more of a ruin than a home; everything having a scavenged, jumble-sale look about it. She looks at the rusting guts of the tractor and horsebox abandoned at the side of the path. Considers the child's swing, upended and half-submerged in thistles and nettles. The dog shit by the door; the dry slime varnishing the five-bar gate which opens into the courtyard and its panorama of rotting furniture and unbegun restoration projects. It never looks like this when she is sitting outside with Jude, but here, now, infected by Jay's presence, she suddenly feels as though her fairy-tale castle is very shabby.

The door of the Audi swings opens. Jay climbs out. Gives her a blank look. Turns away. Then spins his head back towards her.

'Liz?'

She doesn't have a chance to answer. The passenger door opens and out climbs Anya. She's grown a little. Filled out. Her face creases into a wide-mouthed expression of surprise and delight as she takes in her former stepmum, standing on the footbridge in wellingtons and straw hat, holding a basket full of wildflowers.

'Liz!'

Betsy isn't sure how to greet either of them. Can't make herself smile or frown or force her feet to run back to the safety of the wood. Instead she moves forward and snatches off her hat, pushing her sweat-soaked hair back from her face. Jay looks at her as if she's something that the cat has thrown up. He can't seem to help himself. He looks the way she had known he would: striped polo shirt tucked into beige chinos with expensive mountaineering trainers, spotlessly clean.

Anya scampers around from the far side the car and runs to Betsy, who finds herself instinctively opening her arms for a hug. There is a collision of bodies, a tangle of hair, and then she is sitting on her backside while Anya hugs her tight and the air fills with the scent of fresh-picked sprays of honeysuckle. Betsy colours, feeling even more ridiculous, as Anya starts laughing and disentangles herself from the fulsome embrace. She manhandles Betsy to her feet.

'Oh my God, you look amazing! You barely even look like you, and wow, that tan looks like you've been to Tenerife. We saw a bird of prey on the way – a real one, I don't think it was an eagle, though it might have been, but Dad said he doubted it, but maybe you'll know, it had white feathers underneath, but anyway wow – you're all sort of firm, like a boxer, but in a good way, of course, and—'

'Anya,' says Jay, barking out her name as if calling a dog to heel. 'Stop your chatter. You've seen her. That's what you wanted, wasn't it? Now, I have places to be.'

Anya turns to her father, who is opening the rear of the car and pulling out three bin liners, each tied neatly at the top with lengths of twine cut to precise lengths. He drops them at the grass verge as if they sicken him. 'Your clothes. A couple of books. A phone charger. There wasn't much else.'

Betsy realizes she still hasn't spoken. Feels Anya's eyes on her. Turns to the girl and manages a smile, even as a swarm of different feelings buzz at her insides. She feels disgusted with herself when she remembers the reason for his rage.

Of course he'll be angry, of course he'll be distant – you sent his private pictures and messages to people whose opinion matters. Then you left him. Went off with another man. What did you expect – a bunch of flowers?

'I wish I'd known you were coming,' says Betsy, addressing her remarks to Anya. Then, as if reading from a script: 'I've missed you.'

'Don't lie to my child,' says Jay, giving the slightest shake of his head. He looks genuinely sickened by her appearance. 'You don't miss her. Not the way she misses you, though God knows why that might be. Been a misery guts for weeks now. Wouldn't give me a moment's peace. Pushed and pushed until I told her the truth of what you'd done. Where you'd gone. Who you were with. And she still wanted to come see you. So look, Anya' – he sneers as he says it, looking as though he would gladly throw down a petrol bomb and drive away – 'look at the princess in her palace. Back in the fucking gutter.'

Anya's face twitches, a prelude to tears. She bites her lip. 'I don't need to know about the nasty stuff, Liz – I just wanted to see how you were doing good, and, well, Mum said maybe you and I could still see each other sometimes, if you were OK with that, and she doesn't think Dad's told me everything . . .'

'Another lie,' spits Jay. He looks at the crumbling walls of the bastle. 'Not much up from a pigsty, is it?' He sneers at her, looking pleased with himself. 'I should imagine that right about now you're just starting to move from being delighted with the novelty of all this, to grumbling about the imperfections. I should imagine that the bits which were making your heart glow and your bits throb a fortnight ago are starting to irritate you a little bit. I'd imagine you're starting to miss some of the luxuries. You're offering helpful bits of advice about things you know nothing about. You're talking about how things aren't quite what they used to be, and maybe a holiday would help, or a new pair of shoes, or perhaps if you could just go and get your hair coloured at one of those posh places that charge eighty quid for a blow dry you might start feeling more like your old self . . .'

'Don't . . .' protests Anya, urgently, staring up at Betsy, who still can't seem to make herself speak. 'Don't say that, Dad . . .'

'I know you better than anybody, Liz. I always knew what you were but I figured you could at least be house-trained. Didn't even need the whip to do it, did I? I mean, you weren't much of a maid or a cook or even a particularly decent showpiece on my arm, but I stuck with you despite it and all I asked in return was that you try and smile and act like it was appreciated. And what do you do? Self-harm, suicide attempts; drama after fucking drama, and then all this BPD bullshit, as if having an interesting syndrome means you're entitled to act so . . .'

Betsy jerks her head, eager to hear the final insult. 'So what, Jay?'

'So atrociously,' he says, and his whole demeanour is of a man eager to bang his fist on a boardroom table. 'You've got your hooks in this one, I see. Poor sod doesn't know what he's letting himself in for, does he? I should have brought him a gift, really – or at least a receipt. This is what you think you are now, is it? Some local yokel, some country bumpkin, living with a man who probably killed his first wife!'

Betsy feels Anya slip her hand into hers. She looks down at her and sees herself reflected back on the brown of her irises.

Jay snarls at the pair of them, shaking his head in disgust. 'I've tried and I've tried to work out what any of you want and all I come up with is that you want everything. Everything and more. And then you still act as if it's some sort of chore – as if every man is a punchline.'

In the distance, Betsy hears the low rumble of a quad bike. She isn't sure if she wants it to be Jude or not. If he turns up she can't see it ending well for Jay, but how can she let her new man knock him senseless in front of Anya? She looks at the girl and feels her heart double in size as she sees the desperate pleading in her eyes.

'It's funny you chose today,' says Betsy, as brightly as she can. 'I was actually thinking of you when I was up in the woods collecting flowers. Well, it's called a dingle, actually, which is a brilliant word. And I was remembering how good you are at drawing, and I thought "I wonder whether Anya would be able to draw these flowers" and maybe if it were good enough I could put one in a frame. It would have to be good, of course – you'd have to give it your best. So how about I send some pictures to your mum's phone and you draw them and send them to me, and we'll stay in touch that way for a while, eh? It's lovely here. Maybe it would be best if it was your mum who brought you, though – it's not really fair on your dad.'

'Fair on me?' spits Jay. 'Do you know what she said when I told her what you'd been doing? She said there were two sides to every story. Do you believe that? My own daughter!'

Betsy ignores him. Bends down and picks a tiny flower at random from the mass of stems and petals in her basket. She places it behind Anya's ear. 'I only know this one because I asked about it the other day,' confides Betsy. 'It's an ox-eye daisy. Look at the yellow in the middle – it's the brightest flower I've seen. If it's still OK when you get home, draw me a picture of it in one of your notebooks.' She crouches down, knees creaking. 'I'm pleased you've missed me. I've missed you too. But maybe things are all a bit raw for now, eh? And much as I want you to meet my friend it might be best if we save that for another day.'

Betsy falls silent as she hears the louder rumble of an approaching vehicle, moving up the track far faster than Jay had done. She doesn't recognize the sound of the engine. She climbs on to the bottom rung of the footbridge over the drop and sees the top of a dark blue van. Jay has heard it too, and Betsy can tell from the look on his face that he is concerned the driver will go straight into the back of his treasured car. He waves his hands as if signalling the driver of a train, and visibly shrinks in on himself as the van comes around the corner and slams on the brakes in a shower of dust and stones and pollen; little *ting-ting-tings* of shingle hitting the rear of Jay's vehicle. In the driver's seat, a big man with a goatee, clearly uncomfortable in a shirt three sizes too small. Beside him, the man who had brought her the four thousand pounds that day after the accident. Brendon.

Betsy has been waiting for this. Has, at times, been eager for confrontation or at least a chance to score a victory of some sort – to show Jude she can handle herself by sending one of his tormentors packing. But there have been no visitors. No altercations. No proof that Campion has been doing what Jude claims. And now, with Jay and Anya in the forecourt – and Jude God knows where – this is when they choose to make their presence felt.

She suddenly feels an overwhelming urge to run.

Anya slides her hand into hers again. And they stand, two statues, locked together, as doors slam.

A small voice, deep inside Betsy, telling her not to worry – that he will be home soon.

The valley, cruel in its silence.

TWENTY-NINE

She can hear her own blood moving in her veins. Can feel the pulse and thump of her heart. Beneath her skin, aphids and ladybirds, prickly ferns; honeysuckle climbing up her spine and threading through the struts of her ribcage like roses through an arbour . . .

She hears the catch in her voice as she tries to speak. Coughs. Tries again. Her tongue, a salted slug, turning to mush behind her teeth.

'Liz?'

Anya's voice is a spark. She finds herself chattering. Gabbling. She wants everybody gone. Wants to retreat to the wood and sit with her back to the trees and her feet in the grass and stay blissfully hidden away from anything real, or cruel, or ugly.

'. . . well, I don't know if this has been what everybody wanted but there's lots to be done and I think these men have some business interests to discuss so maybe it would be best if you rescheduled, like I said . . . Jay . . . Jay, you should probably be off . . .'

A sheen of sweat glazes her skin. She feels all hot inside, her tongue puffy. She's light-headed, overwhelmed by a sudden exhaustion. 'Jay, are you listening . . . it's not good for Anya . . .'

He isn't paying any attention to her. He's watching the big man climb down from the van and stretch his arms out, crucifixion-style, as if he has been sleeping in too cramped a space. He looks at Jay, then at his posh vehicle. Gives a little nod, appreciating the model. 'That the diesel or the petrol?' he asks. 'I like the whitewall tyres. Kept it nice. I know what they say about Audi drivers but it hardly seems fair. Engine better than a Beamer, so I've heard.'

Jay seems to grow two inches in height. He loves his toys. Likes nothing more than to head into the garage and slide himself under his big beast of a car – his spotless blue overalls ironed to show off a razor-sharp seam. She doesn't think he actually knows what he's doing, but he always seems very pleased with himself after spending half a day on his back, staring up into the greased mechanical guts of his pride and joy, wheeling himself around on the little plastic creeper; the jack taking the strain; bland pop music drifting from a state-of-the-art stereo on his pristine workbench.

'Petrol, of course,' purrs Jay, proudly. 'Gives you that extra kick. You don't want to be changing down the gears looking for that extra few miles per hour. Not in the back of beyond. You get one chance to overtake a tractor or some little old dear in her Citroën, you want something aggressive under the hood, am I right? Wonderful engine under there.'

The man sucks at his cheek, peering down to look at the bodywork. 'Our mam drives a Citroën. French for "lemon", isn't it? Seems a poor choice of name from a marketing point of view. Pretty apt, though.'

'Worth saving up for. Some good deals too.'

'Yeah? Fancied one myself last time I was between vehicles. Ended up going for the Nissan. I know, I know, but the missus reads all the guides on value for money versus security and somebody filled her head about the bloody Nissan, so I'm stuck with it. I'm jealous, mate. Well jealous.'

Betsy gives Anya's hand a little squeeze. There's a chill to the air, suddenly, as if a storm is gathering. She watches the exchange between the two men with a sense of rising panic; an intuition that the pleasantries will not last long.

'You'll be paying for it, I presume,' says Jay, with a little smirk. 'I reckon that means you get the biggest say.'

The man looks at him, angling his head slightly and staring at him in a way that Betsy remembers from childhood. She's seen teenage lads act like this – making themselves still, their eyes hard, their whole demeanour transformed into a clenched fist just by the subtle jutting of their jaw.

'What was that, mate?'

'I'm saying, I bet you'll be paying for the car.'

'What makes you say that? Got a good job, our Belinda. Brings in a good wage. Bit presumptuous of you, if I'm honest.'

Jay doesn't notice the warning signs. He's still high on pride. 'Well, they do say that it's the exception that proves the rule.

Not sure I'd be lucky enough to find a partner who earns what I do. I know we're not supposed to think it, but it's hardly surprising that there aren't as many woman once you get past middle management. It's the temperament, isn't it? I'm sure your wife is a grafter but even the best of them are too emotional to make the big decisions.'

Brendon is smiling, looking at Jay as if he's a funny YouTube video. He glances at Betsy. 'Does he mean this, or is he practicing an act?'

'Dad, not everybody thinks like you . . .' begins Anya, urgently.

Betsy takes a few steps forward and Brendon raises his hand. 'You stay still, love. We'll get to you. You and I have got to have a proper little chat about monies owed.'

'Really, Liz?' Jay looks at her and shakes his head, delighted with this nugget of information. 'This quickly? Messed up good and proper, haven't you? Anya, take a good look at what she chose over us. Look what happens when you think you're better off on your own . . .'

The man walks across to Jay in three brisk strides. Betsy sees what is about to happen before Jay even registers that he may have caused offence.

'Jude's money, is it . . . what we owe? Well, him, not me, but I guess we're a couple so what's his is mine and all that . . . I've been waiting . . .' splutters Betsy, her voice loud. 'I can sort that now, actually. Do you want a chat? I'll just say goodbye to my friends here.'

Brendon, the punch unthrown, his fist opening out like the teeth of a Venus flytrap. He looks to Betsy and the child who stands beside her. Something passes between them. He gives the faintest of nods.

'You off, eh?' he asks Jay, his face uncomfortably close. He's shorter than Jay, but looks as though he could snap him over his knee. 'Well, you drive safe. I'd move the van for you but it's not great at hill starts so I'd carry on up the lane and down the track to the road. Bit bumpy but a car like that can handle it, eh? I've heard the suspension's peachy.'

'Not a problem,' says Jay, a reedy nervousness suddenly bleeding into his voice. 'Anya, come.'

Betsy hugs her. Kisses her. Presses her face against hers and tells her to keep the daisy safe. She finds herself hoping that he really does see her again soon.

'There'll be a letter from my solicitor on its way,' says Jay, in parting. He jerks his head, flares his nostrils, as some insect briefly troubles him. 'I've been left with some debts that I don't feel are my responsibility so I've given your details to the enforcement agents and you can expect a visit. Sorry to have pissed in your paradise.' He moves to climb back into the car but can't seem to resist one last sneering look at the bastle. 'Suits you, this place. Gone to seed. Well past its prime. Looks interesting from the outside but rotten all the way through.'

Brendon furrows his brow and looks at Jay from under dark eyebrows: a thumbprint crease opening up on his forehead. 'Wow, mate, first impressions but you really do seem a prick.'

Jay's eyes widen. He seems about to reply and Betsy finds herself hoping that he does so; that he gets himself smacked insensible and that she gets to enjoy every kick and punch. But Anya would see too. And that simply can't be allowed to happen.

'Do you want to come around the back?' asks Betsy, trying to keep her manner bright. 'As the actress said to the bishop . . .'

'Be seeing you,' smiles the man, and gives Jay a friendly slap on the shoulder. He flinches as if ducking a rock, and Brendon lets out a peal of laughter as he follows Betsy to the gate.

As she unloops the rope and pushes open the mossed-over wooden gate, she gives one last glimpse back at the track. Jay is revving his engine, his face white with embarrassment. She looks out across the valley imploringly, trying to fill it with the sound of a quad bike, the barking of Marshall; the broad-shouldered outline of Jude moving purposefully towards them. She sees nothing.

She closes the gate. Drops the noose back around the fence post. Trudges around the angle of the house and into the cool of the overgrown, rubbish-strewn courtyard, her basket banging against her hip. She feels sick. Doesn't know whether she has somehow succeeded in making things worse. Starts telling herself off. Hears the old voices, sneering, mocking, asking how she's going to fix things now; what the hell she thinks she's doing . . .

He'd seemed OK, hadn't he? Brendon. Stuck up for her? He'd thought Jay was a prick, and that had to count for something.

'Shall we sit outside? It's cold inside.'

'Aye, I've been in. Like a mausoleum.'

'Takes a lot of heating but glorious in summer.'

'I can imagine. Hope it works out for you, love. I really do. Bit different to where you were when I brought you Candy's money.'

'Yes. Candy, you said? Not her husband.'

'Big difference between the person who writes the cheque and the bank that cashes it.'

Betsy watches as he pulls up a plastic seat and sits down, legs spread, and gives her what might be described as a kind smile. Then, almost apologetically, he pulls out a mobile phone from his inside pocket. 'Here,' he says, and tosses it, under-arm. She drops the basket. Catches the phone.

A call is active. The screen shows that it has been listening in for the past ten minutes.

She raises the phone to her ear.

'Ms Zahavi,' comes a voice. 'My name's Candy. I want to talk to you about Jude.'

Betsy finds herself muttering something incomprehensible. She feels silly, and lost. She wants to run back to the woods and feel the forest close around her.

'He's really not what you think he is,' says Candy, and her elongated vowels mark her out as somebody for whom money has rarely been a problem. It makes Betsy feel like a housemaid in contrast, as if she should be carrying a silver tray and dropping into curtseys; forbidden from eye contact with the owner of this rich, imperious voice.

'I know exactly what he is,' she replies, looking at Brendon, who gives a shrug of apology. 'He's what I want.'

'Yes, well, he does make a good first impression.'

'You don't, love. You come across as a stuck-up cow.'

The words surprise Betsy, who had not known she was about to speak until the words were already leaving her lips. She plays them back in her head. She suddenly knows, with absolute certainty, what he means to her. She's not just in love with him – she's addicted.

'Maeve thought that,' says Candy, with a soft laugh. 'And Maeve's dead.'

'It was an accident – we've spoken about it . . .'

'No,' says Candy, flatly. 'No, you haven't. There are things you need to know. I'm trying to be a good neighbour. My husband's staff have some very strong feelings about Jude and it is only by my good graces that they are resisting carrying out my husband's instructions to the letter. I believe I am at the very least owed a reciprocal gesture. That gesture is half an hour of your time, and perhaps a glass of something refreshing. I will be at the Lord Crewe in Blanchland at three p.m. So will you.'

Betsy doesn't like the way she's being spoken to. Her face twists in anger. 'I will, will I? Look I don't know what you think you're doing but I know all about your little crush on my boyfriend and the way your prick of a husband has been trying to run him out of this place and I think it all sounds horribly ugly. I can give your man here a little cash as a gesture on Jude's behalf until we sort something out long-term, a payment plan, or some-thing, but as for becoming best buddies and meeting to compare Jude stories, you're out of your mind. He'll be back any moment—'

'No he won't. He has a job over at Whitley Chapel. He'll be gone until this evening.'

'No . . . no . . . you don't get to know more than me about my boyfriend,' spits Betsy, colour rising in her cheeks.

'I know a great deal, Elizabeth,' says Candy. 'The Lord Crewe. Three p.m.'

'You're off your head, love,' spits Betsy. She looks around her, gazing out across the valley; the rise and fall of stone walls, abandoned farms; the green-and-brown patchwork of land honeycombed with old mine workings. She feels a million miles from any kind of life she understands. 'Anyway, how do I get there?'

In the chair, the man raises his hands, palms up – a shrug that says 'sorry – I'm under instructions'.

'You'll go with Brendon, of course,' says Candy, sweetly. 'And his friends. Rough gentlemen, but from what I've heard, that's just what you're in the market for.'

The line goes dead.

Betsy stands still, open-mouthed and furious. 'You don't think

I'm really going with you?' she asks Brendon, bending down to pick up her spilled flowers. She feels dizzy. Nauseous. She looks up, and he's standing there, legs apart, towering over her; the sun obscuring his features.

'Yeah,' he says. 'Yeah, I do.'

THIRTY

Betsy is pushed up against the glass of the van; the man beside her stretching out his legs and pinning her against the door. She isn't complaining out loud but on the inside she's fantasizing about what she would do in the event of a sudden crash. He's not wearing a seatbelt and she keeps picturing him going through the glass and skidding along the country road in a spray of pinks and reds and shattered bones. She likes the idea of sitting down, cross-legged, and watching him breathe his last; smiling as he begs, raspily, for her to go fetch help.

'You been here before?'

This from Brendon, at the wheel. He's tried to engage her in conversation throughout the half-hour journey across the steep moors and winding, forested roads. She's given him little in the way of acknowledgement.

'Nice place,' he says, cheerily. 'You should get Punch to bring you here for a feed one night. They do cocktails. He'll know that, of course. Very much a regular, though there aren't many pubs around here that haven't enjoyed his patronage from time to time.'

'Fancy though,' says the man beside her, nastily. 'You need to dress up a bit. Can't wander in any old how.' He sniffs the air, theatrically. 'Maybe a wash and brush-up, know what I'm saying?'

Betsy changes her position so she can look at him properly. He's got bad skin. Blackheads across his nose and something like a boil peeking out of his hairline.

'I'd insult you back, but I'd tire before I ran out of things to say,' says Betsy, flatly.

In the driving seat, Brendon lets out a laugh. 'Told you, Tench. Told you she was a livewire.'

'You told me she threw herself at you,' says Tench, nastily. He glares at Betsy. 'Reckoned you were a cat on heat. That right, love? You a cat on heat? Bit of a slag, are you? Not happy unless you're flattening grass or banging your head off a cistern in a disabled toilet, eh?'

'I don't know, Tench,' says Betsy, looking at him with disdain. She's not frightened of this one. Compared to the man she met at the pharmacy, he's as intimidating as mince. 'I do know that you have the look of somebody who spends a lot of time wanking into a sock.'

'You're a bitch,' hisses Tench.

'And you have a limited vocabulary, you spotty little twat.'

'Here we are,' says Brendon, as they emerge from a tunnel of tall trees and into an impossibly perfect village. 'I'm sorry to say we've arrived at our destination. Shame. I was enjoying that.'

Blanchland is every inch a filmset: a flickerpad of sturdy, honey-coloured cottages; matching red doors and elegant hanging baskets, all holding hands around the high, crenelated rectangle of the village pub. There are a few cars parked on what passes for the main street but they look like anachronisms in this setting. Horses should be tethered here; footmen in gleaming livery should be standing beside lacquered coaches; men with splendid whiskers should be sitting outside the alehouse, supping from pewter tankards and admiring the ankles of serving girls hurrying to the wash house.

'Told you,' says Brendon, to Betsy. 'When you get home, tell him you like it here. Make a fuss. Pout a bit. Always works for my wife. Can't say no, can I? She can wrap me around her little finger. Bet you can do the same with Punch, eh?'

She flicks a hard stare at him as he manoeuvres into a parking space, tucked in between a Porsche Boxster and a Maserati. Betsy doesn't know much about cars but she can tell what's expensive. 'Punch?' she asks, tired of hearing the word.

'Come on, love – Jude. Judy. Punch and . . .'

'Oh. Right. Didn't know he had a nickname.'

'It's not a nickname,' says Tench. 'You don't say it to his face unless you want trouble.'

Betsy shakes her head. 'I don't think that's his problem with you, Tench,' she says, staring out at the square. The glass is dusty and fly-smeared and turns the warm blue day into a view that is foggy and storm-laden. She reaches for the handle, eager to be out of the vehicle. She realizes she still has Tench's attention. 'He's not some thug who just hits people for no reason. Any problems you've had with him are because you've brought them on yourself. He's one man against all of you.'

'Have you heard this?' laughs Tench, addressing his comments to Brendon. 'Poor old Punch, eh? Being picked on by the nasty men. Jesus, you've swallowed everything he's fed you, haven't you?'

'How am I getting home?' she asks Brendon, ignoring the man between them.

'I reckon you can afford a taxi,' he says, apologetically. 'Whether you can get one is anybody's guess. Anyhow, don't keep her waiting. She's inside.'

Betsy realizes she's being dismissed. She gives her nastiest smile and pushes open the door. It bangs against the panel of the Porsche. She turns back to Brendon, whose eyes are closed, shaking his head. 'Soz,' she says, and slams the door so hard she nearly falls with the effort.

On the street, she stands still, considering her options. No phone. No purse. No way of contacting Jude. And inside the bar, a woman who fancies her man and wants to tell her all sorts of horrible things. She realizes that even if she should turn away from the pub and start walking away in the general direction of home, she would always regret not hearing her out. She has never been able to resist an impulse. Curiosity; a bloody-minded need to know, has been her prime motivator her whole life.

'Bugger it,' she mumbles, and crosses the road.

There's something distinctly forbidding about the door to The Crypt Bar. It's a big, studded slab of oak set in an ancient stone archway. Betsy has to put her weight behind it, hampered by the dangling roots and creepers of the colossal hanging basket that droops down beneath the big metal sign, creaking like a gibbet. The cool of the old stonework enfolds her as she makes her way down the ancient steps and through another cloistered arch, emerging in a small, narrow bar. It's a grand but comfortable space: stained-glass windows and high-backed wooden chairs made comfortable with squashy tweed cushions and woollen throws. At the bar, a trio of men in matching camouflage sup from chunky pint glasses; two gundogs asleep at their booted feet, trying to absorb some of the chill from the flagstones. Above, a wrought-iron hoop, the sort that should contain candles. Its likeness is reflected in the mirror behind the bar, almost obscured by the row upon row of high-class gins and mixers. Betsy fancies this is not the sort of pub that serves Carling, although she's briefly encouraged by the sight of a huge jar of pickled eggs at the far end. She squints. Double-takes, disappointed as she realizes it's just water, full of wedges of lemon and lime.

'Ah, good, you survived.'

Betsy spins in the direction of the voice. It takes an effort of will to keep herself from bursting out laughing. Candy is not at all what she had pictured. She had imagined a tall, swan-necked femme fatale: golden hair and pearls, costly breasts and teeth like sugar cubes; the sort who looks good testing the flex of a horsewhip and never feels like a tit when ordering Pimm's. Betsy hasn't prepared herself for the reality. The woman before her is pushing sixty and has the kind of rum-dark, sun-hardened skin that calls to mind disinterred mummies and bog bodies. Peperami, at a push. She's grey; her hair a mess of jagged cuts and haphazard scissor-strokes: her fringe snipped back almost to the hairline. She wears a blue T-shirt, exposing strong, wiry arms, and her sturdy, weather-beaten legs stick out from faded shorts, roped with thick veins. She wears sturdy sandals; their soles thick with crusted mud. She's drinking Guinness and there is a paperback novel, splayed at the spine, face down on the wooden table. She's smiling, but if she covered the lower half of her face with her hand it would be impossible to tell her state of mind from looking at her eyes.

'I would stand up but I've had a few and can't find the energy to be unnecessarily courteous – I hope that doesn't start us off on the wrong footing.'

Betsy glances towards the men at the bar. They have the look of experienced eavesdroppers. If they've heard Candy's opening gambit they aren't going to spoil their afternoon's entertainment by alerting her to the fact that her volume is set a good few notches above 'discreet'.

'I don't think that's what will sour it,' says Betsy, her volume matching Candy's. 'I would ask if you want a drink but seeing as your blokes picked me up without even letting me get my purse, I guess this one's on you.'

Candy smiles, pleased with the riposte. She looks past her. 'Freddie!'

From behind the bar, a good-looking man with a shaved head and nice spectacles pops up like a jack-in-the-box. 'Yes, yes, yes,' he says, in a thick French accent. He looks rather smart in his collarless shirt and healthy tan. 'Aha, my lady, my maharina, I did not hear the door – you walk like a ninja, yes – you wear rabbits on your toes, I think, yes, yes, yes . . .'

'Something fabulous for my friend here,' says Candy, giving the barman an indulgent smile. 'Enough to make her comfortable but not horizontal, if you catch me.'

Freddie gives a big smile. 'Oh yes, I understand, and as you English say, "challenge accepted".' He sounds like an Englishman doing a bad impression of a Parisian motivational-speaker, all big movements and huge vowels. He's so French it seems like he's putting it on.

'We don't say that,' mutters Candy, to herself. 'I mean, we do, but it's not exactly a saying.' She shakes the thought away. Looks up, brightly.

'What do you want?' asks Betsy.

'Sit yourself down,' instructs Candy, pushing a small, uphol-stered stool across the floor towards her; wood screeching against stone. Petulant, huffing, Betsy plonks herself down. Gives Candy a hard look. She's more curious than cross. Wants to know what the hell is going on.

'So,' says Betsy. 'I'm here. Can't say I'm happy about it but I'm trying to tell myself that country folk have country ways, and maybe this is normal.'

Candy raises her glass. Takes a pull of Guinness and wipes her mouth with the back of her hand. She looks at her guest appraisingly, making Betsy feel like a paint-blackened carthorse inspected by a trainer of thoroughbreds.

'Shall I strip?' asks Betsy, unpleasantly. 'Do a little dance? I could lie down and you could do a brass-rubbing . . .'

'He was right about you,' says Candy, decisively. 'Pretty as a picture. Bit common, but something in there worth polishing.'

'Common? You can go fu—'

Freddie the barman appears from nowhere, proffering a tall glass full of a near-luminous orange concoction, garlanded with fruit, paper straws and crushed ice. 'Et voila, mademoiselle,' he says, with a flourish. 'Do not ask me the secret ingredient, eh? But tell me if you enjoy – I put on my list to give special customers.'

Betsy, mentally off-balanced, takes a sip through the paper straw. It's potent and fruity and makes her mouth water. 'Fab,' she says. 'Tastes a bit like Skittles.'

'Mademoiselle?' asks Freddie, unsure. 'Skittles? Like in tenpin bowling? I not understand . . .'

'Run along, Fred,' says Candy. 'Grown-ups are talking.'

He does as instructed. Bows, like a footman. Betsy gets the impression that everybody does as instructed when it's Candy giving the orders.

'He said I was pretty?' asks Betsy, surprising herself. 'Jude?'

Candy grins. 'Smitten, he was. Deep smit. Never seen him like that for anyone, though he's not one who tends to give much away.'

The choice of tense jars with Betsy. 'Like that, you said. What, moved on already, has he? Had his fun? That's what you want to tell me, is it? Is this going to get all playground? You've been tasked with telling me it's all over, have you? Wants me gone? Found somebody else?'

Betsy realizes that the very thought of it is an agony like no other. A fist is squeezing at her heart, a foot on her throat. She feels sick and lost and her cheeks burn.

'I need to speak to him,' she says, gabbling. 'He doesn't need to do this. We're meant, I know it. Whatever I did wrong, I can do it differently. How am I supposed to know . . .'

Across the table Candy starts tapping her solitary gold ring against the wood, the sound getting louder with each beat. Betsy stops talking, realizing how mad she must sound. Takes a slurp of drink and has to fight to stop it coming straight back up her gullet.

'My goodness but he knows how to pick them,' says Candy, shaking her head. 'Not quite so full of histrionics as Maeve, but then you haven't been with him as long, have you? Maybe this time next year you'll be as much of a howler monkey as she was.'

'Maeve?' asks Betsy, wiping her nose with her sleeve. 'Is that what this is about? Because if you're going to say he killed her then I don't want to hear it.'

Candy rolls her eyes. 'You have your suspicions, do you?'

Betsy screws up her face. 'I have no reason to doubt him about anything.'

'No, but you do,' says Candy, her voice dropping a little. 'There's a voice in your head says there's something wrong. You don't believe everything he says. You've got a million questions but you don't want to ask them in case the answers pop the fantasy, am I right?'

'You don't know me,' says Betsy, scratching at her arms. She doesn't notice how hard she is scratching until red welts start to appear on her skin. Panicking, she covers the affected area with her palm. When her skin goes red it shows the white lines she carved on herself in her teens: each fine white scar a reminder of past pain.

'I know Jude,' says Candy, simply. 'Known him since he moved in with Maeve. By God she was into him. Obsessed doesn't even cover it. Never seemed the sort for a relationship – liked being a free spirit too much – but she fell for him the way animals do. Hungry. Savage. Willing to fight and die to safeguard their territory.'

Betsy feels her stomach heave. Sips at her drink then pushes the liquid back down the straw rather than swallow it.

'He fell for her too, of course,' says Candy. 'Must have done to come and move in to that knackered old place. She never saw what other people saw when it came to the bastle. Thought she was a queen in a fairy tale if you ask me. Half-killed herself making it habitable and did things she wouldn't thank me for talking about in order to get permission to build.'

Betsy catches her eye. 'Your husband, you mean?' she asks, pink spots burning on her cheeks. 'Toad of Toad Hall?'

'Touché,' says Candy, raising her glass in salute. 'He's told you about that, has he? Ah, he must have fallen for you properly if he's opened up about all that nasty, mucky business. Yes, it would be fair to say Campion and I come at life from different directions, though we do meet in the middle from time to time. I believe that's known as successful marriage. I keep him from indulging to excess, I think. Marriage keeps him relatively respectable, though he does enjoy himself when opportunity arises and I have the good grace not to mention it. He's grateful for that. For me. Most of my advice pays off, in the end.'

'So romantic,' sneers Betsy, feeling the scars sing with pain beneath her hand. 'You should write romances.'

'It wasn't a match made in heaven,' says Candy, licking her lips. She has strange eyes, up close. They're bigger than they should be, as if somebody has drawn a person from a description alone. There's a stillness about her that Betsy finds unnerving. It seems as if she's conserving energy for when it might be required.

'Why do I care about you and your husband?'

'Maeve and Jude – not Campion and I. She was very set in her ways and he was . . . well, I suppose you would say it all got a little Lady Chatterley for a time. She always rather looked upon him like he was a servant who'd done well. She was from old money, was Maeve. Good stock. Turned her back on it, but it was still all boarding school and lacrosse and humping on the riverbank with the sons of curates and cabinet ministers. Living in squalor didn't change that. And she was jealous beyond anything you can imagine. Wouldn't leave him be. Wouldn't trust him. I was her friend, as much as she had such a thing, and there was no comforting her. She convinced herself he was screwing half the valley.'

Betsy can't help herself. 'And was he?'

'Not then, no,' she says, without softening her delivery. 'After she died, he was like a prisoner let out on day release. Broke a few hearts. Flattened a lot of grass, shall we say. But he really did try to make things work with her, even as she treated him like he was something she ordered in the post.'

Betsy glances towards the bar. One of the men has gone. One of the dogs, too. Freddie, polishing a glass, gives a somewhat incongruous wave.

'This is what you wanted to tell me?' asks Betsy, at last. 'That his relationship sucked and that he's shagged half the valley? Well, thanks. For the drink, too. Think I'll leave it there.' She starts to rise, tempted to run. Candy waves her back into her seat, mildly exasperated.

'Just wait a moment, will you?' asks Candy. 'Jesus, no wonder he's looking all doe-eyed and dozy – poor sod's brain is probably battered insensible. Look, just be quiet for a moment and listen, OK? Jude and I have a sort of understanding. I don't want to sound like a Smart Alec but here's the thing – I'm a lot cleverer than most people. I don't ask to be this way, but one doesn't get to pick one's strengths and weaknesses.'

'No, one fucking doesn't—'

'Maeve was a very intelligent lady as well,' says Candy, without pausing. 'One of the cleverest I've known. Bookish. Would have made a wonderful lecturer had she taken that path. Taught Campion a thing or two, and not just to get her own way over the planning application.'

'Good for her,' mumbles Betsy.

'She thought she'd got a bit of rough in Jude. He's tough, you've spotted that, I presume. Fists like hammers. You know in the old cowboy films when the new kid tries to make a name for themselves by challenging the old gunslinger? Jude's had that since he was growing up on his dad's farm. People have always wanted a piece of him. That's men for you. Just apes in shoes. She knew that about him, right enough. Maeve, I mean. Knew he was a bit handy to have around the place. Introduced him to me and I expected to see this great bruiser of a fellow. Saw through it all in about five seconds. He's smarter than she ever was. Smarter than me. You can see it in his eyes.'

Betsy stays silent, unsure whether to be proud or angry.

Across the table, Candy is lost in memory. 'I watched him in here one night,' she says, dreamily. 'There was a party of American academics in – we get a lot of them here, hiking the Roman wall and looking for their roots. Chess players. That was how they knew each other. Good ones too. Maeve had been a whiz at university so she challenged them to a friendly match. Beat three in a row and then came up against this loudmouth with a beard who loved nothing more than talking himself up. He backed it up, too. Wiped the floor with her. Jude sat there, barely speaking, watching as this big-mouth beat his partner eight games in a row. He'd have let her carry on losing if she hadn't had one of her episodes. She couldn't accept she was losing, and Jude did his best to mollify her. He said she hadn't lost. She'd kicked their arses and now she'd had one too many drinks to be at her best. And Big-Mouth laughed at him. Said he was pronouncing the word wrong. Said it was 'asses'. Jude was calm as you like. Told him he'd play him, if he had no objections. Winner would pay for the other's bar tab. Ordered himself a bottle of sixteen-year-old malt from the cellar, just to show he was serious. Then he told the Americans that if they were really as confident as they seemed, he'd play them all at once. The bar staff rustled up six boards and all the Americans chucked money in the pot. Jude took them all on.'

'Seriously?' asks Betsy. She can't stop herself smiling.

Candy grins at the memory. 'Won inside twenty minutes. They couldn't understand it. They thought he'd cheated somehow but there was no way to prove it.'

'They paid his tab?'

'Tried to weasel out of it but the locals weren't having that. Drank like kings and queens that night, I tell you.'

Betsy chews her lip. 'I didn't know he played.'

Candy shakes her head as if sorry for her. 'I don't think you know very much about Jude other than the fact you go all wibbly on the inside when he looks at you. But I *know* him. I know he's always half a dozen steps ahead of everybody else. I know he wasn't happy with Maeve, but I don't believe any of the rumours that he killed her. She died because something in her head broke. If Jude had wanted her dead, there wouldn't have been any suspicion. He's the sort who could get away with murder without a stain on his character.' She pauses, seemingly unsure whether to continue. 'I've warned Campion to let things drop. He doesn't believe me about Jude. That's why I want you to talk to him.'

'To Campion?'

'No, to Jude. That's why I wanted to talk to you.' She spreads her hands on the table. 'Look, it was as much of a shock to Jude as it was to everybody else that Maeve left him the house and the land. Campion thought he was doing him a good turn by offering to take it off him for a decent price but he played it all completely wrong. Told him things nobody should hear about their dear departed. And Jude, God love him, well he's his own worst enemy. Stubborn as a bull that won't go through a gate.

He told Campion he owed him nothing. Told him to do his worst. Gave him a little bit of a bloodied nose.'

Betsy finishes her drink. Shivers. 'What, figuratively, you mean?'

'No, I mean he smacked him like he was a puppy who'd pissed on the carpet. Campion doesn't get treated that way. Only person who doesn't do what Campion says is me, and I've earned that particular right. And ever since, Campion's had one thing in his mind – getting Jude out of the bastle, whatever the cost. I've been stuck as peacemaker. I've always got on with Jude, much as my husband hates our friendship. I've tried time and again to get him to see sense – accept a decent offer and go start again somewhere. He won't have it. He's driving himself mad.'

'Your husband?'

'No, Jude. For months he didn't sleep. Up all night guarding his property, setting traps down by the river, neglecting the animals. It half-killed me seeing him like that and it was worse knowing it was my own family causing the mischief. It was my idea to get him to come work at the estate – to try to mend some bridges – but that all led to trouble. Jude knows the way things should be done and my husband, unfortunately, doesn't like being told when he's wrong – least of all by somebody who's given him a thump. It all ended terribly – some of Campion's men from the city heard they could get in his good books by walloping Jude, and Jude didn't cooperate. Put them on their backsides. Then he took a chainsaw to the big oak – the one that's stood in the grounds of our home since the Wars of the Roses. He didn't even lose his temper. Just carved his initials in the bark and stuck the chainsaw in like Excalibur. It's still there: a rusty handle sticking out to remind Campion that he'd been shown up. Again.'

Betsy pushes her hair from her face. Wonders if she has earned another drink.

'You've made him whole again,' says Candy, not unkindly. 'That night he sat in here texting you all those soppy messages – I was the friend he was neglecting. He told me you'd wrapped yourself around him like ivy. Said as soon as he looked at you, he knew. And I swear, he's been sprightly as a newborn foal these past few months. That's why I know he'll listen to you.'

'Listen to me about what?'

'He needs to come clean,' says Candy, and the plummy tones sound momentarily strangled, as if there is some peach-stone of emotion wedged in her trachea. 'Things can be fixed. We'll still pay a decent price and we can take his secret to the grave but he has a family, Elizabeth. People who deserve to know the truth.'

Betsy feels as though she is reading a book and has turned over two pages at once. Her face twists in confusion. 'You've lost me.'

Candy, agitated, rummages around in the small bag at her side and removes her mobile phone. She thumbs at the keys and then slides it to Betsy. She puts it on speakerphone and presses 'play'.

'. . . no more warnings. No more cautions. This is final. You come on my land, or knock on my door, or look at me or mine in a way I find objectionable, and I will burn your house to the ground. I will turn you into ashes and fucking bone. Send as many of your lads as you can afford and I'll send you them back a piece at a time. Cut your losses. And tell Mick Hewson and his brother to say their goodbyes. He's going in the ground . . .'

Betsy feels cold fingers running across her skin. She can't seem to catch her breath. It had been Jude, but at the same time it had been somebody completely alien. His words sound not so much a threat as an unmistakable prophesy of what will follow. Her mind is a blur of pictures and projections. When did he leave the message? It must have been after the fight at the pharmacy. He'd needed to put himself back together. To stand tall after what he viewed as a humiliation. What else might he have done in order to avenge a loss?

'They've both played nasty,' says Betsy, quietly. 'He doesn't mean it—'

'Mick hasn't been seen for fifteen days,' says Candy, retrieving her phone. 'His family are about one more day from going to the police. They understand the value of silence but they want answers. I can hold them back. I can stop them. All they need to know is where he is and then we can come up with a story that saves everybody's blushes. You can sell up, start again – but you need to show Jude this is the only option open to him. His brother . . . look, just give him a different future. The only other way is more pain, more bloodshed, and him going away for however many . . .'

There is a sudden thud just beyond the arch; a sound like a
bag of potatoes falling from a height. Tench tumbles backward
through the door, nose bleeding, bloody spit on his chin:
pinwheeling over in a crash of chair legs. There is a squeak, as
if somebody has stepped on a mouse, and then the black gundog
is skittering across the flagstones, yelping as if beaten with a
stick.

Jude follows. His face is grey; there's darkness beneath his
eyes. He's panting, as if he ran here. Betsy spies the red on
his knuckles. Sees his fists, still clenched . . .

'You don't talk to her,' says Jude to Candy, his teeth grinding
together, jaw bulging at the hinge. 'You don't talk to me. You
stay away. Your men – they stay away. Your men's dogs – they
stay away. A leaf from one of your trees blows across my garden
and I swear to God I will bring it back and stuff a branch down
your throat. You've played this wrong, Candy. So fucking wrong.
There is now a gap on the map. My land. Mine. And by Christ
if you stumble into it by accident then I will hurt you until your
bones feel like damp cement.'

Candy begins to stand. All of her poise, her confidence, has
left her. 'Jude, please, I have to try . . . this is becoming too
much . . . she deserves to know the truth . . .'

Jude turns away from her. Looks at Betsy, eyes aflame. 'Do
you want to come home?'

She doesn't hesitate. Nods. Takes his hand in hers. She feels
the stickiness of freshly-spilled blood, and rubs at it with her
thumb, staining her own skin.

'Jude, please . . .'

Candy is starting to stand. A look from Jude puts her back in
her seat. He swivels back to the bar. Freddy gives the slightest
of nods.

Tench is starting to get to his feet. Jude's face twists in anger:
an animal sighting a wounded foe. He takes a step towards him,
bringing his boot back like a rugby player attempting a penalty.

'Jude, don't . . .'

He turns back at the sound of Betsy's voice. Gives a little nod
of thanks, as if she's saved him from himself. Then leads her
back up the stairs and out into the light.

THIRTY-ONE

E vening comes and goes. Betsy says little. Jude tries to make her laugh. Tries to stroke her shoulders as she sits, static, at the kitchen table. She flinches as if touching cold metal. He offers a massage. Asks if she wants tea, or cake, or whether she would like a hot bath. Perhaps he could read to her. He writes a poem – dashing off a few lines about the way her mouth reminds him of ripe fruit; his longing to reach up to pluck her juicy lips from the vine. She gives a dead-eyed smile and returns to her position: a statue glaring at the same whorls in the old wooden table.

He doesn't lose his temper. Keeps himself busy, pottering about the house and the garden. Takes a bath. Shaves himself a goatee, the way she had suggested, off-the-cuff, a couple of weeks back. Changes into one of the stripey collarless shirts that she always seems to like peeling off him. She barely registers the change to his appearance. Doesn't even look up as he takes down the saxophone from the hook on the wall and plays the solo from 'Careless Whisper' – something she has been begging him to do since that first night.

Eventually, beaten, he takes himself to bed. Her bed. When she does not join him, he pads down the hall and returns to his own room, climbing under sheets that have grown cold these past weeks.

A little after two a.m., she comes and sits on the foot of the bed. Watches him. He's not breathing right. He's not asleep. He's just lying there in the dark. She can hear the din of his thoughts even over the racket of jumbled conversations playing in her own head. She'd feel sorry for him, if she were capable of feeling anything.

'This is how it's going to be, is it?' she asks, in a voice she barely recognizes.

He struggles upright, reaching out to click on the bedside lamp. It illuminates a room that still carries traces of Maeve. African batiks on the wall; little perfume bottles on the dresser; patterned sleeves dangling out of the coffin-sized ottoman at the foot of the bed. Her books are still piled up against one wall; academic tomes and biographies of people Betsy hasn't heard of. She feels overcome with loathing for the woman who used to sleep here; who built this place; who used to curl up with Betsy's man in this big brass bed; who climbed on to him and slipped under him and bent over in front of him as fancy took her. It makes her want to set fire to the bed. Makes her want to burn the whole place to the ground and piss on the ashes. She is not Betsy, now. Not Liz. She is the teenager that got taken away because her mum used to beat the shit out of her and used her as a debit machine to pay off her creditors. Each time she let some nasty, sweaty man touch her in places she shouldn't be touched, Mum owed a tenner less. Usually, the sex hurt less than the beating she would receive if she acted up. Usually. Not always.

'Betsy, I know this must have been the most horrible day . . .'

'I don't want to hear it,' she says, flatly. 'No. You listen to me.'

He seems to bristle a little, unused to being spoken to like this. She delights in the feeling. Seizes on it; a dog chewing on a heart. 'Feeling pissed off, Mr Punch? Not like being talked to like that by your fairy-tale princess? Yeah, welcome to reality.'

He looks like he wants to speak. Presses his lips together in case anything comes out that can't be unsaid. She knows, now – knows for a fact that he's been reading the *how-to* guides. He's been on the BPD forums, just like Jay. Been trying to work out how best to manage the unmanageable; to get his half-mad, half-bitch girlfriend to toe the line and behave like a normal human being. She hates him, suddenly. Hates him completely. It is as if there are spiky tree branches pushing out through her ribs and through her skin; as though she is transforming into something that is all sharp edges and snarled roots.

'Betsy, just look at me, sweetheart – I've been trying to talk and you won't listen.'

'Is that what you called her?' she spits. 'Maeve? Your sweetheart. Or what about all the others, eh?'

'Betsy, listen to yourself,' he says, moving towards her.

She lashes out, cat-like. 'Stay the fuck back. Mr Punch, isn't it? Yeah, makes sense now. You knew what it meant and you didn't tell me.'

'I didn't want to scare you . . .' he begins. 'We've talked about this . . .'

He's looking exasperated now. Looks close to rolling his eyes. She needs to push him that bit further – needs to get the reaction that will prove her right in despising him.

'I've heard things,' she says, and she is clenching her jaw so tightly that she barely moves her lips as she growls at him. Her eyes are hot pokers. He disgusts her, now, sitting there letting her talk to him like this. Why doesn't he stand up for himself? Why doesn't he tell her she's a nasty bitch and boot her out the door?

'Don't go down this road, Betsy,' he says, quietly. 'I don't deserve all this. You're all I care about, I swear.'

She shakes her head, appalled at his weakness. 'Jay came to visit me,' she says, with a flourish and nasty leer. 'Today. Dropped off my stuff and delighted in telling me what a disgrace of a human being I was. Did it in front of Anya too, just so the one person who actually thinks I'm worth something gets to see the truth.'

'Jay came here? Did he touch you? Hurt you?'

'Oh yeah, that's right, get all fucking alpha male on me. You can do that, can't you, Mr Punch? You can hurt people, as if that's something to be proud of. Well, he got to see as Brendon and his mates picked me up like I was a parcel and then dropped me off for my little sit-down with that grotesque little gargoyle who thinks the sun shines out of your arse. And oh yeah, she told me things. Things that have made me realize what an idiot I've been. How reckless and irresponsible I was coming here instead of listening to Carly. I don't know you and I've just let myself be hoodwinked again. I always said I'd never be so stupid to let myself be led astray and let my heart do the talking. I knew in the beginning it was off. All the bullshit about waiting and not pressuring me into doing anything I'd regret later was all just to seem the perfect guy . . .'

'Betsy, you need to slow down – this is all coming out of nowhere.'

She presses on, ignoring him. She's not even speaking to him now. Just letting words smash together in the air; all venom and rage. 'You knew how to be exactly the opposite of everything that had come before – to seem as though you were right. I know I'm a shitty person for going and digging around but you are such a closed book!'

He starts shaking his head. She can see him fighting with himself. He knows the right thing to say is nothing at all but he's so bloody cocksure of his own power to make everything better that he's going to ignore everything he's read. He's going to say it, she thinks. He's going to blame the BPD.

'Betsy,' he says, softly. 'Please, look . . . do you not think maybe some of this is down to your condition? I mean, it's textbook splitting, isn't it? Something's triggered you and now all this venom's pouring out and I know it has to go in one direction and I'd rather you threw it at me than at yourself but maybe if you just lay down for a bit and let me talk to you properly you'd feel differently. We've got such a good thing going, it doesn't have to be like this.'

The scream that erupts from Betsy's throat is a roar of pure, unadulterated rage. She has never felt so disgusted, so let down. How dare he! How dare he suggest that she is not really feeling what she thinks she's feeling! She sees at once how he is even more controlling than Jay. Every time he tells her he likes her in a certain outfit; likes her hair a certain way – he's trying to mould her. To make her something she's not. He even dressed her in his dead wife's clothes! Suddenly she cannot stand to be here. She needs to be alone. To think. And sleep. She's bone-tired, suddenly, her eyes red and aching. She needs to sleep. She looks at him, eyes half-closed, and decides that tomorrow will do. The bed looks comfy. Jude looks all sort of grumpy and sad: little marcasite tears sparkling on his dark eyes. She suddenly wants to be held. Wants nothing more than to fold herself inside his arms. She slithers up the bed. Pushes his arms apart with her head. Lays a cheek against his chest and feels the beat of his heart. She is asleep in moments.

Jude lies still as a corpse. He doesn't want the breeze to change direction. Doesn't want to summon up whatever vibration in the atmosphere caused her to turn into the raging, vengeful facsimile. Only when he knows she is fast asleep does he slide, silently, out of bed. He dresses without a word. Doesn't make a sound as he moves down the stairs. Calls Marshall with the faintest click of his tongue. Freewheels the Land Rover down the track and doesn't fire the ignition until he's far enough away from the bastle not to be heard.

His hands, on the steering wheel, white as snow.

He is home before Betsy wakes. She looks embarrassed. Sorrowful. She holds him and he holds her and they both agree to try harder. He will talk more, she will listen more. It will get better. It will be like it was before.

At eleven thirty, while she is making conciliatory cheese scones, the landline rings. It's Anya. There's been an accident. A terrible accident. Jay's dead.

THIRTY-TWO

Now

hristmas is coming.

C Above the valley, a full, ice-white moon: a drunken eye peeping through a curtain of sugar-sprinkled black.

Inside the bastle, Betsy hunched over the laptop, Scrooge-like in her robe and fingerless gloves, stopping from time to time to warm her hands on her mug. In the grate, the fire is a rippling collage of reds and golds.

Jude, pulling on his boots, fastening his padded work shirt and polishing off a bacon sandwich, flicking the crust for Marshall. At his belt, the knife. The handle is made from reindeer antler and the blade sits in a soft, deer-hide sheath. Unsheathed, the blade is so sharp that the air around it appears to hum.

'Love you.'

'Love you back.'

She listens to the echoes of his departure, her heart beating faster, harder, increasing in intensity with each step he takes away from where she can see him, hear him, feel him. She listens, trying to steal one last echo of his footsteps from the uncooperative air. Hears Marshall, barking. The new chickens: clucking and squawking their way across the damp yard. The quad, its soft roar echoing in the still valley air. And then she is alone. Alone, with the voices in her head.

What the fuck has happened to Mick? Why hasn't he made good on his threats?

Then, coldly: he's killed him, you silly girl. he's killed him, like he killed his wife . . .

She sits at the kitchen table, staring at the laptop. Jude brought it home a month ago. Second-hand, but restored to its factory settings, so he claimed. She recognizes it, of course. She has no doubts about its origin. She unearthed it from the hole beneath the floorboards weeks ago. If he's given her it as some kind of test, she passed with flying colours. Her face didn't betray her, and there was nothing in his expression to suggest he was doing something sly. She doesn't know when he pried up the floorboards but she has grown used to the idea that he can do things and get away with them.

Betsy's only money is still the untouched four thousand pounds from Campion. It lingers in the biscuit barrel by the sink. She intends to take it back to her bastard benefactor when she finds the right moment. She's looking forward to throwing it in his fat smug face and telling him he can keep his filthy bribe. She's been imagining it ever since watching the video – he and Maeve, rutting at the riverbank, tears and sweat and face contorted in passion and pain. She knows that giving the money back will make Jude happy. He hasn't so much as taken a biscuit from the barrel since she tucked the cash away – as if to do so would risk contamination. But she does rather like having it handy. Her mother has only ever given her three useful pieces of advice: don't rely on the withdrawal method as a contraceptive; don't shave your legs above the knee, and always have access to enough stashed cash for a train ticket and a night in a hotel.

She picks up her mug of tea and realizes it's gone cold. Sets about refilling the kettle and placing it back on the stove, building up the heat in the Rayburn with another fistful of coals. She glances up at the clock – the one she found at the bottom of the bin liners that Jay had brought her the day before his accident. It's an Alice in Wonderland timepiece; childish, blue and rather lovely. It doesn't fit in with the faded grandeur of the Georgian and Regency furniture but it's hers, and it matters to her.

The accident . . .

She grips the tabletop, overcome by a familiar wave of anxiety. Sweat oozes out through her pores. She takes a deep breath and exhales as slowly as she can. It emerges ragged, rasping. Spots dance in front of her eyes.

No, she tells herself. *Don't. Don't think about it. It wasn't your fault. It was an accident. An accident!*

It's been weeks since Jay went into the garage to tinker with his beloved car. Autumn has made way for winter; the trunks of the trees cold as slate and a hazy, cobwebby mist huddles in the valley like milk in a saucer. She isn't sure if she's grieved for her ex yet. Isn't sure whether she should, or if she has any right to. She's run the details of the accident through in her mind countless times but can't stop herself doing so again. Marie has told her what she knows. He hadn't been able to sleep – too churned up over his visit to the bastle, and Anya's desperation to see Betsy. He'd gone to the garage to check that the journey over the dirt tracks and gravelly roads hadn't caused any damage to the underside of the chassis. He'd jacked the big SUV up on his treasured hydraulic pump, providing a crawl space underneath. Conscious of waking the neighbours, he closed the garage door. Turned the key in the ignition. Slid underneath the vehicle and began picking bits of gravel and shrapnel from its innards. All the while the space around him slowly filled with tasteless, colourless fumes. When he began to choke; when his vision began to fade, he tried to haul himself free from the space beneath the car. In so doing, he kicked the handle of the jack.

It was Anya who found the body; legs sticking out like a shop dummy.

Betsy glances again at the clock. It's only 8.04 a.m. Anya will be arriving mid-morning. This is her first overnight stay. She's visited twice. It's gone well. She's enjoyed the animals, visited the dingle, leafed through the old books. Hugged herself into Marshall's sweaty fur. It has done her good, according to her mum. She's got on with Jude better than Betsy expected. He hasn't been awkward or shy. Hasn't said the wrong thing. Just told her details about the local area; the types of trees; the best place to see animals. Anya has listened, and smiled, and laughed at his jokes. Jude never once mentioned Jay. Walked away whenever Betsy brought him up, as if it were none of his business. Anya's doing as well as anybody has the right to expect. She's quieter than she was. More inward-looking; more withdrawn. But the intelligence still sparkles in her eyes and it does Betsy good to know that she somehow appears to be the person most capable of cheering her up.

Ting.

Ting.

She glances at the laptop. The new internet provider has worked some kind of miracle on the broadband fibres and the bastle is now inescapably hooked up to the outside world. Betsy has largely resisted the siren call of social media – not really knowing how to tell her few Facebook friends about the changes to her life these past weeks and months. But she's been back on the BPD forum. Even composed a post about self-sabotage and the compulsion to spoil her own happiness. It's clearly struck a chord. She's receiving thumbs ups and kind words from users across the world, all encouraging her to write more. She thinks she might take their advice, though for now she isn't sure her brain is sufficiently elastic to be pulled in so many directions.

Do it. Do it now. You've earned it . . .

She gives herself a talking to. Tells herself to concentrate on the jobs she's given herself. Buy the goat. Wash up. Put a wash on. Jet-wash the courtyard. Stroll up to the top field and endeavour to fix the sagging wooden poles that are dragging down the gates to the cow field. She doesn't need to do anything else. Anything she looks up online will merely throw white spirit on the embers of paranoia, still smouldering away in her gut. There are so many questions she wants answered and she has no doubt that if she were to ask Jude, he would give her no end of replies. But she doesn't want replies – she wants truths. Certainties. She wants to know if the man she has fallen for is deceiving her.

Admit it, she tells herself. *Admit what you're really afraid of . . .*

She wants to know if Jude is a killer.

She pulls up a search engine. Grabs an unpaid bill from the pile and rummages through the cutlery drawer until she finds a pen. Then she starts to jot down a list of words: names that she's filed in the chaos of her mind.

Campion
Candy/Candace
Maeve
Mick/Michael Hewson
Brendon?

She loses herself for a time, thoroughly absorbed in the task of digging around in the digital world for any clue that could vindicate her paranoia. She finds no shortage of positive press about Campion and Candy: pillars of the community both and largely

responsible for breathing financial oxygen back into the valley.
There's little mention of the methods they have employed or their
rows with tenants over the rent increases. Little on their plans
to open up a site of Special Scientific Interest to grouse hunters
and their guns.

She keeps typing. She allows herself a smile when she finds
something unexpected: a furious, spit-flecked epistle left on a
forum written for and by animal rights activists, principally aimed
at changing the laws on the use of snares. The message was
posted in May, 2017, by a user named DanBrompton, under a
thread entitled 'Still At It – Fat Cats Couldn't Give a Damn':

> Shaking as I write this. Those who know my name will
> probably be rolling their eyes that I'm still surprised by
> people's actions but I have never lost my faith in human
> nature, even after 30 years of campaigning to ban snares
> and hunting with dogs. You may also know I've paid the
> price for my efforts in dismantling snares. 16 convictions
> at the last count, and jail twice for refusing to pay the fines.
> Why should I? I don't agree I'm in the wrong. You might
> also remember that I've taken a few bad beatings when
> I've got on the wrong side of gamekeepers, farmers and the
> various thugs whose job it is to make sure people like me
> don't interfere with rich people's delight in killing animals
> of all shapes and sizes. This weekend I came as close as
> I've ever come to paying the ultimate price for what I
> believe. I know there will be repercussions if I name names
> but this is too important to keep quiet – even if the toadies
> in the Press have refused to listen. I am pointing my finger
> at the owners of the Swinburn Estate: Campion and Candace.
> He's nothing but a thug done good and she'd step over a
> dozen burning babies to go and save her favourite saddle.
> I spend my spare time looking for traps – yes, often on
> private land, why not?! – and on Sunday I had the misfortune
> to find a house cat caught in a snare. The cord had gone
> through to bone and there was a maggot infestation that
> had clearly begun long before the creature died of its injuries.
> I did what the experts say we should and immediately
> phoned the RSPCA and the local police. Police couldn't

care less – all bought and paid for! – and the wildlife protec-
tion officer and me have history so nobody turned up.
Nobody except the assistant gamekeeper Brendon Whistler
and his hired thugs. We've got no shortage of history either!
He's been using the same group of nasty sods to scare off
the saboteurs and the activists for years. Been inside for it
but Campion still keeps him on. I've been wise to what
they're capable of ever since the attack at my property –
another disgusting cover-up. I swear if there hadn't been
some ramblers nearby I wouldn't still be here! Keep up the
good fight. DanB.

Betsy's tea has again gone cold. She reaches into the biscuit
barrel for sustenance and her fingers brush the envelope of money;
the thrill of illicit contact sending a shiver down to her toes.

She types 'Brendon Whistler' into Google. Scans the first
article she finds. Whistler had helped knock the stuffing out of
a couple of hunt saboteurs who'd disrupted a chase by laying a
false trail through woodland. One victim, unnamed, required
surgery to have their ear reattached. The other suffered multiple
fractures to their ribs and severe bruising to their legs and knees.
There was evidence of an attempted lynching, though the
sentencing magistrate said that the accusation was 'barely cred-
ible'. He sentenced Whistler, then thirty-two, and co-defendant
Rufus Hewson, twenty-four, to eight- and four-month prison
terms respectively, saying they were previously of good character
and had been 'sorely provoked'.

Betsy skips on. Finds what she's looking for.

> Speaking outside the court, animal rights campaigner and
> Allen Valleys smallholder Maeve Ducken, said: 'If the
> regular person in the street saw what happened that day,
> they would be appalled. These men are paid specifically to
> deter hunt saboteurs and animal rights campaigners and they
> seem to think they can do so with impunity. People might
> wonder why we're still fighting all these years after hunting
> was banned, but that's because the ban doesn't work and is
> barely enforced. More than that, there are far worse practices
> being carried out right under our noses – the violence

towards animals is truly shocking and there are some unscru-
pulous landowners who seem to think that nothing matters
except making money from the rich folk who come here to
blast over-fed, half-tame grouse. It's disgusting.'

Betsy sits back, her knees jiggling up and down. She's learned
something, she's sure, but she doesn't understand whether it
matters. Jude has told her the bare bones of this already, hasn't
he? Her head is starting to hurt.

Jude.

Guilt floods her as she thinks of him. They've barely argued
since that horrible night. He's tiptoeing around her, holding her
so gently it's as if he's trying to pick up a cobweb without it
coming apart. She feels horribly disloyal, sitting here unstitching
his stories and looking for loose threads.

No, she tells herself, bristling. *No, you've got every right. You
may be paranoid but you might also be really astute. You were
right about Jay, weren't you? You always knew he didn't really
love you enough to put in the effort. Didn't even fight to keep
you, did he? And now the same voice is saying Jude is lying
about something. That night – the night Jay died – you were
dead to the world. He could have slipped away, couldn't he?
You don't know. The way he was with Anya – that was sort of
awkward, wasn't it? Like he couldn't be near her if she was
going to talk about him. Could that be guilt? And what about
Mick – the one Candy told you about? And Jude, with his dead
wife. The one who nagged and belittled him and who left him
everything when she died . . .*

She pushes the laptop away. Puts her hands to her face and
groans into her palms. She glances towards the clock. It will be
another hour at least before Anya arrives. She can get plenty
done. She could collect the eggs, make a cake before she arrives.
Could use her time wisely.

She pulls the laptop back towards herself. She has a sudden
sensation that she has missed something important. She re-reads
the articles. Then she sees it – the shared surname.

Rufus Hewson.

Mick Hewson.

Missing Mick.

She types both into Google. There's little on Michael save a couple of articles in a local paper in Newcastle: a local man raising cash for Army veterans with sponsored athletics challenges at a community gym. He's pictured with a woman described as his partner. Donna Embleton, thirty-two. She's the woman from the river; photographed before she shaved in the Mohawk and before she slimmed down from the hulking bodybuilder physique she sports in the picture.

There's plenty on Rufus, and all of it ties up entirely with the vile specimen who'd fought with Jude at the pharmacy.

She feels sick as she reads. He made headlines shortly after being released for his part in the assault on the saboteurs. The article, printed in the national *Daily Mail*, details the 'sickening and ultra-violent assault' carried out by habitual offender Rufus Hewson on a man and a woman in a row over a parking space. The man was left with 'life-altering' injuries having been struck around the head with an item believed to be a steering-wheel lock. The woman suffered facial injuries and lost a hunk of hair from her scalp. An earlier charge of attempted rape was dropped for lack of evidence. Judge Arthurs, sentencing him to six years, said he was 'an extremely dangerous' individual.

Betsy looks up as she hears the car crunching up the path. She smears the heels of her hands across her face and practices a quick smile. It feels wrong. Everything feels wrong. She starts to rise from the table when some inescapable impulse stops her. She pulls up Facebook and logs on, quickly, ignoring the seemingly endless messages and notifications that begin pinging into her profile. She types Rufus's name into the search facility. She finds him at once. He's puffier in his face than he was in the photograph that accompanies the article. Sallow skin. There's a tattoo on his neck: something that might be the wing of a bird of prey. He's pressing his cheek against the jowl of an elderly lady; her smile falling well short of her eyes. Not much of his information has been set to 'public', but he's tagged in pictures taken in February by one Anthony Bede. Betsy clicks the link. Sees Rufus, beady-eyed and sweaty, holding a bottle of Newcastle Brown Ale, his beefy arm slung over the shoulder of his brother, Mick.

'Boys are back in town', screams the caption. It has eighteen likes. Two responses. One from an Alan Graves:

Glad to see the madman's out. Can't keep a good
man down, eh? Tell him to drop me a line, eh?

In response, a comment from Mick:

No worries Gravesy. He purely <u>beasted</u> his welcome
home party! Still a legend and he hasn't lost his taste
for the ale or the ladies. I reckon he'll be useful to
you. Mr Punch won't know what's hit him!

Betsy closes the laptop. Pushes her hair from her face and
hurries outside. She doesn't like keeping people waiting, though
this aversion has never succeeded in making her change her
ways.

Anya's waiting by the gate, struggling with the loop of damp
rope coiled around the fencepost. She jabs a thumb over her
shoulder as she sees Betsy approach, signalling with her hands,
her face, her whole manner, that she's not alone.

On the road, hands on his hips, looking a lot like Mussolini
in his jodhpurs, is Campion Lorton-Cave. He's red-faced. Sweaty.
There are briars snagged on his coat and a splash of dirt on his
face. Over his arm, as casual as if he were holding a discarded
coat on a too-warm day, a double-barrelled shotgun, open where
the chamber meets the barrel.

Anya opens the gate. Hurries towards Betsy, her bag banging
on her back.

'Miss Zahavi,' says Campion, and there is a slur to his words
that suggests the red face may have been helped by a bottle.
'Miss Zahavi, I think we may have to have an overdue
conversation.'

Betsy stands perfectly still, her heart thumping in a way that
makes her think, incongruously, of a boot slamming down, piston
fast, on the pedal of a bass drum.

'I'm not sure we have anything to say to each other,' she
begins, her voice faltering. She is about to tell him to get off her
property; that Jude will be home any moment, and then she hears
it. The still, cold air carries with it the song of warring sirens:
police, ambulance; the valley filling with the sound of frightened
livestock and angry drivers.

Betsy shivers. Catches the scent of damp grass and the disturbed silt of the riverbed. Something feels wrong.

'I told your wife and Jude's told your lackeys – we're going nowhere. You'd best be going. I won't tell Jude you were here.'

He shakes his head. Stumbles forward and rights himself. 'Miss Zahavi. Or is it Betsy today? Liz tomorrow, is it?'

She shakes her head. 'You can have your money back. I don't care. But we don't need to ever have a conversation . . .'

He swings the gun lazily up, as though following the path of a butterfly. He shrugs, almost sadly.

'Yes,' he says, almost apologetically. He clicks the shotgun closed. Unloops the rope around the gatepost and trudges, muzzily, into the courtyard. 'Yes we do.'

THIRTY-THREE

U p close, there's nothing particularly impressive about Campion Lorton-Cave. He looks old: in poor health. There are little bristly patches in his jawline that he has missed while shaving. His eyes are yellow and shiny, the way Betsy's go when she is holding back tears. His hair, scruffy and sticking up, has a greasiness to it and where it fails to cover his scalp she can see patches of psoriasis, blooming like mildew on stone. It's the gun that changes things. The gun that glares at her: two perfect round eyes, glaring holes in her chest. The gun that makes her listen.

'We can sit here, if you like,' mutters Betsy, pointing at one of the crates in the courtyard. 'No need to go inside.'

'Cold out,' he replies, and his voice carries a whine. 'Doc's orders. Stay warm. Tea would be nice.'

Betsy can't stop herself giving a little snort of laughter. She wonders if this is normal in the countryside.

'Fine, tea, whatever,' mutters Betsy, leading him in through the back door. Anya is waiting inside, her face white.

'Mum had a meeting,' she explains, hurriedly. 'Said she had to go. She says to say sorry.'

Betsy hugs her. Kisses her head. 'You go and put your stuff in the spare room, yeah? I'm going to talk with the man. This is Campion. He owns most of this area.' She glares at the man in the doorway, the gun still over his arm. 'He's a very important person.'

Campion looks as though he's struggling to stay upright. He leans in the doorway, eyes sliding shut. 'Best stay with us, love,' he mumbles, to Anya. 'Don't want you ringing anybody, do we?'

'Leave her be – you didn't even know she'd be here,' snaps Betsy. 'Talk to me, if it's so bloody important.'

'Do as you're told.'

Anya stays still. Betsy, pissed off as much as afraid, starts banging about with mugs, filling the big black kettle and placing it on the stove. She pulls a log from the stack and chucks it into the Rayburn, the heat briefly warming her face.

'Just so you know, Jude's coming home for his lunch,' says Betsy, trying to sound smug. 'He's not hugely keen on cold-callers.'

'He won't be coming home,' mumbles Campion, shaking his head. 'Maybe not ever.'

Betsy stops, perfectly still: a rabbit hearing the tread of a fox. She finds herself smiling, fretfully, the sound of her own heart thumping in her skull. 'Not ever, you say? Don't talk soft. You done him in, have you? Decided that a bit of land and some access rights are worth killing for? I doubt you'd even be able to do it. I can see you enjoying turning a grouse into feathers and mince but Jude? No, hiring thugs is more your game, isn't it? And they haven't had any impact on him.'

Campion waves a hand, vaguely. He seems to be having trouble seeing properly. Keeps opening his mouth as if to relieve pressure in his ears. 'Not me,' he mutters. 'Gone too far already, hasn't it? You can't control a man like that. Can't get him to see sense.'

'Jude?' laughs Betsy. 'Control Jude?'

'No, that monster. Mick's brother. Brendon brought him in – said he and Jude had scores to settle. And Brendon knows what he's talking about. I just wanted things settled. But he won't listen. Won't leave things be.'

'He nearly blinded Jude,' spits Betsy, and feels Anya's eyes upon her. 'In front of everybody. Called him out and started a fight.'

Campion shakes his head, looking pained. He grimaces, suddenly. 'Water,' he mumbles. 'I can't breathe . . .'

Betsy finds herself moving towards him even before she makes up her mind whether to help him. She helps him to a chair, and tells Anya to bring him a glass of tap water. He sips it, gratefully, nodding thanks. Holds it like a toddler with a cup.

'You seem ill,' she says, putting her hand on his forehead. He's clammy. She snatches the hand away as a memory floods her vision: Campion holding a riding crop to Maeve's throat, his arse flashing up and down on the riverbank. She turns away from him, stamping back to the stove.

'You've heard a lot about me,' says Campion, more strength in his voice. 'These past months you've heard what an evil bastard I am. The power I have over people. The way I manipulate my position and ruin lives, yes? Campion Lorton-Cave, the evilest man in the valley.' He shakes his head, dejected. 'I don't defend myself against it because I'm big enough to know that people need somebody else to blame. And whining so-and-so's have been blaming the rich for their problems ever since we were living in caves and some poor hard-done-by bastard felt he deserved a bigger share of somebody else's shit-pile. I get that. That's the way it is. And I wasn't always well off, you understand that, yes? I worked hard. Worked until I bled. Had to marry damn well. Had to grease up plenty of country gents and gentry cunts to become what I am.'

'Jude,' says Betsy, not caring. 'What did you mean about Jude?'

'He's told you lies about me,' croaks Campion. 'Not his fault – he believes what he's saying to be true.'

'That you're an evil bastard who forced his wife to sleep with you in order to get planning permission for her house?' Betsy shoots a look at Anya. 'Cover your ears, sweetheart.'

Campion scowls. 'Yeah, thought that might come up.'

'Why do you care what I think anyways?' asks Betsy.

'I don't,' shrugs Campion. 'You and I got off to a bad start, didn't we, but I put things right. Candy was right about that. Doesn't matter how shit your driving was, I'd had a few and I shouldn't have left you. The money was an apology. Can't be all bad, can I?'

'You've had men trying to force him out of his home!' shouts Betsy, banging the kettle down on the sizzling hotplate. 'Animals killed. A deer strung up in the bloody trees – earmuffs please, Anya – and you're sitting here with a bloody shotgun telling me he's never coming home!'

'Police have found Mick,' says Campion, softly. 'Couple of cave-divers found him down one of the disused shafts, three miles back up the valley. I have friends in the police. They're coming for Jude.'

Betsy shakes her head. It feels like there are cold stones in her stomach. 'He wouldn't. He didn't . . .'

'Rufus thinks he did. Thinks his mortal enemy has done his brother in. And the police aren't going to be arresting Jude until they've got more evidence, which means he's out there, now, with a psychopath after him. After all he holds dear.'

Betsy shakes her head again. 'No. Jude's not a killer. I've had doubts, sure, but—'

'There are those who say he killed my Maeve,' whispers Campion.

'Your Maeve? How the hell was she your Maeve?'

'We had something special,' he says. 'We couldn't be together, not properly, but she mattered to me and I mattered to her.'

'Yeah, I saw the footage!' snaps Betsy, before she can stop herself. 'You with a riding crop to her throat and tears streaming down her face.'

Campion snaps his head up as if tugged by a rope. 'What? What footage?'

'Don't act like you don't know. The day she died she burned a DVD showing you and her at the river. And she wasn't enjoying it, Campion. Didn't look consensual to me.'

'No,' protests Campion, colour rising in his cheeks. 'No, every time was special. Rough, but special.'

'Oh yeah, the "she liked it rough" defence? Bollocks. She had Jude at home – why would she want you?'

He bristles at that. 'Why does anybody fall for anybody? They were wrong for each other, just like Candy's wrong for me. We found something in each other. Sure, she told Jude that it had started so she could get planning permission for this place but afterwards it was never about that. I sorted that out for her because I cared for her. We had something together that she and Jude could never have. She had the most exceptional mind. Understood the truth of things. We may have had different political views but none of that mattered . . .'

'And you think she'd have wanted you to treat Jude like this after she died?'

Campion creases his face into something like a smile, even as sweat breaks out on his forehead. 'Like what? She left him the house. The land. I made a fair offer to take some of it off his hands and he threw it back in my face. Smacked me in the mouth, like I was a dog that needed scalding. He didn't understand the way things were . . .' He stops, quietly, as something occurs to him.

'Go on,' prompts Betsy, desperate for whatever pain he's going to give her.

'Jude must have filmed this footage you're talking about,' he whispers, half to himself. 'But why make a copy? Who was she giving it to? And if he made it, he must have known the truth about us – that we were still seeing each other . . .' He screws his eyes shut. 'Maybe that's where the punch came from.'

Betsy finds herself unable to reply. There are too many feelings and emotions log-jamming in her larynx. 'Why are you here?' she mumbles, closing her hand around the handle of the kettle, feeling the sting of hot metal on her palm. 'What do you want?'

'To warn you,' he says, distractedly. 'Get yourself gone. Rufus isn't listening to Brendon or to me. He's coming for Jude and he's coming for you.'

'Tell somebody, then!' shouts Betsy. 'Tell your police mates there's a nutter coming for Jude. Tell them he's innocent. We saw Mick at the hospital. Somebody had hurt him.'

'Yeah. It has to have been Jude.'

'No, I saw that happen at the riverbank. He fired rocks at him but it didn't do all that damage. Mick was in real pain at A & E. Somebody had done him over . . .'

'Rufus is convinced it was Jude. Word is getting round.'

Betsy is shaking her head, still holding the kettle. 'Why the gun? Why point a gun at me if you're trying to do a good thing?'

Campion looks at the gun as if seeing it for the first time. 'I needed you to listen,' he mumbles. He scowls again, his thoughts elsewhere. He shifts his position, grimacing in pain. 'I don't know why she made a copy. Or did he make it? But on that day? She wasn't meeting me, I know that.'

'Jude says they argued,' snaps Betsy, dismissively.

He shrugs. 'She left without saying goodbye. He didn't see her again until she was dead on the riverbank. And I've heard nothing about a disk. There was talk of some footage of what happened with the poor lass during the shoot but as for anything else . . .'

Betsy's head is spinning. 'He didn't kill her. Didn't kill Mick. Is he OK . . .? Please, is he OK?'

'So far. Can't find the bastard.'

'He's innocent, I swear,' mumbles Betsy, wondering what she truly believes, deep down. She, who has doubted him from the very first moment.

'Didn't kill your ex, either, did he not?' says Campion, giving her a nasty glare. 'Jesus, how naïve are you? Why do you think Maeve wanted me? She was scared of him. He's worse than I'll ever be. He's got the devil inside him, you must have seen that. The lasses he brought back after Maeve died? Fights in the gutter with anybody who'd take him on. Drank himself into a stupor and still had enough fight in him to embed his chainsaw in the big tree at the front of the manor house! Sits there like fucking Excalibur, taunting me, and Candy giggling like a schoolgirl every time she walks past, making me look a fool.'

Betsy has heard enough. She needs to find Jude. To warn him. Question him. Her brain is hurting too much to disentangle her feelings from her thoughts. She glances at the kettle in her hand. It's iron. Heavy. Full of boiling water. One swing and she could put the lying bastard down. Take the gun. Take Anya. Run . . .

Run where? With Rufus out there, looking for vengeance. She looks again at Campion. His wife has always been on Jude's side. She'd offered to help, hadn't she, back in the bar. And nothing could happen up at her big house. Two miles, across the valley – she could do that on foot. She just needs to get away from this horrible man, with his twisted versions of the truth and the shotgun in his hands.

She grips the kettle. Glances at Anya. Hopes to God she gets the message to duck . . .

Campion jerks in his seat. Stutters. Coughs, as if a little explosion has gone off inside him. Blood sprays from his lips. He slithers down in the chair and his coat opens to reveal the blood: a great patch of it staining his shirt, sticking to his skin, where an ugly puckered wound peeks out from beneath a sodden cloth.

Betsy starts forward, unable to fight her instinct to help. 'What? What happened . . .?'

'It's nothing . . .' he mumbles. 'Told him not to come for Jude. For you. Stuck me. I just need a lie down . . .'

Betsy lets go of the kettle. He's been sitting here dying. Been bleeding beneath his coat while baring his soul. She looks at Anya, who has her hands over her eyes.

'No, not again, not again, not again . . .'

Betsy runs to her, kneels down, takes her by the wrists and tries to get her to meet her gaze. She knows what the child is seeing. Knows she is looking again at her father's dead body.

'Anya, it's going to be OK. The man's had an accident but we're going to make sure he's OK. Then we'll find Jude and make everything better, yes?'

'He said Jude killed Daddy. He didn't. I know he didn't. Why did he say that? Why?'

Betsy tries to stay calm. Controls her breathing, but her heart feels like it is trying to punch its way out of her chest.

'Anya, listen to me . . .'

There is a clatter as the gun lands on the stone steps. Campion slithers to the floor like a ragdoll.

'Anya, get the phone, it's in amongst the papers, call an ambulance right now, I'll try and stop the bleeding.'

She races to Campion's side. Rips a strip from her dress and presses it to the ugly wound. 'You're going to be OK,' she says, and doesn't know if it's true, or whether she wants it to be.

'He's the devil . . . the both of them . . . so many bodies . . . so much blood . . .'

His eyes flutter. A reedy groan whistles from his wet, bloodied lips.

'It's not working,' yells Anya. 'There's no dial tone. No sound at all.'

Betsy turns just in time to see the figure appear in the doorway.

Sees Rufus, grinning as if this is the best fun he's ever had. He's got a riding crop in his hand. His red hand. Red, as if he has been stirring paint.

Betsy scrambles for the gun. Turns, swinging it toward his chest. He crosses the ground so fast she barely sees it. Yanks the gun from her and swings it like a club.

There is impact and pain and then the world is a funny colour and it seems as if gravity has stopped working, and she is on her side, looking up, tasting blood: watching helplessly as he punches Anya in the jaw; a red mark on her white face as she crumples like a stringless puppet.

Then he is squatting over Betsy. Smiling at her: a biologist looking down at a pinned rat.

His face is the last thing she sees before the darkness swallows her up.

THIRTY-FOUR

P ain.
A strange stinging sensation; too hot and too cold all at once, like numb toes coming back to life in a scalding bath.

Her shoulders ache. Jaw, too. There's a swollen, tender area on her left cheek. She wants to pat it. To check for swelling or blood. Tries to move her hands and finds herself unable to move.

Out of nowhere, a vicious yank of her arms. The feeling of being jerked like a bad dog.

A face, against hers.

'We are going to have such fun.'

She manages to keep her eyes shut. Fear is swelling, unfurling like the petals of a flower, but she has the sense to stay still. To keep her eyes closed. She knows she will learn more by feigning continued unconsciousness.

Footsteps now: boots on the wooden floorboards. The clatter of metal on wood. Metal on the flagstone of the fireplace. Grunting, now. God how she wants to open her eyes. Countless hideous images flash through her mind. She sees Anya suffering. Jude. Campion, if the old bastard's even still breathing. Every cell in her body is telling her to open her eyes.

A burst of static: the hiss and fizz of a broken TV. '. . . you arse in here, I can't budge it.'

Panting, now. Curses. Metal clattering again and the roar of pain.

She allows herself to open one eye the merest fraction. Through the lattice of her tangled eyelashes, she sees Rufus, shaking bruised, bleeding knuckles, a crowbar in his hand. He's trying to dig up the floor . . .

The creak of the door. More footsteps.

'It's the angle, I think. And the nails are bent over on themselves. Somebody's had this floorboard up before.'

'You're paranoid. Get it up.'

More heaving. The splintering of wood. The sound of timbers torn in two.

She knows what they're looking for. They want the laptop and its contents. The camera too. They're going to be disappointed. Jude's already removed the clear plastic sack from the hole where she left it. He's wiped the contents and given it to her as part of whatever little game he's playing. They're going to lose their minds, she knows it. Rufus will want answers. He'll hurt her in order to get them. Hurt Anya. She wonders how long she'll hold out before she starts making things up.

'Nice one, Billy lad. Pull it up now.'

She opens her eyes. A tall man with a bulbous gut is dragging the sack out of the ground. It's exactly where she left it. She doesn't understand. How can it be on the table and in the ground at once? Unless he's replaced the one in the ground with a fake? Or, and the thought chills her to the bone, the computer she's been using has never belonged to Maeve.

'Spread the word, eh?'

Sitting in the rocking chair by the fire, legs spread, Rufus lifts a black walkie-talkie. 'You there?'

In reply, comes an electronic beep. He gives a nod, clearly pleased with the response.

'Package recovered,' he says. 'Exhibit deposited. Gundog's nabbed two birds. Winged but definitely able to fly. Finish them off?'

A pause. Then two long beeps. Rufus spits into the fire, unhappy with whatever coded message he has received.

'We did talk about occupational perks, yeah? Maybe just inspect the plumage, check what we've got . . .'

Two more beeps, long and loud.

Rufus stands. His colleague, Billy, has plugged in the laptop. He extends a white lead and connects the little camera. From a pocket, he removes a small, tablet-sized device. He connects this to the laptop. In a moment, the screen of the new device is filling with images, a blur of colours and pictures, flicking by too swiftly to disentangle.

'I would be more convincing,' says Rufus: a kid begging to be allowed to have chocolate before dinner. 'Won't even leave a trace, I promise.'

Two more bleeps, louder and more insistent.

'Eye for an eye, yeah . . .?'

He's nearly begging: the desperation in his voice truly grotesque.

Two beeps. *No.*

Betsy allows herself to open both eyes, looking out through the crossed swords of her lashes. 'Liz! Elizabeth, I can't move my arms. Liz!'

Anya's voice, tearful and afraid. Betsy doesn't move. Her half-closed eyes are fixed on the computer screen, watching as Billy scrolls through the catalogue of images and stops on a video clip. Presses 'play'.

The footage is jerky, as if whoever is holding the camera is being pushed and pulled by unseen hands. She sees blue skies; a distant, hazy sun. Heather, soft and purple and inviting as a feather bed. Now a face, looming into shot. Campion Lorton-Cave. He's furious; his face pillar-box red; hair plastered to his face beneath a damp flat cap, He's dressed in his best tweeds. He's roaring, bellowing obscenities at the holder of the camera. The angle swings down, showing the shotgun he holds like a club. Betsy can barely make out the words – just snatches of obscenity-laden venom.

'. . . back in the fucking gutter . . . you think that'll make a difference, I swear to God I will blow your fucking head off your neck if you spoil this for me . . .'

The camera swings right. The man she knows as Brendon has the protester she knows as Moon by the throat. He's pushing his face into the heather. Behind him, two other men dressed in rural tweeds have somebody else on the floor. The nearest, a thick-set man, is lashing their captive with a stick, too thick to bend.

And then the camera is down in the heather, staring up like a sightless eye. And she sees Maeve, arriving as if the earth has spat her out. And she's dragging Brendon off Moon. Kicking. Spitting. Turning to Campion and demanding he intervene. From the heather, a figure rises up. Her face mask has been pulled down and her Hunt Saboteur T-shirt has been ripped down to her waist. She's maybe thirteen.

Betsy has to stop herself from crying out. She watches as

Campion raises his gun. Points it at Moon, trying to find his way to his feet.

Fires.

Fires wide.

The girl falls.

And Maeve is snatching up the camera.

Then the film cuts out.

Billy turns to Rufus. Shrugs. 'Not too late. Could make a fortune from this.'

'The money's good as it is.'

'So we're going?'

'Yeah.'

'How've they got away with it this long? Even the coppers around here could put together a case without the video footage. Shotgun, wounded girl, witness testimony . . .'

'All easy to hush up with money or muscle. A video – that does the rounds before you can blink an eye. Once it's outside the valley, it's outside their control.'

Billy stands up. Tucks the laptop into his coat and the tablet into a pocket. Drops everything else into the bag and throws it on the fire. It starts to melt at once: black toxic fumes belching out from the ancient fireplace.

'Liz, please!'

Betsy raises her head, feigning sudden consciousness. Anya is hog-tied on the floor, legs and arms behind her. Betsy realizes she must be similarly bound.

'Anya . . . it's OK, just look at me, everything will be OK . . .'

A sudden pain. Rufus pulls her upright by the rope and a handful of her hair. Wraps his hand around her throat. Forces her to look at him, her eyes swivelling in their sockets. She sees him grin, and is horrified to see a true happiness in his eyes, as if this were the best fun he could imagine.

'Been a big day for you, hasn't it? It's sweet that Campion used his last breaths to try and warn you about me. Didn't listen, by the looks of things. To be honest, he never was very sharp. All this has kind of sailed over his head a little. Thought he was in charge, didn't he? Thought it was all about leaning on a few people and getting a bit of comeback on Mr Punch. But he never understood. He was only ever a piece to be moved around the board.'

Betsy can't find the words. She just wants him to let go of her arms. To let her slither back to the floor. To let her rest.

'Jude . . .' she manages, her throat squeezed almost shut.

'Still waiting for him, are you? Jesus but you're slow on the uptake. Your Jude's in custody, love. Coppers picking him up right about now, I'd say. Tip-off. Some decent member of the community warning he was about to do a runner. They'll have him for my poor brother. They'll find Campion dead in his living room when they get here. They'll find his girlfriend buried in the woods, beneath the tree where he killed his first wife. He'll be lucky they don't bring back hanging. Throw in your ex-husband and this poor lass here . . .'

On the floor, Anya starts to thrash around, her bruised face a mask of tears and spit.

Betsy tries to speak. 'Why . . .?' she asks, and the word is barely a whisper.

'Why?' repeats Rufus, and permits himself a proper laugh, right in her ear. 'Your man – St Fucking Jude. How many insults am I supposed to stand? He put my brother down, love. And he doesn't deserve to have somebody like you in his bed. Nor like his last tart. Why him, eh? What's so good about him? I'll show you, I swear – show you he was never all you thought he was. And he's going to cry like a fucking baby when he sees what I've done to his lass.'

She struggles in his arms, trying to throw her head back and into his face. She hears him laugh, disappointedly, then he slams his fist into her stomach, and throws her down on the floor. She slips in Campion's blood. Opens her eyes and sees the dead man staring back at her.

'Fire's taking,' says Billy, who hasn't spoken during the exchange. 'You'll be wanting to make a move.'

'Thanks Billy,' says Rufus, with genuine gratitude. 'He's a pal, is Billy. Met him inside, I did. Knows his stuff. Not much of a one for the rough stuff though he doesn't mind enjoying the benefits afterwards, if you understand me.'

Rufus picks up the shotgun from the floor. Snaps it open and checks the cartridges. Takes a knife from his pocket and casually slices off Campion's nose. Throws it in the fire. Gives a shrug, by way of explanation. 'Symbolic, innit? Stuck-up, snouts in the trough. Coppers will lap it up . . .'

He bends down and cuts Betsy's rope. She feels blood rush into her legs and ankles. Then she is being dragged upright again. Shoved towards the door. Billy is doing the same with Anya, who makes a feeble attempt to run. Rufus steps forward and hits her in the back of the head with the shotgun stock. She shrieks, and drops, and Billy hauls her up again.

Through the door, and into the darkening air; blue and black, the clouds promising snow.

Each step an agony.

One word, repeated, over and over and over.

Jude.

Up the valley, towards the dingle; trudging like witches to the pyre.

THIRTY-FIVE

The digger is all right angles and points; damp earth clinging to the teeth of the bucket that has clawed a trench into the earth. She spies a twist of deeper darkness. Even in the swirl of her terror, she identifies it as a yew tree: its circumference vast, its branches splayed out like the fingers of an upturned hand. There are great scars in the trunk; the bark ripped away and the wood exposed. She finds her vision blurring as she gazes into the face of the ancient tree. Sees knotholes become eyes, a porcine snout, a hanging mouth of obsidian black.

'You can't,' she whispers, and the cold wind snatches the words away. 'She's a child. She's done nothing wrong. Let her go and I'll do what you want . . .'

'You'll do what I want anyway,' says Rufus, enjoying himself. 'I make it my business to know about the people I'm going to take apart. I know you've always had one foot in the grave, love – a willingness to die. Well, I know this isn't how you'd choose for it to end, but you'll still get what you want.'

Betsy feels as though somebody has cut a vein at her ankles. Feels her energy, her hope, gurgling into the ground that will soon close over her, and the child she has failed.

'Liz? Liz, what's going to happen . . .?'

She looks into Anya's pale, frightened face: big circular eyes in a mask of blood and dirt. She wants to speak, but nothing comes.

She feels the pressure at her wrists suddenly slacken, and then Rufus is beside her; the barrel of the shotgun pressing beneath the hinge of her jaw, his lips to her ear.

'Tacitus,' he whispers. 'You remember, I'm sure.'

And she does. Remembers the story that Jude had told her, as they stared up at the mess of dead stag in the tree. The story of what the Germanic tribes did to those who peeled the bark of a living tree. *They slice the culprit's navel, and secure it to the trunk of a sacred tree. Then they force them backwards, until their guts are unwound about the trunk – decorating it like tinsel at Christmas. The life of the tree was equal to the life of a man.* He'd smiled as he said that; correcting himself, the way he did when he misspoke. *Or woman, of course.*

Betsy needs to see. Whatever it costs her, she needs to look into this killer's eyes and make one last desperate plea. Needs to explain. She understands how it feels to be filled with the whispers of something incessant and demonic; the uncontrollable impulse to sabotage, to cause pain, to do harm.

She turns, her mouth opening, a babble of pathetic entreaty spilling from her bloodied lips.

She experiences a moment of sensory overload; heat and noise and pain and a sensation of being both within herself and without.

Then blackness.

Silence.

Then nothing . . .

. . . The world returns in a flood. There is wetness on her face. Hot, clammy liquid coating her skin, matting her hair. And she can hear a high-pitched whine, like a dog whistle, not quite there but also drilling through her head like wire.

She turns around and sees that Rufus is on his knees. Billy, behind him, has snatched up the fallen shotgun and is desperately waving it around, jumping at every sound. Anya is on the floor, trying to regain her feet.

Betsy swivels her gaze back to Rufus. There's a reindeer handled knife sticking out of his cheekbone. His face is twitching, one hand clenching and unclenching, a red drool spilling from one corner of his slack mouth.

'Jude!' shouts Betsy, and in this moment she doesn't give a damn what he's done before. 'Jude!'

Billy spins the gun towards her. 'Shut up!' he hisses. 'Shut the fuck up or I'll shoot.'

'You need your cartridges,' hisses Betsy, her eyes flashing gold. 'Don't waste them on me. Not when he's coming. Not when he's right fucking behind you!'

Billy spins on the spot, raising the gun, and Anya lashes out from the floor. She catches him in the knee. He grunts. Turns his back on the shadows. Raises the gun, just as Betsy kicks him square between the legs. He doubles up, gasping for breath, and Betsy pushes past him, desperately helping Anya up with her foot, trying to yank her hands free of her bonds, and then both are running, jumping over the ice-hardened tree roots, the wild-flowers, the mossy rocks. She glances back just once.

She sees a figure she takes to be Jude. He has Billy by the lapels. And he's picking him up as if made of damp paper, and ramming him – skewering him – on to the teeth of the mud-coated digger; the metal emerging from his gore-covered chest to gleam, silver and red, in the moonlight.

He watches her go.

Turns his attention to Rufus.

In the darkness, his smile is a knife.

THIRTY-SIX

Faster. *Faster!*

Stumbling and rolling, they slither their way down the far side of the valley. The ground glistens with the promise of tomorrow's frost. Above, the moon illuminates a perfect V of rooks: an arrowhead pointing them back the way they've come.

The air, Bible-black; cold as the kiss of dead lips.

'Nearly there . . .' stammers Betsy, her teeth chattering, her bones threatening to come apart. She glances at Anya, her face almost swollen shut on one side. She tugs again at her ropes and feels them suddenly give. She must have snagged them on something sharp as she slithered down the jagged slope behind the dingle, making her way to the one place she hopes and prays she will be safe.

'Yes,' she cries, exultant, as the tattered rope suddenly comes apart. She grabs for Anya and with frozen fingers begins trying to unpick the soggy twine that holds her.

'Are they coming?' asks Anya, her voice chopped up into tiny icy utterances. 'I thought they were going to kill us. Did Jude throw the knife? I don't know where it came from. There's blood on you! Betsy, there's blood all over you . . .'

Betsy says nothing. Just tugs at the rope until it comes apart, loosening it far enough for Anya to be able to hunker down and slide her feet through the loop, tying herself in front instead of behind.

'Just there,' whispers Betsy, and wraps an arm around the girl. 'That's the house.'

They stagger down the slope, slithering over stone walls, scratching themselves on barbed wire. The manor house, always just over the next dip, remains a distant blur, a softly-lit rectangle peeking out from a stand of trees.

Betsy feels her feet go out from under her and she slams into a low wall, winding herself. Anya, behind, makes a grab for her and then they are both tumbling over the old stones and landing in a tangle of cold, damp grass, staring up the driveway to the house shared by Campion and Candace Lorton-Cave.

It's an old house. A fortified farmhouse, just like home. It looks like something from a period drama; a hunting lodge built for Henry VIII; all rough-hewn stone and old slate, with thick drapes at the darkened windows and torch-holders bolted to the brickwork. The driveway is lined with tall trees, each cobwebbed with a fine mesh of frosted cobwebs, and in front of the colossal double-fronted door, where the driveway opens out into an attractive courtyard, stands a gnarled oak tree; the ridges and hollows of its trunk contorted into the face of a screaming gargoyle. Through the place where the eyeball might be, Betsy sees the rusting handle of a chainsaw, its blade embedded so deep as to touch the heartwood.

A security light comes on as they half-run, half-fall their way up the shingled driveway.

'Where are we?' begs Anya. 'Whose house is this?'

There are no cars in the driveway. A double garage at the far side of the courtyard stands locked. 'Please be in,' mumbles Betsy, as she runs up to the door and starts hammering at the wood. 'Please . . .'

They wait for what seems like an age. They hear the wind in the trees, the bloodied gasp in their lungs. The house is completely silent. It seems as if the world is holding its breath.

Finally, Betsy hears footsteps, and almost sags with sheer relief as the door swings creakily open and Candace Lorton-Cave peers out at her like a gaoler in a Dickensian novel.

'What on earth . . .?'

Betsy gathers Anya up in her arms and they tumble into the half-dark hallway. A great warm wave engulfs them and it is all Betsy can do not to let it drag her immediately into a blissful, beautiful sleep.

'Oh my God, what's happened?' demands Candy, peering at the blood on Betsy's face and turning frightened eyes on the sobbing, shivering child. 'Come through, can you walk . . . I'm in the parlour, it's warm, I'll get drinks, the first aid kit . . .'

'Campion . . .' stutters Betsy. 'Men at the house . . . Jude . . .'

'I can't understand you,' says Candy, pushing Betsy's hair

back from her face and looking for injuries. She's brisk. Business-like. Checking her over as if assessing a horse.

'Stay there,' she commands, and hurries off down the long, wood-panelled corridor, oil paintings glaring down from the walls; a gallery of hunting hounds, ruffles, crinoline and curls. Despite the pain, the exhaustion, Betsy notices a little of the lady of the manor in each of the disapproving faces.

'Are we safe? Liz, are we safe?'

Betsy can't pretend to know. She manages to haul Anya back to her feet. She drags her the way Candy had gone, feeling the burning gaze of the men and woman in the oil paintings. She wonders, for a moment, how it must feel to be Candy – to have to measure up to such a rich history. She has never had such problems. She doesn't know anything about herself save the fact her mother was a drug addict and that her father paid for her services in heroin. She's never met him. Wouldn't know him if he turned up on her doorstep. All her mum recalls is that he brought her a present when she *told* him she was expecting. A pair of earrings, from the Elizabeth Duke range at Argos. Gold and cubic zirconia. She'd got fifteen pounds for them, apparently. Even named Betsy in their honour.

She tries a handle, trying to find the parlour. Opens a door into darkness and fumbles for the light. Her fingers find it and the warm golden glow illuminates a large study; the sort of place that puts Betsy in mind of a gentleman's club; leather and wood and great towering shelves of old books.

Anya pushes past her, into the room. She half slithers to the floor.

'Rug's all wet . . .' she mutters, her eyelids flickering. 'Soaked.'

Betsy turns to go and look for Candy, just as she hears the burst of static. It's coming from the draughtsman's table by the tall window at the far end of the room, where a lyre-backed swivel chair is softly turning, as if pushed by the breeze.

Betsy steps across the sodden rug and crosses to the table. Unrolled on the board, the edges pinned down, an old map of the valley; all whorls and contours, like the print of a palm. The lettering is spidery; some of the place names completely alien. But there is a perfect circle drawn around the house where Betsy now stands.

The hiss of static again: loud, insistent. She feels the world slow down. Her thoughts become sluggish, her vision blurring, dilating, as the exhaustion begins to catch up with her.

Concentrate Lizzie. You're a little sneak, aren't you? Do what you're good at, you silly girl.

She finds the walkie-talkie in the desk drawer.

Holds it up to her face and presses the button on the side of the slick black handset. Sends the high, electronic beep to the other receiver.

There is a moment's silence, and then the voice. His voice. Each word the smack of hammer and chisel upon stone as he carves his prophesy into rock.

'I know what you've been doing, Candy. And I swear to God, if you hurt her, or the girl, I will burn your precious house to ashes and shove them down your fucking throat!'

'Jude . . . Jude it's me,' hisses Betsy, desperately. 'Jude, what's happening? I thought she was your friend, that she was on your side! What did you do to those men? They said such awful things about you, about what you've done, and I don't know what to believe and I'm so scared, Jude, so scared . . .'

From the doorway, a small voice. It's calm and controlled, and almost apologetic.

'I did say to stay there, Elizabeth. It wasn't a difficult instruction. But I suppose you're not operating at your best, and even at your best, you're not great.'

Beneath the desk, out of Candy's line of vision, Betsy keeps her finger over the button on the walkie-talkie. She stares at the small, goblin-faced woman in the archway of the old door. She's holding a short, antique weapon: carved wood and gleaming brass; ornate scripture running down the barrels.

'It still works,' says Candy, with a little smile. 'Flintlock. We keep all the hunting rifles under lock and key in the lodge but this stays in the manor house, with me. I clean it more than I should. I enjoy it. Taking things apart and putting them back together again – it's always been something I enjoy.'

'Campion's dead,' says Betsy, without emotion. 'Rufus did it. Stabbed him. Trying to frame Jude.'

'So sad, so sad,' says Candy, with a shake of her head. 'I had hoped he would listen to reason but he never was one for the bigger picture. His petty little games with Jude, well, it was all a bit macho, don't you think? Dick-measuring, I believe some people call it. Sending the boys to rough him up – I ask you, it's almost embarrassing.'

Anya looks up at Betsy from the floor. She raises her hands. They're wet, and red.

'Betsy?' she asks, desperately.

'This is where he stabbed him?' asks Betsy, closing her eyes. 'Rufus?'

'Yes. All a bit Cluedo for my liking: "the thug with the knife in the study". I was surprised he made it as far as the bastle, but he always did have the capacity to surprise a person. Can I presume things aren't looking at all rosy for Rufus and Billy? Apparently the local bobbies made something of a pig's ear of the arrest. Brendon was there to enjoy the show. Two squad cars and a dog unit and Jude slipped through their fingers like a soapy eel. I will admit to a genuine fondness for him. In another time, he'd have been quite the swashbuckler, don't you think? Doesn't really fit in the world, but then neither do you, and I will admit to feeling very much out of place from time to time. I really don't ask for very much. I want the Cave name to prosper, that's all. I'm the last of the line, you see. Never could manage to conceive, try as we might. Even gave the old IVF a go. Nothing stuck. More miscarriages than any person should have to endure, and nobody should have to endure a single one. Of course, it didn't help that Campion was wasting his seed on that ungrateful cow Maeve. Who knows – perhaps one of those wrigglers would have finally done the job for me. Too old now, of course. I'm the last. But I do want it to be said I've left the estate running smoothly. Making a profit. Building for the future.'

Betsy shivers, the cold seeming to climb inside her. Her breath is all icy vapour; each exhalation the ghost of something precious.

'The bastle belonged to this house,' explains Candy, pointing the ornate gun at Anya. She shrugs, by way of apology. 'Sorry you got dragged into this. You and your poor dead dad weren't ever part of the plan, but it can do no harm at all to have a few extras tagged on to Jude's account, and if you want my opinion, he probably did kill him. He's crazy about Elizabeth here and he's a bit of an alpha male when it comes to protecting his harem.

Even after Maeve passed on, he wouldn't use what he had on
Campion to get his own way. Didn't want to betray her memory,
you see. Didn't want people thinking ill of her. Thought he was
doing the decent thing hiding that footage away beneath the
ground as if it were a bomb. All he had to do was watch a few
other clips and he'd have found the one that mattered. Would
have seen Campion shooting that silly girl. Cost a small fortune
to tidy all that away, it really did.'

'You knew,' splutters Betsy.

'Knew?'

Desperately, she looks around for something she can use as a
weapon. Spots a spherical paperweight, bubbles and cogs trapped
inside. Slides herself ever so slightly in its direction, millimetre
by painful millimetre. 'When we met, you said you knew about
their arrangement – what she did to be given planning permission, letting him have sex with her . . .'

A look of distaste grips Candy's face. 'That was not the
arrangement, Elizabeth. She seduced him. Gave him what he
wanted and in return he pulled some strings and allowed her to
get her own way. Of course, he was infatuated. Couldn't accept
that she had fallen for Jude, couldn't stop trying it on – threatening to tell her new husband what she'd done, unless she carried
on letting him enjoy himself. Convinced himself she loved him,
poor sod.'

'The day she died . . .' begins Betsy. 'The disk . . .'

Candy shrugs. 'She felt so guilty when I told her I knew about
the affair . . .'

'Affair? He was raping her!'

'We tell ourselves the stories we want to hear, my dear,' replies
Candy, acidly. 'After her operation, it became clear she wasn't
going to get well. She certainly couldn't stay at the bastle. She
was going to need proper care. I wanted to buy the place from
her. Do you know how much money we make from the grouse
shoots alone? And the field that comes with the bastle, under the
old covenant, is precisely where we will place the access road
for what will be the finest grouse shoot in this country. I have
old friends, you see. You may laugh at the notion of ancient
familial bonds but a favour is a favour and I have old chums
who will be only too happy to remove the red tape. Site of Special

Scientific Interest, you see, which means the environmentalists will be choking on their mung beans. But a little bit of muscle and they do tend to go away. People like Rufus are very good for that. Things haven't really changed in this valley, you see, Elizabeth. People want their share, and what they have, they want to keep.'

'But you're setting him up as a killer!' blurts Betsy. She stops, her face creasing in confusion. 'The disk. Why did you ask her for that disk?'

'Silly girl thought she was meeting Campion,' smiles Candy. 'I sent the message from his account. You see, Maeve had shown me rather embarrassing footage of poor Campion shooting that unfortunate youth, during something of a melee on the moor. She used it to exact certain favours not just from my silly husband but from me, too. Certain promises with regards to our future involvement in country pursuits. She wanted us to cancel the grouse shoots. To give areas of prime shooting land over to re-wilding and new forests.' She says the word with a sneer. 'What choice did I have?'

'You killed her?'

'I told her, as Campion, that I would do everything she said but I wanted a copy of the footage. Couldn't send it to me – not with the broadband the way it is here! So I asked for a hard copy. She did as requested, though she didn't bring the original. No, she tucked that safely away somewhere. And she didn't bring the footage of the accident – no, she chose to show Campion what she had on him: the footage of her – as you would call it – "rape". Set up a camera herself, the sly so-and-so. Who would do that, eh? You see what kind of woman she was, I'm sure.'

Betsy holds herself still as the dead. So many times in her life she has wanted to die. And she has spent so many of these past months looking for reasons to ruin her happiness. Here, now, she wants to live. She wants to get Anya out of this place and spare her young eyes from witnessing more ugliness. She has already seen her father's corpse. Seen Campion's too. And the things that happened at the dingle . . .

'She was bloody surprised to see me,' says Candy, reliving the memory. 'Wouldn't hand over the disk, and I don't know why because it didn't even contain what I wanted. I'm afraid I lost my temper. You don't realize how easily a skull can crack, do you? Honestly, it's like Blackpool rock. Just shatters as soon as it hits the stone. Of course, it came as a disappointment when I watched the video.'

'You're mad . . .'

'It helped that Jude was so broken up and that Maeve had kept him in the dark. He confided in me, after the police had gone. Said that he'd watched the footage himself on the day she left – it was sitting there on the screen like she wanted him to see. And not content with that, she left the whole place to Jude, with instructions he never sell to us. Campion did what Campion does – sent the boys in. But the boys knew how the land lay. Campion might be the big man with the fat wallet, but it's wifey who this valley belongs to and wifey who calls the shots. And it was wifey who told Rufus to push things as far as he could – to create a scenario in which it would be believable for Jude to kill Campion. When he's locked up and festering he'll need money for defence lawyers and I think he'll be glad of whatever we offer him for that place. And when the bulldozers come in, I'll enjoy knowing that every demolished brick is another rock on top of Maeve's coffin.'

Betsy suddenly realizes she's stopped listening. She's looking at Anya, sprawled on the rug, bloodied and bone-white.

And she's looking at her own hand, white-knuckled, still gripping the walkie-talkie.

Slowly, she raises her hand.

Nods at the button beneath her thumb.

She releases it.

Hears the crackle of static, and then a voice she doesn't recognize.

'. . . this is DCI Kelly Fisher. Mrs Lorton-Cave, I need you to tell me whether the hostages are safe. We have a team en route to your address but we require confirmation that neither Ms Zahavi or Anya has been harmed in any way . . .'

Candy's face darkens. Her pupils swell, irises darkening, face becoming stone.

'. . . no . . .' she mumbles, and the threads holding her sanity begin to fray and snap. 'No, that can't . . . no!'

She raises the gun.

Betsy grabs the glass orb. Hurls it like a baseball pitcher.

Heat and spray and the sound of smashing glass.

Then Betsy is slithering down the map, smearing blood on to the rendering of the ancient valley, head spinning. It feels as if her arm is on fire.

And Candy Lorton-Cave, Lady of the Manor, is lying on her back, staring at the ceiling, blood leaking from the corner of her left eye, her ear, her nose.

In the centre of her forehead, a lump the size of a fist, and getting bigger.

Then there is just the sound of sirens, the whir of helicopters, and the soft sobbing of a child.

EPILOGUE

New Year's Eve.

A serpent of fire and tar snakes its way through the streets of Allendale. A brass band marches at the head of the procession, leading the 'guisers': men and women born in the Allen Valleys and selected for the dubious honour of carrying a flaming barrel over their heads; yelling and bellowing and quaffing mead in the very traditions of their Pagan forebears. The blood of the valleys is here, and potent as gunpowder.

For Betsy, still taking strong painkillers and inclined to sup a couple of mulled wines before heading out, it's all a hallucinogenic affair: painted faces and old-world costumes; swirling troubadours and ancient, Norse-sounding chants. She would be afraid, if she were not holding Anya's hand in the crook of her good arm, and were it not for the reassuring presence of Jude's arm around her waist.

The streets are heaving; locals and outsiders both. She sees faces she recognizes among the crowds. Sees heads bowing to allow lips to find ears, and feels endless eyes upon her. She's known, now. She's the one who put her Ladyship in a coma from which she's unlikely to awake. She stayed strong, allowing the police to record Candy's confession, even as she and the child were staring down the barrel of a gun. And even when it was all blue lights and interview rooms, she managed to do right by Jude. Told the coppers just enough. Took down two hired guns, tied them up, called the police and is willing to give evidence to ensure that whatever's left of them after their hospital stays will be left to rot in prison for a very long time.

'It's going to fill up pretty soon,' says Jude, in Betsy's ear. 'May get a bit much for Anya. Her mum's already having kittens about letting her come back here after all that's happened, much as she likes having cool Aunt Betsy to call upon when she wants a quiet night.'

Anya, somehow, hears above the din. 'Relax! It's fun. It's like we're visiting a different time, or something. Honestly, I love it, and it's the safest place I can think of. Enjoy yourself. You could have been having a much worse New Year than this!'

Betsy can't argue. She presses her head against Jude's cheek. Enjoys the closeness, and the smell of him. They've talked a lot, these past few days. Both have been interviewed time and again by police trying to tie together half a dozen different investigations. Betsy needed a pen and paper to explain most of it to the rather bemused DCI Fisher, a pleasant-faced, somewhat wide-eyed woman with dark hair, who'd gone to the trouble of finding Betsy's social services record, and who did most of the questioning through a rather unprofessional haze of tears.

It's over, now. The police have a lot of answers to questions they weren't even asking. Nobody believed that Maeve's death had been anything other than an accident. Jay, too, was never likely to be treated as a murder enquiry. And Mick, his body stuffed down a mineshaft out at Oldman Bottom, had a musket ball in the back of his head, compatible with a flintlock rifle. He'd known too much. Keeping him on side was going to become more costly than securing his death.

'The chess games,' she says, as the unanswered question raises a hand. 'You beat a load of American tourists.'

He allows himself a flash of smile at the memory. 'Six of them, in a semi-circle. All better than me. I was the black pieces on the first board. I let the best player start. Mimicked his move on the next board over and did the same along the row. They were playing each other and didn't notice. Just a trick, really.'

'Wouldn't that only work if they all made identical follow-up moves? And the first player would beat you, wouldn't he? You must still be good. Must be.'

'No,' he says, as if it's important she accept his version of events. 'It's just a trick.'

A blue-faced woman in baggy white dungarees spirals past, her face illuminated by the flame. The beat is growing stronger; the rhythm starting to pulse like a heartbeat. On such nights, Betsy can believe herself healed. She knows it is fantasy; knows she is merely high on atmosphere, but in this moment, amid the maddening, pounding feast of saturnalia, she feels oddly peaceful, as if this were home.

'You want to stay?' asks Jude.

'What, until the party? Yeah, course.'

'No, I mean, long-term. Here. In the valley. We can go anywhere. None of the other stuff seems to matter, I thought I'd lost you, and it was as if somebody had hollowed me out and filled me with ash. I can't be without you.'

'I'll never be properly well. I'll always be a nightmare.'

'They're much more memorable than dreams.'

She squeezes him. Kisses him. Hears Anya say 'yuk' and urge them to get a room. She's recording the procession as it goes by, sending footage to her mum, who's never experienced a New Year without her but is revelling in the opportunities afforded by having 'cool Aunt Betsy' in her life.

A man with a flowing white beard stomps by, his flaming torch throwing ribbons of fire into the black sky.

Betsy watches the fire. Feels the pulse of the dance. Lets the street turn into a serpent beneath her feet and sways in time with its gyrations.

There will come a time when all of this matters, she thinks. A time when she will feel like the devil for her part in all this blood.

But not tonight.

Not when the demon is dancing with so much more gusto than God.

And soon, there is just a man, a woman, and a child, watching the procession, and ushering in the new.